Acclaim for Books by Kendy Pearson

FIRES OF INJUSTICE is a fascinating historical novel based on the late-1800s plight of human-trafficking of Chinese women and girls into San Francisco and other west coast cities. I loved the broad spectrum of this story told from Yakira's point of view, who works at the Occidental Mission Home with Miss Culbertson, and Grant, an attorney for the Chinese Six Companies (established to protect and manage the Chinese communities). Even though I researched this era extensively for my own historical novel, I found new insights and information as this story follows the intrigue, dangers, and complications of dedicated people fighting against the injustices toward a disadvantaged population. *FIRES OF IN-JUSTICE* combines beautiful writing with an important part of history that shouldn't ever be forgotten. A real page-turner!

Heather B. Moore,
USA Today bestselling author of
The Paper Daughters of Chinatown

In *FIRES OF INJUSTICE*, Kendy Pearson brings to life a little-known chapter of American history and tells a compelling story of courage in the face of injustice. This engaging and deeply emotional novel follows brave women and men determined to protect the vulnerable, even amid deep prejudice. I couldn't put it down!

Karen Barnett,
award-winning author of
Through Water and Stone

I could not put this book down. I had no idea what I was in for. It was beautiful. It was heart wrenching. It was so perfect! (***When the Mountains Wept***)

Redeeming Lit Podcast

Kendy Pearson brings to life the Kanawha Valley's explosive Civil War history in this multi-faceted jewel of a tale inspired by true events. Endurance, faith, and love shine through ***When the Mountains Wept***, the first book in what is sure to be a stellar series.

Laura Frantz,
Christy Award-winning
author of *The Rose and the Thistle*

When Heaven Thunders is a Civil War romance that beautifully weaves historical detail with deep emotional resonance. The characters are richly drawn, and the narrative unfolds at a deliberate pace, allowing readers to fully immerse themselves in the era and the heart-touching journey of the protagonists. A captivating read!

Lynnette Bonner,
USA Today Bestselling author of
the Wyldhaven series, The Shepherd's Heart series,
the Oregon Promise series, and more

Kendy Pearson's devotion to history and faith shines through every chapter of this novel. Brimming with heart, ***When Heaven Thunders*** is an emotionally charged journey for characters and readers alike. A must-read for fans of well-researched, immersive Christian historical fiction.

Jocelyn Green,
Christy Award-winning author
of *A River Between Us*

In Tempest Winds tells a captivating tale of family, war, love, and hope. Kendy Pearson skillfully brings the turbulent days of the US Civil War to life with historical accuracy, poignant description, and a cast of characters whose lives are tossed by the tempest winds many of us can relate to. With everything that matters at stake for Zander and Lola, readers will not want to put the book down.

Michelle Shocklee,
Award-winning author of
Appalachian Song and *All We Thought We Knew*

Gifted storyteller Kendy Pearson makes ***When the Mountains Wept*** spring to life with her vivid storytelling, every character so expertly sculpted that I found myself missing them when I closed the cover. Augusta and James stole my heart, and I rooted for them from page one until the very end.

Karen Barnett,
Award winning author of *When Stone Wings Fly*
and the Vintage National Park Novels

Also by *Kendy Pearson*

West Vrignia:
Born of Rebellion's Storm

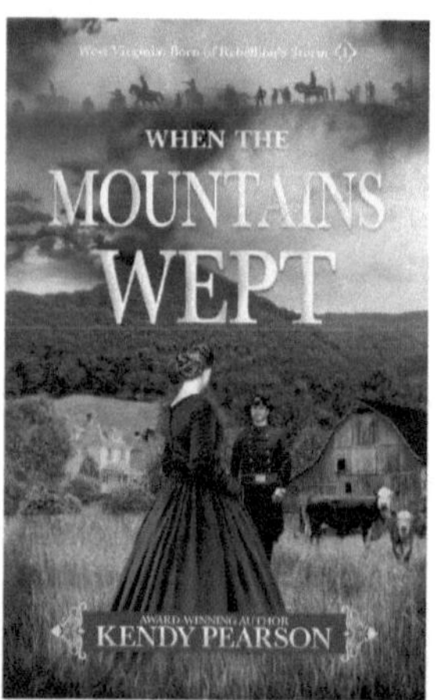

The Award-Winning Series

Sign up for **Kendy's Newsletter** at **kendypearson.com**
to see what's coming next!

AMERICA'S FORGOTTEN WAR

FIRES
OF
INJUSTICE

Heart of History
an imprint of
PEAR BLOSSOM BOOKS

To those who go where others will not;
who welcome the stranger, bind up the broken,
and shine His mercy in desolate places.
Inasmuch as ye have done it unto one of the least of these,
ye have done it unto Him.

Glossary

bairn—child, infant
dinna fash yourself—don't worry, don't trouble yourself
douce—sweet tempered, gentle
fash—fret, worry
ghaist—ghost, haunting memory
guddle—mess, complicated situation
haud yer wheest—hold your tongue
hungert—hungry
ill-trickit—troublesome
ill-scrappit—harsh, ugly
jings—expression: good grief! or my word!
ken—to know
loosome—delightful, charming, lovable
michty me—my goodness
peely-wally—queasy, faint
shooglie—shaky
sonsie—comely, pleasant-looking
unco—uncommon
wheest—hush, quiet—listen

Prologue

Canton, China, 1863

"*Hang hoi*! *Hang hoi*!" (Move out of the way!)

A rickshaw sliced through the crowds, and Avery veered left with his laden cart. It tipped dangerously, searing his blistered palms anew. But mindful of Cait's grip on his belt, he pressed onward. Weaving through the crush of humanity, he passed a silk factory where girls sat with hands in boiling water, uncoiling the silk cocoons.

Turning into a narrow alley, he searched for a place to rest. Beside the tall, carved doors of an ancient compound, skeletal beggars clutched wooden bowls, hoping for a portion of rice.

He continued on several paces and dropped the cart. After sweeping bits of shattered brick from the packed earth, he unwound layers of bloody strips from his palms. Back muscles wrenched as he bowed in noble fashion and took Cait's calloused hand. "Have a seat, me princess."

With a comical simper, she sank to the ground. "Not feeling much like a princess today, your highness. But given time, I'll be back in me royal mood." Her brave chuckle faltered as she dug three hard-boiled eggs from her bag and passed him two.

"Ah, a feast fit for a king." He gave thanks, and they ate in silence for a time.

She fingered the cork of the water jug. "Should we have stayed, do you think? Even despite—"

"Despite losing our heads? Is that what ye mean to say?" How many times must she worry the matter? The warlord's edict was final—and enforced by the two thugs that trailed their exodus from a short distance.

She pressed her lips together and looked away.

He calmed his voice and reached for her hand. "I'm sorry, my love. Our hearts will always be here. Our prayers ever with the Tang people. Painful as it is, ye know as well as I, 'tis time. Mayhap 'tis only goodbye for now, aye?"

He leaned his head back against the hard bricks and let his eyes drift shut, quelling the din of the city. Cait tapped his shoulder. He thought she dozed. More tapping. He opened one eye.

"*Jóusàhn.*" (Good morning). A boy, not fully Chinese, bowed, continuing in Cantonese, "You are traveler? For small fee, SiAh will pull cart." A fine-looking goat stood tethered with a rope. Its smooth coat, clean beard, and round belly were an odd pairing with the ragged lad.

"Is this your goat? And do not lie to me," Avery warned in the local dialect.

"*My* goat. No one else. Where are you going?" The boy smiled at Cait as she awoke.

"To a riverboat. Then on to Hong Kong."

"And to America?"

Was the lad just friendly or a conniver? "What is your name?"

"I am SiJin. You are going to America?"

Avery scowled, still skeptical, while Cait stood, yawning.

She brushed the street from her trousers. "Hello, SiJin. We are missionaries from Scotland, traveling to America." Her light touch to Avery's wounds relayed her thoughts, and the glimmer in her eyes begged agreement. "We are pleased to hire you and SiAh to pull our cart."

"Cait . . ." She was too trusting. A gong tolled the hour, a reminder of their urgency.

The boy swiftly hitched goat to cart. "SiJin knows shortcut to riverboats. Follow me."

The alley emptied onto a busy thoroughfare. After several minutes, they turned down a brick path, shaded by a crumbling rock wall, hoary with cinders that dusted much of the city.

"Did you hear that?" Cait raised a hand in silence and stopped. She narrowed her eyes, cocked her head. "'Tis a *bairn* I hear. A verra new bairn."

SiJin waved them forward. "I think this way." He turned to make sure they followed.

The cry mewled again.

Avery pointed. "There!" A basket hung from a gnarled branch—its base wedged against the wall. He reached it in several long strides and gradually worked it free. Avery lifted it gently, already knowing what to expect—China's way of dealing with unwanted female infants.

Tiny, wrinkled eyelids blinked. "A *Go-Away Girl!*" The words fluttered on Cait's breath.

With their gazes rapt on the babe's sweet face, silence settled over them. The infant squinted back, shiny spots on her red cheeks where tears had dried.

Cait's eyes captured his, and unspoken words convicted him.

Avery braced his resolve, hating the need for it. "No, Cait. We canna."

"Don't you see? God has given us a precious piece of China to have with us always."

The set of her jaw, the pinch of one eye, the quirk of a smile—all brandished hope. Iron-strong and lethal. *Och!* It chiseled through his will. Through his common sense. Through the thick barricade he'd built over the years that had guarded him from an impossibility—*family*. After fifteen years, hadn't they accepted God's provision—the men, women, and children of China as their family? Hadn't these noble people filled that gaping void in their marriage?

She picked up the child—surely a grave mistake. "She's so new. But well fed, it seems." A pink mouth bowed in a yawn as Cait fingered the swaddling cloth. "Such exquisite fabric."

"Cait . . ." If they didn't intervene, death would be a mercy, though likely the lass would be found and sold, bound for a hellish existence. The wretched thought coiled tight in his belly.

"She's but a week or two old, Avery. Not like most Go-Away Girls. Someone kept her for a time—a mother who loved her too much to drown her in the pond." She quivered at the mention of the horrid tradition.

Och! In her mind, she was already in America with a bonny daughter. But a grand obstacle would squash her *douce* heart. "Ye have no way to feed the bairn, Cait. If there was a way, but there isna." He reached to take the weanling from her arms, and she twisted away.

"*Sīnsāang*" (Sir), the boy interrupted. He squared his shoulders and stroked his chin as if weighing a serious offer. "If you wish to take this child to America, Mr. Avery, SiAh will go with you—for a few coins. She has very good milk. Baby will grow fast, strong."

Cait turned, her eyes wide. "You would do that?" Lips atremble, she touched Avery's arm.

The moisture glistening in her eyes suddenly surfaced in his own. He was a strong man. Always had been. Strong in body, mind, and spirit. But Cait could slay him with a mere look, when she had a mind to—for a strong spirit was no match for a pure one.

"SiAh will be very happy American goat." The boy stroked the animal's knobby head. "Maybe I visit SiAh one day." His smile leveled as he asked in English, "Where you live, Mr. Avery?"

"Where did you learn English?" This he wanted to hear.

"Mother. Where you live, Mr. Avery?"

"Mitchell, Avery Mitchell." The lad had spunk. "We will live in San Francisco for now."

"Very good luck to meet you, Mr. Avery Mitchell of San Francisco. But now we must hurry." He squinted into the distance before tugging on the goat's ear. "Riverboats do not wait."

An hour later, rusty stacks belched black smoke as the dock surrendered their boat to the Pearl River. SiJin waved eagerly from shore, cheeks spread in a toothy grin. As Avery lifted a hand to wave back, two men seized the boy. An open hand clouted SiJin, snapping his head aside. The boy shuddered and turned his gaze to Avery. A jagged grin etched his round face, and he yanked one hand free, waving again—before he was knocked down, kicked, and dragged away.

Avery tied up SiAh in the corner of the ship's square cabin. He cocked his head to one side to avoid the low ceiling as he rigged a miniature hammock. Cait laid the wee bairn on the woven mattress to undress her. He stared at the tiny dark eyes probing him—casting a spell on him as a bubble swelled on a plump bottom lip.

"Avery."

Something inside him waxed warm and sweet. "Mmm?"

"Avery. She isna Chinese." Cait's whisper danced at the edges of awareness.

"Nae, my love. Now she will be a Scot or American?" He chuckled to himself.

"Did ye hear me? She isna Chinese."

"Not Chinese?" A surprise indeed. "Weel now."

She stripped the bairn and tenderly turned her over. "No cabbage birthmark." Cait's moist gaze met his. A spark of something he barely recognized flared.

"Oh, Avery. God has heard me cry after all these years." Rivulets washed her cheeks and dripped from her chin. She pressed palms to her cheeks and laughed. "I feel like Hannah of old. Surely God has a plan for this wee one."

"Aye, of that, I am sure." The bairn puckered her pink lips—a private kiss for her new da.

Face aglow, Cait snuggled the tiny form. "Beloved of God, my dear child." A quick intake of breath. "We shall call her *Yakira*—beloved."

He stroked the riot of downy black hair. "And *Jean*, for she is truly a gift. A *verra* unexpected gift." The sweetness of it all pained his chest and burned the back of his throat.

"Yakira Jean. It suits her." Cait pressed a kiss to his lips, and he returned it heartily.

The weeks tumbled by like sea foam, and wee Yakira stole not just Avery's sleep but also every nubbin of his heart. Already, in his mind, the future's every facet gave way to his new daughter.

"Her hair is thicker every day. The same color as me own." Cait looked up, the blue of her eyes riveting. "Avery . . . I dinna want anyone to know she is adopted."

He took a deep breath. Never would he crush her hopes, but . . . *this?* "Wouldna be honest, my dear. We'll love her like our own. Always she will feel loved."

"It willna go well for Yakira should others discover her beginnings—that she was unwanted." Her lids shuttered and throat bobbed. "To think of her thrown away like so much . . . rubbish." The last word cracked her voice—and his resolve.

"Now, Cait. Listen to me, please. 'Tis only the family need know anything. Others will assume she is ours. 'Tis not so unusual to be adopted."

Setting the bottle aside, she shouldered Yakira and patted her back. They swayed with the sudden roll of the ship. "But 'tis our daughter I'm thinking of." Her gaze smoldered to slate. "Avery Mitchell, you look me in the eye and promise you'll say nary a word to Yakira about her beginnings. I'll not have our daughter thinking for one minute she was anything but our dearly begotten child."

"Now, Cait—"

"Promise me, Avery. Here and now, we must agree. Yakira can never know."

He sighed, raking fingers through his hair. He'd never been a heavy-handed husband. Was there no middle ground here? An ache mounted the back of his neck. Yet he buckled. "I promise."

She placed the dozing bairn in the hammock and turned. Her lean frame stretched so her face was within inches of his own. "You're a good man, Avery Mitchell. 'Twas not an easy thing for you to promise, but I love you for it." She kissed him softly, and his arms encircled her as a low wail sang through the seams in the ship's hull.

"My bonny Cait, ye are me first love, and Yakira me second." His words brushed against her raven locks as the floor listed. The round window framed a charcoal sky on the horizon. "Looks like we're in for a nasty bit o' weather."

Avery checked the door and turned with a stagger. SiAh snorted, and the hammock rocked. "At least Yakira will sleep peacefully through the frolic." He guided Cait to the lower berth and pulled her down beside him. "I think we're safest staying right here. Where I can keep me arms about ye." He winked and nuzzled her neck, rewarded with a girlish giggle.

The tempest plunged the world into shadow, and the shifting room rose higher and crashed lower. The moan and snap of a thousand strands of timber plucked an intolerable tune. Their attention followed the sway of the little hammock as wind whined and ocean battered the square-rigger's hull. Cait fussed, wanting to check on Yakira.

"She's fine," Avery assured. The berth shifted. They reeled again. "Finer than we, it seems."

A shriveled cry vibrated from the hammock. Cait sprang to her feet, and before he could grab her, she pitched forward, hands splayed. Her head cracked the small table with a sickening thud. She crumpled to her knees with a moan.

"Cait!" He stood, thrown immediately back to the berth.

She groaned, cradling her head. He breathed a prayer and reached for her in the dappled glow. "Are ye hurt?" He fixed her onto his lap. She squeezed her eyes, and tears puddled. "Cait? Are ye injured?" Fear goaded him at her silence. Yakira mewed and then quieted.

Cait pressed her face against his neck, muffling the slow answer. "That. Hurt."

His fingers felt her head, checking for blood, and the great crowning knot he felt there tightened a strap about his ribs. He could fetch the ship's doctor, but with no wound to stitch, what could be done?

"Mayhap I should fetch the doctor," he said, not wanting to chance something more serious.

"Och, 'tis but a bump. I dinna need a doctor."

After a few moments of inner battle, he dismissed the notion and said a prayer for her. Feet planted wide on the roiling floor, he helped her to lie down and drew up the musty blanket. He kissed her cheeks and settled her head on the pillow. "Rest now."

"Yakira?"

"I will tend her. I am her da, after all."

"You're my hero," she said, the darkness hiding the smile that must've shaped her words.

Chancing to light a candle, he checked on his sleeping daughter. SiAh would not be called into service for another few hours. Avery gathered his bedding from the top berth, settled on the floor, and slept—until a mighty squall from a most tiny lass jarred him fully awake.

Confident that Cait was already at milking, and the hungry cry would soon resolve, he pulled the pillow over his head as he'd taken to doing these past four weeks. Minutes slipped by. Now Yakira's protests threatened a nuisance to other passengers.

"Cait?" He blinked against the brilliant shafts of light that spilled through the window and striped the floor. "Cait?" Her form lay still upon the bed. *Too* still.

An anchor crushed his lungs as he kicked furiously to untangle shoes from blanket. He scrambled to her side, desperate. "My love?" The words scraped raw. He shook her less gently than intended, yet on she slept, face pallid and peaceful. Anguish stretched itself into every limb, every sinew of his body.

Even before he laid his head upon her, begging God for a heartbeat—he knew. The truth swallowed him whole.

Judgement is turned away backward,
and justice standeth afar off;
for truth is fallen in the street,
and equity cannot enter.

Isaiah 59:14

One

Sᴀɴ Fʀᴀɴᴄɪsᴄᴏ, Cᴀʟɪꜰᴏʀɴɪᴀ

November 1884

Yakira dropped the sweet potatoes into her market bag one by one, attempting to hold her tongue. The attempt failed. She squared her shoulders and skirted a row of tall rice baskets, to part the caustic space between Azalea and the awful woman, seeking to set things right. "Pardon me, madam—"

"Mrs. Hickman. Mrs. *Reginald* Hickman." A ridiculous feathered hat complemented the woman's beaked nose and chicken-necked pose.

"Well, Mrs. Hickman, you are gravely mistaken. My lovely cousin here is not now, nor has she ever been—"

"I know a Mongolian prostitute when I see one." The woman sniffed, scrutinizing Azalea from hat to shoe. "And dressing like a white woman doesn't change what you are. You . . . heathen!"

Yakira bristled at the venomous insult. God forgive her, she wanted to slap the woman. 'Twould not be the first time her temper dunked her in hot water.

Azalea tugged on her arm. "Yakira. It is all right. Let us leave." Brows pleated, her gaze jumped to the half dozen spectators gathered for a feminine row. Another tug.

Yakira ignored her cousin's warnings and plunged ahead. "Tread carefully, Mrs. Hickman, lest God judge you for your hateful attitude toward His children. Children who are simply different from yourself. I, for one, am thankful that Azalea is nothing like you—for she is kind to strangers, whereas you have proven sorely lacking."

"Well, I never!" The woman blustered, and crimson quickly mottled her cheeks.

Pulling on Yakira's arm again, Azalea gained a couple of inches for the effort.

"And furthermore, Mrs. Hickman, if you were to loosen your corset and lower your nose, you would see that people are people everywhere, regardless of how they look or what they do or from whence they've come." Yakira cringed as Azalea's fingernails knifed into her flesh. "There is none worthy, Mrs. Hickman."

The woman gaped like a carp on the fishmonger's cart.

Azalea squeezed between them, forcing Yakira to step back. "Good day, Mrs. Hickman." She donned a sweet smile and bowed before trotting away with Yakira in tow.

They'd gone a full block before Yakira unclenched her fists and panic set in. *What had she done?* She yanked Azalea to a stop. "Please don't tell Da what just happened. Or Aunt Lara."

Azalea smoothed her bustle and fingered the lace confection pinned atop her sable plaits. "And let them find out I nearly had to break up a fisticuffs? Why ever would I do that?"

"Women like her . . ." A very un-lady-like growl purled in her throat. With a slow breath, she banked the fire inside and took Azalea's hands. "I'd fight to the death for you. You know that."

"You are my *laotong*—we are sworn sisters for life. Of course, you would. And I for you." Azalea hooked her arm through Yakira's, and they turned down Dupont Street, the only other street in Chinatown where they were allowed to walk without an escort.

They sidestepped a huddle of older children tossing sticks while a young child dressed in the split pants of a toddler watched-on. Yakira knelt and smiled at him. *"Jóusàhn."* (Good morning.) She paused for a return grin before they continued walking. "I'd like one of those someday."

"A little Tang boy?" Azalea chuckled.

"Any little boy will do, actually." She hugged the familiar ache of paper dreams. "We are officially spinsters, you know."

A red-robed Taoist priest skittered past, wide sleeves swallowing his hands and snapping like sails in the breeze. The long hem flailed against black trousers with every clipped step.

Azalea urged her on. "Well, *I* prefer to think of myself as a lady in waiting—waiting for God's choice for me. Mother says God chose me. Then she and father chose me. Now God will choose a husband for me in His timing, not mine. For now, I am content." Azalea bumped her shoulder. "You are not?"

"You know me better than anyone. I am more than content in my work. And I can do without a husband if God will give me children." How ridiculous she sounded. But her cousin understood her heart. Did Yakira truly not care if she ever married? Unbidden, her traitorous mind flickered an image—a beardless face, a mischievous smile. It poked at a corner of her heart, still bruised even after all these years.

"God knows your desires, my sister." Azalea comforted, seeming to read her mind.

An eatery door opened and closed, wafting aromas of boiled rice and fish. On the corner, an enterprising young boy hawked his wares.

He rattled a basket of peanuts—a symbol of prosperity. "You buy? Good fortune to you."

She fished out a penny, and he dumped two handfuls of peanuts on top of her potatoes. "*Dōjeh*" (thank you), she said, amused by the way he bit the coin before tucking it deep into his pocket.

They halted at Jackson Street and turned around. Any farther would take them too near the gambling dens. And too near the cribs where the Chinese prostitutes hawked their services through barred windows or beckoned from guarded upstairs rooms. It was Da's rule, and she'd not give him cause to distrust her. They would return on Friday—but with Miss Culbertson. And a mission.

They crowded together to permit a man room to pass, but he kept pace beside them instead, uncomfortably close. "Please walk," said a female voice. She wore a man's quilted jacket and wide-brimmed hat. "You from Mission Home?"

"Yes. I am Yakira." A finger of warning drew down her spine. She scanned the sidewalks and streets, watchful for the black hat and coat of the *Tong*.

"I am Dong Ju. I go with you?"

"There." Azalea indicated two men just exiting the alley across the street. *Tong men.*

The girl had to come with them now, or she might not live through the beating she'd receive when those men caught her. In seconds, Dong Ju would have no choice. Not ever again.

Yakira shoved her bag into the girl's arms. "Cover your face," she said in Cantonese. She tossed a coin to a weaver, asking to borrow a large basket. He nodded, and she propped it onto Dong Ju's shoulder.

"Just keep walking," she told the girl. Two more blocks and they would be out of Chinatown and too near the police precinct for the Tong to trouble them.

"Jíng hái douh!" (Stay There.) One of the Tong men pointed straight at them; his face twisted with rage.

"Hurry." Azalea caught the girl's hand, and they all ran.

"Follow me." Yakira turned into a shoe shop and rushed straight out the back door. She cut across the alley, into another shop, and out through the front. Blood thumped in her ears as she strained to hear shouts or heavy footsteps.

"Wei Ming." Azalea's breath puffed behind her. "He will help."

Yakira darted into the herb store, her senses slammed by the sharp aroma of ginger and wormwood. Wei Ming sat behind the counter, pretending to read an American newspaper.

"Tong. Behind us." Yakira's frantic words spurred him into action.

He tossed the paper, ducked under a rack of hanging herbs, and locked the door before pulling down the shade. His long queue swung with a quick turn. "You wait here. They go."

Four sets of eyes stared at the door. Breaths heaved in the stillness. Yakira squelched a ripple of fear and reached for Azalea's free hand.

The doorknob rattled. A booted foot bashed the door, quaking a shelf of clay jars. One crashed to the floor, casting shards of crockery and dried seahorses across the floor. Curses. Fists pounded. Wood shuddered.

Soundless minutes ticked by before Wei Ming chanced a peek. "They gone. Think you go out back." He unlocked the door, and they thanked him. He turned to Dong Ju, tenderness softening his brown eyes. "*Síusām di*" (be extra careful).

Running now would only call attention, so they walked up Sacramento Street with a comfortable silence between them. The familiar brick building with its rounded windows and stately chimneys rose into view.

Yakira caught Azalea's gaze and smiled knowingly. Dong Ju's entire world was about to change.

Yakira wilted with relief as she opened the door to the Occidental Mission Home for Girls. "You'll like it here," she said, ushering in her newest student. They stepped onto a bright rectangle of sunlight painted across the floor.

Aunt Lara descended the stairs—dignity and sweetness gracing every inch of her tall frame. "And who have we here?" Her fingers grazed the few silver threads at her temple. "I am Mrs. Campbell," she told Dong Ju in Cantonese.

Azalea hugged her mother, and Dong Ju's eyes rounded at the sweet exchange. It was likely she had never seen such love between a white woman and a Chinese girl.

"This is Dong Ju, and she found *us* this time." Yakira set the borrowed basket beside the door. "Where is Miss Culbertson?"

"She is in the classroom." Aunt Lara dipped her head. Searching out the girl's gaze, she touched her hand. "You are most welcome here, Dong Ju."

The girl nodded, a quivery tilt of her lips adding to her striking beauty. She took in her surroundings with a hundred questions scribed across her face as she scratched one arm.

"Let's get you to your room, then I will show you around," Azalea told their guest, removing the man's hat from her head. "Do you speak English?"

"Little," she said, staring in wide-eyed wonder at the framed photos on the hall bookshelf. Dozens of Chinese girls, all wearing lovely Western dresses, smiled back at her.

"Every one of those girls lived here, or still do. You will meet some of them soon." Azalea motioned for her to follow and led her by the hand. "I will show you the Home."

Garlic and herbs permeated the house, taunting Yakira's stomach more with each step closer to the kitchen. She greeted Cook and deposited the sweet potatoes and peanuts on the counter before heading down the hall to the main classroom. Her fingers caressed the warm woodwork as she walked. How hard her father and Uncle Errol had worked to start the home—just a year after Azalea came into their lives.

Perhaps she would never leave this place. Perhaps she would die here—a happy spinster, content to impart God's grace to all who walked these halls. Or perhaps God would grant her fondest desire—a mission home of her own. She tussled with Him at times, racked between contentment and hope, between what was and what could be. If only she could build on her father and mother's legacy—blaze her own mission field with her own Home for Girls.

Miss Culbertson sat at the desk, hedged-in by stacks of papers. She looked up, and her drawn face brightened. "Well, you are a welcome sight. I can't seem to find the repair list." She sat back with a huff and smoothed a lock of pewter hair that had eluded her snood.

Yakira opened the desk drawer, dug for a moment, and withdrew the list. "Don't feel bad. I looked for it for ten minutes only yesterday."

Chagrin tilted Miss Culbertson's smile as she snatched it from her. "Your father is due from a meeting. I want to make sure he has it. The door hinges will not replace themselves. Oh, I do wish he would approve a new handyman."

"I brought home a new girl. She found us at the market."

"She *found* you?" Miss Culbertson stepped around the desk. "Were you followed?"

"At first, but Wei Ming took care of that."

"Bless that man. Well, she is safe now. What is her name?"

"Dong Ju. She is very young."

"Who is verra young?" Her father filled the doorway and tipped his head to clear the threshold. "Do we have a new resident?"

Yakira greeted him with a kiss to his bearded cheek. "We do, and she is thirteen at most." Hopefully, he wouldn't ask any questions about her outing today. She could only pray he didn't learn of her exchange with Mrs. Hickman. "How was your meeting with the Chinese Consul?"

He dropped into the nearest chair and tossed his derby onto the table. "It seems Six Companies is engaging the services of a fancy east coast lawyer. The Chinese Consul, Mr. Bee, isna particularly happy about it at this juncture, but says he will abide by the Federation on behalf of China's districts. I think he's expecting more trouble in some of the other Chinatowns across the west."

"There you are." Aunt Lara strolled into the room, a twinkle in her blue eyes. "What did I miss?"

Yakira excused herself, hoping for a bit of rest before the noon meal. She found Azalea stretched across their bed, holding her brother's picture.

Azalea looked up and brushed away tears. "Do not say it, Kira."

"Do not say what?"

"Do not say, 'Why do you do this to yourself?' That is what."

"Is that the way I sound?" The bedsprings complained when Yakira plopped down beside her. A worn-smooth, years-old weight pressed on her conscience. "I'm sorry."

Azalea sniffed and rolled onto her back, setting the frame back on the bedside table. "I know you miss him too. What if he never comes back?"

Yakira shared everything with her laotong—all but her deepest feelings about Grant. He'd been so much more than a cousin. He'd been her closest friend and confidant, her only playmate before Azalea. His presence tangled with all her best memories. And just when Aunt Lara needed him most, he left.

He left *her*. Her fourteen-year-old heart had missed him so fiercely that she had cried herself to sleep every night. Pierced anew, she drew in a quivery breath.

Her finger grazed the bronze frame. She had memorized every nuance of that sixteen-year-old face—the dark brows and firm jaw, the serious indigo eyes that had probed her deepest thoughts. Would she even recognize him today? Was he tall like Aunt Lara or shorter like Uncle Erroll?

"Kira?"

She swiped at her wet cheeks and squeezed Azalea's hand. "Just reminiscing."

Two

TRUCKEE, CALIFORNIA

"Truckee!"

California. Nearly home. Grant Campbell leaned over the velvet-tufted seat and buffed a misty spot on the fogged window with his sleeve. Cloaked in white, the Sierra Nevada enfolded the town in its wintry embrace. Three days on his backside, even in first class with an entire country for viewing, had taken a toll on his long legs. Striking out over stationary ground was just what he needed. And no amount of snow was going to stop him.

He collected his papers, sliding them into his valise as brakes screamed against iron and steam billowed outside the window. Truckee was just an overnight stop to meet with railroad magnate Charles Crocker. Establishing a strong alliance with the man was paramount to leveraging Six Companies' influence in Truckee. And he was just the man for the job. And if he wasn't? He snuffed a hiccup of doubt. He was home to stay, come what may.

People milled about on the wide platform of the Truckee Hotel, apparently only a simple one-stop layover. But it would do. He signed his name in the register and collected his key from the clerk.

"Room 205, Mr. Campbell. Enjoy your stay," the older man attempted a weary smile. "The train pulls out at eight o'clock sharp tomorrow evening, continuing to Sacramento and San Francisco."

"Thank you." Grant passed him his baggage claim ticket and slid a dime across the counter. "Might you point me toward the Sisson and Crocker offices?"

The clerk's eyes widened at the coin. "Across the tracks and to your left, just past the restaurant."

Grant thanked him and strode off for his first official meeting on behalf of Six Companies. The first meeting of many that he hoped would make an impact. An impact on something that truly mattered for once.

Across the tracks, to the visiting eye, Front Street bustled with the familiar attractions of a mountain town, but he'd done due diligence. With more than its share of saloons and bordellos, Truckee also harbored the second largest Chinatown in California—and the reason for this meeting. He stepped into Sisson, Crocker, and Company's General Merchandise, stomping muddied snow from his shoes and doffing his hat.

"Mr. Campbell?"

Grant turned to a mountain of a man, fully his own six foot plus. A patch of snow-white hair topped his round face, a match to the uncut goatee that reminded Grant of the old Tang men.

"Yes, sir. You must be Mr. Crocker." His photos hadn't done his formidable presence justice.

"I heard the train and decided to come down and meet you myself before my clerk got any notions about the handsome young lawyer in town." His eyes creased with humor.

"Mr. Crocker. I would never . . ." A mousy young woman behind the counter blushed furiously, her bespectacled eyes pinned to the floor.

"I jest, Milly. I jest." A chuckle quivered his words. "Well, Mr. Campbell, do you prefer we speak in my office or the restaurant?"

"Your office will do. I have everything I need right here." Grant patted his valise and perused the store. Canned goods, kitchenware, and groceries on one side. Saddles, sewing machines, paint, and hardware on the other half. As finely stocked as any city mercantile.

Once they settled into the office, Mr. Crocker laid out the town's ongoing problem with anti-Chinese activities and troublemakers among the businessmen. "Moving Chinatown across the river was the best option. Hate-mongers burned it down so many times I believe I lost count."

"It was good of you to donate the land, Mr. Crocker. The Chinese deserve a safe place to live and run their own businesses. Six Companies believes this is key to minimizing the aggression toward them. While we would prefer peaceful integration, segregation is a far better option than the violence Truckee has experienced over the years."

Mr. Crocker went on about how the rough logging town had grown, graduating to all the problems of Virginia City, just one hundred miles away. "It was *my* idea to bring the Chinese laborers to America, Mr. Campbell. The way I see it, I can do no less than everything in my power to see them allotted the same privileges as any immigrant who comes to these United States in search of a better life."

Better life? He couldn't agree more. But the Exclusion Act cut the throat of that concept with its new category of *inadmissible* aliens! And after two years, it still boiled his blood thinking about it. Even Congress was working against the Tang people.

Mr. Crocker's broad shoulders slumped, and he shook his head. "I am ashamed to admit this country isn't ready to swallow their prejudices for yet another race of people. As a nation, we have a weak citizenry."

"Thank you for all you do to herald the Chinese man's plight, Mr. Crocker—to give them a chance to make their way. You have been instrumental in saving the lives of perhaps millions of starving Chinese in Kwangtung Province."

A slight nod acknowledged the statement before Mr. Crocker's gaze targeted the window. His vision seemed to lay hold of something beyond the frosted panes. "Mr. Campbell, this town is a powder keg." He snatched a folded newspaper from the desktop and slapped it against his palm with a grunt.

Mr. Crocker stood, his bulky frame dwarfing the carved desk. "The increase in vigilante violence is not *'nonexistent'* as *The Truckee Republic* and other papers claim. Not a fortnight passes without gunfire between the rival Tongs and cruel vigilante acts toward the peaceful Chinese." He tossed the newspaper back onto the desk and tapped his finger on an article. "Propaganda. Every word of it."

Grant read the article, its words denying in black and white everything he had already discovered about the environment here in Truckee. He looked up. "Who is this Robert McGleason?"

Mr. Crocker crossed to the window, looking over the street and railroad tracks with a scowl. "Depends on what he's up to, I guess." He walked over to the humidor and retrieved a pipe but no tobacco. "He's a lawyer first and foremost, but worse than that, he's the editor of *The Truckee Republic* newspaper. Likes to raise folks' eyebrows, if you get my meaning. He's your best friend or your worst enemy, depending on the issue. And he takes his meals with the most devout of haters. The most vocal. And even the most vicious."

"Vicious?"

"A few years back a secret society called the *Order of Caucasians* was formed. Had more than 10,000 members throughout California. Three hundred of them right here in Truckee, meeting in the open every Saturday night—not so secret, eh?"

Grant nodded, already familiar with the white supremacist group. A Ku Klux Klan of a different color.

"Howard Dannon, a grocer here in town, started the whole thing along with the doc, William Curless. Now, Dannon, he's got some pretty harsh ways of dealing with what he calls the 'Chinese Problem.'"

This kind of opportunity to glean information was hard to come by. He'd dig if he had to, but if he didn't have to? All the better.

He slipped a small notebook and pen from his coat pocket. "Was *he* behind the vigilantes who attacked the Chinese woman last week?"

"Not that a person would testify to. The sheer number of blind eyes in this town is mindboggling. Upstanding citizenry, church-going folk, all completely *unaware* of any wrongdoing—right under their own noses." Mr. Crocker shook his head and resumed pacing.

"What can be done on our end, Mr. Crocker? What will save this town's Chinese citizens? What will douse this powder keg?"

"There are still a number of good, God-fearing folks here, Mr. Campbell, don't get me wrong. They just have real timid voices. Right now, the lot of them are afraid we're going to find ourselves in the middle of a war—and it won't just be the Chinese Tongs. It will be a blood bath. Send us a marshal, Mr. Campbell. It's the only way. Maybe then, men like Dannon will back off. The weight of the U.S. government on his head just might be what it takes to squash him and his cronies."

Grant stood and offered his hand. "Thank you for meeting with me, Mr. Crocker. I believe you've opened our eyes to an area where we might affect some influence."

Mr. Crocker smoothed his chin whiskers and shook the proffered hand. "I appreciate you taking my request to your employers, Mr. Campbell. Tomorrow, I have business to tend to, or I'd show you around town."

"I'm comfortable making my way alone, sir."

"Chinatown can be a bit . . . surprising for some, Mr. Campbell."

"I was raised in San Francisco's Chinatown, sir. I doubt I'll see anything I haven't already."

"Is that right? I didn't think you a purebred Harvard man. Good for you! Are you familiar with the Occidental Mission Home for Girls, then?"

Grant gulped. He'd thought to remake his beginnings as he had back East. "Um . . . yes, sir. Many people are." That was truthful. He followed Mr. Crocker down the stairs and to the door.

"A fine work Miss Culbertson is doing. I've financially supported the home from its inception."

Dangerously close to a conversation he didn't want to have.

"Would that we had a mission home in Truckee. That is one venture I would surely get behind. Say, you wouldn't happen to be related—"

"I will have a full report on Mr. Huang's desk Monday morning." Grant donned his hat as fresh fire kindled inside him. At last, something on the agenda besides lining someone's pockets. "Good bye, Mr. Crocker. It was an honor meeting you."

San Francisco, California

"Why am I not meeting with Consul Bee this morning, Mr. Campbell?" Judge Kerrington shuffled papers and removed his glasses. Wheaten brows drew down as he peered across the bench.

"He's tending to a situation in Washington Territory, Your Honor." Three grueling days of depositions and paperwork had robbed Grant of all but minimal sleep. His stomach growled. His temple pulsed. He could feel the searing gaze of the churchwomen behind him, fanning their miasma of smug ideals.

"I believe we have a cause of action for presentation?" the judge asked him.

"Yes, Your Honor. You will find the documentation thorough. All requests are signed by both the Consolidated Benevolent Association representative and Mr. Huang, Consul General."

"Mr. Campbell, I understand you have everything well in hand, nonetheless, the people will be heard in this courtroom today." As Grant sat, the judge turned his attention to the plaintiff. "Mrs. Hickman?"

The woman stood, garnering a hush from her compatriots. She stepped into the aisle with a sheet of paper and cleared her voice before eyeing Grant with a schoolmarm's scrutiny. She bore a stork-like stance and an air of old money, which rankled him to no end. Another deep-pocket mogul. The very reason he'd left Boston.

"Your Honor, I represent San Francisco's Christian Women for Chastity. It is my understanding the *SS Oceanic* is carrying fifty-three women and twenty-two female children. All are *celestials*, brought to our lovely city for immoral purposes." A dramatic pause extracted admiring looks from her allies and stoicism from the judge.

"I ask that you ponder the backbone for your decision before making it, Your Honor, taking into consideration the base purpose of this ship's mission. Is it not to add to the current excess of Mongolians in our city—whose sole purpose is debauchery, hedonism, and vice? Is it not to lay further waste to a city awash with a most despicable race of slothful, addicted prostitutes who spread disease even unto respectable citizenry? Is it not—"

"Objection, Your Honor." Grant sprang to his feet. "Mrs. Hickman may believe she has demonstrated due diligence as it pertains to the Chinese Consul's request. Indeed, she apparently is insinuating a breach of moral law, waving the banner of malfeasance, which does not apply to this application of Civil Law."

"Objection sustained." The judge's shoulders slumped beneath the black robe as he sank back in his chair and motioned for Grant to sit. "Mrs. Hickman, is there any cause of action you can plead under the civil law to *not* dismiss your organization's claim at this time? And what remedy do you think you are entitled to?"

"I . . . uh." She wavered, then spurred on by her cohorts, "We would like for you to demand that ship return to a Chinese port and take those heathens back to where they belong . . . Your Honor."

"Thank you, Mrs. Hickman. You may sit down."

A simple request had turned into a dog and pony show. And a miserable showing for Grant's first case back home. He needed to turn the tide quickly. He stood, shooting his opponent a weighty gaze.

"Mr. Campbell, would you like to say something before I hand down my decision?" Judge Kerrington sat forward and cocked an eyebrow. A reporter in the corner scribbled madly in his notebook.

"Yes, Your Honor. I implore the Bench to consider the totality of the crew and passengers who await your decision, some of whom are white Europeans. They have been anchored beyond the harbor for six days awaiting entry—sustenance and fresh water dwindling. Is it fair to leave them to languish? Or is it right to return them on a thirty-day-plus voyage because a faction of white European-American women has misgivings about the morality of a minority of the ship's passengers?"

He raised open palms at his sides in a dramatic gesture, chuckling inside at a matronly gasp from the gallery. He imagined the women behind him, hankies clenched and faces pink with exasperation. "The Chinese Consulate rests, Your Honor." He sat, gaze pinned to the judge, watching for some sign of pragmatism.

Judge Kerrington glanced at the clock and scrawled ink across a document. "I am granting temporary landing rights to the Steam Ship *Oceanic* until such time as Mr. Huang can be heard on his Writ of Habeas Corpus." The gavel cracked. "Good day, Mr. Campbell." He nodded as he stood. "Ladies."

A flutter of *I-nevers* and *we'll see about that* and *this isn't finished* flapped about the courtroom as the gaggle of women migrated through the exit to champion yet another cause.

Grant stepped to the front of the room and waited for the judge to sign the clerk's documents. He would deliver them himself to the harbormaster and other official channels. If he hurried, the ship could dock by morning.

Briefcase in hand, he jogged to catch a cable car. There'd been no time to take in the sights since he was put to work the moment he arrived. A yawn claimed his entire face before he could free a hand for cover, and he suddenly realized just how little sleep he'd had since leaving Boston. Plans to sleep away the entire train ride were upset by *The Adventures of Huckleberry Finn*, begrudgingly rationed for the evenings. And then there was the riveting countryside he'd not seen in seven years.

Now, the familiar chink of the cable car rails and the conductor's prattle tugged him backwards in time. He found himself counting the tiers of homes on the hillside, just as he had as a boy.

He sucked in the sea air, and a torrent of memories drenched his heart. And all of them included Kira. He grinned, trying to envision a grown-up version of her. He didn't even know what his own sister looked like. Did Azalea still possess that indomitable optimism that used to drive him mad?

Guilt gnawed a hole in his conscience. He should've telegrammed his mother that he was coming. But it would be a nice surprise this way. He pounded his thigh. Who was he kidding? He was a selfish fool to leave the way he did. And a bigger fool to stay away. But it was the only way. An *escape*. It was supposed to be but a couple of years. Then three became five, and the pull of success was just too strong.

Grant crossed Waverly Place and continued up Clay Street with buoyant strides. The sights and sounds of his childhood enveloped him—a familiar blanket he had shed in desperation, exchanging it for the raucous Boston milieu.

He dodged two small-footed Chinese women with several servants in their wake. When he tipped his hat, they shrank back, wide-eyed.

More Joss houses had sprouted—places where the Qing worshiped any number of deities, ancestors, or folklore saints. Da had called them houses for lost souls. Behind them were just a few of

Chinatown's many cribs, where pale faces peered out from locked rooms. Even now, shattered voices advertised their trade in a crude, but businesslike fashion.

"*More lost souls, owned by other lost souls,*" Da's voice echoed in his head. A voice Grant had successfully ignored—for years. But here in San Francisco's Chinatown, his father was everywhere.

He stripped off his jacket, flung it over his shoulder, and strode on. The pungent stink of opium assaulted his nose—a reminder that men don't change. Had *he* changed? He'd certainly grown wiser. More self-possessed. Would his mother forgive him? But the simple truth was razor sharp. Even a mother has limits.

One block beyond the white brothels, he stopped. A gleaming bronze sign read CHINESE CONSOLIDATED BENEVOLENT ASSOCIATION. He stood there outside the Six Companies headquarters, wondering if his office door sported a new nameplate yet. It felt good to be a part of something bigger—with more reach than his meager efforts in a courtroom.

He sailed through the front door and smiled as he opened his office, one finger swiping over the shiny letters of his name. After slipping a folder from his desk and another from his valise, he headed down the hall to meet with Yung Wing and Mr. Huang.

"Tea, Mr. Campbell?" Yung Wing's ample cheeks obscured his eyes as he smiled. "We have a victory today I hear."

"You heard correctly. Are you spying on me?" Grant grinned, lifting the fragile cup, letting the herbal steam touch his face. Trussed up in western suits, both men were impeccably dressed—and obviously more relaxed than he was.

Mr. Huang laughed. "No, no, no. I was not spying. I received a telephone call from Judge Kerrington. He said you have now met Mrs. Hickman."

"That I did. I assume she will become a regular nuisance." Exactly what he didn't need.

"Actually, unless Mrs. Hickman decides to leave the city, I doubt you will see much of her. There are a number of concerns for you to tend to in other cities. I hope you do not mind the train."

The train? His bones were still bereft of rigor from his cross-country ride. Thank goodness for the stop in Truckee. "Did you read my report about the meeting with Mr. Crocker, sirs?"

"Yes," Yung Wing said. "You have confirmed some of what we suspected. Do you think a marshal will make a difference?"

"I do. If it is the right man. A man who cares for justice and holds no prejudice. A wise man. Unfortunately, we are at the mercy of the U.S. government to assign the marshal."

Mr. Yung leaned in. "But surely a qualified marshal would be recommended for the job?"

"Let us hope so, sir. I will send a telegram."

Three

SAN FRANCISCO

Yakira dangled the cloth bag in the air, testing its weight before untying the string. With one quick jerk, coins clattered and money bundles struck the tabletop. "Oops." She lunged to slap a hand onto four runaway coins.

Azalea squeezed her eyes tight, rocking back and forth to some unheard rhythm. "I am praying for a loaves-and-fishes miracle. Count slowly so the money will grow."

"Good. That is exactly what we need at the moment." Yakira laid out the paper money and then counted silently, sliding small piles of coins into larger piles. "Fifty-three dollars and sixty-two cents."

"Count again." Azalea clasped her hands beneath her chin, and her lips moved in a soundless plea to heaven.

Yakira scooped the bills and coins into a mound and began counting all over again. The *Oceanic* would soon dock, and there was but a small window of time for them to act.

Aunt Lara stepped up to the table and added another folded bill to the piles. Her brow rumpled, eyes glued to the meager piles. "How much?"

This money would make the difference between life and death for one Chinese girl on that ship. "I'm counting again." Yakira twitched her head toward Azalea. "Waiting for the loaves and fishes to multiply."

"Well now, they just did, did they not?" Aunt Lara settled an arm around Azalea's waist. "Did you check the safe twice?"

"No, but you can," Yakira said, disappointment rusting through her hope. "*Sixty*-three dollars and sixty-*three* cents."

Azalea opened her eyes, her typical smile not quite blooming. "But God will still use what we have."

Da breezed into the room, teeth gleaming between grizzled whiskers. "That He will, ladies. That He will."

Aunt Lara stepped toward him, sparking of mischief. "And ye've a reason for such optimism, I assume?"

"That I have." He waved an envelope. "Our latest benevolence from our favorite benefactor. And I've permission from the board to assign its use."

Yakira kissed his cheek and craftily slipped the envelope from his fingers to peek inside. "Two-hundred dollars?" But for her commitment to adulthood, she would've bounced up and down and squealed like a six-year-old.

Azalea grinned from ear to ear, her eyes closed, hands still folded piously beneath her chin. "Thank you, Father, for your provision. And for the loaves and fishes."

"Loaves and fishes?" Da turned a quirked eye to Yakira.

"Yes! Loaves and fishes!" Azalea beamed, hands clapping and feet bouncing—a complete *lack* of commitment to adulthood.

Yakira laughed and touched Da's hand. "I'll explain later. Now we have two hundred, sixty-three dollars and sixty-three cents. Let's pray all the way to the docks."

"I heard that. Praise the Almighty!" Miss Culbertson rushed in from outside, her face flushed. "We must hurry!"

They bustled out the door, but Aunt Lara barred Azalea with one arm. "I'm sorry, my sweet girl. You know we canna have you down there this time. Someone could snatch you up, and we could lose you."

Azalea stepped back, her enthusiasm soured to a pucker. "I thought I'd grown old enough to not have to worry about that, Mother."

Aunt Lara wrapped her in a quick hug. "You know you are my treasure. And I will keep you from harm, always."

She knew It stung her sweet friend to stay behind, but Azalea bore it with dignity, something that would've come hard for Yakira. "Perhaps next time a disguise?" She squeezed Azalea's wrist. "Pray, dear cousin. Pray our money will be enough!" She kissed her cheek and rushed after the others.

Seagulls soared, their cries complemented by the milling crowds along the wharf. The *Oceanic* bobbed gently as workers attached a gangplank. Stevedores stacked crates and trunks on carts and then worked in tandem to prevent them from rolling away and crashing into the dock.

A cargo net swayed mid-air, suspended by a long beam, prepared to deliver the heaviest cargo. Yakira stumbled backwards when the net above her groaned loud and long with its burden. Da pulled her closer, always her protector.

White travelers made their way off the ship, greeted by chittering family, friends, and servants in white livery. Long moments crawled as the welcoming crowds thinned, only to be replaced by others. Wagons began appearing, pulling up close to the crowds. Three men, each with a whip looped at his side, stood at the bottom of the gangplank.

Aunt Lara grasped Yakira's hand as Chinese children of all ages, most of them girls, scurried down the plank, hustled about by another man, waving his arms. "*Fáai dī!*" (Come on, hurry-up.) A sheen of hunger haunted frightened faces. Rags draped most of the gaunt forms. But every face had been scrubbed clean—for the buyers.

Dear Heavenly Father, please. Please let there be just one we can save. Never would Yakira ignore the incessant ache that gnawed away at her heart. These were God's precious children, but evil called them merchandise. Evil called them disposable. She swiped at a tear and sucked in a quivery breath, determined to be strong.

Chinese women followed the children. An arranged *groom* would meet those of a higher class—obvious in their pleated skirts and wide-sleeved jackets. But most of the girls wore the loose-legged *kuzi* and coat of the peasant class, having been sold, perhaps by the family patriarch, to feed other mouths. All these girls had ever known was the countryside farms, green with happiness—before surrendering to a blight of starvation.

Yakira swallowed down grief, but it met anger coming up and lodged in her throat. Most would share the same fate without some kind of intervention. They would disappear into Chinatown, and few would live to see the end of their six to eight-year indentures.

Men herded the children aboard one wagon, and while the women were loaded into a different wagon, a scuffle broke out. Da's hand tightened, swallowing Yakira's own. One child began crying. Then another. One of the older girls pulled away from her wagon, determined to soothe the first child with a protective arm.

Yakira shook off Da's grasp and rushed to the older girl's side. "You must go back or they will beat you," she said in Cantonese, tugging on the girl's arm. Only then did she notice the twisted hand, surely expertly hidden all this time. The girl's eyes snapped in horror that Yakira had noticed.

"She is my sister," the girl said.

Yakira nodded her understanding, determined to make a difference here. If only God would make a way. "What is your name?"

"Gao Zhen."

"Show them your hand," she whispered to the girl as she ushered her back to the women. "Show them your hand."

Miss Culbertson looped arms with Aunt Lara and pushed on ahead as they followed the wagons to the auction site. Yakira clung to Da, praying for a miracle. Another miracle. Hadn't God brought in the extra money?

The wagons halted in a warehouse yard. Money flashed. Voices buzzed. Fingers pointed. Hands fondled. Teeth were checked.

Yakira looked on with her family as wicked men auctioned off the young women like livestock.

"Six hundred twenty!"

"Six hundred forty!"

"Seven hundred!"

She cringed with every triumphant "Sold!" from the auctioneer.

A frock-coated man in a fine derby sat at a makeshift table recording the indenture details and dispensing documents. A liveried servant stood statue-still, suspending a black umbrella above the official's head.

They would have to bide their time. She remembered the day Aunt Lara and Uncle Errol brought Azalea home. From an auction just like this one. Her dearest laotong. Such a gift, bought with a mere $400 on a rainy, wind-swept day.

"Oh, the children," Miss Culbertson groaned. "Such beautiful children. Lord have mercy." She dabbed her eyes with a hanky before pulling back her shoulders, determination setting her jaw. "Two-hundred sixty-three dollars and sixty-three cents, Lord." The words—a whispered prayer—became Yakira's own.

"*Mh hóu!*" (No, don't.) Gao Zhen's little sister screamed as a man ripped her from her sister's arms. The air cracked with a slap, and Gao Zhen crumpled in a heap.

"No!" Yakira squirmed, ready to intervene, but Da's grip was a vise.

She fought back tears as every child fetched a hefty price, whisked away as quickly as their new owner could sign the indenture paper. She swallowed back bile again and again as her stomach threatened to erupt. A silk-robed merchant, flanked by Tong bodyguards, purchased four of the young girls, including Gao Zhen's sister. How she ached for the sisters. Surely there was a special place in hell for such men as these.

The crowds thinned quickly as the indentures disappeared with their new masters. They were like ghosts vanishing into the darkest recesses of Chinatowns throughout the West. With only a sickly young woman and Gao Zhen remaining, she drew Da closer to the invisible line where *shoppers* stood. Miss Culbertson clutched the bag of money, her lips silently forming the most ardent of pleas to the Almighty.

A guard jerked Gao Zhen to her feet. She barely stood upright, as if she'd collapse at any moment. Her face hidden beneath a stringy black waterfall.

"Gao Zhen. Show them your hand." Yakira spoke the words for her ears alone in perfect Cantonese.

The girl looked up from the ground, finding Yakira's eyes, a question in her own. Yakira nodded, repeating the plea.

With gazes locked on one another, Gao Zhen seemed just now to understand. She pulled up her sleeve and thrust her hand into the air. Gasps and grumbling peppered the air. One man stomped off, obscenities trailing him.

The guard struck Gao Zhen in the back, and she hurled forward, knees slamming to the hard ground. Yakira winced. "Foolish girl," he hissed. He jerked her upright and half-dragged her to the auction block, gripping her arm so her sleeve covered the withered hand.

But the secret was out, so the disgruntled crowd quickly dissipated. And there was an opening bid.

"One hundred dollars." Miss Culbertson stretched up a hand.

"One hundred fifty," sneered an ancient little Chinese man, his glare attempting to send a message to his opponent.

Miss Culbertson challenged him, lightning in her eyes. "Two hundred."

"Two hundred fifty."

With one hand to her waist, she stepped closer, a mere two feet from the other bidder. "Two. Hundred. Sixty." Her words could have chinked a mountain.

Seconds ticked by.

The man lifted his whiskered chin and spat. "You are old yak!" He whipped around and trudged away.

Yakira glanced sideways at her father, giddy to see his own lips twitching to stall a smile.

"Sold!"

The gavel *CRACKED*!

Miss Culbertson marched directly to the man at the table with a jaunty lilt to her step and an envelope in her hand.

The beginning of a new life for Gao Zhen! Laughter trickled from Yakira's throat, and joy warmed her like the summer sun. She exchanged excited looks with Da and Aunt Lara. They would celebrate later. For now, it was all business. And thank God, they were going about the Father's business.

Avery bade Lara sit, for he was not sure she would welcome his news. It was a grand step, and it felt right. It was time for a new chapter in his life. In his precious Yakira's life, too.

"Avery, I dinna like surprises. You know that." Lara scooted to the edge of the brocade chair, sea-blue eyes watching him. "Out with it. Now."

He sat and then stood again. "I've been approached by the Mission Board in New York to head up a joint ministry with a Methodist, Ira Harrington up in Eureka. A ministry to the Chinese."

Her sweet smile met the news. An insincere one—for the lack of a dimple in her left cheek exposed the foible. "That's wonderful, Avery. But your work here. Do ye feel it is finished?"

"Och, Lara. My work isna ever truly finished. There are others here to carry on." He paced to the window. Silence screamed, knotting his insides. He returned to face her. "There's a good-sized Chinatown in Eureka, and there isna one church that welcomes them. The fields are white for harvest, my dear."

"And what of Kira? What says she about this?"

"I've not told her yet." He scratched his neck, wondering why the room had warmed so. "I thought to tell you first."

She chewed her lip. "And when would ye be leavin'?"

He sat on the adjacent chair and almost grasped her hand. "*Weel*, now. Not so verra soon. In a fortnight."

"I see." Her mouse-like reply brought a lump to his throat.

"This isna just about me, Lara. A house has been donated to be used for ministry as I see fit. Tell me the truth, now. Do ye think Yakira is ready for her own Mission Home for Girls?"

She brightened, and the *douce* dimple emerged. "Oh, Avery, she will be thrilled for the opportunity. You might ask Miss Culbertson, but I believe Kira is ready."

On impulse he covered her hand with his, surprised at how like Cait's it seemed, if only for an instant. They were sisters, after all. So much alike in many ways, from their stately form to their coal-black locks. Striking women, both of them.

"I will miss your bonnie face, Lara Mitchell." He grunted, tamping down a measure of reluctance. "I dinna like leaving you and Azalea here alone."

"*Wheest*! None of that. In a house full of girls, how could I possibly be alone?" She slipped her hand from his touch and stood, looking down at him. "But Avery, we must talk."

He knew that tone. And the way her eyes switched to stormy waters, he had an inkling as to the subject matter. He sat back. Waiting.

"You are about to take Yakira from the only home she has ever known. Already ye have waited too long, Avery. She is a woman grown, and ye need to tell her."

"Lara—"

"I know. 'Tis always one reason or another ye've got in your head. Always a reason to wait another day. She is twenty-one years old, Avery. She deserves to know the truth."

"Ye ken I promised Cait."

"And my sister would have come to her senses long before this, had she lived, God rest her soul."

It was like climbing uphill. The steepest of hills with this one. As it had been with Cait when she set her mind to something. He bent forearms to knees and clasped his hands. A defeated man he was. "I will tell her."

"You'll tell her." She crossed her arms, grilling him with a look that robbed him of a foot of stature. "*When* will ye tell her?"

"I . . . I will *try* to tell her before we arrive in Eureka. On the boat." Surrounded by people. Witnesses to the cowardice that had haunted him much, much too long.

The Pacific Ocean

Avery aroused from a lazy nap to the discord of seabirds. Their noise sailed above the muffled rhythm of pistons and waves pounding the metal hull of the *SS George W Elder*. He licked his lips and raised his gaze to the gray curls of smoke gusting from the tall, black stack and bare riggings beyond. Casually stroking his beard, he rolled the tips of his wide mustache, self-consciously taking in his surroundings. How long had he slept?

A dozen men and women soaked up the sun from deck chairs, having stolen his idea for repose. Blanketed and bundled against the brisk ocean air, most engaged in muted conversation. The few passengers engrossed in books sadly missed out on the intoxicating beauty of the Pacific coastline.

Jeweled water glistened to the west. To the east, waves drenched the foundations of gray and blue monoliths, here and there eclipsed by shrub-less, angry crags. Green velvet blanketed rolling hills beyond. Such splendor.

"You're awake." He turned his head at Kira's nudge. Her bonnet brim shaded chestnut eyes, and pink ribbons anchored it lest the healthy breeze whisk it away. *Treasure Island* lay neglected on her lap.

Despite the chill, her smile warmed him. Always a treasure, this daughter of his. Why had he promised so long ago? If only he could've seen into the future, to this day. An impossibly difficult situation, it was. *Cait my love, you've put me in a hardscrabble place.*

"It's beautiful, isn't it?" Kira gazed out over the gentle waves. "Oh." She handed him a newspaper. "The porter gave this to us. I thought you might find a Eureka newspaper informative."

"Ah, Yakira Jean. You've made me a proud father, ye have." He winked and touched the side of his nose.

"Now that's the second time since we left San Francisco you've said that. And I've done nothing." She swiveled, cocking her head to one side. "Feelin' *peely-wally*, Da?"

He chuckled at her Scots. "Nae." Ah, his bonny girl. Such a joy to be had. Thankful for the distraction, he shook open *The Humboldt Times.* A large advertisement instantly assaulted him. WE DON'T EMPLOY CHINESE HELP read the notice above the ad.

Turning the page, he perused the news. "Appears there's trouble aplenty in Eureka. More so than I had thought. There is an editorial here calling for the destruction of Chinatown. Apparently, it stinks."

"It stinks?" Kira looked over his arm, her gaze following his finger. "Oh. It stinks. Well, why doesn't the town take care of the sewage trouble?"

"From what I see here, they would sooner just burn it all down. They have Tong troubles up here too, it seems."

"I had hoped we left that behind in San Francisco." She picked at her fingernails, and her shoulders slumped.

"Ah, now." He patted her hand. "Reverend Harrington assures me things are different there. He has made some converts among the Chinese. If that is any indication, you will surely find the churchwomen supportive of your endeavors."

She brightened. "My own mission home. I can't wait. I know I must wear many hats at first, but with God's help, it will become just like the Occidental. Wouldn't that be wonderful?"

Her enthusiasm prodded him to venture less reluctantly into the unknown. His conscience niggled at him again. "Kira?" *Out with it, man.*

"Mmm hmm." She'd taken up her book again.

In the distance, the shoreline crags gave way to trees. Giant ones, from the looks of it. But his insides commiserated more with the starker landscape.

"Your name."

She lowered the book and faced him, curiosity shirring her lips.

"Your mother and I put sincere thought into your name. *Yakira.* It means beloved." He smiled, remembering. "And *Jean*, for you are a gift to two stalwart Scots." What words could ease the jolt of hearing about her beginnings? He pursed his lips, planning his next foray into this volatile truth-telling.

"I know this, Da." She smiled, indulging him now.

"You were . . . you *are* a beloved gift. From God to us." He brushed back a silky ebony wisp from her cheek. "If only your mother could see the *sonsie* woman you've become . . ."

She abandoned her book. Settling her head against his shoulder, she hugged his arm—his undoing. "I love you too."

He sighed and covered her hands. And asked forgiveness for his cowardice once again.

Four

San Francisco

Grant stared at the heavy oak door, one arm balancing flowers and gifts—the other arm a lead weight at his side. He swallowed, gathering courage as sweat trickled down his back.

The building—the Occidental Mission Home for Girls—hadn't changed in the least. But *he* had. And he hoped it was enough to leave his past behind and begin anew. As much as his arms ached to embrace his sister and mother, his feet urged him to run. To turn away and pretend he'd never come to San Francisco instead of risking their rejection. He didn't deserve their forgiveness. Da was dead because of him. His mother's grief compounded because of the way he'd left. He had once tasted of grace. Now he needed it more than ever.

Hand aquiver, he laid it to the knocker. But his fingers hedged, unwilling to tap this fragile shell lest it shatter what hull of a family he had left. He had stood nose to nose with dangerous criminals, gang bosses, and corrupt politicians. But facing his mother and

46

sister would be the hardest thing he'd ever done. Drawing a shaky breath, he pulled back his shoulders.

He knocked once. Twice. The door opened, and a petite Chinese woman peeked out. Spice-hued eyes framed a heart-shaped face. His parched throat convulsed. *Steady on.*

Suddenly her eyes widened, and a hand flew to her lips. The door swung wide, and she stepped forward, starbursts in her smile.

"I am here to see Azalea and Lara Campbell," he said in rusty Chinese.

"Your Cantonese is still no so good, brother." Her laughter brimmed—a musical thing, with all the soul of a hearty Scottish reel. She flung her arms wide, pinning flowers and packages to his sides as she planted her head in his middle with a boyish squeeze.

"Azalea?" This beauty was his little sister? A sea wave crashed against his heart, dousing his throat and flooding his eyes. Abandoning the gifts, he lifted her slight frame, smothering her in a stout hug as if seven years had never happened.

"I knew you would return to us. I knew you would!" She gazed up at him through a shower of tears, and he set her down and brushed away his own.

"You, little sister, have grown into a *verra sonsie* woman."

"And you, my brother, have grown into a *verra* tall man." She giggled and looped her arm through his.

He handed her the flowers and retrieved the packages. "I come bearing gifts."

"You are gift enough. Come, let us find Mother."

But for a chair here and there, nothing had changed in the home. Girlish voices carried from the classroom. A housekeeper, whom Azalea introduced as Elizabeth, flitted through the hall. A girl bounded down the stairs, appearing unwell with her flushed cheeks and soot-rimmed eyes. She halted at the sight of them. Azalea motioned for her to come, saying something he didn't quite catch.

"Brother, this is Gao Zhen. This is God's *mui tsai*."

"You have an indentured girl?"

Azalea's eyes smiled. "Not I."

Understanding dawned—*purchased.* As Azalea had been when he was only thirteen years old. He bowed to Gao Zhen. "*Néih yáuh fūk.*" (You are blessed.)

Her guarded expression dissolved, and she bowed a thank you before looking to Azalea for dismissal. Only then did he notice her deformed hand.

"It was Kira's doing, otherwise we would've come from the *Oceanic* empty-handed." She hung his coat and hat on the hall tree.

The *Oceanic.* Satisfaction swelled along with all the other emotions battering him just now. He had done something right. Something good.

"Mother should be finished with her class in a few minutes. Let us sit for tea." Azalea tugged him toward the parlor after requesting tea service from Elizabeth. "I want to hear all about your life in Boston. Or wherever you have kept yourself hidden away."

No indictment weighted her words, and for that he wanted to kiss her. He sat, still holding her hand, words buried beneath years of pent-up lament. His gaze stole to the doorway, hoping Kira would appear. Shamefully, the want to see his mother was wavering. But Kira could pave the way, settling his doubts. Unless her own fury was more than he could bear.

"Where is Kira?" he asked finally, slapping his thigh to settle his bouncing knee.

Azalea frowned. "I am afraid you missed her and Uncle Avery by only two days. They have moved to Eureka to take a mission."

"Eureka?" Disappointment slammed him, surprising him with its intensity. "A mission?"

"Uncle Avery is helping with the Chinese there, and a house has been donated for Kira to have her own mission home. It has long been her dream." She searched his eyes as if to see through him. "Do not be sad, brother. This is a good thing for them."

But he wanted Kira. *Needed* to see her. He forced a smile. "I am happy for them."

"Your eyes tell me something else." She squeezed his hand and stood as voices followed Elizabeth into the room with the tea service. "I will get Mother."

Steam swirled from the teapot, briefly mesmerizing. He gathered the gifts into his lap nervously, a schoolboy about to be taken to task by the teacher. The mantle clock chimed thrice, much louder than he remembered. His forefinger tapped out a rhythm against the brown wrapping paper before setting the gifts back on the floor.

Four Chinese girls peeked into the room as they scurried past the doorway. "Ladies," he said, brandishing a polite smile. Whispers and giggles followed them up the staircase—friendly ghosts of his past. Happiness had always filled these halls. A fine place for a girl to grow to womanhood. This home was his mother and father's legacy. How many girls did this place save from a hellish existence? And now, another mission home was set into motion. He smiled at the thought, for Kira was surely in her element, bossy and protective as ever—helping the helpless, giving them legs to walk.

"Grant?"

His heart dropped into his stomach. "*Mither.*" With nerves like pinpricks, he stood. He wanted to reach out to her, to embrace her, but the soles of his shoes seemed glued to the carpet.

She floated across the room. Moist eyes, more lined at the corners now, shone with a mother's love. She moved a hand to her throat, wonder caressing her sweet face. She touched his sleeve. "You . . . you are here."

All dignity crumbled. He was a boy again. She pressed her hands to the sides of his face, and he felt them tremble when he covered them with his own. Grand tears coursed down her cheeks as her eyes searched him as if to ensure he was all there. She nodded then, jerky little movements until a smile blossomed full and welcoming. And if he wasn't mistaken—oh, how he didn't want to be mistaken—there was forgiveness and acceptance in those eyes. But 'twas a blur, for her image swam in his vision.

"I am home."

She fell into his arms. Which of them held up the other was a mystery as they wept together. Laughed together. Joy cracked wide his shackles, and the freedom felt every bit like love. Like family.

When Grant at last settled his mother into a chair and poured her and Azalea cups of tea, it was cold. But no one mentioned it. "I brought you each a gift. Kira and Uncle Avery also. But I understand I missed them."

"They were eager to be off on their new adventure," Mither said. But her enthusiasm belied her countenance. "Yakira will have her mission home, and Avery a new ministry to the people of his heart."

"She seems so young for such an undertaking." She would always be fourteen to him.

"Too young?" Azalea clattered teacup to saucer. "Kira would have taken on a home of her own years ago if she but had the chance."

He held up his hands in peace. "I take it back. No doubt she is more than capable. It is hard to think of her as a grown woman"—he winked at Azalea—"as it is you, my little sister. It will take some getting used to. But you are not the only one who has changed."

"Changed?" Mither's question poked his heart.

"I am no longer that foolish, selfish boy."

"You were neither foolish nor selfish, son. Just hurting." The kindness in her eyes began to mend the gaping tear inside him.

He stared at the striped wallpaper, where golden flower petals distorted into faces. And they were daring him. His throat burned, but he plunged ahead. "Forgive me for hurting you. For leaving as I did." He had to get this out. "Forgive me for—"

"Wheest! I'll have no more of that." She set her teacup down so hard it rattled.

"But Mither, I have to tell you—"

She grasped both his hands and kissed them, piercing him through with another healing stitch. "Ye are me beloved son, and of course I forgive you. Now, I willna have another word of it."

But she didn't know the whole truth of Da's death. And now she'd fervently overruled his feeble efforts to stand accountable.

"I thought you would be proud of me." Grant paced the floor.

"Son, I am proud of you. I am simply saying that Six Companies doesna always have the Chinese's best interest at the heart of what they do." Mither stood to face him. Though she was a woman of uncommon height, he still towered over her.

"But I will be looking out for the Chinese, isn't that what you and Father would want?" He'd been so sure she would be happy about this career choice. His entire rearing centered on ministry to the Chinese—their welfare, both physically and spiritually. Fair treatment. Fair living conditions. What more could he do?

"Your da would be proud to have you walk in his steps, 'tis true. But mind ye look beneath the surface of what the Federation will have you do by them. I've seen many a time when Consul Bee touted Six Companies policy at the cost of individual men's and women's rights."

"I promise, Mither. I will do everything within my power to fight for the individuals. If Six Companies loses sight of that, I will remind them." He was tired of big business trampling the little man in pursuit of money—of enterprise built on the broken backs of immigrants unable even to support their families. He hadn't seen it at first. All fresh and starry-eyed in his first years of private practice, he'd been thrilled with the paychecks signed by big money. Right up until he saw what the laws were doing to the immigrants. Now it was time to make a difference. To do right by his father.

Five

EUREKA, CALIFORNIA

Avery bowed and offered a smile to the two men walking in the opposite direction as his companion hailed them by name. Hopefully, by this time next month, they'd no longer be strangers to him.

Two-tiered shacks lined both sides of Chinatown's wide, muddy street, many of them built over businesses. A few homes on stilts afforded shelter of sorts for livestock or storage below. A shingle sagged above a window, advertising in big English letters, WASH-ING AND IRONING BY TUNG SING.

The pervasive odor intensified as he strode across the street. He watched as a duck landed to feast on refuse in the slough that cut through the center of the street. Decaying vegetables and filth formed a green scum on the water, its odor mingling with the stink of dried fish and opium.

"I know what you're thinking," Ira Harrington said. "Precisely why we are presenting a united front with the owner of this bur-geoning plot of land."

"There isna drainage to be had?" Avery stared at the stagnant effluence, denying his face a reaction to the stench.

"Now that would be a fine idea, wouldn't it?" Harrington's voice dripped with sarcasm. "There *was* drainage at one time."

They turned the corner, and Avery noticed the same man had been following them since entering Chinatown. The very same quilted gray coat and round hat, not the telltale dress of the Tong.

"I will only be a moment, Ira." He did an about-face, bent on engaging the man, who promptly slipped into a clothing store. *Odd*.

"Is there a problem?" Ira's white brows puckered with concern.

"Not at all. Not at all." He brushed a hand through the air. "Lead on."

The next few blocks took them out of Chinatown. But just as he thought they would exchange the stench for fresh salt breezes, he balked. *More* foulness. Three of the stores they passed sported identical window cards: WE DO NOT DEAL IN CHINESE GOODS. "What is this?" Avery asked. "I've seen these around town."

Ira harrumphed. "Frank Roney's 'Pacific Coast League of Deliverance.' Members pay their ten-cent dues, say a pledge, and spend a dollar to post their prejudices. Wait here." Leaving Avery standing on the boardwalk, he slipped into the leather works store for mere seconds and returned. "Here." He handed over a small card, and they walked on. "Might as well know what you're getting into, my friend."

Avery squinted at the small print. "'I hereby pledge my honor that I will not employ or patronize Chinese, directly or indirectly, nor will I knowingly patronize any person, directly or indirectly, who does employ Chinese.' Och. Is this truly catching on?" He'd expected challenges in Eureka, but not this.

Ira raked his fingers through his salted beard and walked on. "Here and there. But it's the abusive, violent mindset I fear more than anything." He waved to someone through a store window. "There's a sturdy fence between law-abiding citizens and a riotous crowd, but it only takes the right force to knock it over." He halted at the Palace Stables. "We're here."

"We're meeting in a stable?"

"Owned by Casper Ricks."

"Ah. A regular entrepreneur." He chuckled, and Ira opened the door, bypassing the empty office and stepping into the dim barn. Several of the stalls displayed carved plaques bearing surnames, some of which he had already come to recognize. Straw and manure mingled in the air, more welcome than the odors they'd left behind in Chinatown.

"Reverend Harrington. To what do I owe the pleasure?" A stocky man with more hair on his chin than on his head shook Ira's hand.

"Casper Ricks, I'd like you to meet Reverend Avery Mitchell. He's joined me to aid in ministry." Ira passed a knowing look to Avery.

After the pleasantries, Ira wasted no time. "What's to be done about drainage of that gulch down the middle of Chinatown? There's plenty of complaining about the stench, but no solutions."

Ricks shook his head. "You're barking up the wrong tree here, Reverend. You gotta talk to Mayor Wallace. He's the one that spearheaded the new street construction. It was one of those new streets he redone that blocked the drainage outta Chinatown. Not a plum thing I can do about it."

"As if it were done on purpose, then." Avery huffed out the words before he thought better of it. "What I mean to say is—"

"It's all right, Avery," Ira said. "You said what you meant to say and you are not wrong. Go on."

"I assume you collect rent from the Chinese for the dwellings and businesses on your property, Mr. Ricks?" Avery asked.

"Of course. I'm a businessman, Reverend Mitchell. I don't see where that's any concern of yours, though." Ricks crammed his hat back onto his head. "I've got work to do, gentlemen. I suggest you take up your complaints with Mayor Wallace. Good day." He spat a stream of brown juice and strode past them.

"That dinna go so well."

Ira slapped him on the shoulder. "Let's talk to David Kendall."

"Aye. He's on the city council is he not?"

"Yes, indeed."

He followed Ira across the street. Impressive, the way the man comported himself. Somehow, he'd managed to walk the line between white men and Chinese men, bludgeoned by neither side. And his heart was wholly for the Chinese in this town. Conversion to Christianity was a difficult thing, steeped as the Tang people were in ancient customs and beliefs. But God was doing a good work here among them, and grateful he was to be a part of it all. He'd only stayed in San Francisco so long because of Kira. And Lara too, if he were honest with himself.

Still though, he yearned for something else. Something formless and nameless. Indeed, at times he felt as though he'd left his heart back beside his beloved Cait, in that vast watery deep between two countries.

The trek to Kendall's office took them back toward Chinatown, and when they arrived, Ira explained their objective.

"You're wasting your time with the mayor," said David Kendall. "The people that man actually listens to are few. If you don't own a business, he won't even see you." He handed a newspaper to Avery. "Take a gander: 'Wipe out the Plague Spots.'"

Avery scowled, his disposition souring more as he read the article. "'Our readers know and acknowledge that this leper's colony is a curse to the city and its future prosperity.' Pretty harsh words."

"And that, my friend, sums up the pervasive attitude of this town's newspaper and much of its citizenry." David poked the paper. "Keep it. There's more oh-so-cheerful news to read." He offered a cocked smile. "I'm only one councilman. I can't part the Red Sea all by myself. It's going to take an act of God to get the rest of the City Council and the mayor to move toward a peaceable solution to what they've coined, 'The Chinese Problem.'"

Ira gripped David's shoulder. "You're a good man, David. Keep fighting the good fight!"

"I try." David nodded, and they bid him goodbye.

Ira closed the door behind them, a twinkle in his eye. "We need more men like him on our side, Avery."

"Aye. That we do." And he wondered if the churchwomen Kira was meeting with at the moment would have the same attitude.

"I cannot tell you ladies how pleased I am to be in your charming town. I am so happy to be heading up such a valuable ministry. Our Mission Home for Girls will provide the most essential spiritual, educational, and domestic training for young women." Yakira distributed lists to each of the church ladies. "I've taken the liberty of jotting down a few items we will need to get started."

Every copy went to eager hands, and she waited impatiently as they read. Her empty fingers smoothed the embroidered tulips on her bodice. Then she clasped her hands to avoid picking her fingernails. *Breathe, Yakira.* A few murmurs. A few smiles.

"This list is quite comprehensive, Miss Mitchell. Skirts, blouses, slippers, bloomers, stockings, slates, chalk, paper, pencils, chalkboard . . ."

"Yes, Mrs. Carlyle. The young women will have many needs. First and foremost will be spiritual, of course." Yakira smiled, heart racing as she considered the wonderful turnout of ladies and their obvious interest. "I'd like to offer up a heart-felt thank you to Mr. and Mrs. Carlyle for their generous offer of a house for Eureka's first Mission Home for Girls." She smiled at Mrs. Carlyle and mouthed a *thank you*, grateful beyond words, as others joined her in clapping.

"You are most welcome, Miss Mitchell. I heartily agree with your enthusiasm to help those less-fortunate in our community."

A woman in the back row raised a gloved hand. "I can donate my old sewing machine. My Clayton just bought me a new one." The woman smiled from ear to ear. "It's the newest Singer model," she said more to the woman next to her.

"Splendid! Thank you. It will be most useful." Yakira could barely contain her glee.

"And I have a few outdated skirts I don't mind donating. I'll ask around." Another woman offered as she stood, swatting an invisible fly. "Pffft. Why don't you just let me work on getting all the clothing you may need?" She touched her nose. "I have my ways." Chuckles sprinkled the room.

"Ethyl, what you have is a mastery of persuasion!" one woman blurted, and Ethyl joined in the laughter.

Yakira pressed a hand to her throat, awed by their enthusiasm.

"And I'll speak with my husband about donating the school supplies. We already stock most of what you have here on the list. How many girls are you planning for initially?"

"Thank you, Mrs. Olson." Yakira had feared thinking too optimistically, but she felt suddenly brave. "I believe it would be prudent to plan for ten girls in the home to start."

"I notice you have bedding, and beds. Might we have a quilting bee to donate some quilts?"

"Wonderful idea, Caroline. I will host a bee in my home. Next week Thursday?" Ideas flew about the room as women chittered, and Yakira's heart took wing. Never had she felt more ready to step into Miss Culbertson's shoes than right now at *this* mission home.

All her prayers over the last few years had finally culminated in one wonderful, living opportunity. And this endearing group of ladies would meet all the Home's needs.

"Excuse me, Miss Mitchell." Ethyl raised her hand.

"Yes?"

"I notice you didn't mention Bibles. Surely an oversight."

"I did not include them on the list since the girls will first be learning Bible verses by rote in their native language. Bibles will come once they've learned to read and write in English." Yakira stepped forward, clasping her hands in front of her. "It is such a joy to—"

"Native language?" Mrs. Carlyle stood, and silence sucked the air from the room. "Surely you are not planning on housing savages?" Her eyes bulged. She brought a lace hanky to her nose.

Stunned by the woman's attitude, Yakira swallowed a retort and oozed professionalism. "No, Mrs. Carlyle, I am not here to minister to the indigenous people."

Sighs of relief.

"But you said native language."

"Yes. While many of the Chinese girls speak some English, at the Mission Home—"

"Chinese girls? Surely you are not planning to—"

"Yes, Chinese girls." Fire seared her neck, her face. But she charged ahead. "Girls who have been brought here against their wills and forced into a most heinous state of slavery."

Chairs scraped and disapproval hissed through the room as the women stood. Voices rose to a cacophony. Yakira staggered backwards, trapped against the wall, watching her dream crumble—bricks to dust, dust to the wind.

Mrs. Carlyle stepped to the front of the room. "Ladies. Ladies! Please, calm yourselves. I believe there has been either a grave misunderstanding or a shameful sleight of hand. I rescind my offer of a house for this . . . this *Mission Home for Girls*." She spat the words and turned to Yakira. "Young woman, you have done the fine women of this community an injustice by supposing we would lend our support to this . . . this subversion."

Never, ever in her life had Yakira been more at a loss for words. Perhaps Providence stymied her tongue. She waited as the women cleared the room. She stood tall, shoulders drawn back and chin up, chewing the inside of her cheek until she tasted blood.

They'd not see her cry. Indeed, they would not.

Six

En route to Truckee

After a quick stretch of his legs, Grant begrudgingly settled into his seat. The one-day stopover in Sacramento had been fruitful enough, fielding questions for Six Companies. If only this second leg of the trip proved as rewarding. Would he still have taken this job if he'd known how much travel it would require? But the Federation was happy with his work, and already he had introduced the language for possible state legislation in support of Chinese immigrants. The rhythmic *chink* of the rails soon relaxed his knotted shoulders and lulled him into a sleepless stupor.

"Newspapers! Newspapers here!"

The voice dragged him from lethargic depths, and he pried open an eye. He arched his back and licked his lips as a uniformed porter made his way down the aisle with an armload of papers.

"Might you have a Eureka paper there?" Grant asked, his mind suddenly on Kira and Uncle Avery. Surely, they'd heard by now that he was back in California.

"Here you go, sir."

"Thank you. How much longer until Truckee?"

The man slipped out his watch. "About twenty minutes."

Right on time for the meeting Charles Crocker had arranged with the pro-Chinese business owners. Since a federal marshal had yet to materialize, the least he could do was keep his finger on the town's pulse. After Truckee, a case in Humboldt County would take him but a few miles from Eureka. He smiled to himself, wondering if Kira had finally outpaced his pint-sized sister, stretching up like a true Mitchell.

He shook open the *Humboldt Times*, intrigued by the headline, WIPE OUT THE PLAGUE SPOTS.

> *In the very heart of Eureka is a community in which exist slums and festering dens. Our readers will not stop to ask for the location of this leprous quarter, for they know it too well. They know it is where a small heathen horde congregates and acts of riot and assassination are more and more boldly being committed from month to month. They know that it is the pestilential quarter where Chinese gambling dens, opium-smoking hellholes, and the lowest brothels abound.*

This is where Uncle Avery and Kira are? He chuckled. What kind of woman had she become? Had she met her match in a small town with such outspoken abhorrence for the very people she meant to help? Well, he'd know soon enough.

Besieged with thoughts of her, he leaned his head against the window and shifted his gaze to the sun-spattered landscape and distant Sierra Nevada. He squinted at the snowy reaches, imagining her face. She would be lovely; he was sure of it. His lovely, fiery-tempered cousin.

Truckee

CHINESE MUST GO!
HIRE THE WHITE MAN!

Signs danced in the air as men circulated among protesters. They *booed* Charles Crocker as he guided Grant through the unruly crowd. Leaflets fluttered here and there, and Grant snagged one and crammed it into his pocket.

"Chinese must go. Chinese must go." The chant gathered momentum as he and Mr. Crocker reached the door.

He followed Mr. Crocker into the building. When the ruckus dampened with the slam of a door, Grant turned to him. "So, the Workingman's Party has descended upon Truckee, I see."

"You don't miss a thing." Mr. Crocker jammed a finger in his ear and wiggled it. "A noisy lot, eh?"

"What can you tell me about the group in *here*?" He threw a thumb toward a windowed double door. Men and women occupied most of the chairs in a large meeting room, waiting amicably, judging by their muted conversations.

"Well, let's see. You've got your businessmen who depend on their Chinese employees, and they're happy with them. The white women who would abhor losing their Chinese servants. And then the timber barons—railroad and mill men like myself who hold contracts with Chinese workers. Men who consider any contract legally binding."

"So pretty much good people all in all?"

"Can't vouch for that, but they do recognize the Chinese's superior work ethic and penchant for dependability. In one way or another, all these folks are economically dependent on the Chinese people." Mr. Crocker opened the door. "And they have plenty of questions for you."

For more than an hour, Grant doused fearful fires and negated illegal, actionable ideas. Finally, the crowd settled somewhat and started calling out other concerns.

"Mr. Campbell, the majority of Truckee's teamsters are Chinese. They're mostly hardworking cooks and cleaners at the hotels and restaurants. Our town is a busy crossroads, and these services are necessary. You can't tell me there are enough white men willing to do these jobs. And what about the launderers? If the Chinese don't do it, who will?"

"And who's gonna cut the eighty thousand cords of wood each year for the railroads?"

"McGleason says there's plenty of white laborers out there waiting to take these jobs. Where, I ask, where are they? Cuz, I don't see 'em."

"Hogwash!" The gruff voice brought them all up short. "There's white workers aplenty out there—with families and destitute. And just waiting for the opportunity of employment."

Mr. Crocker sprang to his feet. His glare shot darts. "Dannon, what are you doing here? This meeting is for *pro*-Chinese citizens, not hate-mongers like you."

Murmurs sprinkled over the room as people turned in their seats. One man edged his way to the aisle, fingers toying with a sidearm.

"Now, *Charles*, I have just as much right to be in this public meeting as anyone." The stocky interloper leaned back, boot heel to the wall. A cigarette hung limp, dividing grizzled beard and bulbous nose.

"Not when the very reason we are here is to stand against you and your kind." Mr. Crocker motioned to a couple of men flanking the doorway. "Will you escort this trouble-maker out of the room please?"

Dannon threw up thick hands. "If you want to throw me out on my ear, that's fine by me. I'm sure McGleason will find a nice spot on the front page for the account." Steely gray eyes mocked Crocker.

More men stood, moving toward Dannon. "All right. I'm leaving. But you are treading on my citizen rights, and I won't be silent about it."

"I'm sure you won't be." Mr. Crocker crossed his arms, staring the man down until he had vacated the room. He turned to the audience. "I am sorry about the interruption, folks. I don't know why I didn't see him sitting back there."

Grant clamped a hand on his shoulder. "No harm done. And if you think he has a foot to stand on—being asked to leave like that—he doesn't. Now, are there any more concerns you would like to discuss?"

Another thirty minutes passed before Grant offered a bit of closure. "I thank you all for coming today. I can assure you the Chinese Consul, Six Companies, and many ethical, law-abiding citizens across this great state and in our nation's capital are doing everything in their power to assure Chinese immigrants the same freedoms allowed any other immigrant in America.

"And just as the Chinese worker has the right to work for whomever he chooses, so you have the right to hire whomever *you* choose. And *no one*—no one can legally usurp that right from you. If you give in to intimidation through violence or any other means, there will be no stopping the demands these people will continue to make on you, your businesses, and your families."

"Hear, hear!" A smattering of applause.

Mr. Crocker stood, clapping loudly and deliberately, igniting a standing ovation.

Grant nodded once and held up a hand to quiet the crowd. "Stand strong, citizens of Truckee. Stand strong." Words meant to encourage twisted his gut. He knew only too well what men like Dannon were capable of. They spread their poison like a cancer—manipulating even the staunchest moralist with twisted lies and half-truths to shore up their agendas.

If Dannon's ilk were looking for a fight, he'd gladly give it to them.

Seven

EUREKA

"Thank you for coming, Avery. Yakira." Rev. Harrington ushered them into the parsonage sitting room.

Yakira absorbed the neatly furnished home, with its welcoming floral curtains and framed needlepoint sampler. Twin upholstered chairs sat opposite a fringed sofa, and a worn rocker seemed to call to her. If only she had a home even half this nice for her girls. She hadn't even acquired one girl yet, but nameless faces still floated through her mind every day. They were out there. Somewhere. And they needed her.

"Mayhap isna God's timing," Da had said. But how she ached for it to be. Too, too hard was the waiting now that she had tasted the possibilities of her dream. The disappointment choked like a noose, robbing her of a life with purpose—a purpose she had been so sure of until now.

She smiled at a young Chinese man about her own age and an older white man sitting in the room.

Rev. Harrington introduced them. "I want you to meet my good friend, William Lord. Besides some mining interests, William has a general store across the bay in Arcata."

"Mr. Lord." Da extended a hand. The man stood, and they shook.

"William, please," the man insisted.

"Then you must call me Avery."

"And this lovely young woman must be Yakira," Mr. Lord said with a smile. "Miss."

"Pleased to meet you, Mr. Lord." Yakira took a seat beside her father, running her hand across the smooth velvet cushion beneath her.

"And this young man here is Charley Wei Lum," Rev. Harrington said.

Charley flashed a mouthful of large teeth. "Happy to meet," he said, dipping his head twice.

She and Da stood and bowed, returning the respected greeting in Cantonese, raising the man's eyebrows. He returned the appropriate greeting.

"Charley here is one of my converts, and he has been very instrumental in ministry to his countrymen. I have every confidence he will have a congregation of his own someday."

Charley nodded, excitement dancing in his walnut eyes. "As God wills."

Rev. Harrington dragged over a chair from a well-used secretary and motioned for everyone to sit. "Well, let us get right to the point, shall we? It seems the Carlyles have suddenly realized they have a fiscal need to rent out their house on D Street."

"Is that so?" Yakira wanted to laugh aloud but held her tongue. She'd not embarrass Da.

"Kira," her father breathed the word much as one would calm a spirited horse.

Rev. Harrington chuckled. "And although I didn't say it to their faces, my thought was, 'unequivocally, poppycock!'"

She liked this man.

"I believe we are all disappointed that the plan for the mission home has fallen through. I know it was a large part of why you both even came to Eureka. But be not discouraged, Yakira." His words were for her alone now. An invisible thread tied his gaze to hers. "You and I both know God has a plan, and that He loves these Chinese girls every bit as much as He loves us."

Da patted her hand. Tears sizzled at the back of her eyes.

She wanted to throw her hands in the air. "And has the Almighty shared that plan with you, Reverend Harrington? Because I am entirely ignorant."

"I believe I may be able to help, Miss," Mr. Lord said, leaning his forearms on his knees.

"Sir?"

"I have a couple of rental houses here in Eureka. I've been doing some work on one of them, a new roof and such, so it is empty at the moment. I'd be honored to lend it to a worthy cause such as yours. It's not large, mind you, but it's a start." One side of his mouth kicked up, and his hands splayed. "What do you say?"

Her dried-up hopes flowered afresh, the sweet fragrance wetting her cheeks. Whatever was God doing for her? She gripped Da's hand. "Oh, Mr. Lord, I don't know what to say!" She drew a shaky breath. "My insides are about to burst. I'm sure the house will be just perfect no matter its size. And . . . and it will be a place where girls will find new life." She sprang to her feet. "Oh, thank you, Mr. Lord!" She clung to his hand, pumping it up and down like an exuberant child.

Da chortled a full-bellied riot and stole Mr. Lord's hand for himself. "Thank you, William. God be praised!"

"And I will spread word of this Mission Home for Girls among other Tang people as I go about my way," Charley said. "May God bless your ministry, Miss Mitchell." His face waxed solemn, and she noticed the keen lines about his eyes.

Mr. Lord handed her a key, threaded through with string. "This is yours then, dear. My son, Oscar, is over there now. He can show you around. Unfortunately, I have to see to some business up the mountain."

She accepted the key with a trembling hand. And that quiver raced the length of her body and squeezed her chest. That God would care so much for *her* meager dreams! She swallowed, staring at the brass key in her palm. But this wasn't about her. Not really. God loved those girls so very much. And through her, she determined to make sure they realized it.

Ideas for the Home flew at Yakira from every direction as she struck down cobwebs with a broom. She would convert one bedroom into a classroom until it was needed. After that, instruction could take place at the dining room table. A sewing machine could tuck neatly into the corner of the parlor.

"Where do you want this, Miss Kira?" Fifteen-year-old Oscar Lord had been a Godsend.

She raced to help him with the heavy chair. "Let's put that near the fireplace."

"My mother's been looking for an excuse to pass this old chair along," he said. "I don't remember it never being in our house."

"Well, if you find yourself missing it, you are certainly welcome to visit it here," she said with a grin. She picked up a hammer to pry open a large crate. "Let's see what is in here, shall we?"

"Here," Oscar said, reaching for the hammer. "Let me do that for you. Mother said it's just some things from the store you'll be needing. I don't even know what's in it."

"This is fun, isn't it? Rather like Christmas morning."

"Maybe for you. I'd rather have a new shotgun than"—he held up a teacup—"dishes."

"Oh my!" She gently dug through crumpled newspapers until she had collected a full set of delicate primrose-painted dishes, a teapot, and three pans. "This is so generous! I can't wait to meet your mother, Oscar. I have a feeling we will be best of friends."

"She went with my father up to the camps. Probably won't be home for a couple of days."

"Mining camps?" Mr. Lord had said something about the mountain. She just assumed it was to check on his mines.

"Naw. Some of the Chinese married Indian women. Their families live along the Klamath River. We carry their baskets, rugs, and such in the store. In return we trade supplies with them. I usually go, but I thought this would be more interesting. Helping you." He ducked his head, the timid signs of a smitten youth poorly concealed. "It's really beautiful up there, in the mountains. I could take you sometime."

"That does sound lovely, Oscar. But I plan to be very busy right here for a while. Say, would you care to accompany me into Chinatown? Is that something your father would permit?" She didn't want to lead the lad on, but she had to spread the word about the new mission home, and Da was down at the bay.

"My father won't mind."

She grabbed her bonnet. "Then off we'll go."

Oscar offered his arm like a perfect gentleman as they walked down Fourth Street. They crossed to the other side of the street, where a Chinese man was pruning a rosebush. His gaze met hers before he bowed in greeting.

"Good day," she said in Cantonese. He didn't respond, but she could feel his eyes on her as she passed. Perhaps the news had already circulated about her mission here in Eureka.

"You speak Chinese?" Oscar asked.

"Yes. Cantonese. I was born in China, actually. My parents were missionaries there for many years." She pushed back the old ache of missing the mother she never knew. "It is a most valuable thing to know in a mission home."

"Can you teach me a few words? Most of the Chinese people we deal with speak some English, so we don't have to learn Chinese."

As they made their way to E Street, Kira taught him a new greeting. "And you must always show respect with a bow. Like this," she tipped her head and shoulders.

He bowed. "*Néih hóu.*"

"Excellent! That will surely help you start every conversation with respect."

She started to tug her hanky from her cuff to ward off the awful Chinatown odor, but thought better of it. She'd not appear some prissy, white woman, feigning to accept another culture. They hadn't walked far when the familiar characters on a bordello sign drew her attention.

She turned to Oscar. "I want you to wait right here for me."

"Here? But . . ."

"If I'm not back in five minutes, I want you to get my father or Rev. Harrington. Five minutes. All right?"

Oscar shook his head. "I'm not so sure about—"

"Five minutes, Oscar. That's all I need. Then we will head back to the house." She strode to the middle of the block, right up to the bordello door and gripped the wooden latch. She took a deep breath, and her nose shriveled at the stink.

The door creaked open. Letting her eyes adjust, she sent a plea heavenward for success. She walked down a hall of closed doors until she found one open a few inches. Spices and incense mingled in the air, the bite masking any sign of the rank street smells.

"*Sīu jē?*" (Miss.) The door creaked as she nudged it open further. "*Sīu jē?*"

A young woman sat on the bed. An embroidered silk robe draped her thin body. "Who are you?" she asked, shooting to her feet, snugging the robe around her.

"I am here to help. I am Yakira. What is your name?"

"I am Pan Min, but here I am called Violet."

"I have the Mission Home for Girls down on Fourth Street, Min. It is a gracious home where girls can be safe and learn many new skills. Any Chinese girl is welcome to live there under my protection. Please tell others about the Mission Home."

Min nodded, and Yakira backed quickly out of the doorway, leaving it ajar. She was not here to cause trouble for the girl, merely to offer an option. She rushed toward the exit to escape unseen, but when she reached for the doorknob, it flew open.

"Who are you?" The beefy hand of a Tong man gripped her wrist, and then he seemed to think better of it. "You leave here. Now."

Yakira slipped around him and scurried to where she had left Oscar. He was gone. Fear pricked her. She shouldn't have left him just standing here alone. But this wasn't San Francisco. Surely, he knew his way around—the places and people to avoid. She called his name, walked to the end of the block, and called again. At the very end of the block, she spotted him munching on a carrot and conversing with a vegetable peddler. Taller than most Chinese, the man balanced a pole across his shoulders and behind his neck, suspending two large baskets of vegetables. The same man she'd seen pruning roses earlier.

"Oscar. There you are." She joined them, curious about their conversation.

"Yakira, this is Henry. His English is very good."

The man expertly settled his baskets onto the ground. "Pleased to meet you," he said slowly, his gaze drinking her in. Something no Chinese man would ever do to a respectable white woman. He seemed to catch himself and quickly bowed. "Forgive me, Miss Mitchell. I did not mean to stare. Observation. It is my curse." He stared at the ground.

"You know my name?" Did she know him from somewhere?

"You are the daughter of Reverend Avery Mitchell, are you not?"

"I am. I'm Yakira."

He met her eyes again, this time with a broad smile. "Yakira." He said her name as if tasting it. Twice. "Ah. Yes. It fits you." He turned abruptly and loaded his baskets to leave.

"It was nice to meet you, Henry." Oscar waved at the peddler's back as he trotted away without another word.

Yakira watched him for a moment. "Henry, huh?"

"Yeah. He just walked up and started talking to me." He held up the last of his carrot. "Gave me this, too."

Two gunshots rent the air, and she grabbed Oscar by the arm, throwing him flat against the wall. Across the street, in the middle of the next block, people scurried into a shop as two black-clad men dragged another into a building. Henry had disappeared entirely as merchants slammed doors, and women herded children into homes.

"Those were Tong men," she said, looping her arm through Oscar's and heading for home.

"Yeah. That happens a lot around here. That's why I don't get to come here very often."

She halted. "But you said your father wouldn't mind you escorting me down here."

"Oh, he wouldn't. He said I was to help you in any way I could." The grin on his face made her want to punch him in the arm. And for just a moment, aside from his blond hair, he reminded her a bit of Grant at that age.

Bumped from behind, she turned and met the sunken eyes of a young Chinese woman. Horror sharpened her features. "Please forgive. Please forgive," she said, bowing with every word, eyes downcast.

Yakira touched a gentle hand to her shoulder. The woman shrank back. Yakira reassured her in Cantonese. "There is nothing to forgive. We are both in this spot together." She picked up the cloth bag the young woman had dropped and handed it to her. "I am Yakira. What is your name?"

The woman's eyes darted to Oscar, to the shopkeeper on the sidewalk, and finally back to Yakira. "I am Shu."

"Shu, I run the Mission Home for Girls over on Fourth Street. If ever you have need of a safe place, you may go there. You will be under my protection. Girls there can have a new life."

Shu nodded as Yakira backed away from her. "Remember. On Fourth Street." She took another step, her heart aching to hug the young woman, to tell her there is hope, for she recognized the girl's fear. The same fear that haunted so many eyes in San Francisco's Chinatown. "God Bless you, Shu."

She tugged Oscar's arm and resumed her trek toward home, determined to have everything in order for her first girls.

Eight

Eureka

Yakira neatly folded the letter and slid it back into its envelope. Azalea's words were her own. How she missed her laotong. "I feel as if I've lost half of myself."

"Uh-huh." Da sat at the desk, poring over a letter from Aunt Lara. A smile lifted his lips for a moment. A slight shake of his head.

"I said, I miss Azalea. It's as though half of me is in San Francisco, and the other half is here."

He grunted, eyes tracking back and forth as he read. "'Tis the way of it, lass."

"Da? Have you heard a word I've said?"

He sighed and looked up at her, removing his spectacles. "I know you miss her. I'm sure they miss us just as much. You are doing fine on your own, aren't you?"

Was she? No, she wasn't. With Azalea by her side, she'd be braver, smarter. They were a team. She held out her hand for Aunt Lara's letter.

"What?"

"My turn."

"'Tis *my* letter. Addressed to me." He folded the letter slowly. "You have yours, and I have mine."

"Since when does Aunt Lara not include me in her letters?"

"Since today, evidently." He snatched paper and a pen from the drawer.

"You are writing back?"

"Aye."

"Please don't seal it until I write one to Azalea."

"I won't." Already the pen scratched, and a quirk of his lips testified of his mood.

"Have you ever thought of marrying again, Da?"

He frowned suddenly, staring at the page. "Look what I've done now." Crumpling the page, he retrieved a second one.

"Have you?"

He turned to face her. "I'll be taking this to the post in a bit, so why don't you run along and write that letter to Azalea if you want it included."

Ah, now *that* she recognized. Her dear, sweet bear of a father was avoiding her question. Could be no other reason under the sun but that he was sweet on Aunt Lara. And why not? Was her sister not the love of his life? And wasn't Aunt Lara the only mother she herself had ever known?

Before the mantle clock chimed again, Yakira handed Da her letter. She watched him seal it in with Aunt Lara's. "I can post this for you." She reached for it, and he drew it back.

"I'll take it meself if ye dinna mind."

"I've invited them to join us, Da."

"Yakira Jean—"

She caught up his hand and grasped it fervently. "I miss them so. Our family has been ripped apart. First, we lose Mother, then Uncle Errol, then Grant, and now I feel I've lost the rest of my family. All but you. And Da, I love you with my whole heart, but you know we could do so much more with them here."

His eyes warmed. He bent and wrapped her in his long arms, kissing the top of her head. "I agree."

"You do?"

"Aye. Let us see what they have to say."

"Oh, thank you. I know I can survive without them, but I don't want to." And she knew Azalea didn't want to either. But was Aunt Lara willing to vacate her station with Miss Culbertson so soon after Yakira left?

Rohnerville, CA

Grant stood to project his voice across the packed courtroom. "Your Honor, had Pun Loi been born white, we would not be here today debating the consequences of Harrison Lyons's abhorrent actions. To murder a man in cold blood carries the death sentence in the state of California."

"Objection, Your Honor." The defense lawyer jumped to his feet. "Mr. Campbell here is equating a Chinese washerman with a white man. California's mandatory sentencing laws pertain to crimes against white men, not a hedonistic group of individuals that—"

"Objection overruled, Mr. Flagstone." Judge Morison signaled Grant to continue.

"Harrison Lyons engaged the services of Pun Loi to do his laundry. The same services Mr. Pun provided for many of the citizens of Rohnerville. Some of his steady customers are here in this courtroom today." He swept a hand through the air, still thoroughly irritated that only a meager few had actually cared enough to testify. "As we have heard through sworn testimony, not *one* of the witnesses called experienced any kind of problem with Mr. Pun's work. And his services were neither inferior nor untimely.

"When Harrison Lyons refused to pay Mr. Pun for his services, witnesses testify that, although he was within his rights, Mr. Pun did not so much as argue with Harrison Lyons. But did Harrison Lyons simply walk away with his free, laundered clothing? No, Your Honor. He drew a pistol and murdered the unarmed Mr. Pun. In cold blood." Grant paused, allowing the last two words to carve their mark.

"Whether this was pre-meditated is unproven, but the fact remains that a man—a good man from the testimony we've heard here today—was murdered." He turned a slow half circle, trying to read the jurists. "The prosecution rests, Your Honor."

"Thank you, Mr. Campbell. Mr. Flagstone, you have the floor for closing argument."

Flagstone sauntered across the front of the courtroom, stabbing Grant with black eyes. His expression changed when he faced the jury, with a serpentine smile for each juror. "Ladies and gentlemen of the jury, I implore you to consider this matter with the bias owed to a respectable man. The fate of such a man is in your hands today." He ladled up words, thick and dripping with emotion. "A church-going man. A husband. A father. A friend. A brother. A son."

The syrupy ploy sickened Grant, but it was a tried-and-true tactic to garner empathy for the guilty party. The defense was desperate, and it showed.

Flagstone waxed melodramatic, a hand to his chest where most stored their heart. "With grave regret, Mr. Lyons let his temper plunge him into an admittedly, irrevocable action. Of that he is woefully repentant. But to sentence Mr. Lyons to death would be akin to sentencing the farmer to death for shooting one of his livestock—an ill-behaved gelding, a bull prone to gore."

A grave mistake—the attack on the jury's personal convictions would backfire. Grant almost smiled.

The defense continued, "I implore you to consider the many years of life Mr. Lyons has yet to live as a contributing member of society. His sincerity is of no question in my mind when he tells me, with tearful eyes, just how regretful he is of his actions that fateful day."

As if on cue, the defendant wiped an invisible tear and hung his head with a woeful shake. The theatrics chafed. The insolent duo had no decency—nor respect for the system.

"These are the facts I beg you to consider as you examine your deepest moral convictions and place your vote today—as you choose to mark *guilty* or *not guilty* on that ballot. Thank you."

The judge's stony face sharpened. "Mr. Campbell, your closing statement."

He was defending a dead man's rights, but today was more about precedent. Was killing a Chinese man less a crime than killing a white man? The law had yet to catch up with God's order of justice. He hadn't prayed in a long time, but for this, how could he not? He sent an urgent plea for the making of history here today. Somehow.

He approached the jury box, fingers itching to plow through his hair. "Ladies and gentlemen of the jury, you have been presented with ample enough facts here today upon which to form an opinion grounded in both law and conscience. Might I contribute to that opinion by reminding you of something? Just this month, the California Supreme Court ruled in Tape v Hurley that public schools in California are *required* to admit Chinese children."

He changed directions, slowing his pace. "I don't recall ever sharing a classroom with pigs or cows in all my years of schooling. That's because livestock do not attend school. Chinese children are not livestock, as my *confused* colleague alluded earlier. I also ask that you add to that opinion the weight of this single personal conviction: If a man looks and speaks differently than you do, is he less of a man because of it?

"Is a man with different customs, different clothing, and different habits, less of a man for it in the eyes of God? And *if* he is no different in the eyes of God, then do you not cast yourself above the Almighty when you consider him no more than livestock, as my *esteemed* colleague here has indicated?"

Folding his hands, he smiled as he searched for a connection. It was his last chance to tear down any doubt. "Me parents, like some of yours, I'm sure, were born and raised in a foreign country, much like Pun Loy. They had a *verra* different way of talkin'." The jurists chuckled at his hearty Scottish brogue. "They wore skirts and called them kilts." More chuckles. "And they came to this fine country of ours to work hard and make new lives for themselves. Lives that were better for the coming here. My father, God rest his soul"—he swallowed past a boulder-sized lump—"was no less of a man for not being born in America. Neither was Pun Loy.

"He was a man, created in the image of Almighty God, as is every human on this planet. So, as you deliberate, ask yourself, 'Does God place any less value on a man's life because of what he looks like, or where he was born, or what he eats or wears?'" He turned from the jury box to address the judge. "The Prosecution rests, Your Honor."

The judge banged the gavel. "We will reconvene at nine o'clock tomorrow morning."

Grant shuffled papers into his valise, releasing a slow breath. A vise gripped his neck. It would be a while before he relaxed. He turned to a hand on his shoulder.

"Fine prosecution, son." A middle-aged man reached to shake his hand. "Well done."

"Thank you, Mr..."

"Call me Ira. Reverend Ira Harrington. I heard Six Companies had a new lawyer. I'm afraid I can't stick around for the verdict and sentencing tomorrow, but if you ever get to Eureka, look me up, will you? We could use someone like yourself on our side up there."

"As a matter of fact, I'm heading to Eureka as soon as I'm finished with this case. I plan to meet with the mayor about some issues in your Chinatown. It will be a couple of days, what with paperwork and telegrams."

"Very good, then. Regardless of the outcome, Mr. Campbell, you can be proud of the job you've done here today."

But in his heart, he knew if Lyons walked away from this, he ought to hang up his shingle and start a restaurant. What good was it being a lawyer when the law went against everything you believed?

People milled about outside the courthouse, having been turned away for lack of space. Inside, with every seat filled, the courtroom fairly vibrated with a lust for injustice. Grant stood beside the prosecution's table, too nervous to sit. He glanced at the clock. In but a few hours, he would set eyes on Kira for the first time in seven years. Maybe today's outcome would set him aright in her eyes. Maybe.

When the bailiff commenced proceedings, Grant wiped the sweat from his hands and sat, rearranging the papers in front of him. Flagstone leered at him, brushing invisible lint from his lapel. Lyons sat with his legs crossed, looking pleased with his cocky, murderous self.

Grant had tried to pray this morning—for the Tang people's sake, not his, he'd told God. He had attempted to negotiate with the Almighty, and for that, guilt scratched at his conscious. His father's voice, the familiar ghost of his past, had mocked him. *"You know better, Grant."*

The gavel rapped the walnut plate. "Court is now in session." Judge Morison looked to the jury box. "Do we have a verdict, Mr. Foreman?"

"We do, Your Honor." A spindly, fortyish man flourished an envelope.

"Is your verdict unanimous, Mr. Foreman?"

"It is, Your Honor."

"Proceed."

The foreman handed the envelope to the bailiff to give to the judge. After viewing the verdict, Judge Morison returned it to the bailiff for the reading.

"We, the jury, in the case of Pun Loi v. Harrison Lyons, on the count of murder in the first degree find the defendant, Harrison Lyons, guilty of murder."

The courtroom erupted. Grant's heart pounded. He'd done it. No—God had done it. No judge would ignore that verdict.

"I'd like to poll the jurists, Your Honor," Flagstone yelled above the gavel's rhythm and din of protests.

"Order! I will have order in my court!" Judge Morison glowered, his face carved with anger, shading pink to crimson. "Order!"

Two rows populated with Lyons's cronies put up a fuss until the judge threatened them with contempt. They filed out of the courtroom, slamming the door behind them.

"Now then." The judge sat back, his purple face fading.

Flagstone pleaded for polling again, to no change of verdict.

"We will reconvene for sentencing in four hours." With a crack of the gavel, the judge left the bench, and the bailiff engaged two guards to usher the jury out a separate door.

Grant would neither eat nor drink until this was over, so he might as well stay right where he was. Doing his best to draw up the framework for what he needed to submit to the courts and Six Companies, he worked until the judge returned.

Once again, courthouse guards turned people away and refused spectators' pleas to stand in the aisles. When the defendant rose for sentencing, Grant held his breath. The verdict had been precedential. But the sentencing would either go down in history or end up as tinder for some politician's agenda.

After reading over his notes, the judge removed his spectacles. "Harrison Lyons, you have been found guilty of murder in the first degree by a jury of your peers. Due to extenuating circumstances, I sentence you to San Quentin Prison for a period of no less than six years, during which time you will not be eligible for parole." *BANG!* "Court adjourned."

Grant launched to his feet. He flexed his fingers, tempted to pound the table. The judge stepped down from the bench and escaped to his chambers amid the raucous protests. Coarse jabs, crudely hurled at Grant's back, targeted his welfare, health, and his manhood. He ignored them, too busy choking back the scream knocking at his throat.

Six years. Hang a horse thief but slap a murderer on the hand!

Injustice blazed inside him, hot and inciting. For maybe the first time in his life, he understood a bit of what fueled his family's endeavors all these years.

Six Companies would see this as a victory—if for no other reason, simply because the murder wasn't just shoved under a rug. His mother was right. Maybe with them it *was* more about politics than what was best for the Chinese immigrants.

Nine

A fiery orb peeked over the inland hills, and morning fog scattered in wispy tendrils across Yakira's feet. Breathing deeply of the brisk sea air, she ignored the chill of an unbuttoned wrap, donned in too much haste. She relished the workday ahead, for by evening, she planned to have the Mission Home ready for residents.

A basket of supplies jostled beneath her elbow as she quickened her steps. Today held so much promise. God's provision still astounded her. Two of the women from the awful meeting had come to her with donations. Surely more of Eureka's churchwomen would come to see the merit in what she was doing.

She rounded the corner, immediately jolted by what she saw. Her emotions flipped from victory to defeat to determination, as she clenched the basket handle tighter. A dozen women congregated outside the Home. And they had plastered a sign over the front door.

"Look, there she is." Women rushed to form a line on the sidewalk across the front of the house.

Yakira gulped, lifted her chin, and strode forward. She had stood nose-to-nose with Tongs. What was there to fear from a few misled women? "Good morning, ladies." She painted on a smile to hide the rage ignited by the awful sign: NO CHINESE.

"To what do I owe this visit?"

Mrs. Carlyle crossed her arms. "I thought you understood what the women of this town thought about your little scheme here, Miss Mitchell." Each word snipped the air like a pair of scissors.

"I do recall the enthusiasm with which these fine ladies offered donations for this ministry, if that is to what you refer."

"Now see here—"

"And, as you can see, Mrs. Carlyle, while you were financially unable to provide the use of your rental house—"

"That's not—"

"God has provided another house for His purpose." She turned to address the other women with determination and dignity as obvious as her bustle. "Should you have donations, they may be left on the front porch at any time, ladies. And I thank you most sincerely ahead of time for your thoughtfulness. If you wish to assist me in preparing the home for residents, I welcome you. Now, if you'll excuse me, I have a busy day ahead."

Sidestepping Mrs. Carlyle, she marched up the steps, and tore the sign from the door. The key stuck in the lock. She wiggled it. She'd been too smug for her own good. She rattled the doorknob, working the lock frantically as heat climbed her neck, and their daggered looks pierced her back.

The door flew open, and she stumbled over the threshold. She closed the door with every stitch of self-control barely holding her together and leaned against the wall, weak-kneed as tremors snaked up her limbs. Melting like a pat of butter, she slid down the wall. Her bottom *whomped* onto the hard floor, and the basket bounced. Fuming voices faded behind her, muffled by the blood pounding in her ears.

Why? Tears brimmed, and she ground them away with the heels of her hands. She'd not meant to make enemies, but how *did* one make allies of that lot? Surely at least some of them would see how badly Eureka needed the Mission Home. But what she'd seen in their eyes was the reality of it all. They wanted her gone. She sighed, collecting the basket's strewn contents. God would provide—if not through the town's churchwomen, then by some other means. Hadn't Mr. Lord's family and their store already blessed her abundantly?

She worked alone until mid-afternoon, and when she left to meet Da for dinner, six women circled the sidewalk—sporting new signage: NO CHINESE HOME FOR GIRLS.

"Ladies, please. I believe you have made your opinions abundantly clear. This"—she swept a hand toward the sign—"changes nothing." Silence shrieked as the women simply stared. Vultures, every one of them, awaiting the death of the Mission Home before it even got off the ground.

She hiked up her hem with a flourish and struck out at a resolute pace. Had she ever been one to ignore a challenge?

Never.

Yakira marched into Mayor Wallace's office, tamping down the actual words bristling on her tongue.

"How can I help you, Miss Mitchell?" he said, motioning for her to take a seat.

So, he knew who she was. She almost said she'd stand. "Thank you, Mr. Mayor. I am opening the Mission Home for Girls over on

Fourth Street in a house donated for use by William Lord. It seems there are women in this town who disapprove of this particular ministry, who, even as I speak, are protesting its opening on the very grounds owned by Mr. Lord."

"Excuse me, Miss Mitchell. If they are on Mr. Lord's property, he is the one who must lodge the complaint. *If*, however, the ladies are congregating on the city sidewalk, then they have every right to voice their opinions and sleep there all night if they wish. Are they on the sidewalk or the premises, Miss Mitchell?"

His condescending smile rankled. She would find no sympathy here. "They are on the sidewalk, sir."

"Good. Then we have nothing further to discuss."

"But the Mission Home for Girls is something Eureka desperately needs, Mr. Mayor. How can a girl come to my home for refuge if she is met by a divisive assemblage of hateful attitudes?" Her words vanished in the wind, and she knew it. But isn't a mayor supposed to listen? Do what's best for the town?

He stood and looked down at her with his palms propped on the desktop. "My wife informs me your mission home is for Chinese girls—certainly all from Chinatown. There is only one kind of girl in Chinatown, Miss Mitchell. If you want to help girls, I'm sure there are white girls who would benefit from your little project."

"Little project? I have trained under Magaret Culbertson of the Occidental Mission Home for Girls in San Francisco. She has the full backing of city officials, I assure you. But I see that will not be the case in Eureka." She bolted to her feet, a white-knuckled grip on her purse, and a boulder-sized knot in her stomach. "Thank you for your time, Mayor Wallace. I will see myself out."

She strode down the street, battling angry tears. Women or no, she would open that home, even if she must sneak the girls in under cover of darkness. If God was for this home, then He would topple that wall of women or make a way around it.

She approached the small white house, ready to unload both barrels on Da, for he was her greatest supporter when it came to the Mission Home. He'd understand her angst, her frustrations. He'd pat her hand and tell her God was at work.

"Miss Yakira?" The timid voice came from the bushes beside the entry.

"Who's there?"

A Chinese girl stepped out, and her fearful gaze scanned the yard. The street. "You are Miss Yakira?"

The marbled color edging one eye, the slumped shoulders—Yakira recognized the signs. "Yes. Please, please come inside." She glanced around and quickly herded the girl into the house. "Da?" He wasn't home yet. Good.

"Sit here and I will bring you tea," she told the girl in Cantonese. Snagging a throw from the back of the sofa, Yakira draped it around her with a warm smile.

She put on the kettle and rushed back, thankful the girl was still here, for she'd learned long ago just how deep the horrors ran among these girls. "What is your name?"

"I am Lian."

"You are safe here, Lian. My father will soon be here, but you have nothing to fear from him."

Over tea, Yakira listened as Lian spilled her story—a heart-breaking story not so different from others.

When Lian looked positively wrung out, Yakira helped her into her own bed to rest. As she tenderly drew the counterpane over her, she gave thanks for this, her first girl. God's girl. Already, love sprouted in her heart for Lian.

"What's this?" Da's voice whispered from the doorway.

She ushered him out and closed the door. "I'll tell you all about it over dinner."

And as quietly as she could, she vented her frustrations about the protesting women, the sign, and Mayor Wallace. Then she told of Lian and how she'd escaped the white man who had purchased her. For two years he had beaten and raped her, and she had worked as his slave. "She cannot go back, Da. I won't let her."

"Now, dinna *fash* yourself, daughter. God has a plan. You can sneak her into the Home under darkness, but sooner or later her husband will come looking for her." Concern shaded his blue eyes.

"Then I'll fight. I'll fight it in court if I have to." She lowered her voice. "More will come, Da. Lian heard about me from one of the girls in Chinatown I spoke with."

His bushy brows plunged. "I don't recall you speaking with anyone when I was with you."

Twenty-one years old and still she felt scolded. "Oscar escorted me. He was every bit the gentleman."

"Oscar? Oscar Lord is but a lad."

"If I am to do this work, you need to trust me, Da. I'm a woman grown, and I must make decisions, and I must live by those decisions. God has called me to this for as long as I can remember. He is opening the doors for His Mission Home, Da. God is hearing my heart, don't you see?"

"But are you prepared for the consequences? I would simply feel better about you keeping me abreast of what you're doing." He cupped her cheek. "Me bonny Kira Jean, I couldna live if something ever happened to ye."

She kissed his hand. Sorrow gazed back at her, bound up, it was, in a fierce love. She wanted him to be happy, not to live his life worrying about her. Another reason she needed Aunt Lara here. For Da more than for her.

Ten

Grant smoothed his beard and swallowed against a parched throat. Would Yakira recognize him? Would Uncle Avery welcome him after everything he'd put his mother through? If ever there was a family black sheep, he was it. What he wouldn't give to have them both accept him with open arms as his sister and mother had.

He stared at the whitewashed door of the clapboard house. Seven years suddenly seemed like a lifetime. What right did he have just to show up like this? Sweat beaded his upper lip, and he ran a handkerchief across it. Maybe they weren't even home.

He attached a smile to his face and knocked. About to knock a second time, he jerked back his fist as the door flew open.

Squinted eyes scraped him head to feet and suddenly blazed. "You have some nerve coming here. Men like you ought to be hung from the gallows. You think because someone is smaller and weaker, because they're not white—you can treat them any way you want?" She advanced on him, jabbing a finger in his eye-level chest.

"Lian is a woman made in God's image, and you will mistreat her no more! Do you hear me? I will do—"

"Whoa. Whoa there." Grant stumbled back, bemused, hands raised in surrender.

A Chinese girl touched her arm. "Miss Yakira. This is not my master."

Yakira? Hah! He should've recognized that divine temper. Memories swelled warm and sweet. "She's right. I am not her master. I am your cousin," Grant said in Chinese, delighted by the righteous anger crimping her pretty face.

Kira dropped her hand from the doorframe and stepped back. She blinked, and her cinnamon eyes glistened, jaw slack. The fury had sizzled to a mist over her fine features. She was a beauty, as he knew she would be—sable hair in a loose knot atop her head, her neck slender and creamy.

"Grant?" She breathed his name with caution and quake.

The back of his eyes burned, and he blinked away the difficult years swept from their friendship. He nodded, suddenly bereft of voice.

In a wild, wonderful instant, she threw her arms around him. "You're here! You're here!"

Her tears doused his shirt collar as he hugged her. "I've sorely missed you, Kira Girl." The old nickname slipped from his lips, easily and right.

Her laughter was music, airy and delightful. She pulled back to study his face. "Your Cantonese still is no so good." She shook her head before tracing his beard with a finger. She turned to the girl, rattling off something that triggered a riot of giggles.

"Hey now. I understood *rat* and *chin*. Neither of which pertains to me."

They laughed all the harder. "Come," she said, towing him by the arm. "Da will be thrilled to see you."

He followed on wooden legs, stunned and elated. In her presence, he was home again.

Yakira whirled to face him after the brief tour of Mr. Lord's rental house. She fiddled with the key, still in her hand. With Lian settled into her room, she finally had Grant to herself.

"Well, what do you think? Eureka's first Mission Home for Girls. Actually, it's the second one, since the first was snatched away even before we moved in."

"It's a wonderful start," he said.

His sincere smile did something to her middle. Why had she not imagined his voice would be so deep?

"And I'm not the least bit surprised to see you in this venture. A heart like yours must seek out its course, no matter the obstacles."

"And obstacles there have been, including the church ladies who protest out front several hours a day." She gazed out the front window. "It's waning, though. I think they realize I'm not backing down. Tomorrow there is hope for another girl. The word is spreading." She turned back to him. A curtain of silence suddenly separated them.

Grant turned his hat over in his hands, his eyes darting everywhere but to her. He struck a handsome figure in his gray ditto suit and jacquard waistcoat. *Awfully* handsome. But she couldn't let that fine face distract from what he'd done. What he'd left behind.

She chewed her lip, mustering self-control, calling on the woman within to conquer the hurt fourteen-year-old girl. "I'm angry with you." There, she said it. Happy to see him, yes. Relieved he was alive and doing well. Angry just the same. And he needed to understand that.

He nodded, brow pleated as his eyes met hers. "I deserve that." Sadness threaded his gaze, but he didn't look away. He was searching her. Testing her.

"After all these years, that's all you have to say?" A cauldron steamed inside her, filled to the brim with missed birthdays, missed explanations, and missed letters. She walked to the front door, fingernails digging into her curled palms, as the cauldron boiled over.

She spun on him, all decorum abandoned. "You didn't just leave San Francisco, Grant. You left all of us. And after your father's death, your mother needed you more than ever. How could you have been so selfish?" All the hurt she'd tamped down boiled and sputtered like a pressure cooker. Hot, traitorous tears coursed down her cheeks, and she smeared them away.

He crossed the floor. His giant hands reached for her, then retracted. The boy she'd known peeked from beneath his shadowed brow. "I am so sorry. So, so sorry the way I left. I—"

"Sorry doesn't change what you did." The words scalded and convicted her before she could stop them. His azure eyes dimmed, sinking with the painful truth of it. *Good*. He needed to know how his family had suffered. How *she* had suffered.

"Kira—"

"I cried myself to sleep for months after you left. Aunt Lara floated through life in a daze after losing both her husband and only son. And poor Azalea had already gone through so much in her young life, just to suffer loss upon loss." She stomped her foot, stricken with a thought to pummel his chest with her fists, to hurt him back. "We were children, Grant! How were we supposed to go on after so much . . ." What did she care if the words stung?

"I know. I was selfish. I was lost. I couldn't look in my mother's face, see her grief, after what I'd done."

She threw up her hands. "Of course you couldn't. You. Weren't. There!"

"No, before I left. After Da . . . was killed. I couldn't." He wilted. "After what I did." His mouth hardened into a thin line, and his jaw knotted. He stared above her head at the wall behind her.

"That wasn't your fault, Grant. Uncle Errol knew there was always danger in Chinatown. Still is."

"But it *was* my fault, Kira."

His gaze touched hers. She saw in his eyes a sea of regret, deep and tumultuous. But so many years . . . "You're too late, Grant. Too late to mend broken hearts." Conviction stabbed her. She swallowed the condemning words and slumped into a chair. "Forgiveness takes time, cousin."

She had chewed on this bitterness for too long. How she'd prayed to forgive. She'd thought she had, but with him standing in front of her now, the hurt stirred up afresh, barbed and ugly. It wasn't her place to punish him further, she knew. It was her place to forgive. Not forget, just forgive.

She inhaled a shaky breath, unable to look at him. "You were so much more to me than a cousin, Grant." The reason the wound had festered so painfully. She'd not put herself in such a position again. *Never* again.

"Aye. And you were my sister, my closest friend."

She looked up, and his desperation painted his damp eyes.

"Kira, please forgive me. *Please*." His hands swallowed hers as he dropped to one knee. "I'm begging your forgiveness. I'll do whatever it takes, but I cannot continue like this. Alone."

His words chipped her brittle heart. But she needed to be strong. "My cousin you'll always be," she said, staring at the way his trembling hands held hers. "But I fear it's too late for us to be friends." She pulled back her hands, and he drew himself up in one achingly slow movement.

Crossing the floor on wobbly legs, she opened the door—more than bruised this time. She felt severed. "You're too late."

He donned his hat and left without another word.

You're too late.

Just three hours earlier, Grant's hope for reconciliation had been ground to dust, cast to the winds. And here he sat at the dinner table, pretending all was well—a challenging performance at best, despite his knack for courtroom theatrics. Still sore from Kira's rejection, he would take the high road. She just needed time, or so he'd convinced himself. And time, he would give her.

Grant passed up a second helping of rice. "Everything is wonderful, Kira. Thank you." A chore it was to keep his eyes off her during the meal. He'd wanted to study her. To drink her in. She'd changed in some ways, but not in all the important ways. She was hurt, yes, but he could not give up hope that their friendship would mend. Now that she was close enough to touch, he missed her more than ever.

"... court case in Rohnerville," Uncle Avery was saying.

"What's that?" Grant asked, fingering his water glass.

"They tried a white man down in Rohnerville for killing a Chinese man. There was but a blurb in the Eureka paper."

"Yes, actually—"

"Can ye believe it? A mere six years in prison. For murder! It was that new lawyer from back east, probably used to winning cases with fancy words and such. If he was worth his salt, he would've got that white man twenty-five years at least. The only satisfaction would've been a hanging!"

Lian settled her chopsticks beside her plate, wide-eyed and obviously uncomfortable.

"Da," Kira said, "now don't get yourself worked up over it. Change is coming. You know that. God has a plan, you always say."

Grant squirmed inwardly. "But Six Companies considers that a victory, Uncle. At least the court acknowledged there was a murder, that a serious crime was committed. Isn't that something?"

"Something? Och! 'Tis nearer to nothing to my thinking." His uncle gulped a drink of water, set it down, and studied him. "Wait a minute here. *You're* the fancy east coast lawyer Six Companies hired?"

He nodded, locking eyes with Kira, wondering what was coming next.

Silence strained the space between them. Uncle Avery leaned his elbows on the table, eyes asquint. "So, what brings you to Eureka after all this time, son? Business or pleasure?"

"Both. My employer wants a presence here to try to get more protection for the Chinese population. Reports of Tong violence have made the San Francisco newspapers. What's this Mayor Wallace like?" Grant sat back, amused by Kira's sour expression.

"Mayor Wallace." Kira crossed her arms over her chest. "I assure you he would rather see Chinatown burn. A sentiment shared by many of the townspeople."

"It isna like San Francisco, Grant. Eureka's Chinese have made their home on a few square blocks smack in the center of town. Not a week passes without some violence or another—a building burned, a Chinese person accused, gunfire. Nothing happens there without it affecting everybody in town."

"Then all the more important for the mayor to see to the safety of the town's residents. *All* of its residents," he told them.

Kira began collecting dishes, and Lian jumped up to help. "Lian and I are staying at the Mission Home tonight, so you are welcomed to stay in my room, Grant."

Uncle Avery excused himself, stretching as he stood. "Yes. By all means. You stay here with us whenever you are in town." He thumped the back of the chair, about to say more, but suddenly took his leave.

"Your da is not happy with me," Grant said to Kira, gauging her reaction. "I don't blame him."

"It's not an easy thing for him either, seeing you after all these years." She bit her lip, a habit that pelted him with keen recollections. "Would you like to walk us to the Mission Home?"

He hid his joy at the simple request. "It would be my pleasure."

It seemed she was trying to put their earlier conversation behind her, trying to forgive. His hope rallied. But an ocean of unanswered questions still loomed between them—and a stiffness he hated.

Eleven

P ewter clouds parted, and the sun's golden fingers stretched across Chinatown. "At last, a bit of sunshine." Avery stepped from beneath an unpainted awning. Made from cast-off lumber, one store looked much the same as the others. He started to fill his lungs with the rain-washed air, but thought better of it, considering where they stood and the stench.

Kira drew her umbrella closed. "Thank goodness." She stopped in front of the fish market. "Da, what do you think? For dinner?" She tapped the edge of a cask.

He nodded, watching fresh crabs writhe in black seawater. "Aye, a treat."

The merchant fished out two and wrapped them in newspaper. "I'll get that," Grant said, digging coins from his pocket and exchanging them for the bundle.

Kira lifted her basket. "Here."

Grant smiled at her, and Avery noticed she was stingy with one of her own. Something was yet unmended between them—that much was obvious. He had dealt with his own addlepated feelings as well, remembering the sorrow upon sorrow dear Lara had borne with his leaving.

"I've seen but a few Tongs down here today," Grant said over his shoulder. "Are they more active at night?" He stepped around two old men sitting on crates, swimming their hands through *mah-jongg* tiles. Kira veered as he neared.

"Aye. The townspeople canna get a decent night's sleep on some weekends." Avery watched as they walked in front of him. Was it so long ago these two had strolled hand-in-hand, just children, clowning and frolicking down San Francisco's Chinatown streets? One couldna go without the other, so close were they. Even young Azalea had struggled to edge her way into their tight circle.

He couldna look at Grant without thinking of Lara. And he couldna see his bonny Kira without thinking of Cait. Strange how his heart could hold such dear thoughts of both sisters all at once.

"Did you have company at the Home when you left this morning? In front of the house?" Grant asked Kira, facing straight ahead as he walked.

"Oh yes. The usual. Mrs. Carlyle, Mrs. Wallace—"

"The mayor's wife?"

"The very one."

Grant shook his head. "I'm meeting with him later today."

A man watched from across the street, unabashed, and Avery pretended not to notice. The same Chinese man he'd thought was following him a few days ago. The man kept pace with them, casually looking their way. When his gaze collided with Avery's, his eyes widened and he stumbled over a basket of reed mats.

Enough of this! "You there!" Avery called, striking out across the street.

Grant was suddenly beside him. "Who is that?"

"I dinna ken, but he's been following me."

Grant darted around Avery, but the man took off running, a poor match for the long legs chasing after.

"What is it, Da?" Kira caught his arm, tugging him from the path of a horse-drawn cart.

"I'm not sure." They stepped onto the sidewalk and continued in the same direction, but the man and Grant had disappeared. After several minutes, Grant emerged from between buildings, his hand gripping the arm of the stranger.

But he wasna Chinese. Not fully, anyway. Avery's feathers ruffled senseless when the man smiled at Kira.

"We meet again, Miss Mitchell," the stranger said with a bow, hardly a trace of Cantonese accent.

"Oh, it's you." Kira smiled politely. "We meet again."

"You know this man?" Avery asked, completely at a loss.

"Da, this is Henry." She looked to the stranger.

He bowed. "Henry Smith. It is a pleasure to meet you, Reverend Mitchell."

Avery returned the greeting, driven by curiosity. "You were following me the other day. Why?"

Henry dipped again. "I was merely curious, sir. Please forgive."

He couldn't shake it. The smile raised a fog of familiarity. "Do I know you? Your name—do you have a Chinese name? Where are you from?"

Henry's eyes smiled before his lips followed suit. "Oh yes, sir, Reverend Mitchell. I am SiJin. We met in Canton."

SiJin? Panic leached the strength from his legs. *The boy with the goat.* This couldn't be happening. Dear God, it was his penance, wasn't it?

Henry turned his eyes to Kira again, a shimmer settling on their surface. "Miss Yakira, I am—"

"Och. Michty me! SiJin!" He practically shouted, seizing SiJin's hand awkwardly, pumping it like a dry spigot. "Of course. Of course I remember you." He squeezed a dollar bill into Yakira's hand. "Why don't you two get us something to have with that crab?" He shooed her and Grant on. "SiJin and I will catch up a mite."

Kira's eyes sparkled, enthralled by the reunion, no doubt. "Perhaps Henry could join us for dinner. We can get another crab."

"Aye. Of course. Grand idea. You do that."

He watched them walk away, irked at the way Kira refused Grant's arm as they crossed the street. He turned to SiJin. "How in all the earth did you find me? And why are you here?"

"I asked your name when you take baby. Mrs. Mitchell is well?"

Avery recounted the ship tragedy, and SiJin seemed truly sad for his loss.

"Our mother died the day baby was born." The man's features sank.

Our mother? "She is your sister?"

SiJin nodded. "I buried mother, but I still had my *mei mei* (little sister). She was so small. It was just the two of us."

He bid him continue, his recollection of that last day in Canton suddenly keen and bittersweet.

"At first, I stole goat's milk for her in the dark of night. It was almost two weeks before I was discovered. I had no way to take care of her after that. When I saw you and your wife, I knew what I had to do."

Avery's head swam with the realization of what the young lad had done for his precious girl. First losing his mother, then his mei mei. Such a sacrifice, such a loss.

"But, how is it she is white?" Never had he imagined gaining the truth of it.

"My father is many men, but mother was American. From California. I did not know her English name. She said it was safer that way. A white man from California paid to keep her only for him. That man is father to Yakira." Deep lines scored SiJin's forehead before his gaze plummeted to the ground. He seemed every bit the orphan boy again, standing there, feet scuffing the ground.

Avery replayed his last hours in China all those years ago. Suddenly everything made sense. He gripped SiJin's shoulder, and his voice gentled. "That was not your goat to sell, was it?"

SiJin shook his head.

"I saw men take you away. At the docks."

With one solemn, slow movement, the young man nodded.

"Were you sold because you stole the goat? Is that how you came to America?"

"Yes. First to Seattle." He squinted into the clearing sky, his expression hardening for a moment. When I became free, I studied as herbalist for four years. Then I began my search for you. For my sister."

He ached for the little boy so long ago. A little boy who made a man's decision after the most terrible time of his life. A little boy who sacrificed everything to save his sister from an appalling life of slavery or prostitution.

"I am happy about the name you chose for my sister. She is truly beloved—first to me, for she is all I have left, then beloved to you and your wife. I am anxious to know my sister. Anxious for her to know of her mother."

Alarms blared in his head, in his heart. "But she doesn't know. We never . . ."

SiJin's jaw dropped. "Yakira does not know you are not her real father?" Shock twisted to anger, blackening his brown eyes. "Are you not a Christian man? Do not Christians speak truth in all things? Why did you not tell her? Why did you let her believe a lie?"

Fearful of drawing attention, he drew the young man toward an abandoned shop. "I *will* tell her." The promise ripped ragged through his lips. The same words he had spoken to Lara. "I am planning to tell her. Soon. Please, give me more time. It should come from me. This whole *guddle* is my doing."

Was this now the sentence for his cowardice? His back was against a wall. If Yakira heard the truth from someone else, it would crush her. What kind of faither was he to let the deception go on this long? "I *will* tell her."

"For all these years in America I dream of seeing my sister. Now I see she is lovely and kind. She looks much like my mother. I have waited long enough." He crossed his arms in a defiant stance.

"Please, SiJin. Henry." He bowed and steepled his hands, desperate. "I beg you."

Mouth a rigid line, emotions swam through SiJin's eyes for a long moment. "I understand it is for love you have not told her. You fear she will not love you if you tell her. But she will still love you, Avery Mitchell, for you are her heart-father." A slow blink. "I will give you time."

Grant and Kira bustled toward them, and Grant motioned to the street with a frown. "What do you suppose that's about?"

Avery turned to see a gathering of Tong men in the street on the next block. Agitated voices carried on the breeze. This kind of trouble he recognized too well.

The reed merchant's door and other doors slammed in succession. The old men playing mah-jongg spilled tiles on the boardwalk as they stumbled into an alley, and a fruit peddler bustled after them. Accusations arose from the small crowd of black hats, and the sun glinted off metal.

"This way. Quick." Grant herded them around the corner, towering protectively over Kira with one hand on her shoulder.

Avery followed last. Shots rang out in succession, striking the muddy street and splintering wood near his head. Fire sliced through his arm. A painful gasp stole his breath. He stumbled headlong, jarred to a stop when his head crashed against something hard. *CRAACK!* Darkness swallowed him.

PART TWO

Twelve

Eureka

Who would've thought her father could be such a historically awful patient? If only Aunt Lara were here, she would know how to handle his moods. First he needed her. Then he didn't. One minute he was hungry. The next he wasn't. "*Restless*," he said. Yakira couldn't blame him, stuck in bed as he was these past two days. A visitor would do him well. And just as the thought appeared, so did a rap on the door.

Rev. Harrington and Councilman Kendall stepped into the house. "How is the patient today, Yakira?" the reverend asked.

"A wee bit ornery, but shortly better I'm sure, now that you're here." She hung their hats and coats before ushering them into the bedroom.

"Ira, David, what a welcomed surprise." Da winced as he sat up, and she rushed to stuff an extra pillow behind him.

"I'm sure your nurse is taking good care of you, but I wanted you to know we're praying for you. Not just anyone can take a bullet to the shoulder and knock himself silly all in one sweep." Rev. Harrington chuckled.

"Aye. I've ne'er been one to do things halfway." He fingered the bandage covering the top of his head. "Mayhap I got some sense knocked into me." They all laughed. Da clenched a fistful of blanket, pretending the laugh hadn't cost him.

"I hear you have some new residents at the Mission Home, Yakira," Rev. Harrington said, with a twinkle in his eye. "A little bird told me."

She'd not yet grown used to small-town living. "Indeed, Reverend. Three girls have come to me since the gunfight. Lian is helping them settle in for now so I can tend my father. But my aunt will be here soon to help."

"Yakira, ye dinna tell Lara about this little mishap now, did ye? Och. She'll have herself in a tither." Da shook his head and winced as pain pinched his face.

"I telegraphed her straightaway." She smiled inside, knowing what a snarl Da would make of the whole thing. "She'll be here day after tomorrow."

He groaned. "You see what happens when a man is down? The women, they take over."

"Sounds like it's exactly what you need right now," Mr. Kendall said. "Speaking of women, my wife and I would like to have you over for dinner when you're feeling up to it."

"Just as soon as I can escape from the women in me life, I'll take you up on it, David." He rolled his eyes in her direction.

Kira took the hint and backed out of the room. "I believe I'll leave you gentlemen to your conversation."

She busied herself about Da's house, gathering laundry, and planning some meals. As the men set to leave, Yakira handed them their things.

Mr. Kendall lowered his voice. "I think you should know, Miss Mitchell, gamblers up from San Francisco had some part in the Chinatown gunfight. Two were killed. Eight wounded."

Gamblers. She knew from experience the trouble they could attract.

"Not to worry." Rev. Harrington patted her shoulder and donned his hat. "The law actually arrested eight of those involved. They're sitting in jail as we speak."

Arrested. Evidently, Grant's talk with Mayor Wallace held some sway after all.

As she tidied the kitchen, a nubbin of pride made her smile. Her current feelings about Grant aside, knowing he was doing important work—that he was good at it—brought her a measure of satisfaction.

The front door opened and closed. "I'm back." Grant's voice filtered to the kitchen. "Was David Kendall here?"

"He just left. Why?"

"After the Council meeting adjourned, some irate citizens held a meeting of their own. I stood by and listened. I think your father needs to hear this. And there's this." He slapped his hand with a rolled newspaper and headed for the bedroom.

She dropped the dishrag and followed on his heels.

Da was sitting upright, eyes closed, Bible on his lap. His shoulders rose and fell. New lines scored his forehead. "I canna help but feel this city is about to break wide open," he said.

"You got that right," Grant said, approaching the bed.

Da opened one eye. "I wasna talking to you." His mouth quirked good-naturedly. "But you have something to say?"

Grant opened *The Daily Times-Telephone* newspaper and read:

"'Timberman John Vance is calling for all mills and timbermen to fire their Chinese employees. Hundreds of valuable jobs are desperately needed by white men with families to support. But these jobs are had by the family-free Chinamen, who send all their money back to China. Do not sentence your countrymen to starvation and poverty because of the Chinaman.'"

He flipped the page and shook it smooth. "There's more."

Yakira sank into a side chair, suddenly weary to the bone with all of Eureka's divisive problems. She could tell by the glint in Grant's eye that he was just getting started.

"'What shall we do with our Chinamen?' Ahhhh . . . here:

"'We urge the city council of Eureka to face up to the disgrace of having such a disreputable settlement right in the heart of our city and remove the Chinese from the middle of town. Make *them* leave!'"

He snapped the pages and folded the newspaper. Cramming it under one arm, he threw his other in the air and dropped it like a puppet with a cut string.

"*And* there are no fewer than eight editorials in this paper, *The Democratic Standard*, and *The Humboldt Times* in just the last two days. Oh, and lest we forget the article interviewing a woman who swears the city is covering up cases of—are you ready for this one? *Leprosy* in Chinatown. Did I mention there is a sizeable recent sign in the mercantile that says"—he framed an imaginary sign with both hands—"BURN CHINATOWN NOW."

Father groaned, cradling his head in his hands. "I need to be out there. Need to calm the people."

"I'm sure Reverend Harrington is doing all he can, Da. You're in no shape to be up and about." She set his Bible aside and gingerly slipped the pillow from behind him. "Rest now."

"I'm here, and I will do all I can, Uncle Avery." Grant patted Da's arm. "You can count on me."

Until you leave us again. She wrestled with a tangle of emotions. This handsome, passionate man was somehow still her Grant. But he'd leave. If not today, then tomorrow. She couldn't risk her heart. Not again.

She and Grant settled silently in the parlor with steaming mugs of coffee. The door flew open with a bang.

"Yakira!"

"What is it Lian? What's wrong?" Yakira rushed to her and closed the door.

"Master come to Mission Home. Look for me. Shu lie to him. He be back." Panic heaved and buckled her words together like a train wreck.

Yakira wrapped her arms around the girl, comforting Shu like a mother. "Shhh. Shhh now." She'd promised to protect Lian, something she could not do alone. *Dear Father, please protect this child of yours.* She shifted her gaze to Grant, surprised at the hard planes shaping his face.

Suddenly the front door shook with a pounding.

Grant grabbed a candlestick from the desk and tucked it behind his back. He motioned for her and Lian to stand out of view before jerking open the door.

"I'm Arlen Branson. I believe you have something here that belongs to me." A man's voice answered, angry and impatient.

Lian stiffened, and Yakira grasped her hand.

"Surely you are mistaken, sir," Grant said calmly.

"I want my girl back. Now! I followed her here from that Mission Home. She's mine, paid for fair and square."

Lian pressed one hand over her mouth, a runnel of tears soaking her fingers. With the other hand, she squeezed Yakira's fingers numb.

"Here is my card, sir. How does tomorrow sound?" Completely professional, entirely commanding, Grant was obviously in his element.

"How does tomorrow sound for what?"

Lian shook her head violently at the snarling words.

"To see you in court. That is where you will have your chance to receive justice."

"What—"

"Good day, sir." The sharp *clunk* of the door echoed.

Yakira stepped out of the hallway speechless. What just happened?

"You make Master very mad. He will beat me." Lian said, wiping her nose on the back of her hand.

"He will never lay another hand on you, Lian." Grant touched a hand to her shoulder, sincerity weighting every word. "Never."

"Grant, you can't promise that." Yakira said, irked at him for giving false hope. More times the law failed than succeeded in protecting girls like Lian.

"If—and that is a big *if*—I lose this case, I will take Lian away from here myself to a place he won't find her." He snagged his hat and coat from the hall tree. "If I'm to get a hearing with the judge, I need to get down to the courthouse now."

The way he moved, the set of his jaw. She'd never seen him more animated or purpose-driven. He flashed a cocky smile before breezing out of the house.

Lian turned to her. "Your man very brave."

"Yes, he is." She stared at the closed door, more than a bit proud of the man who'd just left. "Oh! He's not my . . . man."

Half a smile puckered one side of Lian's mouth. "Not yet."

Grant exited the courthouse, thoroughly pleased with due process. He'd received a 2:00 hearing time and a guarantee the subpoena would go out to Mr. Branson yet this afternoon. The case excited him more than anything he'd done in a long time, and he knew why—because it was important to Lian. And Lian was important to Kira. And Kira was important to him. If only he could crack the wall of ice between them. Help her see he wasn't the same selfish kid anymore. But even as he wished it so, he knew that until the whole truth was out, he was living a lie.

"Mr. Campbell."

Grant turned to see Henry jogging to catch up to him. *In western clothes?* "I am happy to see you. How is Reverend Mitchell?"

"Oh, he is on the mend. Evidently his head is causing him more grief than the shoulder wound. Say, thank you for helping me get him to the doctor so fast. I couldn't have done it without you, Henry."

"I am very happy to help. Is Yakira well?"

Grant smiled. He recognized the spark in the man's eyes. Henry was just a few years older than Grant, and what man wouldn't find Kira lovely? "You like her, don't you?"

Henry's face did a peculiar dance. "You do not?"

"I mean you are *fond* of her."

Henry shook his head. "I care for her as a sister—uh . . . a . . . friend. She is very lovely woman. Lovely white woman." The words stumbled off his tongue.

"It's all right. She has that effect on everyone." And how oft he'd wished they had not grown up together as brother and sister, for he would woo her, and she would find him enchanting. He smiled, shaking his head. She knew him too well, though. Who was he fooling?

"Do you have some place special you're going, Henry? In *that*"—he indicated the suit.

"Oh." Henry seemed to think through his next words. "Sometimes when I do business with white men, I dress this way. I think they almost forget I am not fully white."

"And what business would that be?" Grant asked, wondering just how many hats the man wore.

"I am herbalist. Always seeking to buy in quantity. Sometimes I make deal with white men on farms. Today I buy bark just before trees are cut. Best that way. I sign contracts with landowner."

"You read and write English?"

Henry nodded. "I learn at a very young age from mother, then from master in Seattle."

"Master? You were *jàhng jái* ?" (indentured servant).

"Yes."

Of course, that's how Avery knew Henry—SiJin. "How old were you when . . . when you came to America?"

"Very young, perhaps ten years, but very strong. I did not suffer the fate of many others." He grew grave. "I have been told that your God was with me. I did not know at the time, but now, I believe it was true."

"Was? You don't believe God is with you now?" The words slipped out—his father's, not his own. For along with the yearning to be free of his past, there was an exquisite emptiness inside him. Da's words tumbled about in that void, an odd comfort.

Henry took off his derby, allowing his queue to tumble down his back. He seemed to give the question a lot of thought as he fingered the felt brim. "After recent events, I am considering that your God is with me, indeed." His pensive gaze scanned a gauzy wisp in the clear sky. "I am most grateful to my mother for my name, for it means *God has heard*." His eyes suddenly slit against the brightness, and with a smile on his lips, he laughed. "And it also means *coming from the sea,* which I did! Is no coincidence, you think?"

The man's optimism was something Grant could use right now. In fact, he could use someone like Henry. Bright, enterprising, bilingual. He had a telegram to send.

"How do you feel about trains, Henry?"

Thirteen

Humboldt County, California

Grant guided a sleek team of matched Morgans along the country road, the hectic big city environs happily packed up and locked away. He breathed in, drawing the sweet air to the depths of his citified lungs. If a man could bottle nature's own infusion, he'd make a fortune.

The proprietor of Palace Stables had been reticent to rent to him until he offered a bit of monetary incentive. As he left the swaying masts of the harbor behind and headed east, the morning light waned amid the majestic Redwoods. Colossal tree trunks sprang from snow-crusted earth and reached lacy fingers skyward. Their entangled canopy plunged him into twilight for a time.

He followed the hand-drawn map, and eventually the Fay Brothers' Shingle Mill came into view. Protesters marched lazily in a twenty-foot oval on the mill's property, directly in front of the door marked MANAGEMENT. Grant set the brake, jumped down, and ventured toward the picket line.

Bedraggled men in heavy boots and cutoff jeans came to life as he neared. They drew themselves up with more energy and struck up a chant. "War to the palace, peace to the cottage!" The shouts burgeoned with emotion at his presence, reminding him of impassioned baseball fans back east.

"Good morning, gentlemen," Grant said with a tip of his hat before wedging himself between the protestors. Foul remarks punched the air as he mounted the two steps. The door swung open. A squat, red-bearded man seized him by the arm and hauled him inside before slamming the door.

As he pumped Grant's hand, a frown drew his face into sharp edges. "Those men are getting to me. I don't want to admit it, but they are. If their intent is to drive a man out of business by making him lose his mind, they've perfected the technique."

"Mr. Fay, I presume." Grant chuckled. "I think I'm just in time."

"Thank you for coming, Mr. Campbell. I didn't know what else to do. When Fred Bee telegraphed that you would be here right away, I cannot tell you what a relief it was."

"Why don't you fill me in, Mr. Fay?"

The man motioned to a chair, and he slumped into another behind a desk piled high with papers. "For a long time now, many of my workers have demanded they not work alongside my Chinese employees. And for months I've rejected those demands. I've changed up the schedule, the crews. I've done everything I can think of to keep the peace."

"Are you dissatisfied with your Chinese crewmen?"

Fay shook his head. "On the contrary, they're the best of the lot, so far as workers go. I'm just not sure it's worth the headache any more to keep them on. Haskell and his IWA cronies are crossing the line with some of their tactics. They've plastered signs around town, threatened my family, camped on my property. Vandalized the Chinese camps, too."

Grant paused him with a raised hand. He'd seen the signs, bordering on libel. "I want you to think carefully, now. At *any* time, have you given the International Workingmen's Association or its members permission to be on any property you own, Mr. Fay?"

"No, sir. I've called the sheriff, and he won't do a blame thing about it. Something about free speech, and they ain't hurting anything." The man crumpled a piece of paper, tossed it, and watched it sail over the trashcan. "I can't abide being bullied into firing good workers, Mr. Campbell."

"Nor should you." He stood. "What you see out there is just the beginning, I'm afraid. I'll see what I can do. In the meantime, I beg you to keep your workers on, and I'll have these protesters off your property as soon as possible." Soon, if the Sheriff valued his job over bigotry.

He took his leave, weaving through the line of angry men. The IWA sought to build trade unions and farmers' alliances throughout the state. But in his labor newspaper, the *Truth*, Burnette Haskell was now brazenly urging loggers to destroy county buildings that kept data on land titles. The crusade was already a powder keg. Pairing such chicanery with anti-Chinese activities would certainly throw fuel on any spark.

As he headed west, the shrouded forest opened up again, and the sea-laden breeze struck him full in the face, watering his eyes. He arrived at the courthouse in plenty of time to draw up and file the complaint, citing the IWA and Burnette Haskell as litigants, hoping for a speedy bench trial.

He glanced at his watch, and as if his stomach had eyes, it churned up a loud rumble. He'd have to forgo lunch. No matter, he'd use the extra few minutes in the courtroom to his advantage. And hopefully, to Lian's advantage.

First to arrive, he opened his valise to review the case details. He made further notes, relishing a keen swell of anticipation—until his empty stomach protested. A handful of people filed in, including Kira, her arm protectively around her girl. Lian wore a striking Western gown with her hair pulled up like Kira's. *Good girl, Kira.* Why hadn't he thought of that?

He stood and pulled out a chair for his client. "You look beautiful, Lian." He bowed slightly, and she offered a fragile smile. "Don't be nervous. If all goes as plan, you won't need to say a word. I want you to keep looking straight ahead, *not* at Mr. Branson. Do you understand?"

She turned to Kira, who stroked her arm and whispered words Grant couldn't make out. Kira looked up at him. "She understands."

He returned to his seat, glancing in Arlen Branson's direction. Good. The lout hadn't had time to secure a lawyer.

"All rise." The bailiff stepped aside as the magistrate entered and took the bench.

"I have here before me a petition to release plaintiff, Miss Zhao Lian, from alleged custody of Mr. Arlen Branson. Miss Zhao is of age and therefore independent of guardian. The petition states that she is requesting freedom from any and all ties to Mr. Branson, materially, financially, and bodily. Mr. Branson, you may present an answer to the petition."

Branson stood, a glower that would melt lead aimed directly at Lian. But Kira had coached her well. The girl stared straight ahead, chin high, with a pleasant set to her lips. Branson started to approach the bench.

The judge lifted a palm. "You may speak from where you are, Mr. Branson."

"Uh. Yes sir. Your Honor. Sir." Branson glanced at the door. "You see, Your Honor, I was hoping my lawyer would be here."

"This is a simple case, Mr. Branson. All you have to do is answer to the petition. Tell me what you object to in the petition before us." The door opened, and a man with a pencil and notepad entered.

Branson angled toward Lian, jabbing a crooked finger. "I am accusing this woman, my wife, of grand larceny." Snickers came from the back seats. "Because, you see, Your Honor, I paid $300 for her passage from China, and in return she agreed to work for me for three years. Now, that three years is not up yet, Your Honor. And I paid for the clothes she was wearing when she left, so she has now stolen from me."

"You are saying you paid in advance for three years of service, Mr. Branson?"

"Yes, sir, that is what I'm saying."

"And what exactly kind of work did she do for you, Mr. Branson?"

Snickers again from the back of the room.

"Well, Your Honor, she did the cooking, cleaning, gardening, sewing. What any wife would do."

"Now you are including wifely duties in her job description?"

"Yes. I mean no, sir." He massaged the brim of his hat, turning it over and over.

"Is there a record of marriage, Mr. Branson?"

"No, sir." He blinked, glanced at the door again. "There is not."

"Is there a written contract between you and the plaintiff?"

"Uh, no sir, but . . ." Branson set his hat on the table and produced a paper from his pocket. "This here is a contract I signed with the man off the ship."

The judge motioned him forward and examined the paper, folded it and handed it back. His eyes darted to Lian. "Did Miss Zhao sign this agreement, Mr. Branson?"

"No sir, but it is—"

"How long has Miss Zhao resided with you, Mr. Branson?"

"Two years, sir. So, you see, she has one more year to work off her passage."

"Mr. Campbell, do you have anything to add?"

Grant stood. "Not at this time, Your Honor." He slid his gaze toward Lian, who hadn't moved a muscle.

The judge did some scribbling on a page. The stillness in the courtroom eventually simmered with muted speculation. Grant schooled his expression, hiding the satisfaction prematurely settling into his attitude. But he had a pretty good idea of what the judge was doing.

The judge frowned, scribbled some more, and laid down the pencil. "Mr. Branson, according to my figures, it is not Miss Zhao who owes you money, but *you* who owe her money—to the approximate amount of two hundred, twenty-five dollars."

A loud gasp from a spectator sliced the atmosphere.

Grant wanted to shout.

"This figure has taken into consideration what you would pay a washerwoman, a house keeper, a gardener, a cook, and a seamstress. And I liberally subtracted the room and board, which you no doubt provided her. Now, if I was to calculate conjugal fees, I am quite certain her lawyer would be charging *you* with grand larceny."

A man in the second row guffawed, and the judge silenced him with a granite eye.

"It is my opinion that this woman has stolen nothing but herself. Under the Thirteenth Amendment, I am emancipating her from any obligation to Arlen Branson, his business, or his heirs." The gavel cracked.

Grant itched to jump up and swing Lian in a merry little circle.

"Court dismissed."

Branson stormed out of the courtroom, a gaggle of observers scurrying off right behind him.

A hand squeezed his arm, and he turned. Chestnut eyes blazed. His mouth went dry. Kira was proud of him. *Proud.* Of *him.*

"Thank you, Mr. Campbell," a teary-eyed Lian drew his attention. Her head bobbed several times. "Thank you. Thank you." She beamed at Kira. "And thank God."

He smiled at the sweet exchange. Kira had been teaching Lian of God.

"Well done, Counselor."

Grant turned to the voice. "Henry?" He eyed him, impressed with the way his sharp, vested suit gave him quite the air of respectability.

Kira gathered the women's wraps. "I asked him to come."

He shrugged into his coat and ushered them toward the door. "Shall we get something to eat? My treat. I haven't eaten since breakfast."

"We may have just enough time," Kira said, taking his arm.

He looked at her hand draped on his sleeve. The icy wall between them was beginning to melt. And if the required warming be slow and gentle, he'd oblige. They started out of the courtroom, and when Henry offered his arm to Lian, Grant and Kira shared an amused smile. And it felt like the most natural thing in the world.

"I'm happy that went well. My biggest concern was that someone"—Grant's gaze darted to Lian—"would have to speak for herself. I'm thankful it didn't come to that," he said, daring to cover Kira's hand with his.

They exited the building and turned left onto the sidewalk. He fought the urge to stare at her profile as they walked, instead mulling over conversation points in his mind. "I hope the process to rid Fay's Shingle Mill of their IWA troubles goes as smoothly." He chuckled. "Yep. I'd say Eureka's sheriff is in for a surprise."

She tugged his arm to a stop. Lian and Henry bumped into them. She chewed the side of her lip, just as she'd done as a girl, all mischief and wonder. "*You* are full of surprises, Counselor."

He gulped, a thousand thoughts battering his brain. "You don't know the half of it." She really didn't.

He chose a restaurant at the edge of Chinatown to ensure they would all be served. One without one of those ridiculous *League of Deliverance* window cards. After they'd placed their orders, rehashed a bit of the hearing, and eaten, he figured it was as good a time as any to lay his offer on the table.

"Henry, I have a business proposition for you."

"You need herbal remedy, Mr. Campbell?" Henry's exaggerated Cantonese accent broadened his smile.

"So, you're an actor, too. I'll add that to your resume."

Lian giggled, and Kira doused an un-lady-like laugh with a drink of water.

"I want to hire you to be my interpreter."

Henry cocked his head and sat taller. "You are serious?"

"Yes, I'm serious. I already have approval to pay you a salary from Six Companies. I've been told my Cantonese is 'no so good.'"

Lian's hand flew to cover her mouth. Kira's cheeks bloomed a fetching pink as she suddenly feigned great interest in her pearled cuff. Her lips puckered and twitched. Henry laughed hysterically.

"You all think that's funny, huh?" He shook his head. "I have no supporters here."

"Yes, you do, Mr. Grant. And I am happy to take this job," Henry flourished a handkerchief and wiped one laughter-leaking eye.

Grant slammed both hands onto the table. "Glad to hear it. It will mean meetings, court cases, and travel. And please, please call me Grant."

"Yes, sir, Boss." Henry stood and bowed.

He growled in jest. Would this guy ever give it up? "And no bowing. And no 'Boss'."

Kira checked her watch pin. "Oh! We have to get to the train station." She and Lian stood.

As he and Henry assisted with their wraps, her words sank in. "Train station?"

Her brows shot up, and she pressed a finger to her cheek. "I didn't tell you?"

"Tell me what?" He suddenly remembered she could be as aggravating as she was lovely.

"Your mother and sister are arriving on the four o'clock train."

His mouth dropped open, and the drought of words prompted her to reach up and close it with two fingers.

Kira bustled on ahead. "We'll need to exchange your buggy for a carriage, then pick up Da. So we mustn't dawdle." She turned around, reaching for Henry's arm. "Would you be so kind as to walk Lian back to the Mission Home, please?"

He bowed to Lian—not a Chinese dip, but a deep, hand to his back, ballroom bow, complete with a flourish. "It would be my honor."

Lian smiled demurely and took his arm.

"Well?" Kira asked Grant, one hand popped to her hip. "Are you coming?"

"Uh, yes. Let me speak with Henry first." Grant pulled Henry aside. "I neglected to tell you that your new job starts this evening. We leave for Truckee on the seven o'clock train."

Henry blew out a low whistle. "I must get all of my suits from washerman."

His grave expression brought Grant up short. *Suits?*

Henry nudged him. "I am making joke, Boss." He smiled, showing all his straight teeth.

The ladies waited by the door patiently. Could they see the heat climbing his neck? "You are not funny." He shoved Henry playfully. "Coming, ladies."

Butterflies flitted in Avery's stomach. No, it was bees. Or was it cotton—little wisps of tickling cotton? Whatever it was, he was a dunderhead for thinking Lara would be as eager to see him as he was to see her. Och, but it had been hard without her these last few months. His breath quickened as the train pulled in amid the screeching brakes and hissing steam. The cars brought a breeze laden with smoke and chill. He touched his hat where it covered the healing wound. Thankfully, he was through with the awful bandage. Tenderness still worried head and shoulder, more so than he'd let on to Yakira, but he'd not stand for Lara seeing to him as some invalid.

Passengers stepped from the train, the conductor aiding the ladies. Kira bounced on her toes. "Oh, where are they?"

"Patience, my dear." He spoke more to himself. Suddenly she was there, raven hair threaded through with angel-wings, and a smile for all of them. But she was looking right at him. Waving at him alone. "Lara!"

Grant cleared the path for Kira to go on ahead and then motioned for Avery to go next.

Lara extended her hand, tugging Avery closer in the crowd. She settled a hand on his chest. "Oh, Avery. We've missed you so. Both of you."

He hadn't planned for this. Och! How could a simple re-union vex him so?

Azalea and Yakira squealed and embraced like two school-girls.

After a hug for Grant, Lara turned, snaking an arm behind Avery with a squeeze. He warmed at her embrace. And for just that moment it seemed there were only the two of them, an island in a sea of strangers.

He pried Azalea away from Kira, pulling her into their little huddle, savoring the wholeness that settled inside him. "Weel, weel. Here we are all together."

"As it should be." Azalea said, clinging to her brother's arm now. "One big happy family." She beamed and tugged Kira to her side with the other arm. "I can hardly wait to see the new Mission Home. And meet your students. I am so excited!"

"We'll get the bags, Mither," Grant said, escorting both girls away from the platform. "You and Uncle can just make your way to the carriage."

Lara hollered after him. "Oh, Grant. You may have to arrange delivery. We brought several crates for the Home. Donations."

He nodded, and the girls chattered away as they headed to the baggage room.

"I couldna stand not being here when I heard you were wounded." Lara said, gently tucking her hand around his arm. "Does it hurt?"

"Nae. 'Tis the other arm," he said with a chuckle. "And the *heed* only hurts when I laugh."

She slapped him playfully.

"Ouch!"

"Wheest! Ye canna fool me, Avery Mitchell. I can tell by your eyes—ye've overdone it by coming to meet me. I told Yakira wasna necessary."

"Nae. I'm fine. Just a wee tired. My first outing and all."

They walked in comfortable silence, and he found his hand upon hers, snug and comfortable. And now it seemed all was put to rights. How he'd missed their long talks and the way she could settle him when he took a notion too far. His bonny Lara. *His*?

"Mother, Uncle Avery. Where have you been?" Grant jumped down to help Lara into the carriage.

As Grant assisted him, heat flamed in his head. Then a bespatter of stars to his eyes, and an ocean wave to his belly.

"Uncle?" Grant's concerned voice seemed to echo.

"He's overdone it." Lara's sweet voice. "Let's get him home to rest."

Avery withstood the jostling of the carriage with a grinding jaw. He needed his bed, indeed.

"I am so excited, Aunt Lara. We have four girls now, and already we've made a few things to sell at a shop here in Eureka and one in Arcata. That's just across the harbor. I've opened an account at the mercantile, and so far I've been able to pay back every supply purchase." Kira rattled on about this and that.

He couldn't have been prouder. She'd made such progress with her girls. And so responsible was her handling of the many details of running the place."

"We can get Uncle Avery settled in, then I'll drop the girls at the Mission Home on the way to the stables." Grant slowed the carriage as they approached the little house. He turned to Lara. "I'm sorry, Mither, but I have to leave for Truckee this evening. It's business." He reached for her hand. "I am truly sorry."

Lara patted his hand. "You have a job to do, my son. Do it with all your might." An unshed tear perched to wet her cheek.

"I know," Avery mouthed, and squeezed her hand. "I know."

"I'll be back as soon as I can." Grant was still trying to comfort her.

"Truckee? Say hello to my old friend, Charles Crocker." Avery flinched as he adjusted his position. "He's always in the middle of any Chinese hoopla, as I recall. Wont to protect his investment. Fine man, though."

"You know Charles Crocker? I've had meetings with him." Surprise shaded his words. "Huh. What else don't I know about you, Uncle Avery?"

He gulped. "Oh, you'd be surprised . . ."

Grant continued, "I'm taking Henry with me. Six Companies has hired him to be my interpreter."

"Who is this Henry?" Lara whispered to Avery.

His head pounded harder. Oh, how he wished for his bed. And less conversation. Especially *this* conversation. "Let's leave that for tomorrow, shall we?"

Fourteen

Truckee

"Well, now. I knew it was no coincidence—you growing up near San Francisco's Chinatown. How is it you know Avery Mitchell, son?" Charles Crocker sat back in the tufted leather desk chair, a reminiscent squint to his eyes.

Grant shifted uncomfortably. "Actually, he's my uncle." It would be a mercy if the man wasn't privy to the hurtful choices of his youth.

"Your uncle, you say? Then you must be Errol Campbell's son, like I suspected." He opened a cedar box and offered cigars to Grant and Henry.

"Yes, sir, I am." Grant passed on the smokes before Henry eyed him, fishing for approval. He shrugged, indifferent, but his regard for Crocker just notched up a mite for his consideration of Henry.

The man nodded soberly. "I attended the funeral. You must've been what, fifteen, sixteen?"

"Sixteen." Less said the better. He didn't need the distraction today.

Henry nipped the head of the cigar in one quick motion, and Mr. Crocker struck a sturdy match. Bending forward, Henry's lips puckered and puffed like a fish until a cloud danced across the room. He inhaled the aromatic smoke like an aficionado. "Thank you, sir. It is not a luxury I indulge in often."

A luxury he didn't indulge in often? Grant shook his head, banishing a snippet of sarcasm. He proceeded to regale Mr. Crocker with news of the Mission Home and his mother's recent arrival in Eureka. They spoke of the climate of unrest and anti-Chinese labor disputes. Of politics and trade. Of cross-country railroads and trans-Pacific routes—all while Henry puffed away quietly on his cigar, content as a suckling babe.

"But you didn't just come for a social call, Mr. Campbell." Crocker sat forward, chair springs complaining beneath him.

Grant smiled. "Ah. You got me on that. As to the reason for my visit today." He settled his valise on his lap and extracted a folder. "I've drawn up a complaint against the vigilantes for destruction of property in Chinatown. Since you technically still own the land where the damage occurred, you will need to sign the statement of damages. If we can get even one eyewitness to testify, this will sound a clarion call to halt further violence against property belonging to the Chinese."

Crocker looked over the document. "But if no one comes forward?"

"Then we haven't a case. *This* time." He shared a look with Henry. "There is a solution, however. If you officially deed the land to the Chinese businesses and the residents who presently occupy it, they will be able to file their own claims in court. But as you know, at this time a Chinese man cannot testify against a white man in court."

"So, if I file for damages, *and* there is an eyewitness willing to testify against these vigilante actions, that would be the better solution."

"Yes sir. By far."

Mr. Crocker drew a pen from a holder, screwed off the top, and signed the paper. He slid it back across the desk. "Whatever became of that federal marshal you requested?"

"I haven't heard anything yet. There are probably some stiff shirts back east hemming and hawing about whether they want anything to do with California's *Chinese problem.*"

Mr. Crocker stood with a grunt. He moved through the smoke-fogged room to inch-open a window. "We could sure use a buffer right about now." Gauzy curtains shivered with a frigid gust of mountain air. "There's a man in jail accused of assaulting a Chinese man, but only because there were witnesses willing to put him at the scene. Oh, I know he'll be out after a hand slap. But what about these troublemaker cliques? They blatantly harass the merchants—robbing and assaulting them. Conveniently, they are never witnessed by any whites. The Chinese's pleas fall on deaf ears."

He harrumphed and took his seat once more. "An entire population of people is either invisible, or the cause of every problem in Truckee. No in-between. And the newspaper reports only one side of the whole affair. They paint the Chinese as base, thieving, murdering pariahs with no rights—who don't belong here."

"I will talk with this McGleason fellow after I file this"—Grant tapped the valise—"at the Courthouse. See if I can't get the man to listen to some sense." He stood. Henry seemed in a quandary about whether to take the cigar with him or snuff it out in the ashtray.

"Give Avery Mitchell my best. I don't get over Eureka way much, but if he is ever over on this side of the state . . ." He shook Grant's hand, then Henry's. "You boys watch your backs. I wouldn't put anything past some of the hotheads in this town."

"Will do, sir." The derringer in the top of Grant's boot pressed against his leg, suddenly feeling more like a .45. A fine bit of insurance he'd learned to ignore. Until now.

"Let's see what this is all about," Grant said, striding faster toward a small crowd with Henry at his side. Pedestrians migrated toward the assembly from every direction.

A man orated from the courthouse steps, punching the air here and there with a fist. A couple dozen people congregated on the sidewalk, many quite enthusiastic about the discourse.

As they neared, Henry checked to make sure he had tucked his queue safely inside his hat. "I am sticking by your side, Boss."

"Don't call me 'Boss'."

"I am sticking by your side, Mr. Campbell."

Grant shook his head. "All right. That works when we are with other people."

"This nation is yet in mourning for five hundred thousand of her best and bravest sons, fathers, brothers, and sweethearts." The voice boomed from the top step of the courthouse.

Grant moved closer. He clenched his fists at the sight of the familiar face. "That's Howard Dannon. I've seen a bit of his tactics firsthand. Tip of the iceberg, according to Crocker."

He glanced at Henry, who seemed to pale before his eyes. Henry ran a hand across his mouth, then his smooth cheek.

"Are you all right?"

Henry gave an infinitesimal nod as his slitted eyes targeted Dannon.

". . . they laid down their lives that their posterity might enjoy the blessings of not just a home, but a *free* country. African slavery was abolished—at an unfathomable cost of blood and so much we held dear, which will continue to cripple generations yet unborn." Dannon did an about-face and took three deliberate strides. "No sooner was this accomplished, but we are faced with a far more dangerous and servile race of slaves than those that it cost the nation so much to abolish."

His thick arms waved across the crowd. He did a sort of shuffle and a handsy flourish befitting a magic act—feeding on their responses. "Look around you. Look across this great state of ours. Hordes of these Chinese slaves only await the bidding of their masters to invade our land. To devour our very substance. To indeed, bring our laboring classes down to their base level."

A woman swooned, almost toppling the young man behind her. Voices grumbled, echoing the sentiment of Dannon's harangue.

Grant had enough. He stood a head above most, easily drawing the crowd's attention. "Mr. Dannon!"

Murmurs ceased, and the crowd parted like the Red Sea. He stepped closer with every word, fixing a sizzling glare on Dannon's steely eyes. "Obviously you are not aware, sir, how very similar your speech is to those who incited the withdrawal of Confederate states. Incited the very war of which you speak. This country was brought to its knees in answer to those very words spoken of a different race of people—a people from a different culture, brought here against their will to do service for the white man. And now you speak those same words about a people we *invited* to our shores—again, to do service for the white man. You, Mr. Dannon, are a white man who has not learned from the past."

"Ah, Mr. Campbell." Dannon tipped his imported bowler. "This, ladies and gentlemen, is a representative of Six Companies." More murmurs. "And I fear his brain has gone soft with all the opium he smokes with his Chinese friends. Or perhaps it has gone soft from the sorted disease of—"

"Dannon! Another word and I'll sue you for slander and defamation of character." Grant launched up the steps and towered over him. "I believe this little show of yours is over." He knew how to play this game. How to hold a stare until his opponent backed down. Seconds ticked past. The soft scuffle of the dispersing crowd. Dannon's stale breath. The subtle blanching of that thick face.

"This isn't over, Campbell. This is *my* town. *You* are just a visitor." Dannon straightened his lapels with a huff. Lifting his chin, he stormed down the steps.

Men like Dannon thrived on conflict. Grant stroked his beard, following the man's stout form and tailored jacket with his gaze. "If trouble is what you want then trouble it shall be."

He turned to a tap on his shoulder. Henry jerked his chin toward Dannon. "That man. He is a very evil man."

"You noticed, huh?"

"He is not a good man. I know him from China. Many years ago."

"That's right," Grant said, a conversation coming to mind. "He worked for Mr. Crocker as a labor broker, recruiting workers for the railroad. You knew him?"

"I knew him." Henry's eyes glazed, jaw flinched. "And not as a *labor* broker."

A single remaining spectator stood on the bottom step, a derby propped jauntily on his head. He scribbled furiously on a pad of paper.

Grant approached him. "And who might you be?"

"McGleason, Robert McGleason of *The Truckee Republic*. I hope you don't mind if I quote you, Mr. . . .?"

Wonderful. What splendid timing. "Grant Campbell, Attorney for Six Companies out of—"

"Yes, yes. Well, you will have your hands full here, Mr. Grant Campbell. Truckee doesn't take kindly to outsiders telling us how to run our town." The man shoved the notes into his pocket and walked away.

"Mr. McGleason, I actually had hoped to have a word with you." Grant called after him.

"Me? Whatever could you have to say to *me*, Mr. Campbell?" McGleason studied his watch.

"If this isn't a good time, we can arrange to meet tomorrow."

McGleason shrugged. "Right here is fine."

"I can't help but notice that paper of yours is more than a little lopsided. Every page holds fodder for anti-Chinese sentiment. By fanning those flames, you'll only destroy everything you've built here."

The man cocked his head and twitched his lips impatiently.

"Now, I know you don't see it this way, but this town *needs* the Chinese. The services they provide are critical to the populace, and I can't believe for one minute that feeding the appetites of the bigoted few is good for the many. Believe it or not, sir, there are laws to protect the very people you want to drive out of here. And wherever those laws are broken, you will find me breathing down your neck."

"Why, Counselor, are you threatening me?" McGleason smirked and started to jot in his little book again.

"There was no threat there, sir. There were statements of opinion and fact. Statements of cause and effect. It's called freedom of speech."

"And I simply write what I see and hear, Mr. Campbell. It's called freedom of the press."

Grant brushed an invisible piece of lint off the man's shoulder. "I don't incite riots with my freedom, Mr. McGleason. How about you don't with yours, either."

The man's eye twitched. His lips flattened. "I'm sure I will be seeing you around, Mr. Campbell."

Grant tipped his hat. "Most definitely."

Fifteen

Eureka

February 6, 1885

"There. That should do for the day." Yakira set the coal bucket beside the glowing parlor stove and brushed a hand across her forehead. She perused the homey room with its collection of donated furnishings, rugs, and draperies. Somehow everything had come together in ways she hadn't imagined. The realization rocked her to the marrow: God saw her—He heard her. It escaped any words she could set to prayer.

The cozy house was perfect for the dear ones she thought of as *her* girls. She and Azalea shared the smallest room, far from a sacrifice in their minds. After all, this place was a sanctuary for the girls, not for them.

"I could have done that," Azalea said, handing her a damp rag.

She wiped her face and hands. "Thank you. I must look a sight."

Quiet little Mei giggled, and Yakira looked at her. "What is so funny?"

The girl tapped her chin. "You. *Múih héi gānjìng.*"

Azalea stifled a grin. "Missed - a - spot."

Mei nodded. "You mees a spot, Mees Yakira." She smiled proudly.

"And where is that spot?" Yakira said, a finger to her chin.

The girl stared at the floor, her eyes searching the gold-green braided rug. Her head jerked up. "Spot on chin!"

Azalea clapped. "Very good, Mei. You learn fast."

Lian waltzed into the parlor with Shu and Zara on her heels. How happy they looked now. The pain of their abused bodies and wounded spirits hidden beneath shining smiles. Everything in Yakira longed for each girl to feel as loved as she did. To know that they mattered. To have a second chance at life as Azalea had—all because of God's grace.

"We make love-lee tea for you." Zara's careful words stretched from rosebud lips. Her tiny form bowed, and her dark eyes sparkled.

"We make cooo-keez for you." Shu said, motioning for them to come.

Lian grasped Mei's hand, and the four girls glided into the dining room.

"Something tells me we are in for a treat," Azalea said, hooking a hand through Yakira's arm.

Azalea had such a way with the girls. Once they heard her story and how much her white family meant to her, they were suddenly less reluctant to imagine freedom was possible—that escape from the horrors they'd lived was actually within grasp.

"Can you believe we are finally doing this?" Yakira faced Azalea and squeezed her hands. "We finally have a Mission Home of our own." The reality floated all around her, too wonderful to restrain.

Azalea glowed. "I think of it as God's Mission Home, and we are merely the caretakers. Here for Him to use."

"Exactly. And I'm afraid I get so excited sometimes that I may forget that. It is not ours. It is His. Truly. Oh, my laotong, how I missed you. It brings me such joy to be here together, doing this." She waved her hand through the air, taking in the fir staircase, the lace curtains, and the somewhat worn settee. "And to have Aunt Lara here to guide us."

"And teach the sewing!"

"Yes, there is that, isn't there?" She chuckled and then grew serious. "What . . . what if my father and your mother ever . . ."

Azalea's brows shot up. "What if they fell in love?"

"It *is* possible. They're not related by blood after all."

"I know they are dear friends, but love? Married love?" Her words possessed an innocence and wonder.

"Did you notice something different at the train station? The way they looked at each other?"

Azalea nodded slowly, her mouth agape. "The way they hardly noticed you and me. Kira, do you really think?"

"I don't know. I just don't know." She guided her laotong toward the dining room, thoughts swimming ahead of her. "But would it be so bad?"

Avery patted his belly, thoroughly sated. "I canna remember when I've had a finer meal. Your bonny wife 'tis a fine cook."

David Kendall chuckled and snugged his overcoat against the vaporous cold as they approached the corner of Fourth and E Street. "I tend to agree with you. I'm glad you finally made it over. Glad you felt up to it." A tern touched down a dozen feet in front of them, its orange beak juddering a nasal call before lunging into the wind again. "You seem to be mending well enough."

Well enough, he supposed, although headaches still raged most evenings. "I shouldna complain, but next week and next month will be better. This I know."

Gossamer fog roiled around them as a few shrouded figures scattered over the ghostly Chinatown street. When more dark movement caught their attention, Avery pointed. "I hope that's not trouble."

"You don't have to walk me all the way to my office, Avery. I can bring the maps to your house tomorrow. Mayhap you should get home and rest up.

"Wheest. I'll not rest when the world is yet awake." He eyed the street activity as they drew closer. Angry voices carried on the thick air as two figures plunged flags into the ground at opposite ends of the block, one of which set not thirty feet from them.

David slowed. "What are they saying?"

"Some kind of dispute about the Franco-China war. Rival Tongs." He'd seen this before. Bullets would fly, and the first gang to chop down the opposing flagpole would win. "We best get out of here." Gripping David's arm, he hustled him toward his office, still a half-block away.

Pedestrians vanished into alleys and shops. Avery and David started jogging. Two boys rounded the corner, clowning and shoving one another.

David paused, waving his arms. "Louis! Get out—"

Shots exploded all around them.

Avery ducked as bullets licked the walls of businesses, the ground, the boardwalk. Glass shattered somewhere. "Get down!" He lurched for his friend's arm. David's legs crumpled, and the boardwalk vibrated with the force. "David!"

He tried to hoist David's unconscious form, but fire seared his damaged shoulder. *God have mercy*! He gripped David's wrists, grinding his teeth in pain as he dragged his friend to the office door. Frantic for shelter, he rifled through pockets for a key. Another shot bit the street. An iron vice racked his head as he jammed the key into the doorknob, fumbling with the lock as another bullet splintered the windowsill. At last the door crashed open.

Fire blazed in his head and shoulders, sparking his vision white as he heaved David over the threshold. He slammed the door behind them as hot breath pumped through him. *Dear God.*

An abrupt silence slapped the air. Another tragic death leapt unbidden from Avery's memory, scraping him raw, jolting him to his knees.

Dear God.

But there—were his eyes deceived? Just now, a slight lift to David's chest.

Sixteen

EUREKA

Breakers of regret tossed and thrashed blame from every direction. They even buffeted Avery's vigilant prayers. "Mayhap I could have stopped the fight before it started. If only I'd gotten David to safety sooner." Had he grown so slow in his later years? He plucked a pencil off the desk and let it drop with a bounce before shuffling across the room once more.

"You know as well as I there is nothing more you could've done, Avery. It was just a foolish, awful, mistake." Ira sat bent over, elbows on his knees as he kneaded his hat.

"He's right," William Lord said, walking to the window. Loss swelled his eyes and drooped his stalwart form.

His friend was gone. It seemed all the misery Avery had known with Cait's loss piled aboard, crushing him. "He dinna even wake to say goodbye to his family."

"They don't blame you, Avery. And neither should you blame yourself." Ira sighed. "There's nothing we can do now but handle what comes next."

He looked up. "What do you mean?" Suddenly aware of a ruckus outside, he joined William at the window. *"Jings!* There's trouble a-brewing."

"We'd best get out there." Ira donned his hat and yanked open the door. "Almighty God, help us all."

"Amen to that," Avery said, last to file out the door.

A small mob of white men swelled before their eyes. Gun-toting citizens and loggers trickled to the perimeter like ants to molasses.

"News travels fast," William said, a hand to the sidearm he always carried.

"That it does."

"Burn Chinatown! Burn Chinatown!"

"Expel the Celestials!"

The angry mob filtered toward Centennial Hall, and the three of them followed. Hundreds filed into the sizable building. Avery, Ira, and William pushed and shoved their way to the front of the crowd, bent on diffusing the situation. A man was dead, and no amount of hatred would change that. But maybe they could stop more violence.

Sheriff Brown took the short platform and flailed the air with outstretched arms. "Quiet down, now! Muted down!"

The rowdy lot, mostly men, wielded garden implements, firearms, and even a few baseball bats. Blazing tempers and blasphemies testified to the only thing on their minds.

Several minutes ticked away until the sheriff's voice cut through the rabble. "Now, I don't want this to become something you'll regret. You need to let the law handle this. I've got a bunch of Chinamen in custody, but I can't tell you which one fired the shot that killed David Kendall or wounded young Louis Blanchard in the foot."

Strength siphoned from Avery's limbs. He leaned against the wall. The boy David had tried to warn. How easily they could be burying him, too.

"You can't tell us, or you won't?" A voice accused.

"I can't." The sheriff waved down the growing discord.

"I say we massacre every Mongolian in the area!"

"Drive them all into the redwoods!"

"Hang the ones in custody. Set an example!"

Avery looked on in horror. He'd invested time in getting to know many of these men. How quickly this vindictive mob had seduced them! The Sheriff's suggestions seemed only to spur on more heinous solutions, all of which included murder, thievery, or fire.

"Citizens!" Ira Harrington had mounted the platform. His voice roared over the mess and squelched most of the outlandish behavior in short order. "Please consider this truth—the Chinese men did not mean to kill Mr. Kendall." His arms spread wide, begging for reason. "It was purely an accident. They pay their rent and keep to themselves. You cannot possibly consider wrecking vengeance on all of the Chinese in town just because of a couple of stray bullets!"

Hostilities buzzed like an angry swarm.

Attorney Bledsoe stepped up beside Ira and clamped a hand to his shoulder. His oily smile didn't sit right. "May I suggest a solution?" Bledsoe hollered, tamping the noise once again. "I suggest a compromise. To avoid the 'wrecking vengeance' element of Reverend Harrington's mention, I propose we banish the entirety of Chinese from our town."

Shouts went up in support, and Avery's sick feeling upended and breached in ire.

Sheriff Brown glowered, looking out over the mob. But he made no move to counteract Bledsoe's plan. William's hand never left his sidearm—his expression inscrutable.

Seeming right happy with himself, Bledsoe strutted like a dandy as he approached the middle of the stage and stood not three inches from its edge. "All Chinese will be put on notice to vacate Eureka within twenty-four hours."

"Now just a minute—" The roar of the crowd quashed Ira's plea.

Stars flashed in Avery's vision before igniting a fire between his temples. He set a hand to his head to ease the pain.

An odious excitement swelled as they chanted, "No more Chinese! No more Chinese!" A frown crimped Ira's darkened features as he stepped down to join Avery.

Bledsoe quieted the ruckus and proceeded to call individual men up to form a line across the platform. Mr. Buhne, the hardware store owner, stepped forward, and another attorney by the name of McGowan. Then Francis Thompson, whom Avery knew as editor of *The Humboldt Standard*.

"What is this?" Avery asked.

Ira shook his head as one of David Kendall's colleagues from the city council stepped up—Dan Murphy, owner of the Western Hotel. Most of the called-out men Avery knew only by name—all outstanding members of the community.

"And this is your committee, people of Eureka," Bledsoe announced. "Fifteen solid, law-abiding citizens to facilitate the evacuation of Chinatown and all Chinese in the area. This day, Chinese residents of Eureka will be served official notice that they must vacate the premises by three p.m. tomorrow."

"But where will they go?" Ira shouted, turning heads.

"Why, wherever they wish, Reverend. So long as they leave Eureka," McGowan answered. Thick copper eyebrows shadowed eyes that mocked and played to the assembly.

Responses were quick: "Yeah. That's right. Drive them Mongolians outa here!"

"There are two ships in the bay, fogged in these past two days," Bledsoe continued. "The Chinese will be peaceably shuttled to them for safe passage to San Francisco."

Avery spoke up at last. "And you can insure it will be peaceable. No violence?"

"Reverend Mitchell," Bledsoe said with an indulging smile, "it is this committee's purpose to simply deliver the options to the Celestials. We have every intention of peaceful removal. But as for a few impassioned citizens . . . we cannot say."

The stirred-up vigilantes began crowding towards the narrow front door of the meeting hall—their attitude and intentions obvious.

"I'm needed in Chinatown. Is there a back door?" Avery told Ira. Maybe his presence would stave off more violence for the peace-loving Tang people. They didn't deserve this. And what little he could do wouldn't be enough. *Ah, Lord. How I need ye with me!*

"This way!" Ira led the three of them down a short hall beside the platform and out the back door into the twilight.

They beat the troublemakers to the heart of Chinatown, but already shops were shuttered, proprietors hidden away, fearing for their lives.

The committee of fifteen swept through the blocks in pairs, pounding on every Chinatown door, delivering the ominous decree. And every committee member wore a gun on his hip.

"So, this is what peaceful looks like in Eureka." Avery mumbled to himself.

A single streetlight at each end of Chinatown did little to penetrate the murky fog as darkness fell. Avery spent an hour checking on the bewildered Chinese residents, wishing he could assure them this was the worst of it all. But was it? Some of the younger men called him *"Old Uncle"* for they knew he loved and respected them. How could they respect him now that he had failed so miserably to help? If they did run the Chinese out of Eureka, what would that mean for him and Kira?

Yakira! The Home could be a target as well. He said his goodbyes and rushed the few blocks to the Mission Home, heart pumping in his ears and a freight train rumbling in his head.

Yakira read yet another Psalm, and Azalea translated as all six of them huddled in the parlor. The soothing words seemed to speak to the girls' fears as boisterous clusters of people filtered down the dark street throughout the evening.

"Here we are." Aunt Lara glided into the room, skirts swishing around her. "Who is ready for more tea?"

Shu slid her cup forward. "Yes, please."

Yakira finished the chapter and set the Bible on Azalea's lap. "It is much quieter out there now." She approached the window. The streetlamp's smothered glow braved the ominous fog, and a few lights shone from nearby houses. A dark figure approached, pulling a long coat tight against the chill. "It's father!"

"*Bethankit,*" whispered Lara as she scurried to unlock the front door. "Praise God in heaven. I was so worried."

"Da!" Yakira ran to the front porch where Da was locked in an embrace with her aunt. They parted so suddenly, Aunt Lara wobbled and Da steadied her. Yakira slowed, unsure of how to proceed. She seized her father's hand and pulled him into the warm parlor light. "You must be chilled to the bone. Sit down. We have hot tea."

"I wouldna let her leave." Aunt Lara said for his ears. "I'll go grab another cup." She floated out of the room, bouncing an odd sort of look from Da to Yakira.

Da smiled at the girls. "Ladies."

When he looked at the Bible on Azalea's lap, he winked. "Good idea, lassie."

Azalea set it aside. "We've been reading to the girls all evening. First gunshots, then the crowds, and such awful shouting out there. Whatever is happening?"

Lara returned and poured Da a steaming cup of tea. "It canna be good. Are ye all right?"

"Och. You worry. 'Tis the poor Chinese who are certainly not all right." He recounted the terrible events, beginning with the sad news of David Kendall.

Yakira wilted at the news, hurting for the Kendall family, her da, the Chinese.

Mei and Zara shed tears, and their faces paled as Azalea translated. When Zara stood to bid everyone goodnight, she hauled the other girls along with her. Lian tugged on Azalea's sleeve and whispered in her ear.

"Oh, no." Azalea said, taking the girl's hands in her own. Then she turned to Da. "Lian is asking if they must leave the Mission Home also."

He reassured Lian in Cantonese, "We will not be separated, my dear, that I will promise. We must all trust in God. He has a plan."

She bowed and thanked him, but concern still laced her eyes.

"Oh, Da. I'm so sorry about Mr. Kendall. And I don't understand how the people of Eureka can just turn on the Chinese like that."

"'Twas an ugly sight, it was. Glad I am that none of you had to see it." Da took her hand. "I know not what tomorrow will bring. That said, I dinna want any of you leaving this house tomorrow." His gaze lingered on Lara with an unspoken trust before passing a stern look back at her. "Yakira Jean? Am I clear?"

She deserved that. Da knew her own willfulness had steered her directly onto folly's path on occasion. As much as she longed to be in the thick of what was happening—to know and understand what it all meant for the Home—he knew best. "I hear you, Da. I'll not leave here. And nor will I let my girls leave."

"And nor will I," Aunt Lara said. "Come what may, we will protect our girls." She cocked a determined smile at Yakira and Azalea, a glint sparking in her eyes. "Won't we, ladies?"

Da's shoulders rose and fell. His mouth opened and closed, yet he held his tongue.

How she loved Aunt Lara. Loved them both.

"You've been mighty quiet." Grant shifted in his seat as slices of forest and carved rock drifted past the window. The scarcity of passengers in their train car made for restful travel. "Henry?"

Seated across from him on the opposite bench, Henry raised walnut eyes. One cheek indented where he chewed it. He seemed to focus on Grant's ear. "It makes no sense. The white demon . . ." The side of his mouth twitched.

The common moniker was often accurate, unfortunately. "Go on," he urged, probing the reason for Henry's sullen mood.

"Well, the white demon does not like us in his country. We are the ones who make it easy for them to come across your land from one ocean to the other. We are the ones who risk our lives and sometimes die to build the railroad that opened up their land. For *them*. Now they forget. There is fortune here for everyone—white men, Black men, and Tang men. All men.

"Chinese come with dreams, but so do whites—and they come by rail, made possible by us." He poked his chest. "Now the whites want our jobs. They are through with us. Throw us out like trash. They want us to go away. But what would they do without us?

They have come to depend on us. We do their laundry. We work in their mills, their mines, their factories.

"Everything you've said is true. If only I could make the courts see it. Apparently, you've given it a lot of thought."

Henry leaned forward, forearms balanced on his knees. "And this is another thought I have. People come from the other ocean, and they become citizens, but we cannot. Even I cannot, and my mother was American. If the *Fàan gwái* (foreign devil) attack us or steal from us or murder us, there is nothing to be done. They can cheat us out of our wages. They can rape our women. But we are like the Indian or the Black man here. No power. No voice. No way to get retribution. It is not like in our home villages, where a man must accept the punishment of the villagers. Here, on Gold Mountain, a Tang man is not even allowed to testify against a white demon."

The landscape flattened, and the gray winter blanketed the terrain. A hawk swooped to the ground, a rodent in its talons, helpless, ignorant of its fate.

Henry sat back, his shoulders drooping with a sigh. "So, we learn to *baai hoi*—to stand aside, to avoid conflict."

"Something I wish more white men would learn." Grant had forgotten much these past few years—like how cruel one man can be to another if he reckoned a life had no value. Everything he'd learned from his parents had to do with valuing other people. Loving them as ourselves. And for no other reason than the fact that we were made in God's image. And that made us brothers. *Brothers.*

"The Tang should be treated like guests in a foreign land." Henry sank deeper into his thoughts.

"No." Grant said simply.

"No?" Henry gaped back at him.

"The Tang should be treated like brothers."

"Like brothers?"

"You are repeating me." He grinned and slapped Henry's knee. "I am proud to think of you as a brother."

Henry blinked several times before his mouth curved up. "And I am proud to think of you as a brother." He dipped his head, and his smile tilted. "Grant."

"Ah-ah-ah. No bowing."

"Was not a bow. Was a nod."

They laughed, and Grant switched his attention to what lay beyond the train window. He willed the miles to speed past so he could see Yakira again.

He nearly dozed amid a daydream of her on a spring day, walking with him on the wharf, her ebony hair whipping in the sea breeze and her hand in his.

"You are thinking of her." Henry's voice interrupted.

Aggravated, he opened one eye. "Who?"

"Yakira. I can tell when you are thinking of her. The same as when you look at her."

"Kira is my cousin." But he knew that. "We were close growing up, and I missed her."

"Uh huh." Henry folded his arms across his chest. One cheek bulged, and his eyes glinted.

Grant squirmed, trying to get comfortable. Leaning his head against the seat back, he stared at the curved ceiling overhead. "She's like a sister to me." He closed his eyes, hoping that was the end of it. Silence. Feeling Henry's stare, he opened one eye again. "What?"

"But if she was not your cousin?"

He glared at Henry. "Just what are you getting at?"

Henry re-crossed his legs. "Just remember I say this—life can surprise you. You remember?"

Grant shook his head, finding his new friend very confusing. And just now, annoying. "Yeah, yeah, yeah. I remember." Now maybe he could get back to his daydreaming.

Seventeen

Eureka

Gray dawn spilled through the glass pane and flooded the bedroom floor with the same lacy pattern as the curtain. Yakira yawned, stretching lazily until her mind jerked fully awake. She sat up suddenly and rushed to the window. Good. No more crowds, at least not in front of the Home. But somewhere, the strike of a hammer chiseled at the peaceful morning.

Oh, how she wanted to slip out and check on the Chinatown residents. But Da was adamant. She poured water into the basin, washed her face, and ran a brush through her hair. Dressing quickly, she went to the kitchen only to discover Aunt Lara had already made coffee and was even now mixing up a batch of Scotch pancakes.

"Good morning, my dear." Aunt Lara poured her a steaming cup of the dark brew and set it on the table.

Yakira covered a yawn and sat. "Thank you." Weary to her bones, she lifted the cup and let the steam bathe her face.

Lara threw a look over her shoulder, the skin beneath her eyes dark against her rosy face. "I didna sleep well either. Too much on your mind?"

She half-sipped and half-blew on the coffee. "Yes." She sighed out the word, knowing her aunt was searching for more.

Aunt Lara dropped large spoonfuls of batter into sizzling grease, wiped hands on her apron, and sat down at the table. "I ken ye're *aflocht*, my sweet, but God has a plan." She covered Yakira's hand with her own. "We'll get through this day, and then there will be tomorrow. This Home, nae, this ministry belongs not to you, but to our Heavenly Father. He willna see it come to naught, ye must trust that."

Of course, her dear aunt was right, but inside she struggled. Struggled with the unknown. She always had. And she'd never been as good at trusting for her tomorrows as Azalea or Aunt Lara, or even her father. As much as she yearned for God to use her to offer new life to these girls, she equally yearned to be wanted herself. *For* herself, not for what she could do. Oh, she knew she was loved. And that in itself was a mighty wonderful thing. For how many girls had she seen come and go at the Mission Home who had never known genuine love?

"Yakira?" Aunt Lara's voice dissolved her selfish thoughts. "Would you like some?" A tall stack of perfectly browned drop scones settled in front of her, thick and steamy. "This may be a trying day. I suggest we all begin it with a hearty meal."

"Thank you." The hammering in the distance continued. "What do you suppose they're building out there?"

She shook her head. "I am as curious as you are, but ye ken what your father said about leaving the house today."

After but a few forced bites, she pushed the plate away. Rocks had settled in her stomach, cold and heavy. Surely, they couldn't make *all* the Chinese leave. Could they?

February 7, 1885

Avery had not yet washed his face when the front door vibrated with a pounding. "Avery!"

Suspenders loose around his hips and his beard uncombed, he rushed to open the door. "Ira. Come in, come in."

Ira stood on the threshold, face drawn and eyes keen with distress. "You need to come with me, now."

Within minutes they were on their way to Chinatown, where dozens of people milled about the streets, unusual for this early hour on a Saturday. Morning draped heavy and taut, pregnant with the day's unfolding. A shiver crept up Avery's spine, a foreboding that penetrated every bone.

They slipped around the corner of E Street and halted. Three men drove the final nails into a crude gallows. "Great God preserve us," Ira cried. "This is insanity!"

A fourth man lifted a sign still wet with paint. Avery's breath caught at the shiny letters: ANY CHINESE SEEN ON THE STREET AFTER 3:00 TODAY WILL BE HUNG FROM THIS GALLOWS.

"Here, now. You can't do that!" Red-faced, Ira reached for the board, only to have it ripped from his grasp and nailed in place.

"Sorry, Reverend, it's long past due, and everybody in this town knows it," the lanky fellow argued. "There ain't nothing you can do about it now."

"We'll see about—"

"Let's go, Ira." Avery pressed a hand to his shoulder. "Let's find out what we *can* do." If only Grant were here, perhaps with the law's backing, this entire spectacle could be squashed.

Four empty farm wagons rumbled past, followed by white men bent on mischief. They cajoled and made merry as if they were going to the fair. Garden rakes and ball bats. Wheelbarrows and shotguns.

Silent fury knifed Avery's lungs. What could only two men do against such outrage?

Shouts rose from the crowd as people multiplied before their eyes. "No more Chinese! No more Chinese!" Fists pounded the air to the rhythm of the words. He and Ira jogged into Chinatown, hoping to head off the malaise surely to come.

Many of Chinatown's merchants had set up for business as usual, but others seemed resigned. Faces somber, they stacked crates of belongings onto the boardwalk. A Merchant's wife hobbled daintily, arms laden with stacks of silk fabric. Working girls lingered outside the brothel, wide-eyed as the crowd approached. If any had doubted the dictate of the Committee before now, there was no mistaking the town's veracity as the empty wagons pulled to a stop along D Street.

Charley Wei Lum met them as they approached the garment store. "I try to tell them they must go, but some think it is not so. I worry for safety. I worry for violence. The working girls say they will stay. Please, sirs, you must help me convince them." He slumped as defeat etched his features.

Avery pounded him on the back, ready to lead the charge. "We must make them understand and cooperate to avoid violence. Ira, you take the other side of the street, and I'll make my way down here. Let us pray, for this will surely be out of our hands."

Charley and Avery translated the committee's demands, beseeching the Chinese to cooperate. It was a double-edged sword, for as much as Avery wanted them to stand up and fight against these injustices, he would have none of them injured. The Tang people were again at the mercy of the white men.

Thankfully, some in Chinatown had taken the warnings seriously. They'd already crated up valuable supplies and merchandise, unwilling to leave their investments behind. Older men and small-footed women piled into two of the wagons for the trek to the harbor, too far for them to walk. Others heaped belongings into wagons and secured them with ropes.

Even before noon, malicious threats peppered the streets. Avery was powerless as men raided Chinese homes and stores, searching every corner for holdouts. Working girls stumbled from the brothel, baskets strapped to their backs and arms piled high with clothing.

He tried to reassure them, tried to encourage them, but his storehouse was empty. What does one say when injustice robs a man of his home, of his livelihood?

Even as they loaded the wagons, vigilantes overturned vendor carts, scattering winter vegetables, gourds, and trinkets.

"Here now!" Avery growled. He thought of the hands that had labored long hours to raise the goods, to eke out a living in this hostile place. But chaos reigned, and no one was listening. Baskets of dried fish, rice, and water-filled barrels of shellfish slurried the streets—strewn about by an incursion of white gangs throughout Chinatown.

Gunshots rang out from the opposite side of the block. Two men with bats beat-in shop doors, the reclaimed lumber splintering with each blow. A raucous bunch ripped the bordello door off its hinges and bridged the sordid gully with it. White men and women carted off armloads of dry goods and supplies while vigilantes scattered Chinese goods and fabrics over the street.

"That's thievery!" Avery yelled. Was there no one to help these people? Where was the law? But the question mocked him. The law was behind this mayhem. Every window seemed shattered. Mah-jongg tiles littered the boardwalk—a symbol of a culture torn asunder. He crossed the street to stand with a huddle of Chinese men and women who watched on helplessly.

A Tang man was trying to protect his wife from flying chunks of leather as a vigilante ravaged the shoe shop. "Stop this!" Avery yelled, hustling the couple out of harm's way.

"Been a long time coming," sneered the wild-eyed man hacking at the bundled pieces.

Insanity. It was insanity. Churchgoing men with families drunk on the wine of bigotry and hate.

"Stand back, Reverend." Pete Braxton and another man shoved over a barrel of seawater, and crabs scattered onto the street. Pete flashed him a satisfied look. "It's about time."

"I never knew you felt this way, Pete." Avery shook his head, bile rising in his throat. How had he missed it? Never once had this sentiment leaked out in his conversations with the man. Pete had even hauled furniture to the Mission Home for Kira.

"Pete gawped, his light eyes blank. He started to say something, but another barrel crashed against the boardwalk, dousing his legs with a wave of seawater. He spun around, swearing a blue streak. Avery backed away.

Amid victorious *whoops* and vile threats, the destruction continued as the first wagons headed for the docks. More wagons had straggled in, now lining two entire blocks of E Street and Fourth. Rough men corralled the first batch of residents and herded them toward the harbor at gunpoint.

Voices catcalled as the working girls passed. Bitter tears smeared gaudy make-up across the girls' faces as they balanced heavy loads. Observers—even the very men who had been their customers—hurled spit at them. A man Avery didn't recognize grabbed one girl and threw her to the muddy ground. When her friends tried to help her up, his accomplices knocked them down too—a maniacal game without mercy. The girls sobbed, struggling to stand, slipping and sliding in the brown slurry as they groped to help one another, only to be shoved back down when they stood. The men laughed, their sordid souls much amused by the sick game.

"Stop this! Stop this now!" Avery charged to the scene, fire searing his veins. His fists wrenched, ready to rack vengeance, but powerful arms strapped him, holding him back. Thank God, Yakira wasn't witnessing this.

Avery settled, surrendering his hands and his fight as soon as the cruel men found other amusement. "I'm fine. Let me be." He did his best to calm the rage in his voice. "Please, let me help Mrs. Yang." He shook off the stranger who had waylaid him and turned his crazed mind to help elsewhere.

Widow Yang sobbed, crawling on her hands and knees outside her husband's shop. From the worn boards, she plucked up tiny seeds—her livelihood. Without them, he knew she would have nothing. He knelt beside her, helping her gather as many as he could in a couple of minutes as the madness reigned around them. He told her, in the gentlest way he could in her own language, that she must leave now. Her bloodshot eyes swam with sorrow, but after tying the seeds into a small fabric bag, she nodded.

Surely her years had already known much heartache. And here was more. Everything she had worked toward, everything but these seeds, was gone, for she was too frail to carry supplies or belongings to the wagons. As he scanned the mayhem, a minor victory sparked in his heavy heart when he saw Charley across the street. He hollered but could not make himself heard. "I'll be right back," he told Mrs. Yang.

He dodged a wagon and clustered agitators, making his way across the sticky street to Charley. He commissioned him to pack up and load as much of Mrs. Yang's belongings as possible so the poor woman would have *something*. Something besides a frayed bag of seeds.

Somewhere, a shout rang out. More shouts split the melee. "Burn Chinatown! Burn Chinatown!"

Avery strode toward the chant with balled fists. There were still people in these homes and shops, for naught but two-thirds were in the streets. He spotted Ira up ahead, no doubt with the same thoughts. Och! What were two ministers against such out-of-control villainy? *Ah, Lord, do I need thee.*

Eighteen

EUREKA

Lian and the other girls huddled in a kitchen corner, secured only by a chair wedged against the back doorknob. Azalea spoke soothing words and shared Bible verses from memory. Yakira paced back and forth from kitchen to parlor. Every time she looked out the front window, the scene was the same—enraged men and their words: "Bring out the Chinese!" When one of them fired a pistol into the air, Mei screamed, and Yakira rushed to her side.

"I won't let anyone hurt you," she said, offering more reassuring words they could all understand. She didn't know yet how she would protect them, but Aunt Lara's words kept circling in her head, "*This ministry belongs not to you, but to your Heavenly Father. He willna see it come to naught, you must trust that.*"

She could do nothing but trust, for where was there to go?

Aunt Lara's voice was frantic as she descended the stairs. "From the bedroom windows, I can see the Chinese leaving. Some in wagons, some in groups." She flinched as another shot tore through the yard. "There is a large mob at the corner of Chinatown."

"They're doing it," Yakira said, hot tears beginning to spill over. "They're forcing the Chinese out of Eureka." She grabbed the banister as strength deserted her limbs. But she would not be weak. She *could* not be weak. Her girls were counting on her. She must trust.

The front door quaked, pounded from outside. Mei cried out again, this time inciting the other girls to panic. Men clustered outside the windows, brazenly peering into the house. Yakira drew herself up. If these hate-filled men were going to give her trouble, she'd give it right back.

As she climbed the stairs, the fight inside her swelled to battle. She collected every basin and pitcher from the bedrooms and then opened the window directly above the men.

"Here's what I think of your demands, fellas!" she hollered—and doused them thoroughly.

"Yakira!" Aunt Lara stood behind her, but the single scolding word buckled into a smirk. "Too bad the chamber pots are all empty," she said with a quirked eyebrow. "That won't stop them, ye know. Sooner or later, they will get in here and take the girls by force."

"Then they will take me too!" She pushed past her aunt and hurried down the stairs.

"Kira, listen to reason—"

"I will not abandon them!" The words that had carved her heart long ago now sharpened with new resolve. Hadn't this been what she'd wanted—a mission home of her own, the chance to make a difference? She stopped at the landing and turned to Aunt Lara, close behind her now. "You've been a mother to me, and I love you for it. You taught me to be strong, and stand by my convictions. This is me, doing exactly that."

Aunt Lara grasped her shoulders, moist eyes penetrating her own. At last, she nodded, unspoken words charging the sweet space between them. Yakira threw her arms around her, drawing strength from their love, for she would need it.

"Smoke! I smell smoke." Azalea's frantic voice in the kitchen drew them running.

The back doorknob rattled. "You won't be in there long," warned a syrupy male voice. The knob rattled again. Wicked laughter accompanied a sound kick to the door.

"They think they can burn us out," Yakira said, trying to formulate a plan of action.

The girls sobbed anew, all of them now, as even Shu gave in. Azalea began reciting the twenty-third Psalm in Cantonese.

They couldn't go upstairs—they would be trapped. Smoke seeped through the edges of the door.

Aunt Lara grabbed tea towels from a kitchen drawer. "We need to fill the cracks. It will buy us time."

Glass shattered, spurring panicked screams as they all ducked behind furniture. A flaming torch vaulted across the dining room floor, igniting the tablecloth. Another torch crashed through the parlor window.

Aunt Lara grabbed more tea towels from the drawer. "Water. We need to get these wet." She started for the sink, and Lian jumped up, working the pump as Aunt Lara soaked each towel. She squeezed them out and handed one to each of them. "Cover your face."

"They're going to kill us!" Mei whined, shuddering at the words.

"No. No they aren't." Yakira peeked through the window onto the small back porch. There was smoke, but no sign of fire. *Trust.* Fire licked at the kitchen doorway as the rest of the house crackled in flames. She stared at the doorknob. It was the only way.

Aunt Lara touched her arm. "Kira, no."

She met each terrified gaze. "Follow me." Covering her mouth and nose with the wet towel, she opened the door, and stepped onto the small, enclosed porch. To the right was the cellar door. It was their only chance of escape.

She unlatched the door and made her way down the rickety stairs. Oh, why hadn't she thought to bring a lantern! She descended into the musty darkness, thankful for the little light flowing from the open door behind her. She followed the earthen wall, skirting splintery shelves and an empty barrel.

"*Shhh.* Everyone, be quiet." Aunt Lara's words sounded from the end of the line of sniffles and shivers, of hushed prayers and humming. "They might hear us." The upper door closed, plunging them all into darkness.

Yakira climbed the carved earthen stairs and put her ear to the large outer door. Men's voices sounded just above, muffled and taunting. If they waited until the men left, they could escape.

Yakira turned back to the girls. Their silhouettes shone through a blushing mist that seemed to settle around them.

Something crashed above them, and Shu jumped. "Hot!" She brushed burning embers from her shoulder and patted down her hair.

"Ouch!" Glowing debris sifted through the floorboards, singeing their hair, their clothing. They began patting each other, snuffing the embers before they could take hold.

"Over here. Shhh." Follow my voice, Yakira said, gathering them to her beneath the outer door above her head. She started softly singing the hymn the girls had been learning, "My hope is built on nothing less, than Jesus' blood and righteousness." Frail voices mingled, carrying the tune meekly through the inky stillness.

Trust. She shored up her faith and let the words of the hymn calm her thrumming heart.

"When darkness veils His lovely face, I rest on His unchanging grace; In every high and stormy gale My anchor holds within the veil."

Pleas broke from her deepest self, begging God to save them all. To save her girls. *His* girls.

Nineteen

EUREKA

"Eureka, next stop!" The conductor announced, walking the length of the passenger car. "Eureka, next stop!"

A smile crept across Grant's face, buoyed by entirely too much anticipation. And, curiously, moths fluttered in his stomach at the thought of seeing Kira again. Perhaps more girls had joined the Mission Home. The girls were drawn to her like bees to a flower. He chuckled to himself. As was he—always had been.

All those years ago, when he'd left San Francisco, he'd loved her—maybe more or differently than he should have. His mood fell somber as he cast his gaze out the window. An old ache stretched his ribs. She had been raised in his mother's arms, as much a sister as a cousin, and anything more had always felt unthinkable. So he had resigned himself to calling her his best friend. And now, as her image taunted him, fully grown and captivating, his thoughts of her bordered on insanity, sandwiched between *not possible* and *never*.

"What is that?" Henry said, peering out the window. "Something is burning in Eureka. Maybe a house fire."

"I hope not." He gathered his hat and valise, eager to disembark. As the Southern Pacific car slowed, people stirred, and frantic natter had people pointing out the windows.

"Not good." Henry shook his head. "Not good."

A sea of wide-brimmed hats and quilted coats congregated on the loading dock. Folks huddled together, many with belongings strapped to backs, others seated on rope-wrapped boxes. All of them wore the same mask of defeat.

A sickening portent snaked up Grant's spine as he watched another group plod toward the harbor, flanked by men with guns. "Let's get out of here," he said, squeezing his way toward the exit before the train shuddered to a full stop. Whatever it was, he was going to dive right into the middle of it. How dare they force those men out of town!

He was the first one off the train, with Henry close behind. They jogged toward the harbor, where Chinese men and women plodded up gangplanks onto two waiting ships. Stevedores transferred a mishmash of crates, suitcases, and barrels from wagons. He recognized one merchant and, with Henry's help, discovered the awful news of the expulsion. Leaving their suitcases at the depot, they raced toward Chinatown, dodging the protracted exodus of a hundred more of its residents.

A Chinese laundry couched within a white neighborhood was in shambles. With tubs destroyed and stoves and cauldrons overturned, it was a complete loss.

They halted at Fifth and E Street. The sight set his blood to boil. "What the blazes?" Amid the rubble-strewn thoroughfare, bands of white men emptied shops, throwing produce and canned goods, fabric, and hats into wagons.

Others manhandled several Chinatown residents, shoving them into a huddle. "Here now!" Grant stomped toward them with a growl. He accosted the fellow who seemed in charge. "This is an illegal act, and I'll have you brought up on charges!"

"Then you're gonna have to arrest the whole town, mister. Now, outta the way!" He shoved Grant aside and fired a shot into the air before joining his cronies again, prodding the Tang people on down the street. "Move it on out!"

Henry yanked on Grant's sleeve. "It's no use. Come. We are only two men. We cannot stop what is happening here."

Another wagon rumbled past carrying a merchant and his small-footed wife. They sat balanced atop a jumbled pile of their belongings—their entire lives forcibly carted off. Their forlorn expressions thoroughly wrenched him. He had to do something. But what?

The cellar door above their heads slammed open. Yakira gasped and blinked against the brightness, her eyes throbbing as the words of the hymn died on their lips.

"Here they are!" A man's voice shouted.

"Come out you China whores! Or I'm coming down there to get you, and it won't be pretty."

Her breath froze in her lungs—all hope of escape dashed to bits.

The panic-stricken girls wept as first Yakira, and then Aunt Lara climbed the earthen steps. The rest followed.

"Well, well. What've we got here?" an oily voice drawled as they stood shivering on the lawn. His black eyes raked each of the girls and stopped at Aunt Lara and Yakira. "You ladies can leave now," he said. "We'll take it from here." He drew a filthy hand across his twisted smile.

Half a dozen other men milled about. Leering stares curdled Yakira's stomach and ignited something lethal inside her.

"Don't touch these girls!" she snapped at the two men whose hands had already begun stroking Shu and Lian's arms. "This is a ministry—God's Mission Home for Girls. You have already brought condemnation upon yourselves for this heinous crime. I warn you, do not multiply your sins further by removing my charges."

The oily-voiced man guffawed, a contagion that spread to his goons. "Don't think for one minute that a little spit like you is gonna tell us what to do, missy. We got us a mandate, and we're just being good citizens." He turned to the others. "Ain't that right, fellas?" More raucous laughter.

Aunt Lara pulled Azalea and Yakira to her protectively. "Let's go, girls. We need to find Avery. He'll stop this."

"No!" The word vaulted from Yakira's throat as fury sprouted roots around her heart. "I'm staying with my girls. You find father, Aunt Lara." She stepped aside, corralling her four girls.

"I dinna like this one bit, Yakira. Please!" her aunt begged.

"Suit yourself," the man said with a shrug. When he tried to herd Azalea into a clump with the other girls, Lara lunged for her.

"This is my daughter, sir. She is coming with me."

"She's Mongolian. She's coming with us."

Azalea's eyes flared as her gaze bounced between Lara and Yakira. "It's all right, mother. I'm going with our girls. Just find Uncle Avery." She grasped her mother's hand for an instant before the man pulled her away to join the other girls.

Yakira locked arms with Azalea, and they each gathered two girls beside them to make a chain of six. She held her chin high as the hymn rose to her lips once again. "His oath, His covenant, and blood support me in the whelming flood." Their voices raised in unison. Six voices, fervent and defiant. "When every earthly prop gives way, He then is all my Hope and Stay." Strength infused her limbs, her spirit. "On Christ, the solid Rock, I stand. All other ground is sinking sand."

Their walk had become a march, the words spurring them on in trust that whatever lay ahead, God was there. He had a plan. But as they rounded the corner, her voice faltered. Armed vigilantes lined the streets. And the dear Tang people shuffled along in clusters—the weight of much loss pressing bent backs and hunched shoulders. And they were all being herded toward the harbor.

All she had feared was actually happening.

"It is not Chinatown that is burning. Only that—" Henry pointed to the center of the street where a barrel belched pungent black smoke. It mingled with the thick gray air.

"Thank Goodness." Grant had been prepared for worse. Much worse.

"All the Chinese are leaving. No need to burn." Henry's eyes riveted, and his jaw slackened. He jerked his arm up, pointing. A black-clad effigy of a Chinese worker hung from a gallows. Above it, words spelled out a foreboding warning and deadline in large letters. Henry looked at his watch. "If these white men are serious, there is not much time."

Grant's blood chilled reading the sign. "*Any* Chinese will be hung? They couldn't mean every Chinese person in town. Surely."

"That's exactly what it means."

They turned to the rough voice behind them.

Shotgun in his meaty hands, the stranger stared at Henry. "*Every* Chinese person better be out of Eureka. That means you, too." He took a threatening step toward Henry.

Grant wedged between them. "This man is an employee of Six Companies. You lay one finger on him, and you'll be standing before a grand jury on kidnapping charges."

The man's eyes bulged, and his face twisted with exaggerated fear. "Ooh. I'm scared." He laughed, shaking his head. "Then that'd be a real long line, wouldn't it?" He stabbed a finger into Henry's chest, his steel gaze shooting darts. "Three o'clock, Chinaman." He huffed and walked away.

Troubling notions assailed him. He took a deep breath, trying to separate what he *could* do from what he couldn't. But one of those thoughts niggled more than the others. *All Chinese.* What about his sister?

Henry pointed to the northwest. "There's the fire." He blanched milk-white. "The Mission Home?" Fear flashed in his enormous eyes as they met with Grant's.

They sprinted off, the sense of urgency unyielding. Dodging jagged boards and strewn fabric, shoving past hateful cheers, Grant's heart pounded faster with every step. His desperate prayer was for his mother, his sister. Kira.

His chest heaved as he staggered to a stop. He stared at the remains of the Mission Home, numbed by the sight. He tunneled a hand through his sweat-soaked hair. Surely they'd gotten out before the fire. His mind refused to consider any other scenario.

The charcoaled skeleton emitted plumes of black smoke only to have much of it settle again atop neighboring homes.

"Yakira." The single word rasped from Henry's lips.

Grant looked at Henry, surprised at the grief he saw there.

Abruptly, Henry wagged his head. "No!" The word struck like a hammer blow. "I will not lose her again." He spun and sprinted off.

The ships.

Stunned by Henry's words at first, Grant followed and overtook his shorter friend, frantic to find the women before the rioters had their way. In but a few blocks he'd caught up to them, chagrined by the way they linked arms, heads high. A song trailed behind them, and a sense of pride tapped his panic.

"Yakira!" He cupped his hand, yelling a second time before she turned her head. Her eyes sparked for an instant with something that made his stomach jump. How well he still knew her. She would stay with her girls, regardless. Spine straight, she sang louder, nose pointed directly ahead.

He caught up with them. "Stop this at once," he ordered the men who flanked them.

"Grant!" His sister's eyes shone bright, and her smile stung his heart. "You came!" She pulled away from Kira, but rough hands shoved her back to the other girls. She looked at him again, desperation coloring her gaze.

The men ignored his appeal. He squeezed between them and strode up to Kira, keeping pace right behind her. "Kira, listen to me. I can stop this. Maybe not today, but surely tomorrow. Come with me."

"You're too late, Grant." Her harsh words scorched the air as she faced forward. "You weren't here. Now you're too late." Her shoulders stiffened and drew back.

Even from behind, he could see the hard set of her jaw.

"I won't leave my girls—not for one minute."

Azalea turned his way, her initial relief at seeing him gone entirely. "And neither will I, brother." The smug smile on her lips caught him off guard.

"This is recklessness! Come with me now, and we'll get the girls tomorrow."

Kira turned her head this time, not quite making eye contact as she flung her words. "They took Azalea. You may have left her behind, but I will not."

Gut-punched, he stiffened, motionless as the stream of people broke around him. So that's what she thought of him. Still.

Henry was at his side, tugging on his arm. "You cannot let her go with them."

"Grant!" His mother's voice pierced the chaos. She was with Uncle Avery and another man in a wagon. She frantically motioned for him and Henry to join them.

"Mither! Uncle! Kira won't—and Azalea—" He plodded toward them, pain pulsing in his jaw from grinding his teeth.

"I know, I know. Lara told me." Uncle Avery said. He introduced the man driving the wagon as William Lord. The man nodded and handed the reins to Mither before wielding a shotgun.

Mr. Lord bounded from the wagon, all fringe and leather—intimidating as a mountain man out for bear. With a revolver on one hip and a long hunting knife on the other, he checked the shotgun's breach. "Let's go get those girls, shall we men?"

"Gladly." Grant slipped the pistol from his boot. "You'd better stay here with Mother, Henry." He struck out with Mr. Lord, Uncle Avery right behind them.

"You've made a mistake, Curtis," Mr. Lord said to the one who seemed to ruffle the most as they neared. "These young women are residents of the Mission Home for Girls."

"What Mission Home?" Curtis sneered, passing an amused look to his cronies. "You boys see any Mission Home?"

"Not no more!" A round of callous laughter.

"You—" Grant's thumb twitched on the hammer, ready to cock it and give these loudmouths what they deserved.

Mr. Lord clamped a hand on his arm. "That was my house you burned, *my* property, and you'll be held accountable—every one of you—unless you step aside and let these ladies come with us right now."

Curtis spit. He passed a squinty look over the girls, then to his partners.

A minute later, Grant and Henry were helping the girls into Mr. Lord's wagon.

Grant's hand moved to circle Kira's tiny waist and lift her aboard. He avoided her gaze, her earlier words still stinging, barbed as they were.

"I don't need your help, Counselor." She stepped away and tried unsuccessfully to jump up into the wagon bed. "Henry?"

Henry shrugged at Grant before lifting Kira into the wagon, a twinkle in his eyes that was hard to miss.

"Thank you, Henry," she said. But her eyes pinned Grant in place.

"You're welcome, Miss Yakira." He bowed his head and stretched a wide grin.

Grant snapped his mouth shut. Did he look as dumbfounded as he felt? Whatever she was trying to tell him with that look, he obviously didn't speak the language.

Twenty

Eureka

Avery climbed into the wagon and wiped sweat from his brow, more than ready to head out of town—and away from the chaos and heartbreak. The sunken faces, the stooped shoulders. These were his people. He'd failed them. He should've done more. Should've found a way.

Grant kissed his sister's cheek, then reached for his mother's hand. "I'm not coming with you," he said. "I need to get to the telegraph office and let San Francisco know what's happening."

"Of course you're leaving. Again." Yakira's vinegary comment from the back of the wagon turned Grant's head.

"Daughter," Avery scolded, "he is doing all he can to help." And hadn't Grant been doing that very thing ever since returning to California? The lad had been working hard, of that he was certain. Mayhap this road was a necessary one—one that would bring healing for them all. In time.

Grant's face sagged as he stared at the back of Yakira's head for a moment before stepping away from the wagon wheel. "Henry and I will catch up with you later."

William shook Grant's hand. "My place is in Arcata, just across the bay. Everyone knows me. Just ask around. Your family will be safe there." He snapped the leads, and the wagon rolled forward as Grant and Henry waved.

"Why do they have to be that way?" Lara whispered for Avery's ears only.

He touched her hand, squeezing it for an instant. "Give them time."

The day's events had worn a path through his senses, and surely it was that way for the others. The story Lara had told of the burning house still weighed heavily. What if he'd lost Yakira? The thought squeezed his heart and just as quickly, guilt rushed in. For every time he looked at her, he thought of the two promises he'd uttered—one to Cait and one to Lara. *Oh me.* A fix of his own creation. Circumventing Chinatown for the girls' sakes, they passed fewer and fewer individuals bent on the awful events of the day.

William flicked a thumb at the handful of men congregating in a yard several houses up the street. "What do you suppose—?"

"That's the parsonage!" Fearing for Ira, Avery glanced at the shotgun on the floorboard.

"What are you thinking?" William said.

"I'm thinking our friend may be in need of help. But I willna have the girls party to it. Let me off here, then go around the block and take the girls home with you." He reached for the shotgun. "Mind if I borrow this?"

"Avery, no!" Lara gripped his wrist. "Ye canna!" Her plea warred with the protector in him.

"Wheest." He patted her hand, prying it from his sleeve. "Dinna fash. I'll just wave it about a bit and let God handle the rest." He thought to kiss her lovely cheek, but steeled himself.

William turned the corner, leaving him to slink over to Ira's house and investigate. He huddled at the edge of a neighboring shed to formulate a plan. Two men crashed through the front door, dragging Charley Wei Lum from the house. Two other men stopped Ira from following. "The lad was only saying goodbye. He will go peacefully, won't you, Charley?"

"I go peacefully. I go peacefully." Charley's frantic words fell on deaf ears. They slapped a Bible from one hand and tied his wrists before marching him back toward Chinatown at gunpoint.

"Stay strong, my son!" Ira hollered as the young man disappeared around the corner.

Avery checked his watch. The only thing left in Chinatown was the gallows, and it was after 3:00. Surely these men wouldn't commit murder. He followed them at a safe distance, praying he wouldn't have to use the weapon. It had been many years since he'd fired a fowling piece, and he much preferred God's intervention to his own.

He jogged as a mighty sense of urgency propelled him onward. When the gallows came into view, instead of the effigy, it was Charley Wei Lum's neck in the noose. Only a small crowd gathered there—their jabs and mockery almost childish. Avery slowed to a walk, willing his pulse less fleet and his prayer more powerful.

"Move aside!" He brandished the shotgun, and the crowd parted for him, their jeering squashed in the course of three long strides. All eyes shifted to him. With full pulpit strength, his voice thundered, clear and slow. "Lads, take that rope off his neck! If you hang him, you'll hang him over my dead body."

It was the quietest Chinatown had been all day. 'Twas but the heartbeat in his own ears he heard. He didn't flinch as he lifted the weapon a bit higher. The two men flanking Charley exchanged looks ripe with resignation. "I ain't gonna be responsible for no violence against a minister," one of them said and began loosening the noose.

Charley climbed clumsily from the gallows, hands tied behind his back, his wide eyes never leaving his two accusers.

"Get out of here then, but you better be on one of them ships!" one man threatened.

"I'll take him myself," Avery said, lowering his weapon.

As weary as he was, he'd see Charley safely to the docks, then pray for a ride to Arcata. The women would be sorely worried if he didn't make it back by evening.

Newsmen converged on the telegraph office, burning up the wires with news of the Eureka purge. Chaos reigned as publicity seekers shoved their way into the crowd to report their own impressions on what was occurring. But Grant knew from experience that not all would report the whole truth here. Six Companies had to hear the truth. From him.

Chinese expelled from Eureka by force. Much loss and damages. After 15 minutes in line, Grant handed the short missive to the telegraph agent to send. He had to get back out there and see what was happening at the dock—needed to witness the loading of people against their wills.

"I can't send this," the operator said, handing back the form.

Grant glowered, stroking his beard, ready to thrash the cocky fellow. "Can't or *won't?*"

The man bristled. "Won't."

He slammed his palm onto the counter. "This has to get to San Francisco!"

"Next!" The agent ignored Grant and waved the person behind him forward.

Henry pulled him aside. "If we go on one of the ships, we can observe treatment of Tang people. Maybe more to report to Six Companies then."

Grant nodded, blowing an exasperated breath. What he really wanted to do was stay on for at least a few days for his family's sake—to make sure they were truly out of harm's way. And he feared for any Chinese who remained in the area.

Growing up in San Francisco, he understood the ways of fog and shipping. Even now, hundreds of Chinese were aboard the *Humboldt* and the *City of Chester*. But there would be no departure until daylight tomorrow—leaving the Celestial passengers to languish without proper food or facilities the entire night.

They headed for the ticket office but turned at the sound of marching feet. Two dozen riders herded as many bedraggled Chinese workers.

Grant approached the nearest horseman. "I am counsel for Six Companies, representing these Chinese residents. What is going on here?"

The man raised a hand to halt the other riders, and the worn-out workers jolted to a stop. The sway of their heads, the slump of their shoulders—never had he seen men so blatantly exhausted—many deprived of even the most basic hat for shade. "We caught these railroad workers up at Blue Lake. They's the ones responsible for killing Mr. Kendall."

"Blue Lake? You mean to tell me you marched them on foot all this way?"

"Yes, sir. Left at dawn this morning." The man puffed out his chest.

Irritation pulsed through him. Men like this ought to be whipped. "As I understand it, Mr. Kendall was killed by a single bullet wound. You are certain these men managed to place all their trigger fingers at the same instant on the same gun to kill Mr. Kendall?" *Of all the ridiculous . . .*

"They's guilty just the same." The man spat and advanced his mount, roughly brushing Grant aside.

"What is your name, sir?" No reply. "I said, what is your name?" Desperate to do something, anything, Grant lunged for one of the men's stirrups, but Henry yanked him back.

"It's no use. There's nothing you can do."

"There's got to be something!" Helplessness rocked him. He clenched his fists. He refused to be helpless. He'd think of something. He had to think of something.

The bedraggled lot trudged past him, a staggering, merciless display of inhumanity. A few heads lifted, and what he saw in their eyes sliced something in him wide open.

The set of Henry's jaw and the fire in his eyes told Grant all he needed to know about how all this was affecting him.

They could only watch silently as the marchers stumbled up the gangplank.

"It does something to you here,"—Grant cleared his throat and poked his chest—"to watch people forced against their will like that."

Henry simply nodded, his silence bearing witness to many years on the receiving end.

"Sorry," Grant said, gripping his friend's shoulder. "It must bring back a lot of hard memories for you." He couldn't imagine.

Henry nodded again, his gaze following the last few railroad workers as they boarded.

"I guess we'd best purchase those tickets before there's none to be had. Then we'll have time to visit the family before the ship leaves. You don't mind bunking with me, do you?" Grant started down the docks, and a chuckle behind him told him Henry had returned from his sad recollections.

But something had been chasing Grant since they left the burned-out Mission Home, and nothing he could come up with on his own helped him make sense of it. "Say, Henry. Back there at the ruins of Kira's house. What did you mean when you said, 'I will not lose her again'?"

"I said that? No, you are mistaken."

Grant took a giant step and turned to face him. "That's exactly what you said, Henry. About Kira."

"Grant, Henry!" Avery strode toward them with a young Chinese man. "I'm glad I caught you." He introduced the man as Charley Wei Lum, one of Reverend Harrington's young proselytes and explained about the near hanging. "Let me say goodbye to Charley here and see him aboard. Then I'll join you. We can borrow a conveyance from the livery and head on to Arcata."

"All right. We'll wait for you over at the ticket office," Grant told him.

"I will go with you, Reverend Mitchell," Henry offered, already striding toward the ship.

"Whoa. If ye dinna want to be snatched up yourself, ye best stay with Grant." Avery shook his head. "I wouldna put it past any of these vigilantes to spirit ye away, too."

Grant snagged Henry's arm and hauled him along with him. "Yeah, ye dinna want to be spirited away, too."

Twenty-One

ARCATA, CALIFORNIA

The Lord home was neither ostentatious nor humble, but it was spacious enough for all of them for a time. Avery looked around, grateful to his scalp for the accommodations and the faithful friend he found in William. And Ira. But sadness soured his hopes for him and his Yakira Jean. With the Chinese gone, there was no reason to stay in Eureka.

Avery shook William's hand. "Thank you, the both of you, for this shelter in the storm, and the salve of a meal."

"Ah." William swatted the air. "It's our pleasure."

"I canna tell you what this means—your offering up your home to Kira and her girls until we know the next step."

"Our home is home to all who need a home, Avery." He had one arm around Eleanor's waist. "I expect we'll be housing *fugitives* in the barn before long. I doubt the witch hunt will end just because Eureka is free of Chinese."

"All the girls are settled into two rooms upstairs," Eleanor said. She turned to Lara. "I'm happy we are able to offer you a room to yourself for now."

"I do so appreciate it. Tomorrow I will write to the Mission Home in San Francisco to see if they can replace a few of the things we lost in the fire. They have such a wonderful group of benefactors. I'd hoped for the same thing here." Melancholy laced her words. She turned to Avery. "I'll walk you men out."

She looped her arm through his, and her nearness soothed the day's soreness.

Grant slipped a pen and small tablet from his pocket. "I'll be along in just a moment, Uncle Avery. I have a few questions for Mr. Lord." He turned to William. "That is, if you don't mind."

Henry bowed to William and Eleanor, and his copious words of thanks elicited a snicker from Grant. He donned his hat, tucking his queue inside as Avery opened the door for Lara.

"The fog is lifting." Avery said, covering Lara's long fingers with his own burly ones. Ah, to stroll with her like this all evening. Contentment purred from her throat, and it sent a surprising rush of heat through him. She made him feel twenty years younger.

"Reverend Mitchell."

He'd forgotten Henry was behind them. "Yes?"

The plains of his face stretched taut, and his eyes strained in earnest.

"What is it?"

"We need to talk about that subject we talked about." Henry's gaze dropped to his clasped hands, then to Avery, to Lara, and back to Avery.

So, this was the way of it. It was two against one, and he felt like a man defeated. "You can speak freely in front of Lara. She knows everything."

Henry's eyes widened. "Everything?"

"Yes."

Henry cleared his throat and stood a little taller. He worked his lips, hesitating. "You have not told Yakira about her mother. About me."

"No, I have not." He could feel Lara's keen eyes upon him. And her disappointment.

"I have kept your secret as I promised I would, Reverend Mitchell. Out of respect for your wishes."

"That ye have, lad." And he had failed to keep his promise to Lara in turn.

"I want you to respect my wishes now, please." Henry steepled his hands.

"Avery, please. Yakira has a right to know." Lara touched his chin, begging his eyes to meet hers. "The longer ye wait, the harder 'twill be for her."

"I want her to know who I am. I want her to know she has a brother. I want to tell her about our mother." Henry's voice bled desperation. "All my life I have waited, I have searched. I am not willing to wait any longer."

Avery's world shifted with a painful crack. It was crumbling around him. The sweet and the bitter parts, the framework of his life's deceptions. The trust his most precious daughter placed in him. "Aye," he said at last. "Let the wounds of today settle. Then I'll tell her."

Grant hadn't meant to overhear. And now the words sawed through his mind like a dull knife. Kira adopted? Henry, her brother? So many questions. He knew she'd been born in China—that Aunt Cait had died in childbirth. But where did truth and lies diverge? Had Mother known from the beginning?

He deftly backtracked from the shadowed yard and began to whistle to signal his presence. He strode toward the carriage with heavy steps, kicking a pebble here and there. Their sudden silence at his appearance was deafening. He smiled. "You weren't talking about me, now, were you?"

Mother clung to his arm. "Of course we were." She tittered, a sign of nervousness he'd come to recognize.

He kissed her cheek. "I don't know when I'll be back this way, but I'll write."

She straightened his lapels. "That would be nice." Resignation crimped her weary face, driving the tiny lines deeper at the corners of her eyes. Unspoken were the words, *"Don't make promises you can't keep."* And, *"You've never been good at writing before, will this be any different?"*

"Go now." She said, kissing his cheek. "You have lawsuits to file, depositions to do whatever you do with them."

Grant mounted the rented conveyance and pointed it toward the docks. As he and Henry wended around the bay toward Eureka, his whirling thoughts jostled no less than the buggy on the rough road. With no moon, the darkness pressed in from all sides, as depressing and heavy as the silence between the two of them.

Many things made sense now. Why had he not thought of it before? Was not his aunt Cait said to look much like his own mother—solid and long-limbed? Yet Kira was small, nearly as small as Azalea. Had he not teased her as a lad about her bug-brown eyes, when everyone else in the family had blue eyes?

His heart slammed to his feet. Kira was not *really* his cousin! Not by blood, anyway.

But what did that matter? She'd formed her opinion of him with such firmness that he knew not how to soften it—to make her see how truly sorry he was for all that had transpired. If she couldn't grant him a measure of grace just for leaving, she would never accept the awful truth of why he'd really left and how he'd paid for his schooling.

Pacific Ocean

Grant leaned on the railing of the *SS City of Chester*, watching the Redwood studded coastline shrink from view. The salt air brushed his face, cooling his entire body. Still, the Boston coat was too warm for the Pacific winter.

He had yet to broach the subject that weighed on him. He'd toyed with the approach, coming at it from different angles. Yet the only thing that rang true was to do what he was trained for—even renown for in the courtroom by some. He wanted the whole truth. But was it really *his* truth to know? Curiosity never trumped a person's right to privacy.

Therein lies the rub. As much as he wanted to understand what had transpired across the ocean twenty-two years ago, perhaps it was not a story for his ears. It was Henry's story to tell. And it was equally Kira's story to hear. So he wouldn't pry or push. He would simply nudge the door and see what happened.

"My first time on ocean as free man." The wind caught Henry's voice, snatching it away, but not before it garnered Grant's attention.

Grant stepped closer, both of them leaning forearms on the railing. "That's a pretty profound thing to say. I've come to think of you as plain old Henry." He bumped his shoulder. "My old buddy, Henry. Yep."

"Not so old. Just not so hairy." Henry stroked the smooth skin around his mouth.

"You're just jealous you can't grow one," he chided, stroking his whiskers and tugging his hat lower to keep it from an unintended offering to the sea.

"Mmm . . ." Henry hooked his queue with two fingers, waving it at Grant. "And *you* are jealous of this. I have here many times more hair than your ugly face."

"Ugly? You think I'm ugly?" Grant feigned insult. "You know . . . you're kind of like a cousin to me, Henry."

Henry sucked in one side of his mouth and nodded.

"Why, that would make you Kira's brother, then, wouldn't it?"

Henry's shoulders slumped. He pulled back on the rail, letting his body dip and sway with the waves. After a minute, he hooked Grant with a perturbed look. "How did you know?"

"I've never been much for lies." Or secrets. But he had his own, didn't he? "I overheard you talking with Uncle Avery last night—completely by accident, mind you. But for what it's worth, I had begun to suspect something anyway."

Henry looked out toward the glowing horizon again. Squinting against the breeze, his eyes turned watery and faraway all at once.

"Care to share the details?"

And that, Henry did. The raw facts spilled forth without slowing, as if someone had turned on a spigot. "Do you understand why I care for Yakira, now? Why I want to know her and for her to know me?"

Greater love has no man than he lay down his life for a friend. The verse came to him, the truth of it suddenly wetting his eyes. It's what a ten-year-old Henry did for his baby sister, trading his own life for hers. His knuckles whitened on the railing. And it's what his father did for him. He gasped as his chest exploded with the most painful kind of truth in the universe—the only truth that really mattered in the entire scheme of things.

"Are you all right?"

Henry laid a hand on his arm, with a pleated brow and so much caring, it stunned him. He only nodded, his voice waylaid somewhere between his stomach and his throat.

They stood in comfortable silence for a time. Finally, Grant formulated his next question. "Kira's father. The American. Do you know his name?"

Henry tugged on his watch fob as if there'd been no question at all. "It is getting late. They will serve a meal soon."

"I'm a lawyer, Henry. I recognize stalling. If you don't want to answer the question, just say you don't want to answer the question."

Henry scowled, but something foreign flared in his dark eyes. *Fear?* Suddenly he patted his belly and brightened. "I don't want to answer the question. I want to eat." And with that, he was gone, listing this way and that as he crossed the bow.

He stared at Henry's back. What had swept him so abruptly from baring his soul to shutting Grant out altogether?

The twenty-four-hour sail had provided a much-needed reprieve from all the recent turmoil. Even though Grant had invested several hours interviewing the Tang passengers, which had proven to be a gold mine, he felt rested and ready. And he had already drawn up the body of a lawsuit against the city of Eureka on behalf of the expelled Chinese residents. If he were to expedite this mess and gain a decent settlement for the immigrants, he would have his hands full for a while.

Mayhem reigned as passengers scurried about. Hundreds crowded the rails with their entire lives strapped to their backs, ready to leave the awful eviction in the past. Tiers of steamers choked San Francisco's harbor, coughing up pitchy clouds against a flaxen sky. Eventually, the two ships from Eureka queued. Once they docked, harbor officials were impotent against the sheer number of homeless Chinese flooding the docks. Most of Eureka's old residents vanished into Chinatown, leaving Grant and Henry standing alone.

"Where to next?" Henry asked, suitcase in hand, looking every bit the tourist in his smart sack suit and crisp derby.

Grant patted his valise. "The Ong Cong Gon So Association." He strode toward a waiting cable car as he talked. "I don't anticipate any problems with them accepting this wording on behalf of the merchants I interviewed. Then breakfast. Then Six Companies."

Had he ever been this excited about anything in Boston? Never. It didn't get much better than this for any attorney. He'd been in the thick of the outrage himself—who better to represent these displaced, violated residents? His mind already teemed with the language he would use.

As Henry boarded the cable car, a wide grin split his face. "Much better than a carriage."

The car climbed up a San Francisco street past three-story brick buildings, gray clapboard offices, and colorful homes, leaving the blue bay behind. A whole different expression lit Henry's face as they converged with a tangle of other lines on Market Street. They changed cars at the Ferry Building, where rails sprawled like spider legs, and the air vibrated with clicks and clinks and commuter conversations.

"Will we be riding cable cars often?" Henry gripped the handle with one hand, his hat in the other.

"Hmm. Yes, I guess." Memories swam in Grant's mind, some assaulting like hungry sharks and others assuaging the ache that was growing by the minute. What he wouldn't give to turn back time—to a time before his father's death. How he yearned for a second chance to do things differently. No one tells a youngster that a single decision can alter the course of their life. Forever.

"This is like a fair!" Henry's voice hitched with excitement.

Choosing to seize the better times, he shoved the rest into a dark closet. "I felt the same way when I was a lad."

Twenty-Two

ARCATA

Yakira scratched at the lacy frost on the windowpane while icy raindrops pelted it from outside. She stared at the two unopened boxes on the bed. Eleanor Lord had graciously supplied all of them with the necessities for continuing school, even a change of clothing apiece. But the thought of simply picking up studies as if nothing had happened seemed wrong. It felt disrespectful—when hundreds of men, women, and children struggled to find shelter from the harsh elements. And how many of them worked long hours, seven days a week at jobs where they were hated?

Anti-Chinese parades in Crescent City had provoked the entire town to follow in Eureka's footsteps. They had expelled most of the homeless Tang people via ships bound for San Francisco. But some of the immigrants had made their way south to Arcata, and every day, refugees sought shelter in William Lord's barn. Rumors of vigilantes rounding up woodcutters in the mountains had them all preparing for another influx of refugees. How much longer would this tiny community remain a refuge?

"They're here!" Azalea's excited voice filtered through the closed bedroom door.

Chatter in the hallway told her that the girls were heading downstairs. She straightened the curtain and joined them, eager to hear about what was happening in town.

Aunt Lara was just closing the door behind the three men to block the biting wind that chased them into the entry. Yakira assisted with their coats as Eleanor swept into the room with a tray of hot coffee.

Rev. Harrington thanked her and began sipping the steamy brew even before removing his gloves. He sighed. "Exactly what I pined for after that circus of a meeting."

"Circus?" Yakira passed a look to Da, and he nodded, reaching for his own cup.

Mr. Lord slapped a wilted stack of papers onto the table. "Here. Good for nothing but fire starter."

Eleanor rolled her eyes. "*Daily Times Telephone*. Publishing every vile comment, glib gossip, and step-by-step instruction on how to hate your fellow man. Come. Sit and tell us all about it." She ushered them all into the parlor.

Shu touched Yakira's shoulder. "We should leave?"

Boredom had driven these poor girls to tears, isolated as they were these last few weeks. Yakira permitted them to stay but warned of what they would hear. Mei and Zara skittered back upstairs, but Shu and Lian settled demurely on the floor, tucking their skirts beneath their legs.

"It's quite apparent the whites want to dispose of any Chinese tradition and culture that ever existed around here," Mr. Lord said, his expression sour. "For all these years, the economy of Eureka and surrounding communities have depended upon Chinese labor and business. The very people who benefitted from them now want to pretend they never existed. How does that make any sense?"

"They're trying to cover their sin, 'tis what I see here." Da shook his head, his wiry eyebrows bunched over slate-hued eyes. "I am much afraid this is only the beginning. If you had heard their hateful accusations—most, entirely without grounds."

Yakira shared a concern with Azalea as they both watched Shu and Lian for a reaction. The girls understood enough to know that the individuals in this room loved them. And that white people were fighting for their countrymen's rights. And surely they knew by now that Yakira and Azalea would be here for them—no matter what. Yakira squeezed Lian's shoulder. Each of the girls had burrowed into her heart and sprouted there, cherished and flourishing. There would be no going back.

Rev. Harrington stood and crossed the floor to peer out the window. "I had a rebuttal for every single one of their ridiculous comments. It wasn't the Chinese's fault the city wouldn't put a sewage system in Chinatown. It wasn't fair to punish all the Chinese residents because of two stray bullets. If the sheriff had been doing his job, those San Francisco gamblers and the Tongs would've left before the trouble got out of control." He turned. "I feel like I've failed all of them."

"'Tis not our battle, Ira, you know that." Da shared a troubled look with Lara.

"They argued about whether to refurbish the buildings and move whites in. But Casper Ricks is afraid of lawsuits since the Chinese still hold leases on those buildings," Mr. Lord said. "And if they burn it all to the ground, he's out several hundred in rent and can't afford to build new again."

Yakira settled on the floor beside Shu and Lian. The heavy silence molded the space between each of them, filling the hurts, regrets, and deep places of buried dreams. She picked at her fingernails, hesitant to ask the question that nagged her. "What's to become of the Mission Home?"

Rev. Harrington claimed his seat again, scooted to the edge, and folded his hands in front of him. "I've given that some thought, Kira. I have a minister friend in Truckee who might be of aid. If his congregation is willing to sponsor a place, might that interest you? Truckee's Chinatown is sizeable, second only to San Francisco's."

Her breath caught. She locked eyes with Da, savoring the way they crinkled at the edges, aglow with tenderness. His lips curved just a bit.

"Well?" he asked, as if it was a difficult decision.

"Yes, oh, yes!" she gushed. "Would you really do that for us, Reverend?"

He chuckled. "It would be my pleasure, young lady."

"What's this?" Yakira entered her room to prepare for bed, buoyed with new hope after considering all the possibilities ahead in Truckee. Instead of chattering girls or Azalea lounging lazily with a book in her hands, Aunt Lara and Da each sat upon a bed.

"Is something wrong?" She shuddered inwardly at Da's drawn face, at Aunt Lara's fixed smile buckling at the corners.

Aunt Lara patted the mattress next to her. "Come, lass. Sit here. We'd like a word with you."

She wanted to turn back, run down the stairs and out the front door. "What? Is someone ill?" She crossed the room and sat in slow motion, setting a guard about her heart for the kind of news that sets a person's life on a different path. A death. A leaving. And at that, her chest stung with a thought of Grant.

"No one ill," Da said, one hand massaging the other as if it pained him. "I . . . I need to tell you something. An ill-scrappit truth, a truth too long in comin'. And . . . and fault lies only with me for that."

A stone settled in her middle. "Da, you're scaring me."

"No," he raised a hand, "dinna be aflocht now. Let me get it out. All of it." His chest expanded, and he blew a slow breath, ruffling his whiskers.

Aunt Lara reached for her hand, an anchor of strength.

From Da's mouth, an extraordinary story poured forth. The stuff of novels and nightmares.

The words wedged against her soul, blunt and bruising.

". . . but naebody could love ye more, though by birth ye're not me daughter . . ."

Not his daughter.

" . . . Henry, you see, was that boy . . ."

She has a brother?

The story's fantastical notions twisted and wrenched, bucked and distorted in her mind. Then Da's revelation suddenly sharpened, chiseling to pieces the bedrock of all she knew.

"I beg your forgiveness for withholding the truth of it."

All these years, he knew and did not tell her.

"Yakira Jean. Did ye hear me? I need to hear it from you. Can ye forgive me?" The shredded words scraped as though torn from his very heart.

But compassion had abandoned her—fled with the tale's telling. And she could not recall its feeling or its purpose.

He touched her knee, and she jerked away.

She stared at the floor. Felt his eyes watching her, searching her for some sign of surprise, or rage, or an unnamed emotion that, like all others, lay outside her reach—save that of disbelief.

Her da would not lie to her. But in keeping it from her, he had indeed.

Memories charged at her—*she had her mother's smile, her mother's keen eyes, she sang like her mother. Her mother had died in childbirth*—the stark reason for the guilt she'd carried, hidden in her depths from even God—*she* was the reason her mother had died. It was all her fault Da had lived her lifetime without his Cait.

She quaked, suffocating—until her swollen heart erupted with choking, wracking sobs. Aunt Lara's arms held her fast.

She was only vaguely aware of Da on the floor before her, weeping. His pleas for forgiveness crashed against her ears, a mere pebble to the boulder that had demolished the fragile life she'd thought was hers. For she was not Avery Mitchell's bonny Yakira Jean, she was another man's daughter. And 'twas not Cait, but a prostitute whose death she'd caused. For indeed, blood was still on her hands, just not Cait Mitchell's, a woman she'd never known.

But greater than the grotesque facts of her beginnings, the mountain that loomed above it all—that cast a shadow above the whole of it—was the deception. How could the man she'd loved as a father have deceived her for twenty-two years? And Aunt Lara!

Kira jerked from Aunt Lara's grasp. She sprang to her feet, turning on her aunt and hissed, "You knew! You knew and you let me believe—"

"Oh, my dear." Aunt Lara reached for her, face stretched in agony. "You must understand that your faither had no choice."

"No! There is always a choice. To tell the truth. Or is that another lie you've taught me?" She didn't care that the words sounded cruel, even juvenile. She balled her fists, longing for a blessed release if she could but pummel something.

Aunt Lara helped her father up from the floor. Bent and frail, he had aged suddenly beyond his years. His eyes were neither the stormy ocean of his ire nor the normal sparkling sea-blue. She saw sunken gray pools, spent and anguished, as his gaze swept over her once more before he turned away and shuffled toward the door.

"We'll give you time, my dear," Aunt Lara said, opening the door and guiding Da out like a small child. She paused before closing it, her countenance a mask of regret. "Oh my dear lass. You are so verra loved. And *that* has always been a great truth." She blinked slowly as if it pained her.

The latch *clicked* shut—a sharp swing of an axe, severing the rope that tethered her to family. And trust. And truth.

She threw herself on the bed, and weeping quaked her until numbness overtook her. She curled up on her side, spent and exhausted. With her aching eyes now a desert, she could only blow her nose and stare at the delicate snowflakes that fluttered beyond the window.

God had always been her comfort. But where was He now? He seemed so far away. So silent. Did He see the ugly fury inside her? The hurt? Had He heard the cutting words she'd hurled at the two people who love her most?

At last, the fire inside her smoldered to ash and gave way to blessed sleep.

March, 1885
Sacramento, California

Was the man daft? Had the California sun blinded everyone on the government payroll? Grant stared at the man and seethed inwardly, so weary of verbally shaking bureaucrats by the collar.

Governor Stoneman tapped a stack of newspapers. "I am quite up to speed on what you are insisting is a problem, Counselor. *Nowhere* in these accounts do I find the events you are mentioning."

How could a man in his position believe the biased rags? "To call what happened in Eureka, Crescent City, and other smaller towns '*a peaceful expulsion*' is a lie, Governor. My family was there. *I* was there. My mother and cousin were burned-out of the Eureka Mission Home for Girls. My uncle rescued an immigrant from the gallows."

The man settled silver spectacles onto the bridge of his nose and proceeded to read the top newspaper. "'It is with great pride that we report of the success of the complete expulsion of Chinese residents from Eureka and surrounding areas. This peaceful expulsion has succeeded in safely ushering more than five hundred Mongolians to destinations out of Humboldt County by way of rail and steamship. In contrast to events leading to the expulsion, this paper is happy to report there has been no further violence in our fair city.' There you have it."

"But, Governor, you know as well as I that newspapers don't print everything that really happens. They don't report about families left homeless, or merchants who have been forced to leave behind their entire lives' investments—only to be ransacked and vandalized by the whites who are *peacefully* driving them from their homes. Homes which many have occupied for decades." *Or the people trying to protect them*, he thought, envisioning the Mission Home's charred ruins.

The Governor stood, his face smoldering a shade darker. "Mr. Campbell, I invite you to lodge a complaint with this office. But again, I remind you, I have received not one complaint from local law enforcements in these communities. If there was a problem, I would have been notified."

Grant clenched his teeth as he stood, recognizing the political stonewall for what it was. He forced a curve to his lips. "I had to try. Thank you for hearing me out, Governor."

Henry's boots clicked on the polished floor as he followed Grant across the grand portico before catching up. "Well?"

"Well, since that didn't work, I'm writing to Washington." He strode faster, sick and tired of swallowing back what he really thought of this whole charade.

"Washington?"

"If I can't get Governor Stoneman's attention, I'll go over his head. The new Secretary of State, Thomas Bayard, will be receiving a strongly worded letter from Six Companies asking him to investigate California's treatment of its Chinese residents. Hang it all! This squeaky wheel is squeaking all the way to the White House if necessary."

"Oh." Henry's lips clamped on the word. A beat, and then his eyes popped wide. "Ah. Yes, you make good squeaky wheel."

Arcata

It was not to be. How could she have been so wrong about something? Yakira dabbed at her wet cheeks again, fighting the urge to throw herself onto the bed and scream into her pillow.

Her time at the Eureka Mission Home had been everything she'd hoped for—the girls, the house, and the perfect way she, Azalea, and Aunt Lara worked together. The girls had learned so quickly, even eager to learn of God's love for them, of His forgiveness, and to memorize His Word. She smiled, remembering the wonder on their faces when Azalea called the Bible God's love letter to them.

Poor Rev. Harrington. He could scarcely look her in the eye when he delivered the news from his associate in Truckee: "*The church board does not engage in mission projects which cater to individual races.*"

She huffed and began plucking pins from her hair. Just fancy words to cover the stench of their bigotry. She wouldn't want the support of people like that anyway.

Ouch! A pinprick oozed blood from the tip of her finger. She threw the offending hairpin onto the dresser with the others.

The crush of disappointment was splintering into anger. She scolded herself. Whatever God's plan, it was obviously not for a mission home of her own. She squeezed back hot tears.

Father, why have you given me this desire—a vision so real I can almost touch it?

She whispered a familiar proverb to the empty room. "Hope deferred maketh the heart sick." *Sick.* She could've written it herself, the way her heart ached. And for all it pained her, that same aching, invalid heart refused to abandon its desire. What if God's plan simply looked different from what she'd always imagined? Or—she dropped onto the bed, struck by a terrible thought—maybe the way she'd held Da and Aunt Lara at arm's length lately was proof of how unworthy she was.

Her hands covered her face as guilt raked through her. She had been unforgiving. But she *wanted* to forgive—she was in the process, wasn't she? And she didn't want to doubt God's design for her. She wanted to put one foot in front of the other and walk in faith, trusting that He really knew the desires of her heart. And that He understood the jumble of emotions swirling inside her.

She was truly an orphan, born to disreputable, godless humans who stood for everything she'd fought against her entire life. And everything she'd ever believed about who she was? False. She didn't deserve God's goodness or His plan. This new failed attempt at a mission home blared an alarm, deafening to her mind, to her spirit: *You are not worthy, Yakira. You are nothing. You will amount to nothing.*

She wilted against the Accuser's words, even as something inside warned they were only words.

The door burst open. Azalea's usual smile sat lopsided beneath somber eyes. She squeezed onto the mattress beside her and wrapped an arm around Yakira's shoulder. "I am sorry about Truckee. Mother told me."

Yakira just shook her head. She was suddenly so, so tired of everything.

"Something else will open up, I know it." Azalea's voice purred with the same hope that had abandoned Yakira. "And wherever God leads us, it will be wonderful. We'll take the girls and more will come and you and I and Mother will help them—"

"Help them what?" She faced Azalea and hardened her heart. "How will we help them? They have no home. No family. No jobs. No future."

Azalea squinted, probing Yakira for several seconds. She pressed her lips into a stubborn line and shook her head. "You are not these girls, Yakira. You have a family who loves you dearly. And as long as you have family, you have a home. You have much to work through"—she tapped her heart—"but now you know without doubt, you have been chosen. Just like me. That makes you very special indeed. Your birth mother could have killed you in the womb, but she chose life for you. Henry could have left you for dead, instead he made a way for you to be saved—"

Yakira chuffed. "You make it sound like Henry was my savior."

"Wasn't he? Mother told me that the goat he sold to your father—so you would have food—he stole. Because he stole the goat, he was sold and grew up *jàhng jái* (indentured servant). He traded his life for yours in a way, did he not?"

How had she missed that? Had she been so consumed with her own hurts that she hadn't considered what her being here had cost Henry? Shame chafed her. How petty she'd been. How selfish. She hadn't considered for a moment what it cost her father to tell her the truth—to risk her rejection. And what it cost him to give his wife the thing she wanted most, only to lose her.

Her throat stung, and so did her heart. "I'm sorry."

Azalea hugged her tightly. "God has such a special plan for us. Let me show you." She pulled a stack of folded papers from the bedside table.

Yakira smiled, perhaps for the first time in days. "Your special verses." Over the years, her sweet friend had collected all the verses that spoke to her the most. She'd safeguarded them in her blouse before rushing to the cellar.

"This one," Azalea said, pressing a fingertip to the page. "'Ye have not chosen me, but I have chosen you, and ordained you, that ye should go and bring forth fruit, and that your fruit should remain: that whatsoever ye shall ask of the Father in my name, He may give it you.' That's John 15:16.

"Do you hear what it says, my laotong? It is for you also. Our girls, they are our fruit. God chose us to continue in this ministry, and we will continue to bear fruit. We need only ask Him to provide."

She read the words again, drinking them in, satisfying her shriveled spirit. The verse took on a life of its own. Why had she never grasped it like this before? She let her tears fall and rested her head against Azalea's shoulder. "Thank you, my sweet laotong. Thank you."

Twenty-Three

"Weel, California shan't be gaining any help from the new U.S. President." Avery slammed a palm to the table, thoroughly disgusted by the American people's choice of leadership. At least President Hayes had been willing to work toward peace.

Lara shrugged, and her lips puckered. "What's to be expected from a man who paid another man to do his share of fighting in the War Between the States? He holds no consideration for the less fortunate nor those who are different than he."

Avery read aloud: "'The laws should be rigidly enforced which prohibit the immigration of a servile class to compete with American labor, with no intention of acquiring citizenship, and bringing with them and retaining habits and customs repugnant to our civilization.'"

President Cleveland's inaugural speech did not snuff the flame of anti-Chinese sentiment. Nae! His speech would fan Chinese hate to a roaring blaze—sure to scorch multitudes of hard-working immigrants.

"Och!" He shoved the newspaper away before it seared his senses further. "Lara, I've made a decision. I am sending a post to Charles Crocker in Truckee to invite his interest in a Mission Home for Girls."

Lara's gaze arrested him, and the balmy affection he'd tamped underfoot arose and glimmered back at him.

"What is it?" His mouth suddenly dry, he swallowed.

"You, Avery Mitchell, are the dearest of faithers. Although Kira is hurting right now, she will come to know that truth once again. And be it your friend, Mr. Crocker, can help with a new home," she winked, "it canna hurt the situation, now can it?"

Mischief twinkled in her azure eyes. He fought the urge to reach for her hands and pull them to his lips. Everything she'd been to him over the years was changing, ripening into something that filled the lonesome caverns in his depths.

The door crashed open, extinguishing the suckling flame. William stepped into the kitchen. "I dare not come farther," he lifted a boot. "The snow has given way to mud this morning. Care to come into Eureka with me, Avery?"

"Aye." Avery downed his last swallow of cooling coffee and cast Lara a hesitant gaze. "I'll get me coat."

All night long, rain had washed snowdrifts into rivulets that snaked across every road, dredging ruts and bogs that thrashed the wagon wheels. As they neared Eureka, more and more campsites dotted the road that skirted the bay. Makeshift tents, wagons draped with oiled tarps, even old prairie schooners housed white men and their families. All had made the trek to Eureka seeking promised jobs, vacated by the ousted Chinese.

"Whatever will the town do with them all?" Avery asked, disgusted by the gross misrepresentations the newspapers pushed. Far more applicants had arrived than were jobs available. And much of the work the Chinese had done was evidently beneath many of the white men, who demanded higher wages to even consider the menial work.

"Ira has been pretty successful thus far collecting food donations to help feed these folks, but I fear the townspeople's generosity will soon wane." Rain sluiced from William's hat as he looked down for an instant. "The hard thing is, some of these people sold everything to come for these jobs. Now they have nothing and nowhere else to go."

Avery adjusted the tarp that draped his shoulders as rain bounced off the oiled cloth. Whatever the town had thought of the condition of Chinatown before, the influx of homeless people would surely be a bigger problem.

Old memories circled of the starving people of China, burned out of their homes and terrorized by fierce warlords. Their resilience was a thing of wonder, the way they would repeatedly begin afresh with nothing. From all he knew and loved of the Tang people, they would fare far better than these white men with all their demands and uppity opinions of labor.

A young boy, ragged and soaked, crouched at the edge of the road, prodding a leaf and twig boat through a puddle. He waved as they passed. They both lifted a hand and a smile.

William chuckled at the sight. "I'm leading another pack train into the mountains tomorrow if you want to join me. Perhaps my last one. Not all of the Chinese left in Arcata are willing to live the secluded life the mountain requires. The rest will probably make their way north to Oregon."

Avery grunted, wishing he could go, but he didn't want to leave Yakira just now. Soon, the only remaining Chinese in Northern California would settle alongside smaller Indian communities—a three-day ride into the mountains. They'd make new homes near rushing streams, tucked into the thick wilderness of the Klamath or Salmon mountains.

He sighed, lost in the imagination of it all. A far better life than living among such hatred.

San Francisco

Grant printed furiously as Henry translated Wing Hing's demands for the lawsuit against Eureka. "Ask him if he has the itemized list of losses."

Mr. Wing dipped his head, extracted a neatly creased page from his wide sleeve, and slid it across the embellished corner-leg table. He continued to talk in earnest as the call to prayer resounded beyond the small second-story window. Somewhere a dog barked, and coarse laughter rose from the street.

Henry nodded and turned to Grant. "He says, 'We want Eureka to pay for what they have done. They must pay for our future earnings we will not have because we were forced to leave our businesses and our jobs. We want them to pay for the humiliation of being driven out by mob. We want back our homes. Our jobs. We want to recover our dignity.'"

A small-footed woman carried in a tea tray, depositing it carefully onto an elaborate waisted stool. She lifted the scarlet silk covering—a finely embroidered heirloom, judging by its golden threads—and poured for each of them. Henry spent the hour working on the list. He translated the symbols into names and damage claims for the fifty men and two Chinese women for whom Mr. Wing was acting as assignee.

Grant paced the square room, pausing to look over Henry's shoulder. "Be sure to separate the actual goods compensation costs from the amount they could've sold them for. We'll handle the punitive damages separately."

Henry nodded as he wrote, and Grant heard the smile in his reply when he said, "Yes, Boss."

Grant fingered the list, satisfied with the details Henry had collected. It was a better start than he had imagined. He'd run with it as far as the courts would let him. The claims ranged from $60 to $7,000 per person.

"Mr. Wing, I want you to specifically collect something else. I am looking for an amount from each of them which represents what they suffered as objects of riot and mob action due to the city's neglect of its legal responsibility to protect them."

Henry scratched his head. "You couldn't make that easier?"

"Just translate it." Grant checked his notes again to be certain he'd covered everything. He waited while Henry translated, pleased when the man's brows shot up. Eyes wide, his cheeks rounded with a big smile.

Good. "Tell him I'd like to meet with him tomorrow at noon."

After a brief discussion, they stood to leave. Mr. Wing bowed first to Grant, and then to Henry, offering fervent thanks. Grant responded in Cantonese before the man left.

Henry cringed. "Uh … your Cantonese is *still* no so good, Boss."

Grant huffed, shuffling papers and deliberating a clever rejoinder. "You're *still* short."

"Ouch!" Henry clutched his chest, eyes pinched.

With a chuckle, Grant slapped a folder against Henry's shoulder. "Let's get some lunch."

Now, if he could just convince Col. Bee and Six Companies to let him file a similar suit regarding every other California town that followed Eureka's example. And if he could get this expedited, it would serve as a warning to any cities sitting on the fence. Maybe even prevent more purges.

The sight of men herding Kira and Azalea down the street sparked in his mind. His ire reared anew. That fire could've killed them. The glint in Kira's eyes, her caustic words—they still haunted him. If only she would let him in long enough to explain. He needed her to understand why he was doing this, why he needed to be here.

Henry bumped his shoulder and tossed a dime into the air. He caught it with aplomb and then tipped his new bowler at a jaunty angle. "Lunch is my treat."

"If you say so." Grant stowed the paperwork, and they left the tiny room above a Chinatown shoe shop and braved the rickety stairs to the alley.

A man dressed as a wealthy Mandarin hurried down the board-walk, a cricket-filled bamboo cage gently swinging from one hand. Grant lifted his chin. "So, you ever bet on one of those fights?"

"Me?" Henry feigned shock. "Why would I want to throw away good money on *sāt séuih*?"

"You have. That's what I figured."

"I didn't say that."

"So, fan-tan is your game then, huh, big spender?"

Henry tugged at his new three-piece suit. He actually looked rather dapper in the starched white shirt and wing-tip collar. A ruby-studded tiepin punctured the knot of the western-style tie that bulged between neck and vest.

"I have more noble plans than to gamble money away." He patted the slight bulge in his jacket. They walked up the block in silence awhile before Henry turned into a shop.

"This is a women's clothing store, my friend. Is there some-thing I should know? Someone new in your life?" They'd been together so much, when could Henry possibly have met a lady friend?

"As a matter of fact, there is." Henry touched the fine embroi-dery of a silk robe.

A small-footed woman approached, chattering away in Chi-nese. Henry followed her through the store, interjecting now and then, amusingly confused. At last he shook his head, and after one lengthy sentence, the woman had a revelation. She disappeared behind a woven jade-green and silver curtain.

"This is much harder than I expected," Henry said, crossing his arms over his chest as he rocked back and forth on his feet.

"What did you tell her?" Grant was still dumbfounded. It was all proving quite educational since he hadn't shopped in Chinatown in many years. And certainly not in a women's clothing store.

"I told her one was for a Chinese woman with eyes of diamond and face like a heart."

Azalea? "Now just a minute, that's my sister you're talking about." It was Grant's turn to cross his arms.

The woman appeared with two embroidered gowns, one red and one blue.

"Two? Isn't that a bit presumptuous?"

"And I told her the other was for an American woman who was Chinese beneath her onyx hair and velvet-white skin."

He stewed. Why hadn't he thought of buying presents? Henry seemed far too pleased with himself as he paid for the gifts and watched the shopkeeper expertly wrap them in colored paper, tied with a fine silk ribbon.

"Whew! Ya got any of your paycheck left after that?" Grant held the door wide with a grin, but his sarcasm didn't bounce back at him this time.

Henry strode on ahead with the bundles cradled in his arms and his mouth uncharacteristically quiet. They entered a small eatery where ginger and garlic infused the air, and an older man hacked away at vegetables on a wooden board. His snow-white queue brushed the floor with every swing of the cleaver. Even before they could sit, a tottering woman, bent with age and absent of teeth, delivered soup. Henry gave her their order, and she disappeared through a bamboo door.

"Do you think she knows yet?" Henry's tentative words exposed the eager boy still inside him. "About me." He blinked and chewed his lip as if hoping to pry just the right answer out of Grant.

"I don't know, but probably. Are you worried?"

Henry puffed his cheeks before his breath leaked out in a slow sizzle. "I have thought of her reaction many times. Perhaps she faints. Perhaps she is very angry. But she always cries. Women cry."

Grant lifted the soup bowl and slurped. "She'll be angry at Uncle Avery for not telling her sooner, no doubt. But I know Kira. She would never be angry at you." He almost said she'd love having a brother, but the words fell back in his craw. He had been her brother once. And more.

"I only want her to know me, and I her. That is all. She is my only family, Grant. All I have in this world." His shoulders slumped, and he pushed his soup away.

"And what of Azalea? Is she a sister, too? Because she and Yakira are laotong."

Henry sat up, amazement touching the edges of his coffee eyes. "They are?"

"Indeed. I was witness to the ash pile when they burned their contract."

"Sisters for life. Very rare." Henry smiled at last.

"Between Azalea and Uncle Avery, Yakira knows much about China and the ways of the people. You were right when you told the merchant she is Chinese beneath her skin. Uncle Avery has passed his love of your people on to her. I hope she remembers that when she learns the truth of it all."

Grant rapped a knuckle on the table and leaned forward on both elbows. "So. You didn't answer my question. What are your intentions toward my sister, *Mr.* Smith?"

Henry seemed to shrink a bit, but his lip twitched. "Only friend, uh . . . sister, *Mr.* Mitchell."

"Only friends, huh? Good. Because as her brother, I would have to approve of any *non*-friend, *non*-sister affiliation." Grant quirked an eyebrow and menacingly stroked his beard. "For he would have to be a verra upstanding lad, with a sharp wit and a level head. And facial hair."

At the last three words, Henry slapped his forehead and dragged his palm over his face, but not before he stifled a grin. "It is good, then, I know herb that will grow man's beard."

The stooped woman delivered steaming wooden bowls and chopsticks. She bowed several times and backed away.

"We better eat up and get you some of that herbal cure, because we are headed to Truckee again tomorrow."

Henry moaned. "I do not like that town."

"Neither do I. Got a bad feeling about that Dannon character. And that newsman, McGleason, is also an attorney. I wouldn't put anything past him."

"But *you're* an attorney."

"Like I said."

Twenty-Four

Truckee

Grant trailed behind as Henry questioned the residents of Truckee's Chinatown in search of a man named Song Wah. This district lacked the architecture reminiscent of the Tangs' ancient homeland, like that seen in San Francisco. But the same colorful banners flapped in the breeze, and signs advertised goods and trading opportunities. And the familiar smells—Grant sucked in the clean mountain air—they were still there, untainted by dank city or cloying bay odors.

Their quest led them down a few rabbit trails before Henry finally stopped outside a gambling den. "Song Wah is in there."

"I've never been in one before." The half-truth bolted from Grant's lips in a guilty fluster, for at once he was transported to a dice game in an alley with forbidden Tong boys. The excitement of the game possessed him—preying upon his daring youth. And his recklessness had sharpened the nails for his father's coffin.

Henry handed Grant his hat and coat. He shook out his queue and stroked his fine waistcoat. "And you need not go in now. If

Song Wah is in here, he will no doubt want to speak with you. It is getting to speak to *him* that is the challenge." With a glint of determination, Henry disappeared into the dark room beyond the unpainted door.

Grant discreetly palmed the small pistol from his boot, feeling a bit foolish. It was a toothpick to the Colt revolvers brandished so openly by the Tongs. After drawing a few suspicious looks from passers-by, he feigned interest in some leaflets tacked to the wall beside the entrance. He'd always found the calligraphy beautiful and expressive. Uncle Avery was the only one who could read it, since Azalea had never learned to read before being sold back in China. His uncle had been teaching Kira when he left. He'd have to ask her if she'd continued her studies.

The door flew open, and an unusually tall Chinese man, fully his own height, blasted through with Henry on his heels. Henry rattled off something he couldn't catch. The stranger spun and glared at Grant.

Grant bowed. "Are you Song Wah?" he asked in his *not-so-good* Cantonese.

The man stared at him, obviously unaccustomed to someone of equal stature. He scrutinized Grant from head to toe. Careful to keep his eyes on the man's chin, Grant introduced himself and offered a handshake. The man said more to Henry, the stony corners of his face smoothing as he spoke. With a grunt and an iron grip, he shook Grant's hand. He strode out across the street, and Henry followed, motioning for Grant to keep up.

"Where are we going?"

"To his house. It is this way," Henry said, trotting to keep pace with the man's long strides.

Within the hour, Grant had all he needed for a deposition. And he hoped, a conviction. Song Wah had been an eyewitness to the murder of two Chinamen during a business transaction. One of the slain was his only brother, Song Loy.

"All that"—Grant flicked a thumb over his shoulder as they left Song Wah's house—"I could not have done it without you. I'd have no case." He slapped Henry's shoulder. "Thank you, my friend. Your partnership is invaluable."

"I'm a partner, now?"

"Of course you are."

"Then we share equal of all income?"

He should've known Henry couldn't just receive the compliment and leave it at that.

"You did say partner."

"*Junior* partner. *Junior* partner."

"Oh." Henry adjusted his tie. "You're still my boss, then. I see."

"Yep, still your boss." He chuckled and picked up his pace. "Come on, let's have a talk with the judge, then I'll buy you lunch."

They strode into Judge John Keiser's office only to find he would not be in until tomorrow. "This cannot wait until tomorrow, ma'am. Where might I find the judge at this time?" Grant loomed in front of the secretary's desk. Overly large gold eyes looked back at him through round spectacles.

"Oh, he wouldn't like that, Mr. Campbell. Not at all," she said, suddenly shuffling papers and looking at the wall clock. The soft *tick* of the pendulum filled an awkward silence.

"Well then, I will inform Colonel Bee posthaste that Truckee has been most uncooperative in allowing Six Companies to deal with this urgent matter."

"Oh, dear." She pinched her lower lip between her teeth for an instant. "Well, you might try checking at his residence, then. It's up on High Street overlooking the town. You can't miss it. It is quite lovely." She folded her hands on the desktop, posture rod-straight.

"Thank you, ma'am. I appreciate your cooperation in the matter."

"You're quite welcome." She blinked several times, her gaze sweeping between him and Henry.

He donned his hat, and they started off once more. Chasing people all over town beat long hours on the train any day of the week. An odd turnaround from his life in Boston. Odd, indeed.

"Mr. Campbell!"

Grant turned in the middle of the boardwalk. "Mr. Crocker. Good to see you, sir."

"Well, I heard there was a lawyer poking around." He chuckled and smoothed the long white tuft on his chin. "Hello Henry."

"Good evening, sir." Henry shook the proffered hand.

"What are you boys up to? Trying to make a dent in the troubles of this town of mine?"

"Trying, but I'm afraid Judge Keiser doesn't plan to help us out much. I just spoke with him about those woodcutters who were murdered a couple weeks back. Colonel Bee has asked me to look into it."

"Ah. Well." Mr. Crocker motioned for them to follow. "You boys eaten yet?"

"Not yet. I'm on my way to shake up the sheriff." His stomach growled, and he caught Henry's smirk from the corner of his eye.

"You'll want to talk to Jake Teeter about that. He's your best bet. But let me buy you boys dinner first."

Mr. Crocker led them into the Fountain Saloon, and when a couple of caustic stares settled on Henry, Grant shot darts of his own.

"Let's have three of those fine steak specials, Milo." Crocker told the white-shirted waiter.

"Yes sir." Milo seemed like a friendly sort, with his sleeves rolled to his elbows and black tie hanging loose. "You want coffee with those?"

"Yes, please." Mr. Crocker shrugged off his coat and settled into a chair as Milo brought the coffees.

Mr. Crocker took a guarded sip. "I got a pleasant surprise from your uncle the other day."

"Uncle Avery? He seemed happy to get the letter you sent with me. I'm glad you two are catching up." Whatever the letters entailed, from the gleam in Mr. Crocker's eye, he figured he was about to find out.

"There's something missing from this town that San Francisco has. Something I've come to rather consider a pet project." Crocker eyed them both. "Want to guess?"

Grant shook his head. "I wouldn't know, sir."

"A Mission Home for Girls. I told you last time we spoke that I felt it was a worthwhile ministry. And I understand from Avery that his daughter was all set up with one in Eureka before the town ran their Chinese out. I've offered to sponsor one right here in our town."

"Here?" Henry's voice cracked. "In Truckee?" He stood suddenly. And sat again. Stood.

Grant leaned over and whispered. "Henry, what's wrong with you? Sit down, you're drawing attention."

"I'm sure they've received my letter by now. It'll be good to see Avery again. And your mother, Grant. I assumed she would've married again." He grew pensive. "After."

When the waiter spread out the fare of thick steaks mounded with fried onions and potatoes, the conversation stalled. They ate in silence for a few minutes. Henry picked at his food. What had gotten into him?

"Well, if it isn't Mr. Bee's fancy lawyer."

Grant paused his fork in mid-air. Dannon's rough voice soured his stomach. But he forced the bite into his mouth.

"I hear you've been snooping around, asking questions about that little accident with the Chinamen a while back." Dannon approached the table.

"If you are referring to the interviews I've been conducting pertaining to the murder of two men in the forest, you heard correctly." Grant speared another piece of meat and chewed, refusing Dannon the satisfaction of disrupting his meal or looking him in the eye. "Do the names Slade Carson and Dan Flint ring a bell with you, Dannon?"

The man's provocative laughter incited a sort of exodus as several customers decided it was as good a time as any to finish up and leave. What customers remained gawked on in silence.

"Now, Howard." Mr. Crocker dropped his napkin beside his plate and stood, a single palm easing Dannon back like a spooked horse. "Mr. Campbell is not looking for trouble. Just the truth."

"Well, then. If that's all . . . Mr. Campbell, meet Slade Carson and Dan Flint."

The meat balled in Grant's mouth, and he swallowed down the leaden chunk. Without so much as a drink of coffee to wash it down, he stood and turned around. "Gentlemen." He indicated Henry with a jerk of his head. "This is my associate, Henry Smith. Mind answering a few questions?"

"Got nothing to hide," one said, glaring at Henry.

"You Slade or Flint?" Grant asked, not missing the way the man's fingers fisted and flexed.

"Flint. Whatcha wanna know?"

"Where were you two men on April twelfth?"

"I was right here." Flint pointed across the room. "Sitting at that bar over there."

"At what time?" He probed, willing him to make a mistake.

"All day. From the time they opened until close."

"Is that right? You've got witnesses?"

"Sure I do." Flint swiveled, pointing a finger. "Him. And him. And him." With each claim, the *witnesses* stiffened.

Grant stepped closer to Slade. "What about you? Where were you?"

Crooked teeth bared yellow as his lips parted. "Why, I was with Flint." He leaned forward, eyes bulging and red. "The whole time." He spoke to the three *witnesses*. "Ain't that right, boys?" They nodded emphatically, mute as one man's clean-shaved face mottled red to white.

Grant caught Crocker's look of disgust in his peripheral vision.

"This isn't over, Dannon." If ever he'd wanted to slap a cocky look off someone's face . . . "Mr. Crocker, I thank you for the meal. I'm sure we'll meet again soon. "Come on, Henry, we've got more business to tend to. And a train to catch."

Twenty-Five

ARCATA, CALIFORNIA

"Oh, Henry, it is exquisite!" Yakira smoothed the blue *cheuhng-sāam* against her body, marveling at the sheen and intricate floral stitching. "I don't know what to say." She stood and kissed his cheek, amused by the pink flush that colored his neck and jawline. The raw truth of what he had sacrificed for her swiftly fogged her eyes. She swallowed, so wanting to get out the words that needed saying.

"You are very welcome." He said, dipping his chin. His toothy grin stretched wide across his fine features, and she saw something of herself in his face for the first time.

She blinked back tears, and a tremor vibrated in her chest. She could wait no longer. "Thank you. For . . . for what you did for me." She set the lovely gown aside before tears could stain it.

His warm fingers grasped hers, and their watery gazes united, robbing her next words.

"I . . . you . . ." She sucked in a quick breath and covered her mouth with trembling fingers. What could she possibly say to this man who'd lost so much—for her? His was a sacrificial love, foreign, yet familiar. Parts of her she hadn't known to be missing had suddenly been found. And with the finding, joy assuaged the bruises of her swollen heart. The wonder of it all clogged her throat and dulled her ears.

Henry seemed to understand her tumult, for he tenderly took her other hand and brought their twined fingers to his chest. With a timid smile, he rasped, "*Mei mei.*"

He'd called her little sister. Something inside her broke. She threw her arms around him, needing to share this ocean of grief and anger with him—with her *ge ge* (brother).

The dam gave way and tears flowed, the release a bittersweet cleansing, healing. His chest vibrated and his embrace tightened. Their grief mingled for long moments until he pulled away, handing her a handkerchief and wiping away his own tears on the back of his hand. *Still sacrificing*, she thought. His smile glowed.

"I have waited for this moment for twenty-two years. The path has been difficult, but I believe your God has made this possible."

She gripped his hand again. "I am so, so sorry for what you've been through. How awful it must have been for you."

"Shhh." He stroked her hand. "It is past. I would go through it again if it would bring me to you."

Tears surfaced anew with the tenderness of his words. She was an endless well.

"Please tell me of my . . . my mother." How oft she'd asked the same of Da.

"Sit, please." He motioned toward the settee and sat beside her. "You favor her greatly." His gaze touched her face and then settled on the floor. "She was beautiful and much desired by the wealthy Tang and white men. She was a shrewd businesswoman, choosing her associates carefully, and only working for herself, never for someone else. I was not ashamed of what she did, for I knew who she was, in here." He tapped his chest.

"But what of her family in California?" Oh, the thoughts she'd had about family who were yet strangers to her.

"She wouldn't tell me of her past because it made her sad. But she was always kind to me, never treating me as the other Tang mothers did their sons because of mischief. She said we would forever take care of one another. She taught me to read and write English, and she told me she loved me very often. I was blessed."

"Forgive me if I am causing you more pain." She hadn't meant to. It was selfish of her to put her own curiosity above his grief.

He stayed her with a raised hand. "It is I who am sorry." He looked down for a moment and then back at her, pointing a finger. "I remember how small and red you were. How you cried when hungry. How you liked it when I would hold you." His eyes shimmered. "How your round eyes would look at me."

She patted his hand, strangled by the emotions chasing through his features with the memory as though it were yesterday.

"I tried to care for you. I did my best, but I was only a boy." He brightened. "And now I have you back. A bit bigger, more lovely, and less . . . wet." His eyes shrank to crescents, and they both laughed.

"And my father?"

He bristled before her, and gravity trounced his joy. He shook his head. "I can tell you nothing of him. I am sorry."

The rest of her questions shattered like crystal. How she had let her mind run wild with speculation. She silently scolded herself.

He stood and shifted his jacket as if it made him itch. "It was kind of everyone to give us the parlor to ourselves. I will let them know we are finished." He pointed to another wrapped parcel and grinned. "I have a gift for Azalea also." He seemed suddenly shy, and again pink snaked up his neck.

"I see." Flashing a knowing smile, she already felt a bit sisterly.

"So, we will be moving to Truckee, then." Da's announcement settled around the Lord family's large dining room table, stunning most everyone.

Excitement warred with caution as Yakira considered all the Mission Home had been through under her leadership. Was this opportunity God's doing or her father's?

Azalea quietly translated for the four girls, and their excitement was palpable.

"Kira, you are quiet." Da pressed a gentle hand against her arm. "Are ye not pleased?"

She was. Why did it feel like she'd touched the stove once too often? Did she really want to touch it only to be burned once more?

"We'll not venture into this unless your heart is in it," he said, concern lacing his gaze.

If indeed this was a door God was opening, then she was once again willing. For the girls' sake. "No. I apologize for my reticence. I *am* excited." And part of her was. "When do we leave?"

The space between them seemed suddenly lighter, less prickly. She felt Aunt Lara's gaze upon her, and when she turned her head, the love that glided across the table stopped her breath. She offered a fragile smile, wanting all the holes to be patched, the ripped places mended. But it would take time.

"I'm happy for you all. This is such a grand opportunity. Although we hate to see you leave, Truckee is fortunate to have you," William said, offering his water glass up for a toast. "Here's to the newest Mission Home for Girls. God's blessing on all you do."

"To Kira," Grant said, his rapt attention on her.

"And to the lovely Lara and Azalea," Da added.

Lian giggled. "To all of us!" The girls tittered as glasses bumped between them.

Yakira turned to Henry. He didn't look at all pleased with the news. She lifted her glass again, trying to coax a smile. It worked, though success was short-lived.

As the women all joined in to clear the table, she whispered to Henry, "Why don't you ask Azalea to join you on the porch, and you can give her the gift without prying eyes?"

Now he looked pleased. The familiar grin was back. When he hesitantly approached Azalea, she looked down. *Embarrassed.* Yakira chuckled to herself. It would take some getting used to—this brother of hers.

"Excuse me." Grant surprised her. "Might I have a word with you?" He had said little more than *hello* since arriving. Now he studied her, lines she'd never noticed carved across his brow.

"All right. I suppose there are enough hands to help with the cleanup. Let me get my wrap."

They walked leisurely, accompanied by the hoot of an owl as dusk fell like a curtain over the small town. Bay breezes licked at her hair, and she shook the wayward locks away from her eyes. "You wanted to talk to me?" she said at last, hoping he'd not probe too near the wounds that had yet to heal.

"Um. Yes." Something in the distance drew his interest as he scratched his beard. Suddenly he lifted his hat to smooth back his thick hair and donned it again as they kept walking. "H . . . how are you?"

"How am I?"

"Yes. I mean . . . you've had a lot to . . . to process. I want to know how you are. About it all. Everything."

Mr. Smooth-talking lawyer stumbles across the simplest sentences, she mused. Did she make him nervous? "I don't think I know how I'm supposed to process all of it." She longed to let her guard down. To talk with her dear friend once again—the boy with whom she'd shared everything. The boy who'd broken her heart. But she was still learning to forgive, and it was hard. The hardest thing she'd ever done. Perhaps if she were candid with him, he'd be the same with her.

"I'm learning to forgive," she said simply, not expecting a reply.

He grunted. An acknowledgment, apparently.

"It's all so hard to take in."

"My mother and Uncle Avery love you like parents, you know. I mean, your da, he is your parent. Always has been. From the beginning."

"I know they do." She'd never *really* doubted their love for her. But not telling the truth felt so much like a betrayal that it had buried that love. And she was slowly unearthing it, a shovelful at a time. She wanted to tell Grant those very words, but she couldn't trust him with her heart as she once had.

Oh, but she wanted to trust. Just as she wanted to trust that another Mission Home would not end up stolen from her or burned to ashes. Just as she wanted to fully forgive her da and restore their relationship. Oh, why was life so hard, so volatile?

"How do you feel about Henry?"

His probing question yanked her in a different direction. A better direction. "I like Henry. A lot. He has a kind heart. And what he did for his baby sister—the sacrifice he made—is something I long to be worthy of in his eyes."

"You don't need to worry about that, Kira." His steps slowed, and he turned to her. "That man saw your value from the moment you were born, and as far as he's concerned, the sun rises and sets on you."

She chuckled and swallowed past the lump in her throat. "He'll see how flawed I am soon enough, I expect." *That man saw your value from the moment you were born.* The salve coated her heart in the gentlest way. She sucked in the night air and stiffened at the nearness of a coyote's yip.

"What did you think of his gift?"

"Oh, it was lovely! Did you see it? He is so thoughtful. I am going to enjoy having a brother again."

Kira's earlier words buzzed in Grant's mind like angry hornets. They came at him from every direction, their barbs sinking deep again and again into already swollen flesh. *I'm going to enjoy having a brother again.*

He struck out into the night. He'd been a brother to her. Now Henry filled that spot. Where did it leave him? He picked up a rock and launched it into a thick stand of trees. So, he was no longer her brother. His claim to the label of cousin was a tenuous thread she seemed all-too-willing to snip. What of the friendship they'd shared? Had he sentenced that to a cruel death by his own actions, too? He'd give anything to turn back the time to those awful moments in a Chinatown alley where his own foolishness had cost Da's life.

He pitched another rock. It struck a tree, sending bark splintering into the shadows. The feelings he'd harbored for Kira when he left were anything but brotherly. He ached with the remembrance—the confusion forced on his body and emotions, the shame he felt when he realized the depth of his love for her. Even these last several years had not fully afforded the distraction he needed.

He had his pick of high-society lasses. The old money, the new money, the darlings of the society pages. They'd swooned for him, pawed at him, fawned over him. He'd tried, really, he had. But it was always Kira's face in his dreams.

Such risks he'd taken coming back, hoping his longings would prove mere disillusions after seeing her again. But laying eyes on her that first time in Eureka hurled his plan to the cosmos.

She didn't want him—didn't even see him as she once had. He flung another rock, wishing he could as easily dispatch his frustrations.

"There you are." His mother's voice called across the darkness, and he turned to see her silhouetted by the waxing moon's glow.

"Yes. I needed some fresh air." He strode to meet her, drawing her arm through his as he headed back toward the house.

"You seemed so quiet tonight.

"There was much to think on, I guess." The whine of tree frogs died away as they walked.

"The girls are so excited to go to Truckee. I'm sure if Mr. Crocker is behind this enterprise, it will be a successful one. He's done so much good for Margaret's Home."

"He's a fine man."

"Son, do you think you could spend some time with your sister before you take your leave again? It would mean so much to her."

His perky little sister may be just the medicine he needed. "Certainly, Mither. I'll take her for a ride into Eureka tomorrow."

Her steps slowed. "Kira's had so much to think about. How are things between you two?" Her shadowed smile faded.

"I don't know." But he did know. *Hopeless* was the word he'd not share with his mother. He'd caused her enough concern for a lifetime.

Twenty-Six

TRUCKEE

May 1885

Grant stood outside his family's new home. The stately house was every bit the tasteful edifice he'd imagined, knowing Charles Crocker as he did. With a colorful bouquet in hand, he hesitated, completely unprepared for the wave of trepidation that washed through him. He straightened his tie before reaching for the knocker, but Henry beat him to it. "You're in rather a hurry," he said, a bit relieved that the decision to forge ahead had been made.

"How do I look?" Henry asked, brushing invisible lint from yet another new suit.

"Like an overly anxious puppy."

The door swung open, and Mither stood with a surprised smile. "Grant. Henry." She kissed Grant's cheek, and he engulfed her in a hug. "What lovely flowers!" She squeezed Henry's arm before ushering them into the foyer. "I wasna expecting you until the morrow. But I'm thrilled ye're here. Let me take your things."

"You look well, Mither." Grant ran a hand down her arm, soaking up the glow that radiated from her. "Are things working well for you here in Truckee?"

"Oh, yes." She hung their hats and coats on the hall tree and led them into the parlor. "Come, sit down. There is a great deal of resistance here, but there are good people, too."

"Are there, now? I've yet to meet those—the *good* ones. Except for Mr. Crocker, of course."

Her eyes were eager. "How long can ye stay?"

"A few days. Then it's off to San Francisco for us."

She pressed a palm to his cheek, holding it there as she used to. "You look weary. Let me get you lads something to drink." She took the flowers. "And I'll put these in water."

A girl Grant didn't recognize appeared momentarily. Her curiosity lingered on Henry as Mother asked her to tell the others about their guests. She shuffled away excitedly.

"Grant!" Azalea swept into the room, tackling him with open arms.

He lifted her off the floor as if he were sixteen again, spinning once before setting her down. "How's my little sister?"

"Not so little. I am a woman grown, you know." She smiled at his teasing, but her gaze slipped briefly to Henry, who stared at her like a love-struck schoolboy.

"You will always be little to me," he said. And just to add to the rub, "you remember Henry."

She pierced him with darts before demurely turning to Henry. "I am happy to see you too, Henry."

Oh, this was too much fun.

"As am I, Miss Azalea. I—I mean I am happy to see you, too. Not happy to see me."

Azalea tittered behind her fingers.

Yakira entered, followed by Uncle Avery and six girls. The ones he recognized smiled, acknowledging him.

His breath stalled as Yakira's gaze captured his, drawing him to her like a moth to a flame—for all of three seconds before she strode toward Henry. "I missed my big brother." She gave Henry a warm welcome, and he soaked it up.

His brave little niggle of hope dissolved at the slight.

"Good to see you boys. How goes the crusade?" Uncle Avery rapped him on the back.

Grant dropped into a chair. "I think we're losing."

Uncle Avery rolled one wiry, grizzled eyebrow between thumb and forefinger. "I'm sorry to hear that, though I'm not surprised. I've been considering you as I read the papers, not sure where you are—in the thick of it or holed up in some office somewhere buried in paperwork."

Grant laughed wryly. "Both. But sometimes I'm holed up in a *hotel room* buried under paperwork."

"While I am making trips to get coffee for the boss." Henry said, earning laughs all around.

"All these purges up and down the coast have prompted an ocean of legal headaches. Colonel Bee has hired two more attorneys to start weeding through the mess. I'm lucky I wasn't sent to Arizona."

"Arizona?" Uncle Avery shook his head sadly. "There too."

"Oh yeah, the cowboys cut cards to determine which points of the compass to send the Chinese off to. One Chinese man was tied to the back of a steer and sent out across the desert." Grant rubbed his eyelids. "Prejudice knows no bounds."

Mither clasped her hands, appearing every bit the saint she was. "I read all about the happenings in Wyoming. Terrible. Just terrible."

"We were there two times." Henry said, finally sounding as weary as Grant felt.

The excitement of homecoming had waned, and the ugly truth of the West's climate was suddenly up for discussion.

"Apparently San Francisco's Chinatown is going to see an influx of new residents. There are fewer and fewer places for people to go for refuge. A few hundred of Seattle's Chinese are heading to San Francisco as we speak. Portland's got problems too, but the mayor's a good man. He's got a handle on it."

"I dinna suppose things are wont to improve with Leland Stanford being elected Senator. How is anything supposed to improve for the Chinese immigrants as long as men like him are in office?" Uncle Avery fussed.

"I did manage to rattle some cages in Washington. Secretary of State Bayard is aware of what's going on in California now. Whether he's friend or foe has yet to be determined."

Uncle Avery fished a folded paper from his pocket and passed it to Grant. "A bit of merriment for your brief visit to our fair new home."

A grotesque representation of a Chinese man with an opium pipe framed the announcement of an Anti-Chinese Rally. "This is tomorrow?"

"Aye. I plan to be there. Hopefully the sheriff will be there too. Care to join me?"

"I'd be negligent if I didn't." All hope of even twenty-four hours of peace evaporated.

Kira was sitting quietly, and every time Grant glanced her way, she seemed to examine the arm of her father's chair. If he could just speak with her.

Azalea chattered about the new girls in the home, but Grant couldn't follow what she said. His concentration scattered like dust motes with Kira sitting there across the room. If he could but catch her gaze. To look into her eyes. To see the truth of the way things were between them. *Look at me, Kira!*

Suddenly she lifted her head, and he held her gaze, magnet to metal through the space between them that had seemed so impenetrable just a moment before.

"Grant." Mither's voice intruded.

The connection shattered, and Kira looked away, leaving his pulse pounding.

"Yes, Mither?"

"I've prepared a room for you and Henry. I hope you don't mind sharing. The end of the hall, on your left."

He nodded his thanks. "I'm done in."

Henry stifled a yawn. "Me too."

Mither started gathering dishes from the low table, and Kira rushed to help her. "Let me, Aunt Lara." She reached in front of Grant.

"Kira," he whispered, begging another exchange.

One side of her mouth curved, and her gaze touched his for a long moment before lifting the cup. His heart inflated. Had his eyes deceived him? Not a trace of malice or pain inhabited those chestnut pools. He swiped a hand over his face, concealing a stubborn smile.

Yakira closed the pantry door and pressed her back against it. Her chest thrummed. She laid a hand to her throat. Heat climbed her neck and floated through her whole body. What had just happened? One minute she was toying with Grant, and the next he'd held her prisoner with just a look. And she couldn't pull away. Not that she wanted to—so sweet was the draw of his handsome face and alluring eyes. She'd wanted to brush her hand across his jaw, feel the softness of his whiskers.

Yakira. What is wrong with you? Was she not furious with him?

But all she felt now was the desire to be near him. And maybe a wee bit foolish for her silly behavior.

Had she forgiven him? A smile nudged from inside. Perhaps that's what she felt. If she *had* truly forgiven him for the years of abandonment, couldn't she then simply love him as she once had? The dearest of brothers? The dearest of friends?

But in her heart of hearts, an impish voice whispered, *"Nae."*

For in the deepest nooks and crevices of her soul, she knew she wanted from Grant Campbell something else. She wanted not the love of a brother, nor the love of a friend—but the love of a man.

And it frightened her.

Twenty-Seven

November, 1885

Yakira pressed her fingers to her lips, hindering the chuckle that threatened to spoil such a special moment.

Azalea sashayed across the study floor in her gift from Henry. "I have never owned anything so beautiful." She traced the intricate embroidery—butterflies winging across the bodice in a graceful arc before disappearing at the hem. She smoothed both hands over the red silk, a delightful shine to her cheeks.

"Is it the gift, or the giver you fancy more?" Yakira couldn't help herself. Ever since receiving Henry's gift, Azalea had mentioned him every single day.

Azalea shrugged, a slow rise and fall of her shoulder, without so much as a glance in her direction as she opened another box of supplies. "I will not honor that question with an answer."

Yakira chuckled. "My big brother is sweet on you." The words danced in a singsong tease. *Her brother.* She'd not seen Henry since their brief visit five months ago. Nor Grant.

She sat and began recording the new inventory with pencil and paper. Grant's handsome face kept appearing in her dreams, making these last months feel like years again. And she hated it—hated that her heart betrayed her, even when she was unconscious—hated that she found herself wondering where he was at any given moment.

It was happening again—this longing for him. And his not being here. The familiar ache rankled her. She should've protected herself better. Hadn't she suffered enough? Hadn't she learned her lesson all those years ago? The pencil lead snapped against the page.

Yearning did nothing to bring someone closer when the person chose to stay away.

Azalea floated about the room as the floor-to-ceiling shelves filled with books and learning supplies. The heavy box of books shipped by rail from Rev. Harrington's church sat on the floor.

"Did they send the picture books we requested?" Yakira abandoned the list and picked through the books stacked on the table.

Azalea leafed through a book. "Oh, look. There is a map of the world in this one. Would it not be wonderful to acquire a globe? I do not think the girls can yet fathom the vast roundness of our earth."

"Always the teacher, you are."

Shu's voice carried from the entry. "There is someone at the door, Yakira." She breezed into the room and froze with her mouth agape. Her hands flew to her cheeks. "Oh! So many wonderful books!"

"Thank you, dear." Yakira smoothed stray hairs, tucking them into the snood she wore around the Home. The girls had been warned not to answer the door, for although they'd been in their new home for some time now, much of Truckee was no friendlier toward her girls than Eureka had been. Sometimes she longed for the frenzied city life of San Francisco, where her every move was not scrutinized.

She smiled, spotting the visitor through the beveled glass side-light before opening the door. "Mrs. Bensman! What a lovely surprise. Please, come in."

The woman hefted a stack of quilts. "Another gift from the women of Second Presbyterian. You'll find the winters around here are much different than San Francisco or Eureka."

"Oh, let me take those from you. You and your ladies are such dears. We are forever in your debt."

"I'll take them, Mrs. Bensman," Mei said, slipping silently down the staircase.

"Oh, all right. I've forgotten your name, I'm afraid."

"I am Mei." She loaded her arms with the quilts.

"I believe I recognize that dress, Mei. It belonged to my daughter once upon a time. She has a family of her own now." Mrs. Bensman glowed. "I am ever so thankful you could alter it to fit."

"I am most thankful." Mei said in halting English. Mei had positively blossomed these last months.

"Are you sure you can handle those?" Yakira asked her, stacking them a bit more securely.

"Oh, yes." She turned and marched slowly up the stairs, her head peeking around the cumbersome stack as she went.

Yakira ushered Mrs. Bensman into the parlor. "The dresses you brought last month have all been altered and claimed most gratefully, every one of them."

"That makes me happy. You've done such a fine job of revitalizing this big old house." Her eyes swept around the room. "And you've made it so welcoming, Yakira."

"I am still amazed at God's goodness—supplying such a large, elegant home as this, through Mr. Crocker, of course." She motioned toward one of the matching Hitchcock chairs with its gilt stenciling. "Might I interest you in some tea?"

"I can't stay long, but tea would be lovely." Mrs. Bensman removed her gloves and sat as Yakira scurried to the kitchen.

Moments later they were laughing over the wonderful mayhem of a house full of young ladies while Mrs. Bensman recounted story after story about raising four daughters. "Ah, how wonderfully fond those memories are."

"Azalea and I have many of our own mischievous escapades as well." Yakira remembered with a chuckle.

Mrs. Bensman scooted to the edge of her chair. "How is the Chinese church coming along? Are the numbers growing?"

"Oh yes!" How thrilling it was to watch Da with his small group of proselytes. "Growing slowly, but already my father has eight men meeting thrice a week in the basement." Da had gained a bounce to his step again. He was teaching and winning the Chinese men with his own brand of devotion and encouragement. She imagined what it must have been like for him, working and living in the villages of Kwangtung Province. Surely Providence opened this door, for it was as if Da's hope had renewed since moving here.

Mrs. Bensman clasped her hands together. "I am thrilled to hear that. I have spoken to the Chinese woman who does our household laundry on occasion, and she wants to know more of the Bible. Her name is Lan. Would it be improper to tell her about your father's little church—with only men being there and all?"

"Why don't you let me talk with my father? Perhaps Azalea can approach her and see where it goes from there."

"Splendid." Mrs. Bensman sipped her tea with elegance as her polished nails played with the light. Creases at the edges of her eyes deepened with a broad smile. "This ministry is the body of Christ at its finest—proselytizing those who know nothing of our Heavenly Father."

"I agree." What would it have been like to have this woman as a mother? Such a dear, dear woman.

"Our next project for your home is to secure warm coats for your young ladies."

"That would be so very generous." And something very necessary, which Yakira had not even thought of as yet.

"How are they supplied with undergarments?"

"We received some from the Occidental Mission Home in San Francisco recently, so I think we're set for the time being, but thank you. Should we gain more girls, we will have need." Already two girls had joined them in the short time they'd been here. Poor Shuang came to them so broken and scarred, the mirror would forever tell of the horrors she'd endured.

"Very well then." Mrs. Bensman pushed her cup and saucer toward the center of the short table. "Oh, I'd nearly forgotten. Mrs. Cletus says she has two beds. I told her I was certain you could use them. I'll have them delivered tomorrow."

Yakira pressed a hand to her chest, suddenly overwhelmed. "Are you certain you don't have angel wings beneath that lovely cape?"

The woman stood, and pulled Yakira into a motherly embrace. "We are happy to help in any way we can, my dear. There is much evil in this town, and any bit of light we can shed, God will make brighter."

Azalea flew around the corner. "Oh, excuse me!" She dipped her chin. "Mrs. Bensman, how wonderful to see you." Her eyes skipped to Yakira, drawing her with a flick of her fingers.

Mrs. Bensman gathered her reticule. "I really must be going, ladies. Remember to watch for the delivery tomorrow."

Yakira showed her to the door. "Thank you again, so very, very much." She bowed, her hands tented in respect, for it was more than a mere thank you.

The woman squeezed Yakira's fingers. "You are most welcome."

She closed the door and turned to Azalea. "What is it?"

"It's your father. He's at the back door. One of his students is injured."

They rushed to the kitchen where Da dabbed a cloth to a man's torn face. She drew in a sharp breath when the man winced.

"Oh, Yakira. If you please. Some bandages. There is brandy in that top cabinet for antiseptic," Da said calmly as if he tended the wounded every day.

She scooted a chair to the cupboard and climbed up to retrieve the brown bottle while Azalea rummaged through the ragbag and tore one into strips.

She handed Da the bottle and suddenly recognized the young man. Ho Wah, the fruit peddler, was one of the kindest merchants in Chinatown. "How did this happen?"

"He was set upon by some of Howard Dannon's thugs. They stole his money and spoiled the entire contents of his baskets. I think he may have a cracked rib."

She tied the torn rags into one long bandage to wrap his ribs. "Here, Da." She watched the tender way her father cared for the wounded man, and her conscience flamed anew with shame. True, his blood didn't flow through her veins, but did it truly make her less his daughter? She knew the answer deep inside. How could she have ever thought it changed anything?

She had only to deal with the grief of betrayal that gnawed a hole in her heart. But for all she knew of her great God, in time, it would mend.

Tacoma, Washington

Grant shot another wad of paper. It hit the rim of the wastebasket and bounced across the floor to join a dozen others.

"Missed again," Henry said, expertly juggling crumpled paper balls.

"I wouldn't have if you hadn't moved it clear across the room."

"What is the challenge in that?"

"I have plenty of challenges, thank you very much. I don't need more." Grant slid back the chair, cursing the too-short hotel desk. His long legs didn't fit under it, yet it was the only solid surface on which to write. Why hadn't he brought his travel-desk? He stood with a groan and bent to stretch his back.

For months he'd been Six Companies' lackey. They'd had him in Wyoming twice to deal with violent riots, instigated by white miners against Chinese miners—all over a labor dispute. The suit he'd prepared covered damages in excess of $150,000. But there would be no compensation for the twenty-eight murdered Chinamen. The stack of papers shipped to Six Companies for typing was a paltry offering to right such an appalling wrong.

"Let's take a walk. If I have to sit here much longer, I'll break this desk into kindling." Without waiting for Henry, he bolted for the door.

Tacoma's fog rivaled San Francisco's this evening, and chill seeped through his jacket as if he were in Boston. An eerie silence settled over the night—a stark contrast to yesterday's madness.

As they walked, a thick, cloying haze of smoke settled all around them. Just a day earlier, vigilantes had set Chinatown ablaze along with hundreds of Chinese settlements and homes. He tucked his nose against his collar to mitigate the stench that would no doubt linger for another few days.

He turned, pulling Henry by his sleeve. "Stay close, all right?"

"You bet, Boss. Thank you for letting me out of the hotel."

He didn't have it in him to banter tonight. And locking Henry in the room yesterday was the only way to ensure his safety. He ground his teeth, still peeved about the whole affair. Personal pleas and petitions from hundreds of influential voices throughout the Pacific Northwest had called for a stop to the mayhem. But Territory Governor Squires ignored it all. The man was an immigrant himself, for Pete's sake!

Infuriated and powerless, he had watched hundreds of laborers and merchants herded into cattle cars. Their cries had torn him from sleep all night. The sheer horror of it sickened him. Small-footed women, hands bound, forced to walk behind wagons, their husbands helpless against the vigilante gangs. He could spend years hunting down all the victims and filing charges. And in the end, what difference would he make?

"It will make a difference." Henry mumbled.

"Huh?" Had he spoken aloud? "You think so? Well, *I* don't. The pile of paper I produce will prove nothing but kindling after the judicial machine gives it ten seconds of attention, and then pitches it into the fire. What does the government care about these people, anyway? Yesterday, the mayor *and* the sheriff hid out at city hall while the *mob* ran the city!" Bile rose from his churning middle. "Newspapers whitewash the truth, and the politicians ignore the voices of the very people they're supposed to be representing."

"I know that look." Henry fished a handkerchief from his inside coat pocket, unfolded it, and produced a small, hard ball. "Here. I only have three left. Maybe you need different job." He handed over the peppermint-ginger creation, and Grant popped it into his mouth. "You are only one man, Boss. But you are doing something that matters." He lagged several feet and then caught up. "Are we leaving tomorrow?"

"Yes, Portland. Again. To speak with the mayor, then to Oregon City. We're taking more depositions from the 150 workers driven out at the Woolen mill. After that, I'll have a talk with Judge Deady. It'll be a pleasure to slap Mr. Pennoyer with a suit for instigating the attacks on the Chinese in Portland. Quite a pleasure, indeed."

Henry blew out a long breath to accompany the obvious sag in his bearing.

Grant clapped a hand to his shoulder. "And then, my friend, we are going home."

"We have a home?"

"Well, so much as home is where your family is—yes, we have a home, Henry."

Twenty-Eight

TRUCKEE

R ank bodies choked the meeting hall, and the air sizzled with expletives and everyday discussions. Robert McGleason waved his arms, calling for attention to begin the rally. Grant leaned against the back wall. He sucked on one of Henry's antacid concoctions as he scanned the ranks of agitated men who had shown up for one purpose—to see the Chinese ousted.

Howard Dannon and his contemptible mug stood near the front with his two hooligans, Carson and Flint.

Uncle Avery bumped his arm, indicating the three troublemakers. "You know them?"

"Yeah. We've met." Something about Dannon gnawed at him. The man was a snake, no doubt about it. The room settled as much as it was going to with this lot.

"If you are a Chinese-lover, you're in the wrong place!" Robert McGleason's gambit prompted a series of applause and *hoots*. "Now, I've been monitoring the activities surrounding the Mongolians in city after city. We've witnessed the peaceful 'Eureka

Method' type purges up and down the coast. From Crescent City in the north to Arcata and Ferndale, and numerous other small lumber towns across California."

Shouts of support rang out, quickly tempered by McGleason. "And we've witnessed a different tactic used up north in Washington Territory—where vigilantes in Tacoma burned two large Chinese neighborhoods, forcibly expelling the residents." More shouts. "This country has witnessed massacres in Wyoming and vile threats to the Chinese populations of Portland, Seattle, and Olympia." His voice cracked as it climbed above the heartening cheers. He tamped the responses back with raised hands.

Grant scratched his chin, wondering where this was going. The man was up to something. And not the usual agenda, judging by his wording.

McGleason stepped to the edge of the makeshift platform, eyeing the murmuring men before continuing. "I ask you. Are these thousands upon thousands of driven-out Mongolians rushing to the ports to purchase tickets and return to their homeland? No! They are not. They are still here!"

An uproar vibrated the air, and suffocating impudence filled the room. Grant folded his arms over his chest, taking in the crowd, trying to remember faces.

Staring at the floor, Avery stroked his shapeless beard. The slump of his shoulders signaled defeat, and all Grant could think of was how much of his uncle's life had been spent in the trenches, fighting for the Tang people's eternal futures.

McGleason continued, "As I monitor the Anti-Chinese climate across our state, it is with embarrassment that I broach a sensitive reality. Truckee has been denounced for having the second-largest Chinese population in this great state of California."

A dissonant symphony of *boos* and *hisses* swelled as fists pounded the air. McGleason flagged down the ruckus for several seconds before he could continue.

"Despite our proactive incentives—our nudging the Mongolians from our midst and our facilitation of needed relocation—they are still here!"

A fire flared in Grant's belly. *Nudging?* Truckee's definition of *nudging* was murder, thievery, and the razing of countless Chinese homes and businesses.

"Do you see businessmen among you here today? What about mill owners and cattlemen? Are there any in attendance?" Mumbling ensued as attendees looked around. "No, they are unwilling to sacrifice business success on the altar of what is right.

"My friends, it is time for something different! A way to drive out the Chinese lawfully. It's time to replace arson and assaults with a concerted, organized, and well-focused *freeze-out.*"

McGleason pushed on quickly. "We will devise a method of eradication that is lawful and humane—and far more effective than shuffling Chinamen from one town to the next with their queues swinging jauntily as they trot out of town."

Laughter erupted and swelled through the entire crowd. Apparently, it was more than McGleason's humor the men found so amusing.

McGleason tried in vain to regain his footing.

Grant seethed at the sight of Judge Keiser stepping onto the platform. *Unbelievable!* The magistrate was walking an ethical tightrope. And Grant had a few ideas about how to bounce that rope a bit. He relished the thought of seeing him topple—disbarred, even.

When the judge raised a hand, silence settled abruptly. "What my son-in-law is proposing can work. It has the possibility of complete success and it is lawful. Hear him out, men. Just hear him out."

"Thank you, Judge." McGleason proceeded to outline a plan. A committee would work to convince each white Truckee citizen and merchant not to do business with or provide services to any Chinese person. "By this," he said, "they will be forced by economic necessity to leave Truckee."

Grant growled under his breath and glanced at Uncle Avery frowning in disgust. Any tactic the town tried would have the same effect—ousting the Chinese.

Dannon's gruff voice sailed over the stirring crowd. "If they won't leave by *incentive* as we have amply offered in the past, what makes you think a bit of economic hardship will make them go?" He'd ignited a flame.

"Yeah!"

"That's right!"

"I say we burn Chinatown and be done with them!"

"They'll just camp out in the forest and eat mushrooms if they can't afford to stay in town."

Dannon shouted again, "They're like vermin. Getting rid of them takes planning, precision—extermination!"

Angry voices and epithets peppered the room. Some men with half a conscience seemed to lose enthusiasm after hearing particularly vile suggestions.

"And that does *not* include squeezing their money bags," Dannon yelled, mocking the new plan.

Constable Teeter stepped up and joined McGleason. "I say we give it a try. If there's a way to persuade them to leave legally, I'm all for it. The violence in this town has got to stop. It's not safe for anyone after sundown."

With outstretched arms, McGleason fairly radiated victory. "It's settled then. If you would like to join the committee to help initiate a boycott, please come see me in my office."

So, this would be the way of it? Grant pressed against the wall and stared at the floor, making room for men to exit. When a cold finger drew down his spine, he lifted his gaze from a pair of silver-tipped boots to a black waistcoat and tie.

Dannon donned a posh bowler atop his collar-length hair. Slivers of white streaked his black beard and eyebrows, a stark contrast to his pale skin. "Well, I guess we haven't seen the last of you then, Counselor."

"Mr. Dannon." Grant ground his teeth. Their eyes locked—two steeds about to tangle.

"Weel now gentlemen." Uncle Avery intervened with a touch to his arm. "I am sure we all have things to tend to. Good day to you, Mr. Dannon."

When Dannon cleared the door, Grant turned to his uncle. "I need a word with McGleason. I'll meet you back at the Home."

He waited until only Judge Kaiser and Robert McGleason were alone before approaching. "Informative meeting, Mr. McGleason. Judge."

McGleason shrugged into a coat. "Ah. Colonel Bee's underling. We meet again. You here on Six Companies business, Mr. Campbell?"

"Where Chinese immigrants are concerned, it is always my business."

The judge grunted. "What do you think of the town's new tactic? A thoroughly legal solution to an ongoing problem."

"I've come with but a warning, Judge." He shifted his attention to the cocky newsman. "I'll be watching you, McGleason."

Yakira handed the green beans to her dad while struggling to keep up with what Aunt Lara, Da, and Grant were saying about the meetings from the day before. The words flitted through her brain, scarcely finding a place to settle.

She drank in Grant's features as he spoke—the earnest set of his full, dark brows, and the comely face. Gone was the boy she remembered, and in his place was a man she was getting to know anew. But the once mischief-sparked eyes had waned, replaced by a somber intensity that sifted through her. The passion of a boy was now the fervency of a man, consumed with others instead of himself. He had changed. And she owed him the chance to prove it.

"Crocker's list of businesses dependent on Chinese labor will be invaluable," Grant was saying. "If McGleason makes good on his threats, we'll encourage them to pull their advertisements from his newspapers."

"Aye, and see how McGleason likes being on the receiving end of a boycott!" Da chortled, his gaze a-twinkle at the idea.

"I'm going to check-up on that U.S. marshal we requested some time ago. If the citizens are foolish enough to climb aboard this boycott business, things could get ugly real fast. Isn't that right, Henry?" Grant knocked her brother's elbow off the edge of the table.

Slack-jawed, Henry blinked. "Yes. Yes, Boss. That is indeed correct."

Azalea collapsed into giggles, spurring a torrent of the same from the other girls.

Yakira couldn't resist. "Boss, huh?"

"I tell him not to call me that, but he listens about as well as he follows a conversation." He scowled at Henry, but already Azalea had usurped her brother's gaze again.

Grant winked. At *her*.

Prickles of heat leapt from her neck to her face. She grabbed the coffeepot from its trivet, quickly turning to Aunt Lara. "Coffee?" Her aunt swiveled attention from Grant and offered her cup, but the crimp of her eyes and curve of her lips made Yakira want to duck under the table.

Aunt Lara reached a hand across the wide table and Grant covered it with his own. "I wish ye dinna have to return to San Francisco tomorrow, son. It's been so wonderful to have you here. Please say you'll be back for Christmas."

"I make no promises, but I'll do my best." His eyes flitted to her for an instant and back to his mother. "With all my heart, I want to be here."

Lian stood to clear the table, joined by the other girls. When Azalea stood, Shu pushed her down. "You stay. Enjoy." Azalea nodded, suddenly preoccupied with her hands as they rested in her lap.

Henry was trying mightily to distract himself. Yakira smiled. It was rude of her to find his awkwardness so amusing. "And surely you'll be here for Christmas if Grant comes, won't you?" she asked her brother.

His expression lit up. "I would like that very much. *Sister*." He said the last word as if he was practicing, and it thrilled her to think of spending her first Christmas with an actual, real-life brother.

The thought of Christmas with Grant stung her eyes as memories of years gone by peppered her mind. Somehow, by God's grace, they had stepped from beneath the dark umbrella of bittersweet into the sunshine of sweetness once again. Though wounds were still tender, now she believed the healing could come. But what that looked like for her and Grant was a mystery. And she'd try her hardest to leave it in God's hands—and not interfere as she was wont to do.

As if summoned by her thoughts, Grant said her name.

"Care to take a walk?" he asked, hope coloring every curve of his face.

She nodded, and he rushed to pull out her chair, offering a hand as she stood.

"Thank you, Counselor." Her sassy retort expertly concealed the wee motes colliding with her insides.

The chilled afternoon mist had transformed into tiny flakes of wet snow, sopping the muddy streets for the occasional passing conveyance. "Are you warm enough?" Grant asked as they turned the corner from Spring Street. Heading where, he didn't know—with his feet nor his heart. But at least they were together. Alone.

"I'm fine. I do love the colder weather." Kira said, snugging her cape tighter.

"What's that? You don't miss the soup-thick fog of San Francisco?" He longed to wrap an arm around her shoulders, to warm her.

"I do not. Nor the horn blasts of the harbor, nor the clang of the cable cars." Her pink cheeks lifted, eyes squeezed into crescents. "You know, as hard as it's been—the having and the losing and the having again of a permanent Mission Home—I am full of gratefulness that it has finally come to fruition."

"And you are doing a wonderful job with your girls, Kira."

She shook her head. "I don't know."

"You are. Mither has told me she is proud of the way you've taken all the girls under your wing. They respect you. And they are so much happier than when they first came to you."

"I didn't realize your mother had talked to you about it."

"Of course she has. Besides, I'm pretty good at asking questions, you know."

She slowed and turned to him with an impish grin on her lips. "So, you asked your mother about me?"

Ha! *Entrapment.* "Uh . . . yes. I wanted to catch up on everything I'd missed. And I can see for myself how the girls have changed. They seem truly content. Most anyway."

Dim lights glowed from toasty homes bundled against the frost and waning light. Not a soul trekked the frigid sidewalks or traversed the miry streets as the town settled. They were blissfully alone.

She clasped her hands and continued at a slow pace. "It has been hard for Shuang. She still needs much healing in her life. But she *is* slowly trusting in Jesus. Day by day." Her countenance lifted. "I know much is unsure, but the rewards are many. Aunt Lara has taught me so much, and I long to be to those girls everything she has been to me."

They walked in comfortable silence for a time, but what he ached to tell her pounded against his chest, begging escape. He groped for more words, if only to hear her voice again. "My sister has grown into quite the *sonsie* lass since I've been gone."

"She has, hasn't she? As lovely on the inside as she is on the outside."

Dare he? He slid his hand over hers and turned her toward him beneath the streetlamp's glow. "And you . . . I always thought you the loveliest girl in all of San Francisco. But now—now you take my breath away."

Her eyes rounded. He squeezed her hand, and she didn't back away.

Deep velvet eyes glinted in wonder. "You thought me lovely?"

His blood warmed. "The loveliest." Slowly, he drew her to him, and she came. And barring his heart against the rejection he feared most in this world, he circled his arms about her. And yet she came. When last they'd stretched this common thread, they'd been young, but sixteen and fourteen. But 'twas a woman pressed against him this time, unmatched by any, and holder of his heart's key.

A quiver. A tremble. She was weeping, or was it he? He pulled back to see her wet cheeks, eyes glistening with years of hurt and—*glory be*—was that hope aglow at pain's edge? He tipped his forehead to hers, undone. "Forgive me, Kira Girl. Forgive me."

Her thumb brushed wetness from his own eyes. With the slightest bob of her chin and a fairy-soft whisper, she spoke the sweetest music to his ears. "I do forgive you." She choked on a laugh, pressing her face into his chest.

He was flying—beyond the moon. Beyond the stars. Soaring.

He lifted her off the ground with a twirl, as he used to. "Ah, lass, ye dinna know the gift ye've given me."

She threw back her head, and delight danced to the melody of her laughter. Lamplight frolicked in her eyes. He spun her once more, and his burden launched into ice-sprinkled air. His back slammed against a tree, wide and shadowed. He crushed her to him, and her fingers brushed his neck. He searched her, filling every crevice of his needy heart and head with her.

The world vanished but for her face near his as he bent to touch his lips to hers. Oh, glory, but he'd longed for this. Dreamed of this. But he'd not scare her away, yet tender as she was.

The sweetness of that single kiss sparked a flame to life, blazing heat through his middle.

She didn't spook. Dare he . . .?

Her fingers roamed the back of his head, combing his hair, drawing him to her with ardor. Nae, with a hunger. The wonder of it so besotted him he wanted to cry out. He trailed kisses across her chin, her neck, molding her limp body to his. A moan rose from her throat. Alarms sounded, brash and intrusive in his head. But still he held her, kissing her hair, relishing the thrum of her own heart against his.

What delightful agony this woman was!

"Kira. My love." The words scraped and clawed from grave to dawn, from death to life. The words he'd spoken in his dreams a hundred times.

"I love you." Her small words stunned him.

He tipped her chin, begging the light to expose the truth in her lovely eyes.

"I think I always have." Her body trembled against him.

His eyes burned anew. "I feel my heart's about to burst." The smile that carved his cheeks refused any temperance. She suddenly shivered, and he adjusted her skewed cape and lifted the hood.

She pressed her hands to his chest, and he could feel her gaze on him, luring him in for more. "You know, I'm not *really* your cousin anymore."

Flames flared again at her touch. "And for *that* I am selfishly, ecstatically, undeniably, grateful." He pressed a long kiss to her brow, wrestling back an illicit yearning to begin again and greet the sunrise with her still in his arms.

She sighed as if reading his mind.

With a grand reluctance, he loosened his hold and deposited a gentlemanly kiss on her cheek. He turned her about and drew her hand through his arm. "Let's get back before all the blather is about us instead of Henry and Azalea."

Twenty-Nine

TRUCKEE

December, 1885

"Has everyone gone mad?" Avery paced the kitchen, his coffee grew cold, right along with the blood in his veins.

"Wheest. Dinna fash now." Lara pulled out the chair at the tiny table and retrieved the coffeepot. "Sit. I'll warm your cup." When he didn't budge, she plunked her hands onto her hips and scowled for a beat before the lines of her face dissolved. "God knows your heart, and glad I am for it."

"McGleason may be a bigoted fool, but he's not stupid. It was one thing when it was naught but a moldering few agreeing with his vile *committee*, but now he's collected some of the upper crust aboard his wretched bandwagon. And they're pestering everyone who employs Chinese workers."

"And you're worried about Kira." She refreshed his coffee and set the pot back on the stove.

Always one to understand what simmered beneath his skin, she was. "Och, Lara. I dinna ken she can take another turnabout of the Mission Home. I fear she'll lose the vigor and want of it and believe she's a failure."

"Our Kira is stronger than you think, Avery Mitchell."

He reached for her hand, and his thumb gently brushed across her knuckles. This woman was gold, she was. "If she is strong, 'tis naught of my doing."

The creases deepened at the edges of her eyes.

"And I've not told ye enough how much I appreciate all ye've done for her—being mither and all that comes with it." The coffee grew cold again, but what did it matter? The affairs of life cared not a whit.

"What time are ye meetin' Mr. Crocker?"

"Och! The time. I've got a bit of business in Chinatown before I meet with him. I'm late now." He begrudgingly released her hand, bereft at the sudden emptiness in his own.

"Is that the last one on the list?" Avery climbed into the buggy next to Charles Crocker, feeling every one of his sixty years. The waning winter daylight had cut his efforts miserably short, for dusk fell even earlier in the forested Sierra foothills.

Charles perused the folded paper and tucked it back into his pocket. "That's the last of them. These businesses employ hundreds of Chinese workers, all told. If they will just hold the line, keep their workers, and withdraw their advertising from McGleason's precious paper, I don't see how this boycott can succeed." With a click of his tongue, the buggy lurched forward.

"Richardson Brothers Mill and George Shaffer seemed a wee *shooglie* to me. Should we be worried?"

"I'll keep on them. George and I go way back. As long as his timber income isn't threatened, he'll stand strong. He's only interested in the bottom line—the Chinese work for less than what the whites are demanding right now, what with their unions and all."

"I hope you're right." Should the timber barons and big mills cave to McGleason's mob, all hope will tumble like a house of cards. And once again the Chinese will bear the brunt of the white man's ire. His small congregation had grown to ten now. With but one exception, they were all babes in their faith, prone to stumble without a firm hand of encouragement. Would their newfound faith count among the losses of what was to come?

"What of your foray into Chinatown? Any luck with that?" Charles asked.

"Aye, the community is in agreement. They will withhold doing business with any member of the committee."

Charles chuckled, guiding the bay gelding onto the main road. "That ought to sting a bit. Give McGleason's ilk a taste of their own medicine."

"That it should." Fighting fire with fire, they were. But the sheer number of whites compared to Chinese severely tipped the odds of the scrap. And with McGleason blasting Truckee's business to every newspaper in the state, their hamlet was quickly becoming the center of attention. And that would not bode well for his people.

"I wonder how long it will be before Six Companies decides to step into the middle of this. Have you heard from Grant lately?"

"Not a word, but I expect he's circling the wagons as best he can from San Francisco." The lad had proved his mettle, but this whole *guddle* could well prove bigger than even the law could affect.

Yakira slid the tin of baking powder and bag of salt across the counter. "Good morning. I'll take ten pounds of flour, and four scoops of dried apples, if you please." She pulled seven peppermint sticks from a jar. "And these, too. That should do it."

She dug coins from her pouch, breathing in the heady odors of cinnamon and anise. Dannon's Grocer had the best variety of food in town, but she'd still need to trek over the bridge to Chinatown if she was to get everything Aunt Lara asked for.

The clerk, about her own age, set the flour sack on the counter. "I'm Velma. Just moved from Carson City."

"Well I'm Yakira. Pleased to meet your acquaintance, Velma."

The friendly woman nodded and began scooping up the apples. White-blond curls framed her face with a fuzzy halo.

"Excuse me." Howard Dannon squeezed in behind the counter. "I'll take care of this, Velma."

She half-smiled at Yakira, shrugged, and backed away. "Certainly, Mr. Dannon."

"Miss Mitchell, I am surprised to see you in my establishment. You know we don't cater to your kind in here." He pointed to the glaring sign on the wall behind him.

"What kind might that be, Mr. Dannon?" She straightened her spine and pasted on a smile as her fingers coiled the shiny strings of her reticule. "The kind of people who run mission homes for the less-fortunate?"

His black whiskers twitched with his smirk. "I've got nothing against doing God's work, Miss. But I do have something against those who would harbor the inferior Chinese with vain hopes of bringing them up to our level."

"All men are made in God's image, sir, regardless of skin color. I even venture to believe that even *you* are made in the image of the Creator." She drew her brows together and touched a finger to her chin. "I think."

"You impertinent girl! Out. Out of my store now!" He strode to the door, opened it, and stood aside, blistering her with a look.

She frowned at the supplies and picked the coins off the counter. When she reached the threshold, she turned to him. Guilt rode her, for her temper had prevailed when she should have been meek, regardless of his own impertinence. She took in the haggard dark eyes and rucked brow, the sleek collar-length hair that had surely once been black as midnight.

"I apologize for my strong words, Mr. Dannon." A slight crack in his stony facade. "We disagree about the very definition of humanity, it appears. And I feel quite sorry for you." *Better—yet true.* She whirled and left, sadness gripping her in a new way. She truly felt sorry for him and others like him, for they were lost as could be.

She made two stops in Chinatown for vegetables and fresh fish before finally heading home. But caution niggled at her as she came within a few blocks of the Home. A feeling she couldn't shake made her stop and turn. There was no one in sight, save for a young child playing with a dog. A block later she turned again, spying a slip of fabric as it disappeared behind a tree. She gulped down a breath and hugged her market bag.

Quickening her steps, she veered into the neighboring yard, rounded the house, and shot through the back door of the Mission Home. Heart pulsing in her ears, she slammed the door, turned the lock, and fell against it. She had nothing for defense save a butcher knife in her basket, and the thought of using it made her stomach lurch. *Oh God, help.*

Aunt Lara opened the kitchen door and peered in wide-eyed. "Yakira? Whatever is the matter, lass?"

"I was followed from Chinatown." She swallowed, but her mouth was dry as a desert.

"By whom?"

"I don't know. I didn't see them."

"But ye're sure you were followed?" Aunt Lara placed a hand on each shoulder and moved her aside. "If they mean us harm, we canna stop them. Whoever followed you may need our help." She unlocked the door.

"Aunt Lara, no—"

A figure sat hunched on the steps and turned suddenly. Just a girl. A Chinese girl, who, by the terrified look on her face, needed help.

"Come, come inside," Yakira told her in Cantonese. How silly she'd been. "You are safe here."

The girl's fear-laced gaze darted everywhere as she stood and hesitantly followed them into the house. The tied silk hat, matching tunic and pants revealed much—a prostitute from one of the highbinder brothels. And if they suspected she was here, the Tong would be on their doorstep as well.

Aunt Lara moved a teakettle onto the back of the stove. "I'll find Azalea."

Yakira bade the girl sit and pulled up a chair so she could face her. Ever so gently, she took the girl's hands in hers and soon discovered her name.

"Ubon, you are under my protection here. If you wish to live here and learn how very much you are loved, you are welcomed to stay." The soothing Cantonese words flowed from Yakira, and the girl—only fifteen—seemed to relax a bit. Ubon nodded, although her dark eyes continued a vigil, probing every cranny in the room. It was the same fear Yakira had witnessed countless times over the years.

Her heart swelled. She could help Ubon, minister to her. But if the Tong found out, there would be trouble. She must talk to Da right away. He would know what to do.

256

Thirty

Three sets of eyes followed Avery's every move. What in blazes was he to tell them? That if the entire house went up in smoke again, it would be because of the new girl? That *all* of their lives were at risk? He strode across the room again for good measure before settling on the sofa beside Yakira.

"Here is the long and the short of it. If Ubon stays here, best be prepared for trouble. But if naebody knows she is here, we might not have any trouble." The Tong considered her their property, and that she was, according to the contract she had signed with them. Perhaps even before her feet hit the ground in San Francisco.

Kira knotted her fingers and shared a look with Azalea. "No one need know, Da. We can give her a different name. She will not leave the house. She can stay away from the windows."

"But, Kira," Lara said, "that is no life for a girl." She looked to him then. "Is there some way we could smuggle her out? To Sacramento, perhaps?"

"Let me think and pray on this. But whatever we do, no one must know she is here, and by all means, change her name, her clothes—whatever you can do."

It was Kira's turn to pace. "I promised I would protect her."

"And we will—all the girls," he told her.

Already McGleason had turned to threats of a full economic boycott and public shaming of merchants who refused his plan. And sure as he knew human nature, bigger troubles were just around the corner. But this time he'd be prepared. He had purchased a shotgun of his own after the Eureka disaster. Now it was time for Kira to have one if she was to offer any measure of physical protection for the Home. God help them mightily if ever there was need of it.

He stood and reached out to his daughter. "Yakira Jean, come with me."

Resolved: That not only the laboring man, but the entire community demand that all individuals, companies and corporations should discharge any and all Chinamen in their employ by January 1, 1886, and refuse thereafter to give them work of any kind.

Acid climbed Avery's throat, souring his disposition further. The ridiculous resolution appeared in every edition of *The Truckee Republican* now—McGleason's insidious reminder to the people to step in line. His Committee of Five was working overtime to *persuade* every person within ten miles of Truckee to take part in the boycott.

"At least there are still those opposing the loss of Chinese laundries," Lara said.

Always the encourager, she was. 'Twas her nature, God bless her.

"Not to mention restaurants and boarding houses so dependent on them. Mrs. Bensman, bless her, has stirred up her group of women in a valiant protest."

"Aye, but McGleason has a card to play for every hand, it seems." Avery held the paper so she could see the bold advertisement from her seat across the room. "Stocks are being sold to raise money for a steam laundry. They've already raised $700."

He read the print in his best imitation of the arrogant editor: "'Not only will Truckee's new steam laundry rid the town of Chinese hand washers, it will create jobs for white women and induce them to move to the masculine frontier.'"

She chuckled, the mirth not quite reaching her eyes. "Masculine frontier, he says. *Hoot*! I canna believe white women will fall for his drivel."

"I want to believe that too. But this new *Labor Bureau Committee*—what a sham—is making a list of all unemployed white men willing to replace the Chinese. When business owners see it, even the most resolute will run dry of excuses."

"But surely there are the big timbermen like George Shaffer who will hold out. They canna possibly afford to pay white wages with the number of men on their payroll."

"I hope so. I pray so." He tossed the paper aside and stood. "I ask you. Am I yet standing in America, Lara?"

She looked up from her needlework, started to speak, but then simply stitched a sad, understanding smile across her *douce* face.

He crossed to the window and stared out at the circle carved by a streetlamp's glow. "Och. Have I traded one set of warlords for another? Is it not the same when one group reigns over another with their narrow definitions of mankind?"

She set the mending aside and joined him, their shoulders pressed and her warmth welcomed. "The girls are settled, but I think not for long. How did Kira do?" Concern shaped her words, and her gaze fixed on the darkness beyond the glass pane.

She didn't have to say it, for he knew their outing with the firearm had weighed on her mind. "She will do well." He felt his lips curve. "She is my daughter, after all." He swallowed past a lump, wondering if Yakira had truly come full circle after her grand shock. There still seemed a moat around her heart, not as wide as it had been, but a defense nonetheless. And he missed their closeness. But teaching her to protect herself with her own gun had proven profitable for both of them, weaving a bit of new trust between them.

"And what of your men, your flock? Do they understand it all? Will you continue to meet?"

"Aye, for now." It was a hard road for the new believers, convincing them that the love God had for them brooked no room for hating their fellow man. "Their spirits are strong."

Footsteps trotted down the stairs. "Da, they're coming." Kira dimmed the gaslight and joined them at the window. "Azalea is with the girls, keeping them from watching."

Ghoulish fingers of light danced at the end of the block. Soon, clusters of men, women, even children, came into view. Their voices chanted as torches bobbed and swayed through the night air. "The Chinese must go! The Chinese must go!" With faces drawn and shadowed in firelight, the mob marched to the cadence of their chants as they had every night since the resolution.

He felt Yakira's hand grasp his. The memory of her spindly little arms about his neck lodged a stone in his throat.

The malicious ruckus passed by. Behind it trailed a single thought—*God help us all*.

San Francisco

Incense and lemon polish mingled with the haze of cigar smoke as gold-threaded dragons stared back at Grant from a mantel scarf. Mr. Huang's office was anything but simple. While the chief consul lived like a king, his countrymen were denied even the most basic rights in this country.

Fred Bee perched his spectacles on his nose and leafed through page after page of bad news. "This newspaper man, McGleason, is telegraphing Truckee's events all over the state. And we need to put a stop to this before it becomes a real row. *The Truckee Republican* is fanning the flames on every aspect of this boycott fiasco. *The Alta California* reports that every employer in the Truckee basin has pledged to discharge its Chinese laborers prior to January first. The timber baron named Shaffer has fired all of his workers already. A large Truckee mill"—he flipped a page, then turned it back.

"Here it is . . . a mill by the name of Richardson Brothers has fired all of its employees. Wing Chung Lung has been forced out of business by this boycott, and a couple of other Chinese firms are on the verge of bankruptcy. The list goes on." Col. Bee looked up, his face harder than Grant had ever witnessed.

Seated across the massive lacquered desk, Mr. Huang leaned forward, hands folded. "Mr. Campbell, you and Mr. Smith are going back to Truckee. Let the other attorneys continue with the other anti-Chinese troubles."

"Yes, sir. What about that U.S. marshal we requested?"

"I don't know what the hold-up is, exactly. I will send another telegram." Mr. Huang stuffed his smoldering cigar back into his cheek.

It was now or never. The idea had nagged him since his last conversation with Uncle Avery. "Sir, if I may broach another topic?"

"Go ahead."

"Currently, there is a stipulation prohibiting the proselytizing of Chinese Immigrants. Sir, even in China, Christian missionaries are welcome. Why? Because the Chinese Government knows they bring prosperity, health, and virtuous character to the people. I humbly request this stipulation be removed. I have drafted an official request." He slid a single page across the desk. "Why should the immigrants be denied a right granted to them in their own country if America is willing to offer it to them?"

Mr. Huang steepled his fingers, one eye squinted, the other settled on the wall past Grant's head. A long moment passed in silence. Then, with a quick nod, he said, "Mr. Campbell, you make a valid point. Due to the changing environment and perhaps the way Chinese workers are perceived at this time, this is something that may be considered."

"Thank you, sir." What opportunities this would open for the Mission Home and Uncle Avery's tiny basement church.

Col. Bee cleared his throat, closed the folder on his lap, and slipped another from beneath it. "There is a second reason you are needed in Truckee." He rolled a section of mustache with his lips and let the folder fall open. "It seems there is a Tong issue in which Six Companies wishes you to intervene. One of the Tong-owned businesses in Truckee is missing a prostitute. It is believed she has run away or is seeking asylum in Truckee somewhere."

Grant chewed the inside of his cheek, disturbed by where this might be leading.

"Since this particular Tong has helped out Six Companies on occasion, they have asked a favor—for you to retrieve their missing *property*." The colonel's jaw clenched at the word. He passed the folder to Grant. "You'll find the girl's signed contract in here. The thumbprint renders it binding, I'm afraid."

He stared at the file in his hand, gutted by what it represented. It was a double-edged sword, sure to sever anew the mended wound between him and Kira. *Lord in heaven, if there be a way...*

Thirty-One

Henry slept peacefully, head cockeyed and chin gently bobbing with the train's motion. If only Grant could do the same.

He pulled his sleeve over his fist and swabbed the foggy glass. Familiar landscape rolled and buckled with green patches of orchard and winter crops. Eventually, snowy mountains overshadowed it all. Always before, the Sierra Nevada had hailed a friendly welcome, but today, the steamy, foreboding mountains seemed angry. They warned him to turn around and go back to San Francisco.

A chill rattled through his limbs. He pressed his temple to the cold glass with a soft thud. He lifted his head and did it again. And again.

"It won't help." A yawning Henry blinked. "I've tried it before, with a wall."

"I thought you were sleeping."

"I was, but something hard was bumping the window. How can a man sleep with that racket?" Henry shrugged the blanket from his shoulders, letting it fall to his lap. He straightened his hat, preferring to keep his queue tucked out of sight in public.

"You can sleep anywhere. Wish I could."

"What keeps you awake?"

Breath sizzled through his lips as he retrieved the folder from his valise. "This." He handed over the Tong contract.

> *I agree to prostitute my body for the term of five years. If, in that time, I am sick one day, two weeks shall be added to my time; and if more than one day, my term of prostitution shall continue an additional month. But if I run away from the custody of my keeper, then I am to be held as a slave for life.*

He'd read it a hundred times, praying for a loophole to jump out and redeem him. "I'm supposed to return some *property* to a highbinder brothel."

Henry handed back the page, his expression grave. "I have heard of such many times. Did you know that a missed day because of a woman's monthly time is considered sick day? Such a contract is for life, because time is always extended. Better to run and take chance for freedom than be slave for life."

Grant tipped his head back against the seat. He scraped fingertips through his scalp and tugged at the roots. This couldn't be happening. All he had wanted was to make a difference. To do some good on behalf of the Chinese people, not to enslave them.

"Pray to your God that you cannot find her." Henry said matter-of-factly. "If He can help bring me to Yakira, He can do this small thing."

Small thing? This was a mountain that needed moving, and it was crushing him. And it was jeopardizing everything he had been asking God for over these past months. But this wasn't only about him and what Kira thought of him, or what his mother thought. No, this time a life was at stake.

Truckee

"Stop this!" Avery flung Slade Carson aside, reaching Ho Wah as he crumpled to the snow-dusted cobblestone. "Haven't you done enough to this man?" He glared at Dan Flint, who made a show of examining his trimmed fingernails, although Ho Wah's blood sullied his knuckles.

"This ain't none of yer business, Reverend." Carson blinked against the large snowflakes on his lashes and wiped a sleeve across his face.

"I'm making it my business." But his words felt hollow, for nothing had come of the assault complaint he'd filed on Ho Wah's behalf last time.

Dan Flint tossed an empty poke at Ho Wah's feet. "This ain't the end of it."

"Oh yes it is." Avery bent closer to Ho Wah. "Can you stand?" His friend nodded.

Carson and Flint sauntered off, their insolence no doubt carrying them off to torment some other poor soul.

"You're coming home with me," he told Ho Wah in Cantonese to make sure there was no confusion. "And there you'll stay."

After settling Ho Wah into the basement of the Mission Home—which also housed another of his students for the same reason—Avery headed straight for Dannon's Grocery. Lord help him, he wanted to knock Howard Dannon's teeth down his throat.

He burst through the door, and the few customers stared at him in shock. The crazed bell echoed in his ears as he realized he probably looked like a madman. He brought himself up with a deep breath and nodded to the shoppers with a fake smile. "Good day, ladies." And a good day 'twould be if he were to best the proprietor.

"Where might I find Mr. Dannon?" he asked the clerk behind the counter.

"He is just back here, I'll get him." The skittish lass backed away.

Avery rounded the counter. "Don't bother, I'll find him myself."

"Oh! But you can't go back there!" Her panicked words trailed behind him as he pushed the curtain aside and skirted crates and barrels, following a narrow aisle to a partially opened door. He barged in, and Dannon's mug snapped up.

"What's the meaning of this, Mitchell?" He stood, eyes shifting to a desk drawer for an instant before his hard gaze bore into Avery.

"Call off your thugs, Dannon. This has to end. Or it won't be just the local authorities I'm appealing to this time."

"Well now, Reverend. I can't see as how it's any of your business, the way I collect my debts."

"So that's what ye call *debt collectin'*, is it? Robbery and assault? Surely not a chosen method for any honorable business man."

Dannon stepped around the desk, and Avery moved toward him, easily a head taller than the man.

"You barge into *my* place of business. You call me dishonorable and accuse me of robbery and assault." His cheeks puffed before blasting breath to the ceiling. "We'll see what kind of charges we can come up with against your precious Mission Home. Like refusing to cooperate with town mandates, manipulating citizens to cross the boycott, harboring thieves. You have just days to find new homes for your stray China dogs, Reverend. After that"—a maniacal chuckle—"well, there's no telling what will happen."

Blood boiled up into Avery's ears, hissing and steaming until he knew he'd not be responsible for what his fists would do. He stepped closer, looking down on the stout little man. He jabbed a finger in his face. "Ye threaten my family, sir, there'll be hell to pay." He turned and strode out the back door, unwilling to collect himself for a few clueless customers.

"It was so kind of the ladies from Mrs. Bensman's church to supply these." Yakira said, opening a brand-new box of fragile ornaments. She savored the holiday spirit flitting inside her. Not since before Grant left had she looked forward to Christmas so much.

Azalea drew long lengths of red ribbon from the mystery box of Christmas decorations. "This is so much fun!" She handed bright bobbles and crocheted linen stars to Mei. "I love decorating for Christmas."

"Oh, these are so beautiful." Yakira dangled one of the etched glass balls in a sunbeam streaming through the window. Ubon touched it, setting it to spin, casting prisms of light across the room. Yakira settled a gentle hand on her arm, guiding her from the window. "Ubon—*Bao*, away from window, remember?"

The girl had been more than happy to cooperate with the rules for her own protection. And she was especially enthusiastic about her new name, for "Ubon" had meant *lotus*, a flower that springs from the filthy sludge—now she was "Bao" which meant *gem*. And Yakira would do everything in her power to make sure she understood she was indeed a beautiful gem, a precious treasure in God's eyes.

Aunt Lara appeared in the doorway with a wide smile and a box in her arms. "Be thankit for His marvelous provisions."

"More food?" Yakira peered into the box.

Mrs. Bensman had procured people to make purchases secretly for the Mission Home, since only Chinese businesses would still sell to the Home. Without the woman's intervention, they would have had little food. Thankfully, the San Francisco Mission Home shipped them other nonperishable supplies.

"Come," Azalea said, bright ribbons spilling from her hands. "Let us dance." After seconds of excited banter, Azalea was stepping gracefully with Lian and Shu in a dance as ribbons swept the air between them.

Lian hummed a mysterious melody that wove its way through Yakira, drawing her thoughts to Grant. Each day of late, she found herself staring out the front windows, hoping to glimpse his tall, lean form striding up the street. Moths fluttered in her stomach, and heat coursed through her body remembering their kisses in the darkness on that cold evening.

It was as though her life had ripped down the middle all those years ago, the painful tearing away leaving but frayed edges. And now something new emerged, sweet and hopeful, woven from those same frayed threads. Only God could fashion such a thing.

"Are you going to help?" Azalea nudged her. "Well?"

"Oh. Yes." She joined in the decorating fun, draping the banister and trimming the tree. When Aunt Lara appeared with cups of hot cocoa, they sipped the steaming treat and admired their work. Soon they were singing the only Christmas song the girls had learned—*Silent Night*.

Surely the night marches would cease for the holiest night of the year. But with the way the angry throngs had doubled, then tripled, she doubted the Savior's birth would be an exception.

The doorknocker halted the singing. Bao gasped. Azalea came to her side, ushering her and all the girls up the staircase. Aunt Lara quickly collected the cups and whisked the tray away to the kitchen as the knocker banged again. Yakira thought of the shotgun, loaded and hidden in the armoire.

She went to the door, peering cautiously out the sidelight. "Grant!" She flipped the lock and flung the door wide despite the cold. "You're home!" She rushed at him, delighting in the way her feet left the floor as his powerful arms engulfed her. She pressed her face to his neck, savoring his scent as all the wonder of that night sluiced through her.

"Uh. Hello? I'm here, too." Henry's words rode a chuckle.

Grant lowered her to the floor in one achingly slow movement, his gaze riveted on hers. His mouth parted slightly, and cobalt eyes shone with such love it took her breath away. His eyes never left her as he said, "Wait your turn, *cousin*."

She laughed aloud at the way the words danced off his tongue. She reached around Grant, pulling Henry into the house and giving him a brotherly hug. "I am equally happy to see you, brother." She winked at Grant.

"Equally?" Grant's lips puckered in a pout, and she playfully slapped his lapel. Sweet was the memory of his silliness, one of the many things she'd loved about him.

"There's me boy." Aunt Lara swooped in, relieving him of his coat before pulling him to her. "Happy I am to have ye here for Christmas. You, too, Henry. Oh, what a grand time we'll have!"

Yakira hung Henry's things on the hall tree and looped her arm through his. "Yes, indeed. A grand time."

Thirty-Two

Yakira considered the many Christmases of years gone by, summoning the best of all her memories. This one she would add, for surely Providence alone had wrought this miracle from such a tumultuous year.

"Let's have no talk of boycotts or night watches or any such thing this evening," Da said, his features aglow with tonight's joyful occasion. "If the Savior can make His appearance in the dank of a barn, we can certainly celebrate His birth amid such ill-trickit chaos."

"Indeed," Aunt Lara said, candlelight dancing in her eyes.

Pine and candle wax infused the air, stirring delight and thanksgiving into a hallowed concoction in Yakira's heart. If only she could capture this moment somehow, and guard it so it wouldn't escape.

How very different this Christmas was from last year. Gratitude flooded her at the sight of her girls, dressed in their finest. Some wore western dresses, but all wore radiant smiles—for this was their first real Christmas. The first time they'd known of a Savior who came for each of them. Even Ubon—*Bao*—had fully embraced the God of grace and mercy. And Father's students, Ho Wah and Shen Bow, had surprised them all with paper lanterns, now displayed on the banister amid greenery and red ribbon.

Aunt Lara passed the vegetable dish, encouraging everyone to eat their fill. "Don't all you ladies look lovely." She winked at Azalea, who positively glowed, attired in Henry's extravagant gift.

"Aye. But 'tis not just the young ones." Da's gaze touched Aunt Lara's before he reached for his glass. "And let us be verra thankful, indeed, to Charles Crocker for the goose. And to Mrs. Bensman's brood for the tasty provisions. No cause for any to leave this table *hungert* this eve."

"Have you celebrated Christmas like this before, Henry?" It was only one of the many questions she had not been able to ask her brother.

"I have not. But I hope this is the first of many." His grin slid promptly from her to Azalea.

Azalea blushed furiously, and she'd never been prettier. "I hope so, too," she said at last, as if he were the only one at the table.

"You've gained another girl, Kira. Perhaps you could introduce her." Grant's stiff words brought her up short.

"I . . . I'm sorry, I thought I had. Grant, this is Bao. She came to us not long ago."

"Pleased to meet you, Bao," he said with half a smile. He ran a finger between his collar and neck.

When the conversations buzzed again, she reached behind Azalea to tap Grant on the arm. "Are you feeling all right?"

He touched his napkin to the corner of his mouth. "Yes, why do you ask?"

"I don't know, it's just . . ." What was it really? "Nothing, I guess." He looked away before she could say more.

But her joy guttered by half. Throughout the entirety of laughter and sustenance, of empty plates and full stomachs, something was amiss. For though the man could hide his thoughts from prying eyes, the boy she knew could not. When she looked really hard at the Grant she used to know, she saw his crimson thoughts leaked onto his sleeve. He was angry about something. And the knowledge of it might just ruin the most perfect Christmas ever.

That, she would not risk.

Male voices carried from the parlor as the women made quick work of the after-dinner mess. Oh, to be a fly on the wall! It had always rankled Yakira to be excluded from a conversation because of her gender.

"I think you girls may be excused," she heard Aunt Lara say before the girls scurried toward the dining room.

She followed behind. "Don't forget to say goodnight, girls," she reminded them.

They curtsied as she'd taught them, each one in turn offering an appropriate "good evening" to the men. Amid re-sewn bustles and girlish giggles, they rushed up the stairs. "Lady-like, girls," she gently reminded.

"Come on, Ubon," Mei said, reaching for her friend's hand.

Yakira cringed. She must speak to Mei about using Ubon's new name.

Grant stood there with his heart in his shoes, drinking in Yakira's every movement. The silk *cheuhng-sāam* caressed her every curve, firing his imagination. As she blew out each of the tree candles, she stretched her sleek neck, and his fingers ached to touch it—to feel her silken skin, the warmth of her. But what he had to say would ruin everything—demolish the bridge they'd painstakingly rebuilt.

"Do you think they will march tonight?" He asked as she pulled the shade aside to peer out the window.

"I hope not, but I expect it." She turned to him, her expression suddenly wistful. Her hand reached out to him. "But for this miserable rain, we could walk."

So, she too was thinking of their last walk together. Taking her hand, he guided her to a wingback chair, for sitting beside her on the sofa would be his undoing. He needed to get through this. He had hardly choked down dinner with the knowledge of what was to come.

"I want . . . need to speak with you about one of your girls."

Her eyes narrowed, and she pulled her hand from his. "Which one?"

"Ubon."

Her lips spread in a tight smile. "I don't—"

"Kira, I heard one of the other girls call her that. Her name isn't really Bao, is it?"

Her shoulders sagged. She picked at her fingernails. "No."

He grabbed both her hands, pleading with his gaze. "Please, please tell me she did not come here from one of the Tong brothels in Chinatown."

She sat up straight, her brow suddenly crimped as she pulled back her hands. "Why? Why is it you ask?"

He unfolded the contract he had kept in his pocket and handed it to her. "I'm sorry." The words cracked from his lips, weighted with a gritty, dirty layer of regret.

Her face darkened as she read. She thrust it back at him. "This means nothing. That girl is God's child now. I will *not* let her go back." Suddenly ire flared in her eyes, and the firm set of her jaw left no doubt. "Are you representing the Tongs now, *cousin*?"

The words stung, for they carried a host of meaning between them. Ten steps forward, fifty steps back. He fought the urge to drop to his knees. *What was he doing?*

He knotted his fists and sucked in a deep breath. "Six Companies owes this particular Tong a favor. I am supposed to get her back for them." There. He said it. She could hurl a hundred bullets, and it would not inflict more pain—he had already given himself up for dead. His mother was right. Six Companies did not have *all* the Chinese immigrants' best interests at heart.

"I can't believe this." She was on her feet, staring him down, her eyes cavernous. "That you would think for an instant I'd let you take one of my girls because of some piece of paper. Or because some highbrow Mandarin owes a highbinder a favor! Is this who you are now, Grant Campbell? Was that night . . . when—"

Her chest heaved, and she looked away. A quiver pulled at her lips. "I was a fool." She spun, clutched wads of her dress with both hands, and fled up the stairs.

He sprang to his feet. "Kira!"

Their fragile bridge shattered, every shard piercing both of them through. And the fresh wound so pained her she hadn't even bothered to ask what he planned to do about Ubon.

Thirty-Three

"I don't believe you've met Tuck Chung. He's an upright sort of fellow." Avery told Grant. "And he knows the ins and outs of Truckee's Chinatown. All the players."

He made respectful introductions between Grant and the merchant. If anyone knew anything that would help Grant's dilemma, it was Tuck Chung.

Grant dipped his head. "Pleased to meet you, Old Uncle."

Tuck Chan acknowledged the greeting and continued with Avery in Cantonese, even though Avery knew the man spoke English well enough.

"What'd he say?" Grant asked when they both chuckled.

"He thinks you are too tall, but handsome enough to be Tang. I told him who you work for, and he said one man isna enough for the problems coming to this town."

"Tell him there is a U.S. marshal coming soon. Perhaps that will stem the tide of trouble."

"He isna ignorant, Grant. These people keep up with the news as much as we do. They know there are already purges and boycotts up and down the coast. One government lawman is powerless against such mania." He clasped Grant's shoulder. "You wanted to find out information about the girl?"

"Yes."

Avery questioned Tuck Chung, disturbed to find out how many immigrants had already lost jobs, but proud that they had not yet left the area. If the tide were to turn, 'twould be better for the town to keep its Chinese residents than to have to manage an influx of strangers. He thought of the tent families outside of Eureka and the children's eyes hollow with hunger. Those people had sold everything in hopes of jobs—jobs that didn't materialize. How could he stand by and watch it happen all over again on a grander scale?

He bid Tuck Chung farewell and struck out with Grant across the frozen street, enlightening him as they walked. Cramped, steep-pitched houses lined one side of the street, shops cluttered the other, and residents scurried in between.

"He says they're searching the town for Ubon. Looking for her at each departing train, besides." He kept his voice low, wary of big ears. "I'll check back with him in a couple of days. He also says he's ordered two crates of rifles—in case there's more trouble from either Dannon or McGleason."

"But that's—"

"There are many laws that tie a man's hand to protect what is his, lad." He grunted. "You need to get your head out of your law books and think about what it was like for your mither and faither in San Francisco's earlier days. Always swimming against the current of gold-hungry whites, they were—just to help the Tang people survive."

"You're right, Uncle Avery." Resignation shackled Grant's words. His stride slowed. He stroked his beard. "You're right."

"I am. I canna condone the killing, but if a man willna protect his own family, he is no man." With the frostiness between Grant and Kira lately, he'd best tell him now, since his strong-willed daughter would have none of his nephew at present.

He entered a vegetable market. It had always amazed him how Tang farmers could grow certain vegetables in the peak of winter. Their secret was well kept. Indeed, it remained a mystery to the white gardeners. He selected several onions before broaching the topic.

"After what happened in Eureka, I bought a shotgun. And I've given one to Yakira as well."

"You can't be serious!" Grant's eyes fairly bulged.

"Now, dinna fash yourself. I taught her how to use it. And well, she did. I trust her to keep a level head should it come to such." He fished money from his pocket to pay for the onions and carrots. He waited until they'd left the store and were well out of Chinatown before launching into his next question. "And if the Tongs know of the girl's location?"

Grant puffed out a steaming cloud. "I don't know what I'll do, Uncle. I just don't know."

"Might I suggest ye make it a matter of prayer? God will hear ye, and if it's an answer ye seek from Him, He'll give it."

Pain laced Grant's eyes and notched his brow. "I've been negligent to my upbringing the last few years."

"I know." He hadn't meant the words as condemnation, only to let the lad know he understood. "Ye canna let the *ghaist* of your past keep you from talking to God, son."

"What ghosts of my past?"

They crossed the bridge in silence as Avery thought on his next words. He greeted an approaching couple. They promptly looked as if they'd sucked on a lemon and brushed past him.

He took a deep breath. "Now, I can understand the ache of a boy on the cusp of manhood feeling so responsible for his faither's death that it pained him to see the loss in his mother's eyes every day—"

"Uncle—"

"*Haud yer wheest!* Let me finish." The conversation was long overdue, and as painful as it was, the wound needed lancing. He slowed his steps, keeping his eyes ahead, giving Grant his privacy. "I even understand that boy running away across the country instead of dealing with the distress of it all." He stopped and turned to him, surprised at how pale his skin appeared against his black beard.

"But what I dinna understand is the reason ye dinna write to soothe your mither's broken heart." A hundred nights Lara had cried herself to sleep, so lost in her grief was she. The remembrance coiled his fingers even as he yearned to see the wrong righted. "And ye havena even told your mither the whole of the truth yet."

Grant's jaw dropped. "What do you mean?"

"Och, son! Ye ken what I mean. Has not God been drawing you to repentance?"

Grant closed the bedroom door behind him and leaned against it. Years had tamped the old fear deep into his conscience, but now that he was alone, it reared up, brazen and hideous. Uncle Avery knew! How? And hadn't told his mother. *Thank God.*

God. Was the Almighty not stripping him naked of every shred of deception? The conviction of his actions and the want to spill the mess at his mother's knee crushed him like an anvil, driving him to the floor. *Oh God! Forgive me.*

The simple words screamed from his mind, his very soul, again and again. He fell to his knees, doubling over, so great was the tearing within him. Groans—so wretched they could not possibly be coming from him—scraped his throat and filled the space with a single plea. Hot tears fell to the rug, but he cared not, for suddenly the only thing that mattered was to try desperately to right the wrong he'd inflicted on his precious mother.

A tap at the door. He stilled. Had someone heard him?

"Grant?" Mither's tender voice.

"*Now*," a voice whispered within.

He arose on shaky legs and slowly opened the door, drawing her in with a trembling hand, closing the door behind her. The concerned look on her face brought tears afresh.

"Mither, come. Sit."

He told of the inheritance money he'd claimed from his uncle in Scotland, requesting that he withhold news of it from her.

"Ah, son. Long ago I forgave ye for the money."

He braved a look at her now. "You knew?" *How?*

"Aye. A letter from your uncle."

And then he poured out the part he'd had in his father's death, festered and putrid as it all sounded to his ears. Suddenly he was in that alley again. The stink of urine pinched his nose. Agony curled him tight against the hard ground as three Tong boys kicked him repeatedly. A roar split the air as Da appeared and heaved away one attacker, then another. But they turned on him. Grant could only watch in horror as they mounted Da's shoulders and restrained him. The third boy rammed him from behind, hurling him headfirst into an unforgiving brick wall. A revolver exploded. Wild-eyed, the boys ran, leaving Grant a crumpled mess, sobbing over Da's lifeless body.

At some point, he'd wilted to the floor and rested his head upon her knee as he had as a boy. Her fingers lovingly stroked the hair at his temples.

"But you were not to blame for your faither's death, my sweet boy."

"But Mither, that alley was forbidden. The gambling, forbidden. If I'd listened to him. It was I who should've died that day, not Da. It was *my* fight. *My* fault. He was protecting *me*."

He ground his sodden face against her skirt. "Forgive me. Oh, please forgive me."

Her silence bade him look up. But he couldn't bear her rejection.

Pain sliced through the cloud of blue in her swimming eyes. Her lips parted, and she shook her head ever so slightly.

Breath stalled within him. *Could she not forgive him?*

"Ye've carried this with you all these years. How verra hard it must have been for you. I am so, so sorry."

She was sorry for him? Did she not hear his plea?

"Of course I forgive you." She coaxed him to sit beside her and settled a hand upon his. "My love will always bid me forgive you. Now, my dearest son, you must forgive yourself."

He nodded, but words failed him.

"I believe, as you are able, you owe some other people an explanation."

He no longer balked at the idea, for the worst was behind now. The anchor that had crushed him so entirely was somehow, wonderfully, miraculously gone. And he wanted nothing more than to clear the air with his family.

Fresh, joyous tears fell, and he smiled from his deepest parts. Inside him was light. Forgiveness. Acceptance. And peace as he'd not thought possible. For the first time in many years, he looked forward to listening to what God had to say to him—listening to what God wanted from him. And not only would God help him set things aright with his family, he had inexplicable confidence God would see to the Kira-Ubon dilemma.

New Year's Eve 1886

"No, you're not taking her." Yakira evaded Grant's grasp, setting her jaw against a very unladylike retort.

"It's the only solution." He slumped into a chair, hands folded in front of him. "It is all I have to offer. Think of Ubon." The contours of his face seemed softer somehow—the sea-tossed eyes settled and calm.

She hated to admit it, but he was right. Ubon's safety was the only thing that mattered. But what would happen to *him* if they caught him? As furious as she was with him, she still cared.

"We must do it soon. I don't know for sure if the Tongs know she's here. How soon can you be ready?"

Henry had been mute, but now his gaze seemed to beg her to agree to this crazy plan.

Da burst through the door. There was a grim pull on his whiskered face. He jabbed a finger at them and strode through the hallway. "You three stay put. Where's Lara?"

"Upstairs. In the alcove. What is it, Da? What's wrong?" She dropped onto the sofa, and Grant merely shrugged. For all that was happening, it was as if they were children again, about to be scolded for some ill-planned mischief for which they had been equally responsible. She shied from the fond memory, determined to stay angry with Grant for his lack of backbone where Six Companies was concerned.

Da returned to sit beside her while Aunt Lara retrieved Azalea from somewhere in the back of the house before joining them.

"Whatever is the matter?" Aunt Lara settled in the chair across from Grant.

"It's happened. The Cigar Makers Union in San Francisco has made good on their boycott threats and fired all their Chinese workers. A train is passing through town tonight—carrying more than 400 union workers from the East Coast to replace them." A look of disgust twisted his face. "Would you believe Truckee's Fife and Drum Corps is practicing?"

"And you're expecting trouble." Grant stood. "I'm going with you."

"Aye. And you ladies will stay here." He pointed a sharp finger at Henry. "And you!"

"Yes, Da. Lights off. Doors locked." Yakira glanced at the armoire. The shotgun was supposed to be a comfort. It wasn't. If ever she had to use it, God would be her strength—and level head. "Are the men downstairs?"

"I don't know, but if they are, they should stay put." He fluttered a hand at Grant. "Weel, dinna just stand there. Get your coat."

Yakira followed them to the door, and before she could close it behind them, Grant whirled.

"Kira . . . be safe." The words trailed as he turned from her with a gaze of longing that branded her heart.

She locked the door, glancing again at the armoire and sending a prayer heavenward.

Thirty-Four

TRUCKEE

Torch flames danced to the peal of church bells as the fife-and-drum corps led Truckee citizens in a march up and down the depot platform. Cheers rose as the train stopped to take on wood. Cigar workers spilled onto each car's end platform, celebrating and *whooping* as others waved from the car windows. While railroad workers loaded firewood into the tender, the parade spread to the streets as more and more townspeople joined in.

Grant cringed at the rabid, repeated declaration from the platform as Robert McGleason touted his message through a megaphone. "The citizens of Truckee will not be responsible for whatever happens after January fifteenth!" The sharp words droned on and on, adding to the maddening ruckus and his own indigestion. And he was out of Henry's stomach drops.

Banners danced in the air: SUCCESS TO ANTI-COOLIE and NO CHINESE NEED APPLY TRUCKEE STEAM LAUNDRY.

He leaned closer to Uncle Avery, trying to be heard over the commotion. "See those red hat bands? They're part of the Labor Union movement. I saw them back east. It means they're willing to go to war over their rights."

Uncle Avery shook his head. His features hardened to stone as he pointed beyond the platform.

Grant tried to follow his gaze, noticing only another of the menacing signs of a rooster: WHEN THE COCK CROWS THE CHINAMAN GOES. A threat if ever there was one.

"The sign?" He yelled above the din.

"No!" Uncle Avery took off at a fast clip, skirting the passenger platform. Grant followed him past a boisterous group of boys and across the tracks. "There," he said, pointing.

Workers off-loaded dozens of crates—an entire rail car of them. He strode closer with Uncle Avery now on his heels. He approached the Chinese men loading the crates into wagons as a railroad official stood by with a clipboard. The white lettering on the crates was unmistakable, even in the shrouded light. *Firearms.* And along with hundreds of rifles was a substantial box marked CARTRIDGES. Well, at least he could tell San Francisco the Chinese are prepared to defend themselves.

"I guess Tuck Chung isn't the only one to order arms." Uncle Avery said as they left the station.

They wandered down Front Street amid vulgar men who stumbled with drink and celebrated the oncoming atrocities. Women waved from second-story windows, and over on Jibboom Street, ruffians fired into the air. Had everyone lost their senses? Marchers snaked through the town, circling block after block.

The Mission Home was dark when they approached, but before they reached the front yard, a light appeared on the main floor, and the door cracked open. Henry and Kira stood in the doorway, their faces shadowed.

"You waited up?" Grant said, ignoring Henry's cocked smile, but hoping for a welcoming one from Kira. They stepped aside, and once he and Avery were in the house, he turned to her. "I should leave for San Francisco in the morning."

"Tomorrow?" Disappointment flashed across her eyes and vanished just as quickly. Her smooth jaw braced with determination. "Then we have a lot of work to do tonight."

"What kind of work?" Henry butted in.

"We're going to save Ubon," she said simply.

The resolve he heard in her voice made him smile. And the spark in her gaze lit a blaze inside him.

She squeezed his upper arm and then trailed her hand down his sleeve, depositing a feathery touch to his hand. Her lips crimped to one side. Ah, he knew that look—could almost hear the words she wasn't saying, words he wanted to hear.

"All will be ready by morning." She turned and walked away, leaving him feeling suddenly very alone.

He memorized the lilt of her step, the way she lifted her hem. The sway of her hips. *Dear God, let this plan work.* For if it didn't, he might not be around to finish what he'd begun with her.

New Year's Day, 1886
Truckee Depot

Azalea had exquisitely transformed to play her part. With her eyes discreetly hidden beneath a wide-brimmed hat and wearing a blue-bustled gown, she plied a matching parasol with aplomb.

Grant took a deep breath. Their ruse just had to work, though fraught with danger as it was. He paraded her on his arm as they entered the train depot, making a show of introducing her as his charge—even to perfect strangers, who met them with curious stares.

In a stage-worthy performance, she tittered and spoke to everyone in perfect English, apparently bored senseless with yet another rail journey this month. Henry excelled in the role as her valet, tending to her many nonsensical concerns as if born for the stage.

"*Do* be careful with that Italian bag. I will not tolerate a scratch on it." Azalea's chin lifted regally, a queen ordering about her servant.

"Yes, Miss." Henry bobbed submissively.

"Are you sure you properly checked-in my steamer?"

"Yes, Miss."

"Do you have the ticket? Do *not* lose that ticket. I cannot abide you losing another, or I will see your wages effectively docked."

Henry's cheeks jumped—apparently his best attempt at squashing his amusement.

But desperate prayers for a successful ruse buffered Grant's own performance. He swept the station with his gaze as they crossed the platform, vigilant for anything that might foil their plan. They approached the train, and he handed Azalea up onto the step.

"Just a minute there."

The deep voice froze him in place. He turned slowly, mind reeling with all of their expected obstacles. Please let this not be one they hadn't discussed.

"Now see here," the conductor said, attempting to protect his wealthier passengers. He quickly stepped aside after his gaze climbed a mountain of Chinese edifice—a Tong bodyguard.

The bodyguard seized Azalea's arm. "You come with me."

"Unhand her!" Grant growled. This bit they had rehearsed.

Henry recoiled and stumbled backward, drawing attention.

Outraged, Azalea slapped at the man's hand. "How dare you! What is the meaning of this?"

He jerked his hand back, stung by her reaction. His wide face crimped in frustration. "My mistake," he said, backing away.

"I should think so!" Azalea huffed, making a show of withdrawing a hanky and wiping her dress where his meaty hand had touched.

Grant winked and drew her close as they boarded. "Now the tricky part," he whispered, amused by the keen lift of her eyebrow.

"Would you care for a bit of exercise, miss?" Henry asked, right on cue and enjoying his role a bit too much.

"Yes, please. Especially after that rude man's behavior." Her voice was surely sufficient for every ear in the car. "I will be sentenced to yet another arduous leg of naught but dreary California landscape soon enough." She flipped her hanky through the air and tapped the parasol on the steel floor, drawing quite an audience.

"Allow me," Grant said, guiding her down the length of the passenger car. "Why don't you secure our berth, *Ah Pok*?"

Henry rolled his eyes at Grant's improvisation and promptly bowed, affecting his part. "Certainly, sir."

Grant opened the door at the end of the car, and he and Azalea stepped outside onto the rear platform.

"Grant!"

His heart flipped at Kira's voice.

Avery stood lookout several feet away as Kira handed up Ubon, whose dress was identical to Azalea's.

Grant pecked his sister's cheek. "Perfect performance milady."

Her cheeks pinked. "I'll pray for you." Her words carried a love he knew was genuine, even after he'd confessed his secret to her. His sister passed the parasol and hat to Ubon and then climbed to the ground. Within seconds, the two blue-bustle-clad women had successfully switched places.

"Come, Azalea," he said to Ubon once she had settled the hat to shadow her face. "We must find our berth." He nodded a fleeting goodbye to the girls and guided her through the door toward their quarters.

Ubon would thrive at Miss Culbertson's Home, for she'd had a grand beginning with Kira.

San Francisco

Weary to the bone, Grant relaxed in the chair and stared at the blue carpet's scrollwork. After an intense meeting with Governor Stoneman in Sacramento, he had continued on to leave Ubon with Miss Culbertson. Then he'd rushed straight here to deliver his report. If his plan had succeeded, he would hear nothing more about the missing prostitute. And his employer would never know what he'd done.

He gnawed the inside of his cheek as Colonel Bee paced the room.

"After your last visit, Grant, Six Companies decided to hire a couple of detectives to glean first-hand knowledge of California's anti-Chinese developments. The successful Eureka purges were such an inspiration to other Californians, we now have nineteen towns to contend with. Each one has drafted bylaws and an-nounced dates to withdraw their patronage of Chinese residents. I'm sure McGleason is taking full credit for every single one of these developments.

"That said, the Chinese minister has pressed Secretary Bayard to demand the U.S. Government intervene before we have a war on our hands. *And,* not only is Six Companies shipping arms to the Chinese, the detectives have informed us that an arms dealer in Sacramento has also shipped an undisclosed number of arms to Truckee's Chinatown."

"I believe I've witnessed the delivery of those firearms, sir. And as you've read in my report, McGleason vows the citizens of Truckee will not be responsible for the safety of the Chinese after January fifteenth. My conversation with the governor was no help whatsoever."

Governor Stoneman had been short with him, insisting repeatedly that no reports of anti-Chinese violence had reached him. And no one had sought his help. He blathered on, blaming the Chinese for crowding the Caucasian race out of different avenues of employment. And while vowing to uphold the law, he still refused to intervene in any of the anti-Chinese rallies—which he "most certainly wouldn't prevent citizens from attending."

Consul Bee rapped his knuckles against the enameled tabletop. "All of that sounds about right. When the Chinese minister asked for the state to protect the Chinese, the Governor offered some hogwash about being capable of performing that duty without the Chinese's suggestion. Bah! The man might as well have announced publicly that every town is free to launch any purge of their choosing."

Grant crossed his ankles and stifled a yawn. "With McGleason's committee targeting every industry, it's just a matter of time before they all give in. His thugs are urging merchants to buy only white-made cigars, and pressure is on lumber companies to rescind every contract for Chinese labor. They're threatening that all Chinese must leave the woods by the fifteenth or else." *And then what? An all-out war?* His blood ran cold. The boycott had taken a turn for the ugly.

There was one thing they hadn't mentioned. He sat up and propped his arms on his thighs. "Sir, what if we were to urge reporters all across the state to publicize the dangerous events as they develop in the Sierra Nevada. It might be eye-opening for those other California towns now considering some of these same extreme measures."

A slow smile spread across the consul's face. The first Grant had ever seen. "You might be onto something, Mr. Campbell. I'll pass this along. And fully recommend it. In the meantime, U.S. Marshal Jonathan Drew will be arriving in Truckee on Wednesday. He has your contact information."

It was about time. Surely a federal presence would make a difference, even with men like Dannon and McGleason.

"And I'm pleased to inform you that Deputy U.S. Marshal Alerman boarded a steamship yesterday. By now he has filed your Wing Hing v City of Eureka lawsuit with the county clerk and is likely serving papers on Mayor Walsh." He clapped a hand onto Grant's shoulder. "A giant first step for the Chinese people to win reparations. And you did that, Grant. With the diligence of us all, there are sure to be more victories ahead."

He'd done that. The satisfaction surged from his feet all the way to his head until he recognized that surely God was responsible for it all. Never again would he assume to understand the Almighty's actions.

"I think that's about it for now. Just continue sending the reports." Bee offered a hand, and Grant stood and clasped it. "Say, what about that Tong prostitute? Were you able to do anything about that?"

He schooled his expression. "I am convinced she isn't even in Truckee anymore, sir."

"As I suspected. I didn't envy you that assignment, but sometimes life gets complicated, even when we try to do the right thing."

Didn't he know it.

Thirty-Five

TRUCKEE

"Mrs. Bensman, whatever is wrong?" Yakira escorted her red-faced friend into the house and hung up her wrap. "Come, sit down." She led her to the parlor and drew her to sit beside her on the sofa. "Tell me."

"I won't be bullied. We ladies demanded Reverend Warren step down effective immediately."

"You didn't . . ."

"How can he preach such hate from the pulpit, claiming to speak for God!" Mrs. Bensman's eyes welled up as she slipped out her hanky.

"What happened?"

"I'm sorry to say he did not take it well, and has instead expelled each of us from the church." She threw back her shoulders as if to cast aside any notion of regret.

"Oh, no. I am so sorry." Was it shock or guilt that pressed against her with such weight? *Dear Father, what have I done?* Had she stirred up a whirlwind by accepting so much help from this dear woman?

"Clarice's husband is furious, so they will definitely be searching for a new house of worship. Belinda and Myrtle have taken to groveling and asking forgiveness for their *lapse in sanity*." Her lips flattened with the shake of her head before her features softened. "And dear, dear, sweet Dorothy will be joining me as we stand by our principles."

"I . . .I don't know what to say. You were expelled from your church because of your support of the Mission Home? Because of me . . ." Tears stung the backs of eyes.

Mrs. Bensman patted her hand. "Oh, my dear. I don't even know if the reverend was privy to that undertaking, unless Belinda or Myrtle told him." Her lips crimped for an instant. "That may be a possibility, but it doesn't bear consideration, as I will *not* sit under such hypocrisy another moment."

"If only more women had your convictions. You are such an encouragement to me. Thank you for all you have done, all you have provided. What a blessing you have been. God has used you beyond what you know."

Her friend smiled, and new lines sprouted from the corners of her eyes. "Oh, I'm not done supporting your Home, my dear. I'm afraid it leaves only Dorothy and myself, but help, we will. No ridiculous boycott or threats will keep these hands from God's work. You just give me a list of what you need, and I will see what I can do."

A single teardrop coursed down Yakira's cheek, and she brushed it away. She hugged Mrs. Bensman, suddenly overwhelmed. If this woman would risk everything for her Home, then *she* would certainly continue to do the same.

Mrs. Bensman stood. "I really must be going, but there is one other reason I stopped by." Her smile faltered. "I overheard that dreadful Mr. McGleason mention that one of the Committee members must pay you a visit."

"But they've been here. Twice." Their benign threats had no claws, just noise. And the Home had continued on just fine, hadn't it?

"I'm concerned this time will be different. Please tell your father, won't you? It would be best if he is here when they come."

Yakira nodded, her gaze darting to the armoire where her second line of defense hid. Her first was on her knees.

"Thank you for meeting with me, Grant, Avery." Mr. Crocker rolled his desk chair around to the front of his massive desk and bid them sit in the two facing chairs.

Grant stared at the photo on the wall. He'd seen a similar photo a dozen times, but this one was different. Instead of only white men posing at the point where the golden spike was pounded into the ground, this photograph was of the Chinese men whose sweat and blood made the venture possible. It told the *true* story, and Charles Crocker knew it. It's what Grant liked about the man.

They sat in silence as Mr. Crocker worked a cigar, fogging the room with a languid cloud. Finally, he slapped a paper onto the desk beside him. "This is drivel. McGleason is delusional: *'Chinese are rapidly driven out of Truckee by peaceful means, departing in large numbers.'* Tell me, Avery, how many residents of Chinatown do you estimate have actually left?"

"No more than a hundred. And the ones remaining suffer lack of food." Uncle Avery crossed an ankle over his knee, leaned back, and laced his hands. "They're tough, the Tang men. They're not easily moved by threats. Families may evacuate, but not the men.

And they are fully prepared to defend themselves when the time comes, of that I'm certain."

"So I hear." Mr. Crocker retrieved a newspaper from the small wastebasket next to the desk. CHINESE ARMED blazed across the front page. "McGleason is stirring up every vein of public opinion against them. He paints the white man as peaceful and the Chinese man as a disease. He can't print the sordid *news* fast enough."

"Even in their own country, 'tis the way of it. The hierarchy with the Chinese villagers and the highbinders . . ." Uncle Avery's eyes glazed, and Grant knew he was remembering his years in China. "Tuck Chan's loan has been called in by the bank. Even if he's forced into bankruptcy, he'll dig in. It willna be pretty."

Crocker grunted. "Folks are flooding in from out of town to take the place of the Chinese. How long do you think it'll take McGleason to realize the truth? Work won't go to Truckee's jobless whites—the folks he supposedly started this crusade for in the first place. Nope. Washerman, mill-worker, and woodcutter jobs will go to transients instead."

Of course. And not before job seekers from hundreds of miles around flood the entire area. Grant ran his hands down the length of his thighs before sitting up straighter. Unsure of where the facts ended and the rumors started, he had to ask. "Is it true there are accusations of threats driving woodcutters out of jobs? Threats to the mills if they don't rescind contracts?"

"I'm afraid it goes much deeper than that. Loans are being called in on a number of businesses—Chinese *and* white. Reputable businesses. Since McGleason has renounced his nonviolence tactic now, I'm expecting a blood bath one way or another."

Uncle Avery dropped his foot to the floor with a thud and sat up. "But surely now that Marshal Drew is here, he'll put a stop to any further violence."

Crocker shook his head. "Not where Dannon is concerned, at least. The man has always had a taste for the rougher ways of getting what he wants, which is why I fired him all those years ago. But McGleason flipping like this, changing tactic?"

The swing from the no-violence pact had Six Companies panicked, too. Stir the pot a bit more, and they'd have the makings of a California civil war on their hands. He ground his teeth, sick to death of feeling powerless.

Mr. Crocker cast a snake of smoke into the air. "That paper-pusher managed to outfit every one of my mill customers with petitions. I'm talking about customers across a three-state area! My partner is prepared to wage an all-out war on the man. I don't want to see it come to that, though. As a matter of business, I have $6,000–$10,000 advanced to my Chinese workers in the form of provisions and supplies. I can't *afford* to fire them."

"You won't have to." Grant stood slowly and crossed the floor, working out some details in his mind. "If it comes to it, let me represent you, Mr. Crocker. As a mediator." And he would investigate the bank contracts on the called-in loans. If Eureka had reaped the whirlwind, he'd make sure the town of Truckee, McGleason, and Dannon reaped something far worse.

February 1886

Yakira lowered the shade, blotting out the sun's friendly rays. Yet another gang of white men tromped down the street with signs and jeers that plainly flaunted their intent. Voices hurled angry shouts—threats no proper woman should hear. They seethed with disdain for all Chinese, determined to spread their vile plague to every citizen in the Sierra Nevada region.

She leaned her back against the wall, the uproar wringing her senses. For the girls' sakes, she must hold it together. And she had decided anger was better than fear. Even townspeople from surrounding communities had joined the frightful night marches. Now the long, fiery parades snaked their way through the streets every night. The entire town was overcome—tempers and maliciousness blazing through every home, every business.

She dropped the heavy textbook onto the table with a thud. Six pairs of eyes watched her. "I am sorry for the distraction. I know it is hard to ignore them"—she glanced toward the window—"but please try. Now, where were we?"

A commotion in the entry drew her attention, so she turned the class over to Shu and scurried from the dining room. Aunt Lara stood with her back against the door as it shook violently, pounded from the other side. She held one finger to her tight lips.

"Open the door, laaa-dies! It's official business." The gruff voice mocked them, sounding altogether drunk. "On behalf of the Committee to purge Truckee of—"

Another voice interrupted. "By order of Committee-man Howard Dannon and the town of Truckee, you are hereby ordered to vacate these premises by midnight tonight. You have been duly warned." The men guffawed, and the door lurched with a kick.

Silence.

"Miss Yakira?" Mei's frightened face poked around the edge of the dining room.

She rushed to comfort the girl. "Just some troublemakers, dear. Go back with the other girls." She turned her about gently. "All is well." But her insides screamed, *all most certainly is not well!*

Mrs. Bensman warned about a visit. Was that it? Poor dear Mrs. Bensman had been discovered providing the Home with groceries and was thus boycotted from purchases of any kind herself.

She covered her mouth with a hand, undone as worry plied its seducing smirk. *Take therefore no thought for the morrow.* Tomorrow. Their stores had dwindled. Once the flour and lentils ran out, what would they do? At least Six Companies had shipped rice for the starving Chinese.

She hugged herself to banish the shiver that coursed through her. The boycotts had been deemed ineffective. And now violence and extreme measures reared up in their place, forcing everyone to kowtow to the hatemongers. *Take therefore no thought for the morrow.*

Azalea pattered down the stairs, a welcome interruption. "I heard." She knotted her hands and wet her lips before speaking. "The girls and I have not left this house for weeks. Perhaps it is time we went to San Francisco. Surely we could make it to the train station with bodyguards."

Aunt Lara wrapped her arms around her daughter, kissing the top of her head. "I don't know. We must pray, seek wisdom." Azalea nodded, melting into her mother's embrace.

Yakira touched Azalea's arm tenderly. "God has a plan, my lao-tong." She wanted to encourage, but the whispered words echoed feebly in her ears. *Does* God truly have a plan? If God chose her, perhaps it was for such a time as this. Like Queen Esther, might she make a difference somehow for the people of her heart?

Hadn't Grant made a difference? He'd accomplished much for Eureka's Chinese, and now he worked tirelessly for Truckee immigrants. Every day he filed lawsuits, drew up depositions, reported the events to big-city newspapers, and sent telegrams to state and federal officials. He was doing what he did best.

Weariness weighed on her heart. Grant had presented countless mills and lumbermen to U.S. Marshal Drew in order to persuade them to stand against McGleason and Dannon. And each one had buckled, save one—Sisson and Crocker. *One.*

If even Grant couldn't turn the tide, how could she ever make a difference?

Thirty-Six

Gut-punched at the man's decision, Grant watched Charles Crocker pace the width of his office. "Are you sure this is the way you want to play this?"

"They've threatened to tar and feather our manager, for Pete's sake." Mr. Crocker raked a hand through the length of his wiry white beard. "That U.S. marshal's certainly not doing his bit to protect people. If he had the grit to haul McGleason and Dannon out on their ears, maybe the decent folks could take back the town." His imposing form wilted as he shook his head. "But I don't see that happening. Do you?"

Grant circled the tip of his pen on the paper. Every ounce of Crocker's frustration seethed in his own veins. "I don't understand why he's not made more arrests, either."

"Well, if he's there tonight, he'll get a taste of Truckee politics at its finest."

Grant huffed, dreading another public meeting. "At my request, Colonel Bee has telegraphed the Governor, Secretary Bayard, and

Congressman Morrow. He's requesting troops to suppress the growing mobs." He hated to see it come to martial law, but if that's what it took . . .

"Congressman Morrow has been seeking to tighten immigration laws, so what McGleason is doing doesn't bode well for his efforts. The entire United States is watching Truckee at the moment." *And watching this cancer spread*, Grant thought.

"And if troops are actually deployed, how long will it take them to get here?"

Crocker's question was legitimate, considering how long it took the U.S. marshal to show up. "I can't say."

Resignation flattened the contours of Crocker's face. "You'll present my final offer to them at the meeting?"

The decision gnawed at him. It just didn't sit right, and it was fully against his better judgement. "If you're sure that's the way you want to play it."

He had asked for the floor, not only on Mr. Crocker's behalf but also for personal reasons. What he had planned would amount to exhausting his last round of ammunition. Whether or not it would make a difference—it was all he had left.

"Order!" James Reed, the constable appointed by McGleason's mob back in December, attempted to commence the town meeting. The crush of bodies afforded but a shoulder-space around the edge of the room. "Order!" The constable raised a revolver, poised to shoot into the air before the crowd finally simmered.

Grant looked at his notes again. The letters blurred on the paper, and he blinked, struck with the thought that God could give him better words than he could ever formulate. He'd prayed earlier, asking the Almighty to intervene on behalf of Charles Crocker and help the people see truth this evening. And by the looks of the crowd, only a miracle would suffice. He stuffed his notes into the box under his chair, making sure his visual aids were still there.

"I'd like to introduce you to U.S. Marshal Drew," Reed said. *Boos* peppered the crowd, and the marshal scowled, passing a quick look to Grant. "And we will be hearing from the Attorney for Six Companies—" Shouts obliterated the rest as loud curses fouled the air from a cluster of men in the front. A brown, viscous wad splattered against the podium.

The uproar rattled his ears, but not his resolve. He honed his focus on the platform and donned his prosecutor face—a bull ready to spring from the gate and throw his rider to the ground.

"And we will also hear from our own Robert McGleason." Applause and hoots erupted, leaving but a few disgruntled faces amid the biased mob. The constable waved down the ruckus before continuing. "Our guest has asked to speak first." He turned to Grant, yielding the floor.

He stood on wooden legs and mounted the platform. Perusing the crowd, he searched for some sense of objectivity. He made eye contact briefly with Uncle Avery, towering a head above most, even from his seat. Henry stood against one wall, arms crossed, hat low, and his queue secreted away. Since Mr. Crocker's approval rating had taken a sour turn, he had chosen not to come at the last minute for fear of instigating a riot.

Constable Reed quieted the room and sat while Grant placed his notes on the podium and the box on the floor. "First of all," he began, "I stand here on behalf of my client, Charles Crocker.

Clamors swelled again.

He turned to the constable. "Sir, if they are going to continue to act like a bunch of rowdy schoolboys, there will be nothing accomplished here tonight."

Reed nodded and stood. "Now boys, we're gonna hear out everyone on this platform, all right? You will silence your comments until we are finished. If you're unwilling to, leave now or spend the night in jail." Grumbles trailed, but no one left.

Grant thanked him and began again. "In response to petitions demanding the expulsion of every Chinese person in their employ, Sisson and Crocker offers to bind the firm to never again employ a Chinese laborer under one stipulation—that the committee allows the firm to fulfill current contracts due to expire on June 1, 1886."

"Uh, excuse me, Mr. Campbell." Judge Keiser stood in the front row. "I'd like to offer a response to this proposal on behalf of the city at this time."

The judge promptly mounted the platform, even as Grant cast a disapproving look at the constable, who simply shrugged. He approached the podium, but Grant didn't budge. He nodded professionally but groused inwardly. Let someone try that in *his* courtroom.

"It has come to light that Sisson and Crocker are at a loss right now of between six and ten thousand dollars due to current investments that would be lost if the Chinese laborers were let go immediately." The judge's voice bounced off the back wall as he waxed judiciously. "That being the case, the merchants of Truckee, without any provocation, have donated a substantial sum of six thousand dollars to offset Sisson and Crocker's losses *if* the firm will discharge all their Chinese employees immediately. This offer expires at midnight tomorrow night."

An unmistakable voice harangued. "Sisson and Crocker can rot with the rest of the Chinese lovers."

Constable Reed sprang to his feet. He overrode the last word with one hand on his sidearm. "This is your only warning, Dannon!"

"My humble apologies," Dannon oozed. "Please, continue." A slippery smile creased his mug as he deferred to the platform with a flourish.

The judge stepped down, and Grant began again. "Thank you, Judge Keiser." He stumbled over his next words, distracted by two men who seemed intent on Henry. They eyed him, shuffling several feet closer, whispering between themselves.

"I . . . uh, will convey your offer to my client," Grant said, forcing his attention back to the moment. "But for those of you who do not subscribe to the *San Francisco Argonaut*"—he produced the newspaper from the box, snapped it open to display and read the headlines. "STORM OF BLOOD ACROSS OUR SIERRA; SISSON CROCKER HAVE THE RIGHT UNDER LAW TO REFUSE TO DISCHARGE."

A disgruntled hum rose in a wave, receding when Reed stood. He remained standing as Grant continued. "I have another item I'd like to show you." He retrieved two framed photographs. Holding up the first one, he said, "Most everyone around these parts has seen this famous photo. It appeared in every newspaper in the country." He made a show of looking at it himself. "I see some pretty influential men in this picture, all of whom you are likely familiar with, including your own Charles Crocker.

"But *this* is the photo that should've been printed for all to see." He held up the picture from Crocker's office wall. "For in *this* photo you see not the brain trust behind the Railroad's construction and completion, but the very men responsible. In fact, you see the actual calloused hands that drove the multitude of spikes and forged the steel."

Good. He had their attention. He propped the photos on the podium and strolled several paces to the left, rubbing his hands together with each measured step. Energy sizzled through him, familiar and empowering. With an affable smile pinned to his lips, he cast his gaze over the audience. He was just getting started.

"Let me indulge you in a bit of a history lesson, if I may. After two years and a mere fifty miles of track laid, Charles Crocker became convinced that the Asian race that had built the Great Wall of China could also build his dream. At first, he was met with resistance—until the white men watched Chinese men dig tunnels through forty-foot snowdrifts to lay track. Even when Avalanches whisked workers away, and tunnels collapsed, still, the Chinese worked on. Come the spring thaw, men were discovered still standing, still holding their tools, faces frozen in death masks."

Only the scuff of his boots touched the silence as he turned to pace in the opposite direction.

"Chinese laborers dynamited through 1,700 feet of solid rock to create the Donner Tunnels, right here in our own backyard. It was the Chinese who built a Central Pacific line that rose 7,000 feet in 100 miles."

His pulse thrummed as words erupted, impassioned and unpredictable. "Chinese who dangled in wicker baskets along sheer cliffs to chisel through granite and shale, carving out shelves on which to lay track. With hammers, crowbars, and dynamite they made the earth yield"—he pounded the air with his fist—"to the ambitions of the Big Four."

He snatched up his visual aid again and stepped around the podium to the very front of the platform, brandishing the true photograph. "And if that isn't enough to stir some measure of admiration for these resourceful, tenacious, industrious people—the very minute that golden spike was placed at Promontory Summit in Utah, 11,000 Chinese workers were immediately out of a job—workers brought to these United States for *our* indulgences!" He needed it to sink in, to change their perspective.

"Fourteen-hundred of these hardworking men moved here, to Truckee. They arrived already skilled in masonry, track-laying, ironwork, cooking, and dynamiting—a fully skilled workforce with tenacious wills." He set the picture back and held out both hands, beseeching. What more could he do to make them see?

"These men brought you the means for prosperity, people. *Prosperity*. And hear this. Before these men achieved what no one else could, this town, your town of Truckee was a mere two-store stop."

He crossed the platform, touching his gaze to dozens. "And just ten years past, it was the Chinese alone who worked tirelessly to reclaim 500 million acres of the Sacramento Delta, where land values soared from one dollar an acre to one hundred dollars an acre because of their work. And every penny of profit went to the white man. I say again. Every penny of profit from their hard work went to white men."

He chewed his cheek a moment and approached the very edge of the platform, towering over the array of mixed expressions. He waited several beats, tossing a prayer heavenward when it seemed his steam had dissipated to the rafters.

"Citizens of Truckee, let me say this one last thing, then I will leave you to your meeting. Former Governor Leland Stanford in his inaugural address called the Chinese an inferior race and said they should be discouraged from settling by every legitimate means. But later that same year, he became president of the Central Pacific Railroad. He very soon discovered his colossal need for Chinese laborers. An embarrassing situation for the man, wouldn't you say?" A few nods of agreement.

"So I ask you, people of Truckee, if our governor can change his opinions, his biases—why can't we? Do you really want the drivel you spew today to end up being the crow you eat tomorrow?" Exhaustion covered him like a lead blanket. How tired he was of the fight. But fight he must.

Palms together, he entreated them to recognize truth. "When you find that life without these unstoppable Chinese people is not all you dreamed it would be, I pray you will remember the words I've spoken tonight." He envisioned the military troops, the mayhem. Kira's Mission Home. "For everyone's sakes, I hope you will not reap the whirlwind."

He collected his box and left the platform. A stream of hisses and epithets followed him to the back of the room, where he joined Uncle Avery. He sat down at last, every inch of him board-stiff. That was all he had.

In the next few minutes, McGleason whipped the crowd into a frenzy. His own venomous threats soundly snuffed his original message of a peaceful boycott against Crocker and Sisson. He raised a call for punishment of all Chinese advocates and finally ended with feral demands that Congress withdraw from the Burlingame Treaty and amend the Exclusion Act so no Chinese leaving the U.S. could ever return.

"We'd better get out of here," Uncle Avery said. He funneled Henry out the door ahead of them an instant before the doorway jammed with a disorderly exodus. Men broke out and across the street, propelling their ferocity in every direction.

Henry seemed to vanish, disappearing into the darkness. Panic squeezed Grant's middle as he scouted the mass of men. "Henry!"

"I dinna see him!" Uncle shouted, already jostled several feet from their position. "Henry!"

Please, God. Protect him. They'd been so careful never to leave him on his own. None of the Chinese left Chinatown anymore. In fact, they'd posted guards at the bridge and along the river to keep troublemakers from sneaking into Chinatown. "Henry!" This was all *his* fault. He'd never forgive himself if anything happened to him. "Henry!"

Someone grabbed his arm, and Grant whirled, hoping it was Henry.

But it was Uncle Avery's firm grip on him, suddenly yanking him along, stepping sideways through the advancing throng.

"We have to find him. There's no telling what some of these men might do to him." He couldn't think about it. *God, please.*

Moving as fast as they could, they pushed and shoved their way to the far side of the building. "Henry!" Grant hopped onto the base of a streetlamp for a better view and yelled one last time. His breath pumped from his lungs, and his hollowed insides screamed, for nowhere did he see Henry.

Grant slowed his pace and turned. "Uncle."

Bent over, both hands on his thighs, Uncle Avery heaved for breath as he waved Grant on ahead.

"He's got to be home by now, right?" Grant said, more to himself. He sprinted toward the house once again. They had rushed home after the meeting, praying Henry would greet them with some silly crack about slow white men. When they realized he hadn't beat them home, they rushed back to the meeting house, looking for him through dark yards and alleys.

Just when desperation sought to overtake him, he spied a crumpled figure on the front steps of the Mission Home and ran. "Henry!" He stumbled to a stop, touching his friend's shoulder. Greeted by only a groan, Grant sat beside him, wishing for a bit of light. "Who did this to you?" Another moan. "Can you walk?"

No response. Uncle Avery appeared down the block and began jogging. Without a word, he held the door while Grant carried Henry into the house and all the way up to their room, leaving a trail of frantic female sobs and questions.

Kira opened the room, sending everyone away but Azalea. Henry moaned, his slitted eyes flashing fiercely when he saw the women. "No. Leave me!" The harsh words brought them up short.

Grant jerked his head toward the door. "I'll tend him."

Uncle Avery puffed his way into the room and batted Kira away. "Leave him to us. You lassies pray." He closed the bedroom door as Grant settled Henry carefully onto the bed.

When Uncle Avery turned up the gaslight, Henry winced and curled on his side like a babe. He brought his knees to his chest. His wet face reflected the yellow light.

Grant sank to his knees with the sudden realization why Henry didn't want anyone to see him. Aside from the scarlet cheek and gashed brow, another wound would be a long-time healing, for Henry's long, sleek queue was no more.

Thirty-Seven

TRUCKEE

"You cannot be serious!" Words like *blind* and *spineless* came to mind as Grant stared down the U.S. marshal, utterly dumbfounded.

"Mr. Campbell, I have no fear whatsoever of lawlessness on the part of whites."

"How can you say that after what they did to my translator?"

Marshal Drew huffed, removed his Cahill Hat, and stroked the felt. "This really isn't my purview. It's the governor's job to protect the Chinese in Truckee, not mine. My work here is done. I will report my observations back to Consul Bee."

Marshal Drew extended a hand. Grant just stared at it, rolling the man's words over in his mind. "I don't know if you're just ignorant or lazy, but there is definitely more you could do. The federal government has much at stake here. Don't you see what Truckee's little game is doing to the rest of California? What about the rest of the *country*? When this cancer has spread from coast to coast rending the already blood-stained fabric of America, *then* will it be your problem, Marshal?" The shiny star on his chest mocked Grant as it rose and fell.

The man donned his hat. "Sometimes things just *are*, Mr. Campbell." He touched a finger to his brim and strode off toward the train depot.

Grant seethed, shooting bullets at the man's back with his eyes. He stood there for several moments to let the fury ease. *Well, Lord, it's in Your hands.* Where it needed to remain.

He marched down Front Street, stunned by the garish new banner tacked up at the Truckee Horse and Engine Company: ORGANIZED TO PROTECT WHITE MEN'S PROPERTY. And over the entrance, a smaller one proclaimed: OUR NEXT GOVERNOR, R.F. MCGLEASON, WHITE LABOR'S CHAMPION.

God help them all.

His head throbbed, and the urge to lie down and sleep for a month drew him toward home, where Henry had spent the last week in bed, more from depression than from his injuries. A Chinese man would rather die than part with his queue. This, he'd known from birth. He ached for his friend, praying that he'd soon let Azalea back into his life, for if anyone could help Henry make sense of it all, it was his little sister.

He kicked at the dirt like a schoolboy, feeling sorry for himself. Mr. Crocker had crumbled in the face of McGleason's mob and rescinded all of his Chinese contracts, taking the financial loss. When a man like Crocker falls, the message it sends is catastrophic to their cause—the toppling of a mighty redwood, earthshaking and gone forever.

Ho Wah and Shen Bow had vacated the basement, and Avery's tiny church was no more. A shepherd without a flock, he was. Mired in a mournful bog, he set one leaden foot before the other, laboring to keep up with Grant as they walked.

He'd faltered in his calling after Cait's death, so lost he was to grief and futility during those first couple of years in America. But for his beloved Yakira, he would have returned to the highlands and lived out his days in a wee cottage—a hermit, tending to a green little garden and a deep well of sorrow.

That same feeling flogged him now. Unless God intervened, 'twas no reason for his family to remain in Truckee, for every westbound train spirited away more Chinese every day. *God has a plan.* The oft-said words begot pity. Surely God *did* have a plan. But what was it?

And what of Lara? The thought of leaving her behind again drove him lower. The time without her in Eureka was a test he'd failed. Her presence was a part of him after all these years—an arm he'd not cut off. Nae. Not an arm. 'Twas his heart he'd be leaving behind this time. *Och!* Whatever was to become of them all?

He followed Grant across the bridge to Chinatown, set on purchasing rice. Instead of a few armed guards, a picket line of over thirty Chinese men met them.

"Why the increased security?" Avery asked in Cantonese, observing the strapped revolvers and rifles. As he conversed with them, the answers soured his already *shooglie* mood.

"What did they say?" Grant asked as the guards parted for them to enter.

"Their stores have been robbed. Everything gone."

"Even the rice from Six Companies?"

"All of it." How would the Chinese stay and fight without food? The *ill-scrappit* truth set his bones rigid. What was next?

They trekked down the dusty street. Gone were many of the familiar faces with whom Avery had spent countless hours in conversation, persuading them of a God who loved them dearly. A God who saw them. He hailed a greeting to Zae Quo, the shoemaker who was packing his sewing machine into a crate.

"I'd like to deliver a message to Tuck Chan," Grant said, keeping a slow pace beside him.

"Of course." In a short time, Avery found the merchant busy in his shop. They talked of the devastating news that both the Central and Northern Pacific lines had discharged all of their Chinese workers.

"It is hard times," Tuck Chan said. He looked to Grant. "Even Six Companies has no power to stop what happens."

Defeat seemed to sag Grant's stature as he handed him a telegram. "This came in yesterday. The Mexican government has extended an invitation for Chinese laborers to seek work in Mexico. It *is* an option."

The proud man's eyes followed an overflowing cart for a moment as it rolled past. His chin dipped in a slow nod as he took the envelope. "I will pass this along."

"I am sorry I can't do more right now." Grant offered his hand, and when Tuck Chan wrapped both hands around his and bowed, Grant stuttered in broken Cantonese, "Please forgive my failed efforts."

Avery warmed at the exchange. He truly cared, this nephew of his. How hard he'd fallen when his faither died. How far he'd traveled in his escape. But now he was home. Truly home. Avery blinked back grateful tears and added his own hands to theirs. He had no words.

After leaving Chinatown, they passed the burned-out hull of a small barn. Vigilantes had decided the owner had not been swift enough in firing his part-time gardener. At the next street, a lamppost tilted at an odd angle, its globe shattered, like many others around town. Such destruction. Such hatred.

He glanced at Grant, not surprised at the stony set of his face. The lad had to know he'd done all he could. He'd fought the good fight, he had. His da would've been proud. Verra proud indeed.

On the corner of River near the livery, a boisterous clutch of men he didn't recognize congregated, no-doubt bent on troublemaking.

Grant shook his head. "Probably came for jobs but don't like the wages offered. Now the townspeople will bear the brunt of their malcontent."

"Aye. And I fear 'twill grow worse. How long do ye think before McGleason realizes his plan is backfiring?"

Grant shook his head in disgust. "The man is blinded by his own ambitions, and he's taking the town down with him." He huffed and walked a little faster.

"Can ye imagine—a Governor like him? It turns me stomach *peely-wally*. If the devil wears tweed, he lives in Truckee, for certain."

Yakira stepped over the glass shards and picked up the paper-wrapped rock. The second one this week. She knew the vile contents before she read them: *Chinese lovers not welcome. Vacate now.*

Azalea stepped from the corner where she had quickly gathered Shu and Lian like a mother hen. She peered out the window and motioned frantically for Yakira.

They watched in silence as a dozen men with torches congregated on the front lawn. Darkness had not completely fallen, but the chilled finger that drew along Yakira's spine told her she had to do something.

"Oh, where are Uncle Avery and Grant?" Azalea's voice whined, uncharacteristically. She wrung her hands and began to pace.

Never had Yakira witnessed such a breach in Azalea's usual peace. Was there a soul who did not envy her trusting, confident nature? Not even when trapped in a burning cellar had her laotong shriveled like this. Yakira looked at the two girls, wrenched by the fear she saw there. They couldn't live like this anymore.

Slippers padded down the stairs, and Aunt Lara appeared. "What was that?" She took in the glass, the paper in Yakira's hand. "Not again." She crossed to Azalea. A mother's arm quickly shored up the dainty shoulders to ease their burden.

Yakira opened the armoire, and Aunt Lara gasped. "Oh Kira, no."

"Apparently those men only speak one language. Let's see if they understand this." Ire sharpened her resolve and honed her determination to a biting edge. *Enough*! She loaded two shells and strode to the front door. With one hand on the doorknob, she cast a long look at Azalea. Her eyes glistened back, and unspoken words floated between them.

It was all Yakira needed.

She stepped onto the front porch, and the mob quieted. "Get out of here! Leave this home at once!" She hated the way her voice quivered on the last word.

Loud laughter. Hecklers mocking her demands.

Anger roiled through her veins. She pointed the muzzle at the clouds and pulled the trigger. The air exploded, striking the men silent. Shocked faces stared back at her. "The next one is for one of you!" She dug in, tenacity sharpening her claws as she thought of the terrified girls huddled behind the furniture by now. She had only one shot left.

A stranger held up his hands. "Don't do something you're gonna regret, Miss. Just put that down nice and slow." He started up the stairs, and she leveled the gun barrel at him.

"One more step, and you'll see just how far I'm willing to go to protect my girls." She moved closer, straight and strong as an oak.

One of Dannon's own, Dan Flint, stepped up to the man, touching his elbow. "Leave it, Mars. It ain't worth it. There's an easier way." His eyes raked her from head to foot, a serpentine smile sending a message that curdled her blood.

She dared not move lest they sense the quiver that snaked its way through her frame. The barrel stayed its target until the men were well away—until she saw Grant sprinting toward her, wild-eyed, cutting his way through the retreating men. He bounded to the porch, wordlessly tipped the muzzle skyward, and took the gun. One muscular arm enfolded her, and only then did her legs give way.

Leaving the shotgun on the porch, he carried her through the door to the sofa and settled her onto the soft cushions. Nausea churned, and her head swirled, but she fought the onslaught.

"Kira girl, are you all right?" His voice covered her like a warm blanket, and she reached for him, needing the strength of his arms again.

How she hated the hot tears that leaked onto his crisp white shirt. And she hated the way his voice crooned to soothe her, his love coloring every word. She'd been so rigid with him, so unwilling to offer grace when he needed it most.

The door banged open, and Da's voice boomed, "What has happened?" He held the shotgun in one hand.

She looked up, just now aware of all the concerned gazes and feeling a bit foolish. She had been strong, hadn't she? But it was apparently short-lived, for now all she wanted was to crumple into a heap.

"Let's get you up to bed," Aunt Lara's voice broke in.

"I'll carry you," Grant offered, rising with his hand still upon her.

His gaze pressed her, determined. Its jeweled intensity speared her with longing. The longing that coursed through her wrung her heart, returning her to when she'd tasted of his passion. Suddenly his gaze moved to her lips. When his eyes rose to hers again, an unmistakable desire blazed there.

A delightful shiver rippled through her. "I can walk, Counselor."

"And I can carry you." His corded arms swooped her up before she could protest further, and he charged up the stairs.

She let herself relax in his arms, her nose buried blissfully in his neck as she smiled at Da's hushed question to Aunt Lara: "What was that all about?"

Thirty-Eight

Yakira watched on as her girls chatted happily and ate their meager helpings of rice. A measure of joy sweetened the satisfaction she felt. These precious young women had changed so much. They positively beamed. Each of them had a story to tell. Tales of heartbreak, rejection, and abuse had sullied their spirits. But no longer were they bound by their past. What a privilege it had been to have a hand in their new lives—God's fingers at work through her to make a difference for them.

Yet the unknown still suffocated her heart. Where would they find food for the next few days? Wherever would they make their home? For it was certain not to be in Truckee. She blinked back tears, suddenly drained of trying and hoping. All she had wanted was to offer what Miss Culbertson had offered for so many. Why, oh why had she been prevented time and time again?

She felt a hand cover hers and looked up.

"We all have heavy hearts these days." Azalea's sweet smile told her she understood.

Oh, the somersaults inside her! The doubts and the searching, the hopes and the waiting—even the way she had badgered God for justice such as the woman in the Bible had demanded from the judge.

"You must eat to keep up your strength, my dear," Aunt Lara encouraged her. "I have a wee treat for us for dinner this eve."

The words were meant to excite, to encourage them to hold on for yet another dreary day. Vigilantes had trampled the vegetable garden, and there would be no more rice from Chinatown. What else could there possibly be? Perhaps something from San Francisco?

Da burst through the back door, a large box in his arms. "'Tis Christmas early, ladies." He settled the box on the table as Zara pushed empty bowls aside. "From Crocker's store. I had to retrieve it in secret, of course." Da stepped back with a chuckle as the girls purred with excitement and dug into the box.

Two large bags of flour and tins of fruit, three dozen eggs and powdered milk! It *did* feel like Christmas. Yakira flung her arms around his neck, something she hadn't done of late. When she pulled back, she found his face aglow, eyes misted. "Please tell him thank you. From all of us."

Hands pulled more blessed food from the box, and she laughed for the joy of such a simple thing. God was truly watching over them.

She looked up to witness the silent communication between Aunt Lara and Da. The spark in her aunt's eye and the subtle tilt of her lips. His nod and the way his gaze linked with hers. It had been their way for years. They knew one another so well. But was that not the way of her and Azalea's sisterhood?

It was also the way it had been between her and Grant. Before.

Unbidden, her skin tingled at the memory of his kisses, and her blood fired. She missed him the moment he walked out the door last week. Why did it seem he was always leaving her? And why was she always pushing him away?

The room was a flurry of cleanup and menu planning. Lian and Shu raced to see who would sweep the floor, and Mei beat them to it. The room tittered with the silly victory, and soon the last of the dishes were set to drain.

Yakira sighed softly, setting a bowl on the shelf with the others. Henry had been so reluctant to leave with Grant this time. It seemed his spirited nature was cut off along with his magnificent queue. He and Grant had argued soundly, and Grant threatened to fire him if he didn't come along. In jest, surely, for she knew they had become the best of friends. Grant needed a friend like Henry. Like her *brother*.

Azalea bumped her hip. "You are very quiet."

"Just thinking too much, I guess."

"Planning our feast?" she said, her lips pursed, brows lifted in mischief. "We will eat like queens tonight."

"Yes. We shall." But across the river, there were those who would go to bed hungry. And she was helpless to do anything about it.

Chico, California

"You want me to ship my produce to Penryn?" John Bidwell leaned back in the leather desk chair, hands folded across an ample belly.

"Where it will all be repacked and relabeled." Grant told him, more than a little eager to suggest such a sleight of hand to the former congressman.

"And then my produce will be sent on for sale."

"Exactly. You'll be selling your goods in Truckee, Reno, Carson, Virginia City—and no one will be the wiser." Pleased as realization lit the man's face, he continued. "Think what it will mean for the boycott if one of the largest growers in the state manages to circumvent it—completely within the confines of its own language. You'll be an inspiration to every grower and business being bullied into cooperation with the boycott."

"And I don't have to fire any of my Chinese or Indian field workers?" Bidwell's mouth finally kicked up in a tilted smile.

"Not a one." Grant stood. "Do we have an understanding?"

"We certainly do, Mr. Campbell." The man rounded the desk, his jowls shaking with a laugh as he extended a hand. "We certainly do."

"Wonderful. I'll just let myself out. Thank you for seeing me, sir." He found Henry right where he'd left him, sitting in a chair out on the boardwalk, one leg crossed over his knee.

"Well?" Henry ran a hand through his shorn hair, plopped on his derby with a tap, and stood.

"One word."

"Home?"

Ah, his friend had not lost his sense of humor after all. "No. *Victory*. The word is *victory*, Henry." He slapped him on the back and started walking. "The sooner we catch the next train to San Francisco, the sooner we *can* go home."

Henry flailed the air with his hat, cowboy style. "Yee haw! Let's get to it, then."

Grant chuckled. Henry was back to his old self. "Let's go home. *Ah Pok*."

San Francisco

"You asked Marshal Drew to return to Truckee?" Grant couldn't believe what he was hearing. He imagined the man's reaction, knowing how he felt about not being needed there.

Col. Bee nodded. "His reply was, and I quote"—he thumped the desk between them—"'I will not return to Truckee just because some accidental drunken row may arise, and violence be done the Chinese.'" A perfect imitation of the pompous lawman.

Unbelievable. "We tried, sir."

"And we will keep trying. Now that McGleason has been elected to the San Jose State Convention of the Anti-Chinese League, we'll be spending more precious months fighting *his* drivel—on top of the boycott clubs created all over California, thanks to him. You've met the man, Grant. I ask you, does he ever sleep?"

"Obviously not. Truckee is already polluted with signs supporting his run for governor."

"Governor? Now there's a thought to keep a man in his cups." Bee chortled. "Fortunately, we're starting to see some disasterous effects of McGleason's scheme. Our detectives have wind of a consortium formed by some of the leading employers. They purpose to reduce the wages of the white workingmen to below those previously paid to Chinese. That ought to add a little sting to the medicine—along with the suffering of tourism thanks to the hotels' and mountain inns' inability to acquire food or staff."

"Exactly what I've observed in the Sierra Nevada, sir. I see ads in every newspaper, but cheap, white labor is not emerging as the entire boycott plan had counted on. Even lumber camps cannot staff their cookhouses. The trickle-down effect is hard to hide."

"You met with John Bidwell?"

"Yes, sir, on the way here. He is wholly on board with my idea of repackaging."

Bee threw his hands in the air. "Excellent! That's no small victory for our side."

"Threats are still blazing toward hold-out businesses, though." Grant slipped an envelope from his valise and handed it to Col. Bee.

Withdrawing a match from the envelope, Bee asked, "What's this?"

"A threat. One of many sent to the last two smaller mills before they folded. I did have success speaking to Schubert and Meyer growers. They've agreed to give jobs back to all one hundred fifty of their Chinese employees after the boycott burns itself out."

"From the sound of things, the writing is on the wall, so to speak. McGleason will probably be the last to recognize it."

Grant passed a thick folder across the desk. "The lawsuit against Truckee, amended with all of my notes. Some witnesses are no longer in the area, unfortunately."

Bee slapped a hand on top of the folder. "Excellent. I'll let you know as soon as I get through it. We need to dot every 'i' on this one. The other attorneys also have their hands full with purges and boycotts up and down the coast. Am I ever thankful that dunderhead, Pennoyer didn't win the Mayoral race up in Portland. And now we have Mayor Gates on our side. He's doubled the number of city police and deputized 300 armed citizens to manage the anti-Chinese *activities*."

"I'm happy to hear that. He's a good man. Committed to the cause. When I first suggested deputizing the citizens, he thought I was out of my mind," Grant said, withholding just how much communication he'd had with the man of late. Colonel Bee didn't need to know *everything* he was up to.

"Well, I'm glad he listened to you. I'm thankful to have you on our side, too, Grant. I'd like to blink and be done with all this nonsense. But then we'd both be out of a job, wouldn't we?" His lips bent in a sad smile. "Ah. I'm quite ready for retirement at any rate."

"Was there anything else, sir?" His foot tapped, ready for the chance to stand and be out of there.

"Ah. Yes." Col. Bee reached into his top drawer and handed over a piece of mail. "This came just yesterday for you. I was going to have it forwarded to Truckee."

Grant noted the return address. *Portland*. He smiled inwardly, hoping it was what he thought it was.

"Oh, yes, one other thing." Bee flipped through a stack of documents. "Well. Where is it?" He huffed and dropped the stack onto the desktop. "At any rate, the Chinese government has withdrawn the ban on proselytizing. Good news for your family's ministry."

He jumped to his feet, grabbed his boss's hand, and pumped it in a most undignified way. "Thank you. Thank you, sir." This day looked better by the minute.

"Until we meet again, Mr. Campbell."

Grant waited until he hit the outside steps before he tore into the letter.

"A letter?" Henry leaned in. "Who is it from?"

He elbowed Henry aside. "I'll tell you in a minute. If it's what I think it is, God has answered my prayer."

Henry smiled. "You sound like Azalea." The statement tolled a compliment.

He read anxiously, thrilled with the missive. All of his efforts had paid off. Now if only his family felt the same way he did about it all. He slapped Henry on the arm with the letter and handed it over. "Let's go home, cousin."

PART THREE

Thirty-Nine

June 16, 1886

A meaty hand crushed Yakira's mouth, pinched her cheeks, and drove her head into the mattress. She pulled in a desperate draw of air, smothered by rank breath. She kicked against the bedclothes, thrashing for her life in the dark room. Panic rattled every cell in her body. A vice clamped onto her limbs. She screamed, draining her lungs, but only a muted sound vibrated through the calloused palm.

The mattress bucked, and she knew Azalea fought for her life also. *God, help!* Hands jerked up her head, and she folded in agony as hair ripped from its roots. Someone forced a foul rag between her lips, severing the edges of her mouth like a dull knife. She gagged, lurching. Vomit scalded the back of her throat, but she couldn't swallow.

Human forms shuffled about in the blackness.

Again she kicked with all her strength. Her nightgown ripped, and suddenly one leg flew free. It connected with flesh. An expletive split the night. *Good!* She would kick at anything and everything until she was dead.

Iron fingers sank deep into the flesh of her legs, and someone sat on top of her, crushing her chest, driving out what little breath she had left. Ropes bit into her ankles and wrists. The mattress shifted, and Azalea was gone. Large, shapeless bodies darted through the dark room.

A single moonbeam shot through the window onto the floor, and for an instant, she saw a man carry Azalea's still body out the door. Yakira's heart shattered. Hot tears blurred her vision. *Fight, my laotong. Fight!*

Cruel hands jerked her upright and threw her over a thick shoulder. Every step jarred, stabbing her puny ribs with pain as they descended the stairs. She strained to keep watch. To stay conscious. Where were the other girls? Bright orbs swam in her vision. Nausea roiled. Other shadowed figures bore girls down the stairs, some fighting, others still. *Fight, my precious ones. Fight!*

"This one bit me!"

Good!

Grunts. Deep, whispered voices.

One of them growled, "He won't be any trouble now."

Da!

"In the wagon."

"Lock her in there."

"Not her. I'll take her."

Flint! Dannon's man. He'd finally followed through on the threats, and it was all her fault. Her head swam. Her nose clogged—her only source of air. *I will fear no evil, for Thou art with me. Oh, God. Protect us. Please protect us . . . Thy rod and thy staff—*

Her body crashed against the floor. Agony pierced every limb. They'd dumped her onto the floor—the kitchen floor. She wrenched her head left and right, squinting into the darkness. Her shoulders throbbed, arms quivered. Her hands, bound behind her, felt severed, numb as they'd become.

The realization that she was now mercifully alone buoyed her. She waited several beats, listening. If she could but roll across the kitchen floor and reach the knife drawer—

Instantly hands jerked her to her feet. She screamed, and they released her. She let herself fall, preferring unconsciousness to whatever these men would do to her. In one violent lurch, hands pitched her over a shoulder again, jostling her down the back steps, then dumped her mercilessly onto a splintery buckboard.

No! No! Where are my girls? Azalea! Tears blistered, and her flimsy cries moaned beneath the gag. She was alone, but for the two figures on the wagon seat, silhouetted when they pulled onto the street.

Kira's full lips spoke his name, and the sweetness spiraled through him, coiling like a spring until he could resist no longer. He claimed her lips, and a jolt shot through his arm. Another jolt—

"Grant!"

He opened one eye and growled, irritated beyond all reason.

"We're here!" Henry licked his palm and patted his hair. "How do I look?"

"You look the same as when we left."

Henry's features rutted with frustration.

Grant ground a knuckle to one eye and sat up straighter. "But you look happier." Much. "Remember, not a word about the surprise, you got it? When the time is right, I'll know."

Henry nodded. "But I want to be there when you tell Yakira."

He stretched his stiff neck and arched his back. "Yeah, yeah." The thought of slipping into bed tonight was second only to his wish of finding Kira still up. No one would expect them back so soon.

The train shimmied to a noisy stop while passengers fussed about something or other. "What is going on out there?" asked a dapper man in a gray frock coat as he craned his neck to see out a window. "I've heard things about this town, but I didn't expect . . ."

Grant bolted from his seat. "Come on!" He worked his way to the exit, not even bothering with polite *excuse-me's*. When he bounded to the ground, the sight staggered him.

Flames unfurled over a section of Chinatown, and black smoke percolated across the whole of Truckee. Townspeople, some in nightclothes, filtered through the streets to join the throngs gathered at the bridge. Grant and Henry jogged to get a closer look. The Horse Hose and Engine remained on the white side of town, attached to a fireplug—doing absolutely nothing.

"Of all the—Why isn't this engine pulling water from the river to fight the fire?" Grant yelled to a hose-man atop the wagon.

"Can't do it."

"Can't or won't?" He bounded up the bottom step and pressed closer.

The man spat and wiped a sleeve across his mouth. "I just do what I'm told."

Right. What hope was there for Chinatown if the fire department couldn't—*wouldn't* help? Grant shoved his way through the crush toward the funneling smoke. He glanced behind to make sure Henry followed. They'd help in any way they could. Surely others would pitch in.

He slammed to a halt. The town had staged a locomotive between the bridge and Chinatown—a deliberate iron blockade to ensure Chinatown would burn.

"No!" Henry's exasperation echoed his own.

All those people! Their homes, businesses. Regret slammed against his chest. How had this happened?

"I order you to move that train!" Judge Keiser barked the order, puffed up and authoritative.

Grant whirled, colliding with Henry. There was hope after all!

"It's staying right there, Judge." Howard Dannon stood shoulder to shoulder with McGleason, their arms crossed in defiance.

The Judge blustered. "Do you realize what you are doing? The entire town will be sued!"

"We're *protecting* the white side of town."

The judge massaged his bare chin and gave a half-nod. "Then at least get the engine over here to draw water from the river in case it's needed. Isn't that what the town paid for it to do?"

Dannon shook his head. "Riverbank's too steep. It's doing just fine waiting at that plug over there in case it's needed."

Grant erupted, charging into the three of them. "I'll have all of you up on charges! If one person over there dies, you're facing murder charges!"

Dannon fired back a smug response, "The fire was an *accident*. A pity the engine can't pull from the river. There's no blame here, *Counselor*."

"We'll see where the blame lies after the investigation. After lives and properties are destroyed." Grant spat words like venom, his aim meant for the judge especially.

Time was just too precious to waste with this lot. He picked his way from the bridge to the shadowy riverbank, trying to make out what was happening. Henry slipped, and Grant reached out and hauled him upright before his seat hit the ground. "Come on. Let's get Uncle Avery. Then we'll row across the river to see if we can help."

They jogged through town, bypassing curious citizens and lit-up homes. A shattered streetlamp left the Mission Home in utter darkness, for not a single light glowed from the Home's windows. *Odd.* And with everything going on in town? He looked at Henry, recognizing the same swell of fear that surged through *him.*

Henry took off, speeding ahead of him. Grant overtook him and sprinted up the front steps.

The hair on the back of his neck prickled—every muscle tensed. *Yakira.* He snagged the revolver from his boot and kicked in the locked front door. Silence hung thick in the house, sinister and taunting.

Henry flew up the stairs.

Grant shuffled through the blackness, checking each room on the way to the kitchen—where Uncle Avery's form lay crumpled on the floor.

Frantic Chinese voices. Angry. Fearful. They carried from beyond a door. Feet pounded past. Shouts. Yakira ground away at the ropes on her wrists. Up and down, up and down. She worked against the splintery post behind her back. Muscles flamed in wooden arms, yet she couldn't give up. Up and down, up and down. Sawing, always sawing. The ropes sliced into her torn skin with every motion. Cramps seized her shoulders, shooting tears to her eyes. *God. Please.*

Where were the other girls? After all they had survived, and after all the healing, only to . . . She shook her head with a pitiful sob when her mind taunted her with the possibilities. *Please protect them, Father. In every way.*

Smoke sifted into the dark room. It pinched her nose and twisted her stomach. *Fire!* No wonder the Chinese were so frantic. If only she could reach something—anything to help loosen the gag. The corners of her mouth oozed, dripping down her jaw onto her nightgown. Lifting her chin, she strained against the gag to swallow the pooling blood that threatened to choke her.

Pushing past the merciless shards of pain, she continued to work the rope against the post. She shifted her attention heavenward, pleading for her girls, for Azalea, for Aunt Lara. And Da. Was he even alive? The thought gouged a hole inside her. She couldn't lose him. She couldn't.

If only Grant had been here. He and Henry would've stopped those men. But he was gone. Again. And she needed him.

There were too many of them, reason shouted.

Old hurts tangled with new ones. She squeezed her eyes shut against the sting of smoke and conscience. *God alone sees each of them this very minute, and He will be their deliverer.*

She shuddered at a dark image of Da, unconscious or even dead. It congealed inside her. Flooding. Drowning. *Dear God, don't take my father from me!* Her tears had dried up long ago, yet her heart's cry thundered for heaven to hear.

The door shook violently. Then something thundered against it, again and again. Her muffled screams tore her mouth afresh.

"I get help!" The Chinese words brought fresh sobs. God saw her. Now, so had someone else.

Forty

TRUCKEE

"Uncle." Grant knelt on the floor, lungs paralyzed. He pressed a hand to the still shoulder. "Uncle." He sat back on his heels in relief at the gentle rise and fall of the barreled chest. Suddenly a ruckus jolted the pantry door behind him. How had he not noticed the chair wedged against it?

"Help! I'm in here!"

Mither! God bless her. He flung the chair aside and threw open the door.

She wilted against him, weeping. "Grant. Praise God!" She slipped his embrace and fell to the floor beside Uncle Avery.

Grant touched her back. "He's alive."

Henry stormed into the kitchen, a barely controlled, heaving inferno. "Girls. All. Gone!"

Gone? The news shredded Grant, stole his wind, and fisted his hands.

Henry's gaze fell to Uncle Avery. He looked back at Grant, his brown eyes charred black, rife with pain.

"He's alive." Grant's meager words barely scraped through a consuming red haze. *Girls. Gone.* He'd kill whoever was behind this.

Mither grasped his pant leg and pierced him through with haggard, swollen eyes. "They took Azalea and the girls in a wagon. I heard them say something about taking them ten miles up the mountain and leaving them. Oh, Grant." Sobs shuddered her words. "I don't know where they took Kira. It was Dannon's men, I'm sure of it."

Dannon! Fury raked his veins, his very bones. He'd tie the man's noose himself!

Uncle Avery moaned, and Mither kissed his forehead. "There now."

Eyes aflutter, he groaned again, a hand to the goose egg at his hairline. His eyes snapped open. "Yakira! Where?"

Grant crossed the room in three long strides, hissing a shaky breath as his mind swam through the mire of emotions to a place of logic. *Think, man!* Both his sister and Kira needed him, but he was only one person. "Henry, you go to the livery, get a wagon, and go after the girls."

"No! They'd never rent *me* a wagon. You need me if you want to find Kira. I have a plan."

"Then Mither, see if they will give you a wagon and—"

"I'll go with Lara," Uncle Avery growled, struggling to sit up, although his face was a mask of pain. He clung to Grant's sleeve as he helped him stand. "Look at me!" Wrath twisted and reddened his uncle's face. "Bring. Back. My. Daughter!"

Grant nodded. "I vow it, Uncle." Nothing would keep him from Kira this time. *Nothing!*

"Take the shotgun."

Henry slapped him on the back and disappeared from the room. Grant bounded behind him, grabbing the shotgun and extra shells from the armoire before racing out the front door to catch up.

"Pray that Dannon is still at the river," Henry shouted.

"He'll wish he'd never been born." Grant had no plan—only the firestorm inside him, wild and unrestrained. He didn't recognize himself. He needed a cool head if he was going to help Kira—if he was going to find her before—No! He couldn't think of that.

Henry hurdled a rock wall with ease, and Grant sailed after with the shotgun in one hand and pockets bulging with shells. They charged down Bridge Street past the stables, not slowing until the crowds halted their progress.

"Give me a hand." Henry gripped a lamppost, and Grant obliged.

"See him?"

Henry shook his head and inched higher. "There!" He jumped down and took off again.

Grant shoved his way forward, nearly losing Henry as he zigzagged through the masses in the dark. He spotted Dannon, standing with his arms crossed, a fat cigar in his mouth, and a smug smile on his ugly face.

Before Grant could stop him, Henry caught Dannon's arm and swung him around. They were eye to eye for but an instant before Slade Carson had Henry in a chokehold.

Grant swung the gun butt, snapping Carson's head aside and giving Henry a chance to run. But Flint instantly seized Henry.

Grant leveled the muzzle at Flint. "Let him go." From nowhere a fist exploded against his jaw. Shards of pain sliced from jaw to eye, cleaving his entire head. Sparks shimmered in his vision. Someone wrenched the gun from his hand.

With a savage growl, he unleashed the fury that had boiled within. At once, an iron grip locked his arms from behind. He threw his head back, rewarded with a sickening crunch. Bodies flew at him again and again. He swung. Fists pummeled. Blood stung his eye, and he wiped it away. Suddenly, a small army was on top of him, jerking his arms back again. A loud *POP* shot needles through his shoulder. They wrestled him down until his cheek scoured the hard ground.

Blades of agony slashed his shoulders and elbows. He ground his teeth, expecting the snap of a bone. His eyes searched frantically for Henry, fearing the worst. Poor Henry dangled helpless and silent in Flint's headlock.

Flint's slippery smile landed on Grant before hurling Henry to the ground and restraining him with a boot heel to his neck.

"Dannon!" Henry's voice screamed loud enough to silence the onlookers. "Call off your goons. Or the whole town will know exactly how you made your money in Canton!"

Dannon's eyes flashed wildly, and he backed away from the widening crowd of spectators. He signaled for Flint to bring Henry, and for the others to release Grant.

They walked thirty paces, and Dannon aimed a cautious smile at Grant. "Counselor." Whatever Henry knew, he had the man's attention.

Dannon nodded to his thug.

Henry yanked free of Flint's meaty hand. "Where is she? Where is Yakira?"

"Why should I care about some Chinese advocate?" Dannon blew cigar smoke into Henry's face.

"Because your men know where she is." Henry's breath churned and his black eyes frosted. "Because she's your daughter!"

Grant gripped his arm and spun him around. *Insanity.* "What are you talking about?"

"I don't have a daughter." Dannon snapped, bravado chinking each word.

Henry pressed, "Do you remember a woman in Canton? Ah Si?"

Dannon halted mid-puff. His eyes narrowed and he lowered the cigar. He stared at Henry, then cleared his throat. It was a lifetime ago. "I knew a woman—a *friend* by that name. What of it?"

"I am SiJin, her son." Henry jutted his chin and raised himself up to Dannon's height.

The man chortled, as he buffed the cigar with thumb and forefinger. "So you're her little brat, all grown up." He seemed to shrink. One eye twitched. "How is your mother?"

Grant watched as confusion chased across Flint's and Carson's faces. His own confusion grew muddier by the second, thickened by this sordid accusation and his urgency to find Kira.

Henry planted his feet, arms crossed over his chest. "She died giving birth to *your* daughter! And right now *your* goons have kidnapped *your* daughter. And you are going to tell us where she is." Every word launched barbs, spearing the dazed man.

Dannon cursed and threw down the cigar, grinding it into the dirt with his boot. "Listen, I don't know what you think you're trying to do . . ." He stared at the pulverized cigar, emotions storming across his mug from one extreme to another.

It all made sense—the way Henry worried over Kira since moving to Truckee. The way he kept her father's identity a secret. Grant roiled as the reality of it all sank in, sickened to think that Kira could be related to this monster.

"He's telling the truth," Grant said. "Reverend Mitchell found Yakira in Canton and raised her as his own. And you need to tell us where she is. *Now!*"

Dannon cursed again. He removed his hat and plowed a hand through his hair. The truth sank in at last. His eyes flared, and he turned to Flint. "Where'd you take her?"

"We locked her in that old storage shed on the edge of Chinatown, Boss."

Chinatown? All eyes turned toward the blaze across the river. Grant stumbled backward, blood singing in his ears. *God, have mercy!*

"You idiots!" Dannon railed. "Idiots!"

Grant and Henry tore off. Dismissing the blockaded bridge, Grant thought to swim the river, but the current was too swift. Movement caught his eye ten yards down the dark bank. A boat! He slipped and skidded along the marshy shoreline, then scrambled down the bank to where Tuck Chan was drawing a rowboat to shore. Henry made quick work of explaining. His eyes blazed wildly when he turned back to Grant.

"He says there is a woman in the shed on this end. He tried to break her out, but he did not have ax."

"I don't need an ax. Tell him we need his boat."

Already the man was motioning for them to get in.

Grant rowed feverishly, muscles heaving to make every stroke count as he fought the current. His shoulder screamed, but his heart screamed louder, drawn to the fully engulfed Chinatown. *Please, God.* He bounded into the water as soon as the bow struck ground.

"Secure the boat," he yelled to Henry as he clawed his way up the bank in the pitch black, scrabbling and sliding backwards twice before reaching level ground. He sprinted toward the end building. Tears streamed as the thick smoke enveloped him.

"Kira!" Flames licked the shed's sagging roofline as he rammed his shoulder against the locked door. Its hinges clattered. He backed up and threw his full weight into the rough wood. A few planks split and ruptured. Once more he rammed it, and more boards fractured. Smoke seared his nostrils and stole his sight as his raw fingers groped for purchase, widening an opening.

"Kira!" He choked, drew his shirt over his mouth, and charged into the black tempest. "Kira!" *Please, God.*

It was no use. Firelight bounced off thick smoke, foiling any visibility. *CRAACK!* He lunged to one side, dredging the dirt with his injured shoulder as a beam crashed to the ground.

Completely blinded, he groped on his hands and knees. Barrels, burlap bags, crates. His hand hit something firm. *A body.* No! Spasms wracked his throat. Fear wracked his senses. "Kira!" He trailed his hands up her legs, arms, her face. She was unconscious, wrists bound to a post behind her.

He dug a small knife from his pocket and sawed at the bindings, freeing her hands. Suddenly there was light everywhere as glowing cinders rained down on them. He ducked against the scorching arrows and threw her over his shoulder. He half crawled and completely stumbled from the building, running smack into Henry.

"Is she...?" Henry skittered beside him as he headed for the riverbank.

"I don't know!" Strangling, suffocating fear screamed through his words. *God, let her live!* He couldn't lose her. The slippery bank aided their descent as he faltered and mostly slid to the water's edge.

He lowered her to the cool mud and stripped off his shirt. Dipping it, he sponged frigid water over her face, whispering her name through a rain of tears. "Come back to me, my love." The words tore at his raw throat. His heart cleaved, refusing to consider anything less than a miracle, for if her life ended, so would his.

Henry sprawled in the wet earth, holding her hand, silent sobs quaking his shoulders.

Her river-washed face reflected the moon's haunting glow as Grant watched for a twitch of her lips, a flutter of lashes. Anything to show she'd not left him. His riven soul keened to his Maker for mercy. Such a wretched place was this—suspended between heaven and hell. He was a lifeless carcass, ripe for the vultures of madness.

"Come back to me, my love." The desolate plea crackled against his senses as he continuously stroked the cold water over her temple.

The smallest movement. Then a trace of a smile.

His chest unbolted, and hope soared heavenward.

"Kira?" He pressed a kiss to her brow. "Och, me bonny lass."

Henry looked up. "She's alive?"

He laughed as joy splashed over him. "That she is. That she is."

Forty-One

Truckee

CLACK-CLACK-CLACK.

Yakira pried open her eyelids, wincing at the searing brightness. She turned her head as a cough racked her body. Her lungs felt afire. Da's grizzled whiskers swam in her vision. She blinked, trying to vanquish the haze in her mind.

Oh the nightmares she'd had—over and over. Flames crackling. Fighting for her life. Her family. Her girls. Da, dead. But here he was. Alive.

"There's me sonsie lass." Da swiped at his cheek. "Bethankit. Bethankit."

She smiled, cringing as knives sliced the corners of her mouth. *The gag. The ropes. Fire.* It all came rushing back to her, the vile nightmare she had obviously survived.

Henry hovered at her side. "Welcome back, sister. You have been sleeping for two days." His toothy smile beamed. "Sip this. It will help with your sore throat." He gently lifted her head and tipped a cup to her tender mouth.

The warm brew soothed despite the bitter taste. She let her eyes drift shut as he tipped the cup again.

"This is *Sang Xing Tang*—Mulberry leaf," he said. "It will help with the cough."

She shallowed her breaths for fear of another agonizing cough attack. Exhaustion sat heavy upon her every limb.

CLACK-CLACK-CLACK. She scowled, trying to place the odd, yet somehow familiar sound.

Grant's soft chuckle drew her attention to the other side of the bed. She turned her head slowly, forcing her heavy eyelids open once more. Cobalt eyes danced brighter than she had ever seen them. His mouth curved, sluicing her ravaged body with sweetness and warmth and all things wonderful.

"You're a sight to behold," he said in an almost whisper.

"So are you." The words scraped raw, costing her. She willed a leaden hand to reach up and touch his face as the fog cleared in her head. *"Come back to me, my love."* The memory made her smile—and wince at the pain.

"Henry is preparing one of his concoctions for your wounds," Grant said. "He's over there pulverizing dried plants just for you."

She nodded. So that was what she heard—a mortar and pestle. A common accompaniment to the girls' cooking.

Suddenly Azalea swooped into the room, sunshine in a skirt. Pressing her head gently against Yakira's chest, she chuckled. "Praise be to God!"

She had never been so overjoyed to see her laotong. "But you—"

"Shh . . . you must not talk until your throat is better," Henry said, dipping his finger into a small stone bowl and dabbing paste onto the corners of her mouth.

"Mother and Uncle Avery found us," Azalea told her. "We were left up the mountain in the middle of nowhere, so we all began walking back home." She yawned, touching her hand to her mouth. "A very long night, but God watched over us all. It is you who have scared us so." She pressed a kiss to Yakira's cheek. "Listen to Henry, he and God will make you well again." She swept a bashful gaze to him, lingering and warm. *Pure adoration.*

Henry lifted Yakira's hand and gingerly dabbed more of the salve onto her wrists. He wrapped a strip of cloth over the open cuts and tied it. "I grind *san qi* weed to make *bai yao*. It will bind the edges of your wounds. Will cause swift healing." A sly grin broke across his face. "In China, soldiers carry this at all times. They call it 'gold-no-trade.'"

His tender care melted her heart. If only they could spend more time getting to know one another. Although he had answered many questions for her already, she had more.

"Rest now, daughter," Da said, his big hand soft on her head. "There are things we must speak of."

His quiet resignation saddened her. Something tore at him. *What?* She nodded as everyone left, except Henry and Grant.

Her brother produced a cup of something else, obviously meant for her.

"Another one of your brews?" Grant said to Henry with a tease. "You are full of surprises."

"And that should surprise you that I am full of surprises?" Henry rolled his eyes, drawing a chuckle from them both. He offered the concoction. "This is *Suan Zao Ren*, to help you sleep," he told her, lifting her head as she drank. He glanced at Grant with a cunning smile and backed away. "I will check in on you later, sister." He patted her hand and left them blissfully alone.

Stillness settled between them. She soaked up his perfect features, the depths of his eyes laced with equal measures of love and concern.

She mouthed a "thank you," and he pressed a finger to her lips before placing a feathery soft kiss on them. Then he kissed her nose, her brow. She watched a battle of sorts flicker across his features.

He was leaving again. The thought squeezed her heart. This thing, this love between them would be nothing more, and wanting it as she did would not make it so. A tear escaped the corner of her eye, and his thumb wiped it away.

"Rest now," he said, backing away, his mind apparently already on something else.

She closed her eyes as more tears leaked before she floated away in sleep.

Mither swept down the stairs, a tray in her hands. "Henry's still with her. He gave her something to help her sleep. After the shocking news about Dannon, I'm glad she is finally resting."

"I'll take this. Come, sit." Grant deposited the tray on the dining room table and motioned her ahead to where Uncle Avery sat in the parlor.

It had been excruciating watching Kira's face as Henry and Avery spilled the rest of her story—the part about Dannon. The storm of emotions he saw there made him long to take her in his arms and board the next train to somewhere far away. Just the two of them.

He chuckled to himself. To a deserted island, perhaps—like Robinson Crusoe. Only not to the island of *Despair*, but to the island of *Delight*. The thought kindled flames low in his belly. He almost sighed aloud.

He craned his focus back to the telegram in his pocket.

Mither patted the sofa cushion beside her. "Sit." But for the threads of silver in her ebony hair, she had not changed a bit from his boyhood. Always patient, always on his side.

"I have good news and bad news and good news," Grant said, slipping the telegram from its envelope before taking a seat.

"'Tis a lot of news." Uncle Avery said, kicking one leg across his knee and settling back in the too-small wing-chair. "After all that," he tossed his head toward the staircase, "good news is welcomed."

Grant stared at the telegram, already having committed it to memory, and still feeling gut-punched. "Apparently Judge Sawyer was a wolf in sheep's clothing. He changed his view on Chinese rights as easy as a pair of shoes, it seems. All these months we've awaited a grand performance, but now we've skipped to the curtain call."

"I take it you have news of the Eureka claims." Uncle Avery scowled. "The bad news part."

"The only claims considered on behalf of the Eureka Chinese residents are the claims for property losses due to the city's negligence. And even those figures will be undercut by the tax rolls." Hang it all, but he'd wanted to see justice. Was it too much to ask? But God knew he'd tried. It was out of his hands entirely.

Avery puffed his cheeks before his lips vibrated with a stream of air. "I'm truly sorry. But was it not that lawsuit which sparked many more? It got national attention. You did that! The good it did is not counted in dollars, son."

The sentiment rang true, but disappointment flogged him just the same. "I guess I know that. I'd hoped for justice for once. That's all. I feel like I have given false hope to hundreds of people."

Mither patted his knee. "God knows your heart, son. 'Tis what's important. Turn it always toward Him, and no matter what others see, He will use you."

He took her hand, conscious of the softness of her skin and the way she squeezed back. She'd always been *for* him, not against him.

Even when he was lost all those years, her prayers preserved him. Brought him back to his family.

"I'm afraid there is more." He waved the telegram. "There's been a fatal blockade in the lawsuit against Truckee."

"Nae!" Mother turned in her seat, gaping at him. "Surely not."

He nodded sadly, hating to dump more onto this whole Truckee debacle. "A loophole. Truckee is not incorporated. There's no culpable municipality, no entity to hold responsible." He shook his head, still miffed. But there was a rainbow in all this. "The other towns, however—Santa Cruz, Felton, and several more—are subject to the same charges as Truckee. And those charges have stuck nice and tight."

Mither clapped. "You see? I told you your work isna wasted."

"Aye. As I said"—Uncle scrubbed his hands together, a glint in his eye.—"Changes are a-comin', mark me word."

"And"—Grant stood—"I am representing the investors of the new Steam Laundry. We're suing the Laundry Association. At least I'll leave here with some sense of satisfaction."

"Leave?" Mother's eyes widened. "You're leaving us again?"

Forty-Two

Yakira breathed deeply of the blossom-scented breeze that danced through the windows and tousled the parlor curtains. Such convincing she had to do before Da would allow her to leave her sickbed after these last weeks. Henry still had her wrists swathed in bandages, claiming they would easily become infected. Except for the lingering cough and persistent ache in her shoulder, she felt almost herself again—physically.

Her mind, however, struggled to fit this new information about Mr. Dannon into some proper place. The way God had chosen the daughter of a prostitute and slave broker as his own—and given her the honor of ministering to the very people her birth father had abused and sold like cattle—it defied comprehension. She thought of Rahab, of Paul, and others. Were they not a most unlikely choice for God to use also?

But with the sting of revelation, the mountain that loomed darker and higher than her past was the question of the Mission Home. Her girls. She pressed a hand against the sudden ache in her chest. Day and night she'd pleaded with God for an answer. Da said they must leave. But what was it *God* was saying to her? Her prayers seemed to fly back to her like a seabird with nowhere to land.

Until she'd awakened this morning.

"Have I not given you these little ones, my daughter?" Her Heavenly Father had whispered the words to her very soul. How ungrateful she'd been. Hadn't the heartache of Eureka brought her Mei, Zara, Lian, and Shu? And had it not been for this time in Truckee, Shuang and Ubon would not have new lives today. She would cling to these truths with every fiber of her weary soul.

"Are you sure you're warm enough? I can close the windows." Azalea tucked the thin blanket around Yakira's legs. "Would you like some tea?"

"I'm not an invalid, dear, just a bit tired."

"And sore and coughing." Azalea settled fists onto narrow hips. "Maybe you are over-doing it." She tipped her head, brow ruffled in concern as if she could see into Yakira's heart with all its aches and yearnings. Her eyes softened. "God has a plan, my laotong. A wonderful, perfect plan."

She nodded, thankful beyond words for Azalea and her strong faith, which she so often shared when Yakira's own well ran dry.

Grant plunked down a chair from the dining room, angling it so he could reach for her hand. "Perhaps Kira might bear with us all a bit longer before heading back to bed."

"Quite a bit longer, I'd hoped," she said, returning the liquid gaze that kicked her heart to a trot. She longed for time alone with him. It had not been easy in a house full of females, each one clucking over her like a mother hen.

He cupped his hands to his mouth and hollered at the ceiling, "Henry! We're waiting for you!" A crooked grin danced across his whiskers. "Is that man ever on time?"

A girlish giggle climbed her throat. Light as air, she felt. So much had toppled in her brief life, but God was at work. She was clueless as to the *how* or *what* of it all, but the suffocating yoke of just days before was gone. Lifted overnight. Such indomitable peace could only come by the Almighty's hand—of that she was certain.

"I wasn't aware there was a meeting." She passed a sly look to Da. "Good thing the warden opened my cell."

He winked, touching a finger aside his nose. "Aye, and the warden will cart ye back up those stairs if the inmate becomes too sassy."

"I'll behave," she said, rewarded with the old sparkle she'd missed of late.

Henry rambled down the steps. "Just preparing another treatment for Yakira's wrists."

"Whatever you are using, I canna believe how well it is working," Aunt Lara said.

Henry started to respond, but Grant cut him off.

"*Now* that we're all together, I have an announcement." He removed Yakira's hand to her own lap and stood. Palms together as she'd seen him do in the courtroom, he paced a few steps and turned to the small audience. "I have been in contact with first, Mayor Gates, then Reverend Partee in Portland. It seems the Second Presbyterian Church has acquired an empty boarding school they wish to refurbish. When I learned they were in a quandary as to its usage, I proposed an idea." He took two steps, turned, and brought his fingertips to his chin.

Henry rolled his eyes with a smirk. "I feel like I'm in a courtroom."

Azalea muffled a laugh.

Grant glared good-naturedly before continuing. "I'll spare you the details of the long distance banter."

"Thank you." Henry wiped his forehead with a touch of drama.

He was testing their friendship further, and Yakira loved it. Loved the way her two men cared for one another. And she adored the way they brought out the best in each other.

Grant cleared his throat. His lips curved, and his eyes captured hers alone. "Suffice it to say, after a glowing recommendation from Miss Culbertson and Reverend Hamilton, Kira has been invited to open a Mission Home for Girls in Portland."

Aunt Lara gasped. A curtain of silence fell.

Yakira stilled as the words penetrated her brain and drifted slowly down to her heart. She couldn't take her eyes off Grant, knowing he was watching for her reaction. He positively beamed, and in that moment she knew this was his love reaching out to her, holding her with a hope that had been battered and refused—until this moment.

"There's more." He tore his eyes from her to address everyone. "Since the Chinese government has lifted the ban on proselytizing, the church will offer salaries for staff as needed. They will only oversee the finances. Other than that"—he closed in on her and reached for both her hands—"other than that, everything would be up to you."

"Oh, Yakira!" Azalea sprang up, and then stilled, waiting on her.

Shock guttered through her. Her peace wavered, and familiar voices badgered her mind. *Dare she get her hopes up only to have them dashed again? Why didn't God remove this yearning if all she did was fail?*

"Kira, lass, did ye hear what Grant said?"

She turned to Da's question, realizing every eye was on her. And like the strike of a match, the prospect sparked to life. She banished the horrid voices. *Yes!* Yes, she would take the chance if God had truly opened yet another door. Sweet Grant, he always knew her heart.

Her throat suddenly tight, she could only nod. And smile.

In one swift movement Grant was on one knee, his strong fingers coiled about hers. His gaze was a sea of brilliant stars, captivating. He blinked several times, and his chest rose with a quiver. "I am quitting Six Companies. I want to work in Portland on behalf of those I can help directly. It's my calling, Kira, and the Mission Home is your calling. God couldn't have fashioned a more perfect plan—for *us*."

One second she was falling into those blue depths, and the next swimming amid the tangle of words that seemed mired in her brain. *Did he just . . . ?*

"Are you asking me to marry you?" Her breath hitched, and a magnificent shiver chased through her.

He licked his lips and tipped them in a timid smile. "Yakira Jean Mitchell, I love you with all my heart, and"—he choked on a laugh—"yes, me *loosome* lass, I am asking you to marry me!"

"Yes." The word drowned beneath the thrum of her heart. "Yes!" She threw her arms around his neck, burying her face, eyes suddenly leaking a river for the joy that seemed a salve for all the years of waiting, of yearning, of doubting. If a broken heart could mend instantly, hers surely had. And the feel of it was a splendid thing.

Aunt Lara was over them, arms covering like a cloak. "Me precious children." She sobbed the words, and Azalea joined in with laughter burbling through tears.

"Am I glad that's over." Henry said. "I didn't think he was ever going to get it out."

"Watch it, *Ah Pok*." Grant shot out a hand and punched his arm. And just as quickly, they clasped hands.

Da wrenched Grant's hand away from Henry, pumping it like a spigot. "Weel done, me boy."

Like the parting of the Red Sea, Lara and Azalea stepped aside. Yakira moved into Da's powerful arms. They engulfed her, and his sturdy frame sheltered her, protected her, as he had all her life. Awash in his love, his unfailing love, how could she ever have doubted that he was the father God had planned for her from the beginning of time?

After tears dried, and Grant had settled beside her on the sofa, Azalea fetched the girls, and another round of joyous laughter filled the parlor.

"If I may," Da was saying as he stood. Silence came hard with all the foofaraw. "Since we are all here together anyway, I've an announcement of me own."

"*Now*, Avery?" Aunt Lara half-whispered, blinking.

"Good a time as any," Da said, drawing her to him. She stood close to his side, two giants of stature and heart, their faces sparked with what looked like the knowing of secrets. Da drew her arm through his own and brought her hand to his lips, a keen smile prickling his grizzled whiskers before he kissed it.

Muted giggles.

Da turned ceremoniously to the rest of them. "Lara and I are to be wed."

Yakira gasped, stunned mute.

Azalea squealed. "It's about time!" She bounced to her feet, descending upon them both with arms wide.

Grant squeezed Yakira's hand, a smile beaming ear to ear as he pulled her to her feet.

Just when she'd thought to burst for joy, the not-so-unexpected news crowded in.

"And once we are wed, we will return to the highlands." Da's voice lanced the air.

Her limbs fell heavy. She dropped Grant's hand. "You're leaving us?"

Lara nodded, moving to hug Yakira. "Aye, for a time." She settled a hand on hers and Grant's shoulder. "We couldna bear the thought of leaving you all for long. And I willna be missing the coming of any bairns to this family." Her eyes sparkled, keen on Yakira's.

A sturdy knock at the front door interrupted.

"I'll get it," Henry said. "Carry on." He returned a moment later. Contention splayed across his normally smiling face as he walked stiffly over to her. "Sister, you have a visitor. It's Dannon."

"Dannon!" Grant's eyes flashed fire as he spit the word. "I'll throw him out—"

"He wants to talk to Yakira." Henry said. "Alone."

"It's all right, Grant." Yakira reached for his hand. "There are things I have to say to him."

Learning that her father was not Avery Mitchell, but some immoral stranger, had been hard. Discovering that the stranger was a slave-trading brigand with a face was even harder. And now the words God had repeatedly spoken to her would find purchase. She picked up the crocheted throw that had fallen to the floor and tossed it onto the chair before striding toward the entry, shoulders back and a prayer on her lips.

Dannon stood just inside the entrance, hat in one hand and a nosegay of yellow chrysanthemums in the other. He seemed sunken into the floor somehow, less formidable as he stared at his fifty-dollar boots. When he lifted his head at her approach, his lips parted. He squinted for a moment, then blinked several times. "Yakira. A . . . a beautiful name."

"My mother, Cait, gave it to me when I was but a few days old," she said, watching near-tenderness play across his eyes for an instant.

He thrust out the flowers. "These are for you."

The bully had shriveled to an awkward human, rife with regrets and, if she wasn't mistaken, bearing a degree of optimism. She accepted the flowers, and thanked him with a polite smile.

"I know I have no right. But if there is a chance for this old man to get to know his daughter, I will take it." His voice was gruff and soft all at once.

He appeared miserable. Did she pity him? Yes. Hoped he would find redemption? Certainly. And for all she'd come to understand these past two years, she knew that anything was possible with God. And only by the Almighty's grace alone, she bore this man, her birth father, no malice.

But neither would she mislead him.

She drew a deep breath and peace settled over her as she remembered what God had whispered to her.

"Mr. Dannon, please know I bear you no ill will. But it matters not who my earthly parents are, sir—not really. What matters is that God chose me as *His* and surrounded me with those who would love me most." She touched his hand, and his bewildered gaze fell from her face to her fingers.

"For you see, I am *chosen*. My *mother* chose to have me, my *brother* chose to save me, and *God* chose Avery and Cait Mitchell to redeem me. I am nothing to you, Mr. Dannon, but to my Heavenly Father, I am Yakira—beloved."

ACKNOWLEDGEMENTS

Many people deserve much credit for contributing to *Fires of Injustice* in some way. Foremost, I am thankful to Jesus Christ, my Lord, and Savior, Who reminds me He chose me to bear fruit (John 15:16). For fourteen years, writing has been fruit-bearing for me. I want to thank the following people for helping me bear that fruit:

My hero husband who indulged my investigative spirit and joined with me to visit Truckee, a Chinese underground, and other pertinent places of interest related to this book.

Mira San Juan for her input on all things Chinese.

Kara Starcher of Mountain Creek Books LLC for her lovely book cover and expert recommendations.

Sarah Forster, editor/proof-reader extraordinaire. Rachel Taylor, Publicity Assistant extraordinaire.

Special thanks to Linda Kruschke for her legal guidance on certain scenes. Special thanks also to Berne McNelly, my railroad consultant and second proofreader.

A more-than-you-know kind of thank you to Melody Roberts, my ever-vigilant critique partner throughout four novels.

And to my readers, for your reviews, emails, encouragement, and ideas on what to write next.

AUTHOR NOTES

Growing up in the Midwest, my school years were steeped in stories of the American Revolution, the Civil War, and the Wild West. Oh, and I mustn't forget the Indian Wars, since places named for Native American tribes surrounded me.

Moving to Oregon introduced me to a whole new pocket of American history. During my years using U.S. history curriculum as a high school history teacher, I noticed that the topic that birthed this book never made much of an appearance in the text books.

One day I traveled to Pendleton, Oregon to visit relatives, and someone mentioned visiting the Underground. That's the exact moment I learned just how naive I was about an entire chapter of American history that so fascinated me; I needed to learn more.

I needed to learn more about **America's Forgotten War**.

I wanted to know what forced the Chinese immigrants to live underground in many West Coast cities. Why were the laws the way they were back then? Why did we invite the Chinese workers here to build our railroads and then treat them unfairly when the railroad was finished? Why did brokers buy and sell Chinese people like cattle, even though slavery had been abolished years before?

Much of what my research revealed was ugly and heartbreaking. I strove to present this pocket of Chinese-American history to you in a way that honored both God and the Chinese immigrants of the United States. History basically wrote this story. I simply invented a family to follow in the steps of many other real-life heroes who dared to fight for justice in this very dark chapter of American history.

More truth than fiction: Most of the events recreated in *Fires of Injustice* are of historical record. I generally like to mention to the reader some of what is actually true in my books. But apart from my fictional family, very little in this story is **not** true. Check out the Suggested Reading section to learn more.

Here are some notes for the reader and a small sample of facts you'll read about in *Fires of Injustice*:

- **The Occidental Mission Home**, founded by a Presbyterian group in the 1870s, operated under the Woman's Occidental Board of Foreign Missions. Several years after the incidents in my story, the home relocated, and Miss Culbertson hired a young woman, Donaldina Cameron, to teach sewing. Although the home changed names a few times, it still stands today as the Cameron House at 920 Sacramento Street. Cameron and her team are credited with rescuing thousands of women and girls.

- **Speeches and newspaper articles** quoted throughout the story are taken from archives.

- **Politically related** statements, organizations, charters, quotes, activities, and politicians are all from historical records.

- **The Prostitute Contract** is authentic.

- **The characters:** William Lord, Rev. Ira Harrington, David Kendall, Charlie Wei Lum, Charles Crocker, Casper Ricks, and many others are of historical record. My character, Robert McGleason, is based on Newspaper-man-turned politician Charles McGlashan, known for developing the "Truckee Method" of expulsion.

- **Regarding first-cousin marriage:** This was quite common in the 19th century, legal in most U.S. states, and accepted by reputable families for its emotional connection, cultural approval, and financial benefits. The cultural shift against it began (after my story's setting) in the late 1800s and early 1900s, when new theories about heredity and social reform movements reframed cousin marriage as unhealthy and backward. At the time this book was published, first-cousin marriage was still legal in 18 U.S. states. Famous men who married first cousins include: Presidents Martin Van Buren and John Adams, Edgar Allan Poe, Charles Darwin, Prince Albert (Queen Victoria). According to global demographic analyses (*World Population Review; Vivid Maps*), roughly one in ten marriages worldwide occurs between first or second cousins. Who knew? In ***Fires of Injustice***, Grant's dilemma reflects the emotional reality of their upbringing—they were raised like siblings—rather than any social or legal taboo.

- **Canton and the Tang people:** Canton is actually the modern-day city of Guangzhou, Guangdong Province, southern China. Victorian-era Chinese immigrants to America (from this area) often referred to themselves as the Tang people. They self-identified more with the Tang Dynasty (618-907 CE) than the earlier Han Dynasty. Cantonese is the primary language of this area of China. Early Chinese immigrants in San Francisco called Sacramento Street "Tang People's Street." This evolved into the standard Chinese term for Chinatowns worldwide.

In my primary resource research, terms such as *Celestials* and *Chinamen* populated the newspapers, speeches, and legal documents. These are terms deemed derogatory today in many circles. I attempted to limit these terms to anti-Chinese/hostile sources in my story. My intent is to honor the Chinese immigrants of the 1800s while staying true to history without causing offense.

Discover more gems from my research and historical novels by signing up for **my newsletter** at **kendypearson.com**.

I sincerely hope I've sparked your interest in this dark chapter of our nation's history, **America's Forgotten War**. At one time, I had this large sign on the wall of my classroom:

THOSE WHO CANNOT REMEMBER THE PAST ARE CONDEMNED TO REPEAT IT.
—George Santayana, 1905

Gifts
just for my readers!

Receive the Free
Extended Prologue
of
Fires of Injustice
(ebook or audio)

Receive the free
First Five Chapters
of
When the Mountains Wept
Book 1 of West Virginia: Born of
Rebellion's Storm
(ebook)

Visit
kendypearson.com
for your FREE ebook or audiobook!

—THE BEST WAY TO THANK AN AUTHOR—

If you enjoyed this book,
please consider leaving
a brief review for other readers
at the places listed below.

Thank you for reading!

Kendy

———— ❈ ————

Wherever you buy your books
BookBub.com
Goodreads.com

———— ❈ ————

See **kendypearson.com** for more suggestions
and to receive the extended prologue!

Keep Reading for a SNEAK PEEK of Book One—
West Virginia: Born of Rebellion's Storm series

West Virginia: Born of Rebellion's Storm 1

WHEN THE
MOUNTAINS
WEPT

KENDY PEARSON

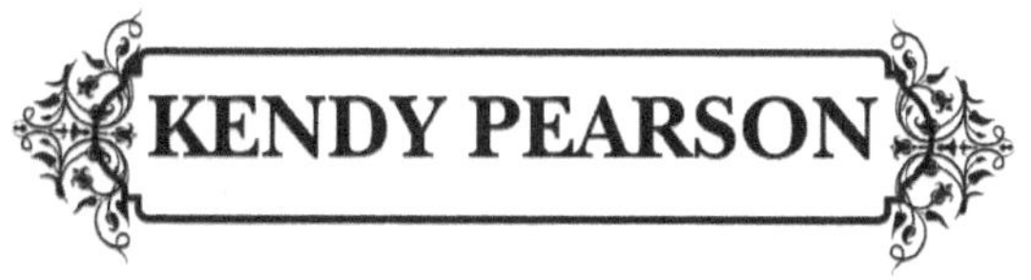

Heart
of
History
an imprint of
PEAR BLOSSOM BOOKS

WHEN THE MOUNTAINS WEPT

Fayette County, Virginia
February 1861

"We can do this, Daisy. Just don't you kick me." Augusta puffed a wisp of hair away and wiped blood from her arm as a new contraction sent ripples through the cow's coppery hide. Daisy's brown eyes widened as she let go a rafter-shaking bawl. Poor ol' gal. "You just hold on, now. It'll all be over soon."

Movement caught Augusta's eye as a woolly spider descended on a single thread. It plunged, paused, plunged again, and settled on the floor. A familiar ache wrenched her already bruised heart. She wasn't so different from that little wire-legged creeper, was she? She had abandoned her dreams only to plunge into an impossible situation.

Two days—forty-eight agonizing hours—until she'd have her answer.

"Did you do it, Gus?"

Augusta's head snapped up. "What, Will?" Twelve-year-old Willamina had been planted at Daisy's other end for the last half hour.

"Can the calf come now?" Her sister slapped at a fly tangled in her unruly curls. "There now, Daisy," Will crooned as she caressed the jersey's blocky head. "You go ahead and birth that little one of yours." She winked at Augusta. "Gus will take care of you."

The cow huffed through inflamed nostrils, raising tiny clouds that vanished in the chilly stall.

"Could be there's something wrong here besides this little fellow not being right where he oughta be." Augusta sorted her tangled thoughts, separating tomorrow's worries from the task at hand as hay and manure odors mingled with the metallic scent of blood.

In the next seconds, one hoof and then another emerged, followed by a bony forehead and flat nose. She dragged the calf into the fresh straw and scraped away the mucous sack with her fingers. Always a beautiful thing—new life.

She massaged the moist nose of the stirring newborn. "Well, I guess the good Lord wanted the Dabneys to have another bull. Not much for milk and butter, but I reckon come time to butcher, we'll be thankful for the roasts."

If they weren't forced to sell the little guy before then. Surely, the Almighty had a plan. He just wasn't sharing it with *her*.

"Aww, I was wantin' a heifer this time." Will snagged her worn hat and stood, shaking straw from her britches.

"You can want all you want, but it won't make it happen. We've got two more due to calve in the spring. Maybe you'll get your heifer then. Now, go set the table and ring for supper."

"That's woman's work," Will grumbled.

"Willamina Dabney! I will not have you complaining. You be thankful you've got family to call to supper and food to put on the table." She swatted the girl's behind. "Now scoot!"

Once the newborn discovered its first meal, Augusta stretched weary muscles and quit the barn, aiming to see to Pap's meal, already simmering on the stove.

She dipped broth from a steaming kettle and made her way to his bedroom. Glad to find him awake, she set aside the cup and brushed grizzled hair from his drawn face. He was fretting, and she knew why. "I'll be fine, Pap. Don't you worry about me. I'll be back from Charleston afore you know it."

"I just wish I was the one going." He wheezed and caught his breath. Moist pewter eyes wrapped her in love. "If we can't get the bank to work with us—"

"I won't let you down, Pap." She'd do anything to keep her family together. Anything to keep their farm. "Zander's coming with. We'll stay with the Carmichaels. You remember my friend, Maudie Carmichael, don't you? From Mrs. Munday's School for Young Ladies?" She stirred the hot broth, refusing to pine for happier times just now. "And Melinda Jane will take fine care of you whilst I'm gone. I wouldn't be surprised if Izzy didn't come sit a spell. Maybe play some checkers, too." She was rambling now, but she'd see him rest from his worrisome talk.

Her dearest friend would watch over Pap, but Augusta still cringed at the thought of leaving him like this. Every day, she thanked the Lord for a little more time. She wasn't ready to see him go on to be with Mama and Jesus. Not just yet.

Pressing a kiss to his hairline, she squeezed his mottled hand. "I'll look in on you later." Grief stole her voice, so she nodded and softly closed the door.

Her sweet Pap. Would he even see Christmas this year?

Charleston, Virginia

Marble columns towered above Augusta's head, testing her mettle. Her hand hesitated on the cold, brass handle of the door as something contrary to peace sluiced through her. Bold script etched the smooth, stone façade to her left–CENTRAL BANK OF CHARLESTON. She hated this place. It was an edifice to the financial ruin of farmers everywhere—plain folk struggling to eke out a living from the land, only to lose it all to the snobbish coat-and-tail types in their hilltop mansions.

But all she held dear was precariously perched upon the shoulders of one Thaddeus Fontaine, Bank President.

"I'm here to see Mr. Fontaine," she told the window clerk. "I'm Augusta Dabney. I believe I have an appointment."

The white-haired gentleman glanced at a schedule and flipped over the tiny OPEN sign. "Right this way, ma'am."

She followed the crisp black suit through the lobby and up a gleaming staircase with the scent of lemon oil hovering in the air. She paused an instant to admire the flawless shine of the floor. Quickening her steps, she caught up to the clerk once more. A carved door loomed at the end of the hall; the transom bedecked with flashy gold lettering—PRESIDENT.

"He'll be with you in a moment, Mrs. Dabney."

"It's *Miss* Dabney," she corrected as the clerk walked away. Drawing a deep breath, she pulled back her shoulders and lifted her chin. She could do this. The door opened and two men stood shaking hands. Her stomach lurched as a jumble of memories frayed her courage in an instant. *Dear Lord, please don't let him be the bank president.*

"I hope I'll be meeting you over at the Pattons' place soon, James. Good to see you again."

The visiting gentleman whirled without warning, knocking her off-kilter. His hand moved to steady her, then recoiled. "Excuse me, ma'am." Half a smile did nothing to soften the stern edges of his handsome face.

"Ah, my next appointment." The banker's eyes fixed on Augusta. His familiar, enthusiastic smile unsettled her. "Dr. James Hill, may I introduce to you Miss Augusta Dabney?"

One eyebrow arched below carved lines on the doctor's forehead. "Are you, by any chance, related to the Dabneys of King William County?"

"Why yes, I am. My father—"

"Good day then." A shadow darkened striking brown eyes before he spun and marched down the hall.

How rude! But she couldn't afford to be rattled.

"Where is Mr. Fontaine?" She frowned, looking past the enormous leather wing chairs for a glimpse of the gray-haired man. Gripping the front of her dress, she pressed down the whirlwind in her middle. If only Fin weren't away on business. Her brother should be here.

"I believe you are looking for Uncle Thaddeus. *I* am now the acting Bank President." His coy expression only sickened her stomach. "I do hope you remember me, Augusta."

She remembered him all right—from her one year at finishing school. After a brief acquaintance and a healthy dose of youthful infatuation, she had agreed to accompany him to a coming-out ball. He had been overbearing and much too familiar. The recollection burned her cheeks.

"I see you *do* remember. It was the Hansford House, was it not? A lovely gala, with quite a collection of beautiful women, as I recall. Ah, but I was fortunate to accompany a particular auburn-haired lass that evening. Was it so long ago, Augusta? You've changed." His fingers touched a tendril fallen from her hat. "More . . . beautiful."

Drawing back just enough, she narrowed her eyes. "And do you recall that particular lass slapping you for being boorish?" She stepped around him and took a seat. "If you don't mind, *Mister* Fontaine, I'd like to talk business."

He chuckled and settled into an oversized Empire chair behind the mahogany desk. "Now, what can I do for you?" He folded his hands and glanced down, seeming to admire his reflection on the polished desktop.

"I've come about the note on our farm. I'd like to talk to you about modifying the terms." She sat a little straighter. Her family needed this.

"I see. What kind of modification do you have in mind, *Miss* Dabney?"

"As you know, we haven't missed a payment in five years on that note. There's not much more owing, and I was wondering if you would accept smaller payments—or perhaps an installment every *other* month." Hoping she sounded business-like, she clutched her reticule to steady her quivering hands.

He leaned back into the tufted leather. "That's quite a modification. It would be highly unusual for me to allow such an arrangement." He paused for seconds that felt like minutes, tapping a finger on the desktop. "Is there anything of value you can leverage against this loan to lower your balance? Livestock or horses?"

"Not right now, but later perhaps, after the spring calving." *I will not grovel.* She lifted her head a bit higher.

More tapping. At last, he retrieved a page of paper and blotter from the top drawer and dipped a pen. "Perhaps we can arrive at a solution that would work for both of us—I mean, for your father and the bank, of course. Mmm?"

"I would be obliged. What do you have in mind, Mr. Fontaine?" A crumb of relief. This was going to work. It had to.

"Why don't we start with an agreement for the bank to accept whatever amount you feel you can afford for now? I will need to draw up a temporary deferment for the full payments. However, you must realize there is still interest. The bank will allow you until August to bring the payments current. Is that agreeable?"

August? So soon. "I appreciate your willingness to work with us, Mr. Fontaine. Might you allow us until the end of the year to bring the note current?"

His bare upper lip twitched into a brief smile. "A shrewd proposal, Miss Dabney."

The mantle clock's second hand thumped its advance. Her confidence wilted.

He scratched several sentences on the paper before glancing up—all business. "Let us say October, then. Is *that* agreeable to you?"

Did she have a choice? "Yes. It will surely have to be, won't it? Thank you for your time, Mr. Fontaine." She stood, conscious of every tenacious corset stay squeezing her ribs. Only God knew how they would make this work.

"I'll have the documents for you by noon," he said, standing.

Her heart clung to a frail hope. She had won only the first battle of the war—a war against a formidable foe. She offered her hand to conclude their business. He looked at it for a moment, chuckled, and clasped it. But when he didn't release his grip, she attempted to pull her hand free—until his eyes pinned her in place.

"I hope to see you soon, then . . . Augusta." One side of his mouth slithered upward as her heart thundered a warning. Finally, he nodded, releasing her hand.

The air shifted in the room, and she bit her lip. This would've gone so much better with the senior Fontaine.

What had she gotten herself into?

SUGGESTED READING

If you are interested in reading further about Chinese immigrants in 19th century America, here are a few books you may enjoy.

- ***Driven Out***: The Forgotten War against Chinese Americans by Jean Pfaelzer

- ***The Paper Daughters of Chinatown*** by Heather B. Moore

- ***On Gold Mountain***: The One-Hundred-Year Odyssey of My Chinese-American Family by Lisa See

- ***Strangers in the Land***: Exclusion, Belonging, and the Epic Story of the Chinese in America by Michael Luo

- ***Idaho Chinese Lore*** by M. Alfreda Elsensohn

- **Massacred for Gold**: The Chinese in Hells Canyon by R. Gregory Nokes

- ***Thousand Pieces of Gold*** by Ruthanne Lum McCunn

Also by *Kendy Pearson*

West Vrignia:
Born of Rebellion's Storm

The Award-Winning Series

Sign up for **Kendy's Newsletter** at **kendypearson.com**
to see what's coming next!

About the Author

When Kendy Pearson discovers a pocket of American history omitted from the schoolbooks, she enjoys digging in and turning that pocket inside out. Her novels merge fictitious characters with historical events, timelines, and personalities—and she always includes a romantic thread to warm the heart. Every story is a journey through tragedy, secrets, regrets, and God's undeniable grace. Her books have received eight literary awards to date.

Kendy is a veteran high school teacher, worship leader, novice bluegrass fiddler, and Civil War reenactment enthusiast. She enjoys public speaking and teaching writing workshops. Her favorite things include ice cream, snowy days, fireplaces, and maple trees. Kendy is the mother of four grown children and five grands. She lives in the Pacific Northwest with her sweet hubby and two amusing miniature dachshunds.

Subscribe to her newsletter to learn more about upcoming books, freebies, and insider nuggets at **kendypearson.com**.

Follow Kendy:

bookbub.com/authors/kendy-pearson
goodreads.com/kendypearson
facebook.com/kendy.pearson.author
instagram.com/kendypearson
threads.net/@kendypearson
twitter.com/kendypearson

www.ingramcontent.com/pod-product-compliance
Lightning Source LLC
Chambersburg PA
CBHW051130130726
47988CB00005B/1783